Praise for *Monument Road*

"Quimby's storytelling, his humane impulses and his lyrical passages on the meaning of love and time, and on the history, geology and botany of the region, will surely impress readers."

— *MINNEAPOLIS STAR TRIBUNE*

"Not to be overlooked is the love, humor and friendship among pain and loss, which makes it a book far more about the richness of life than the finality of death."

— *GRAND JUNCTION DAILY SENTINEL*

"Part modern western, part mystery, this first novel will appeal to fans of Louise Erdrich and Kent Haruf. Quimby's prose reads so true, it breaks the heart."

— *BOOKLIST*, starred review

"The Colorado setting and the author's simple style of prose perfectly complement the complexity of the human spirit in this superb debut."

— *PUBLISHERS WEEKLY*

"*Monument Road* is so rich with landscape, character and event that such a small telling cannot begin to do it justice. Read this exquisite story; it is a joy and a wonder and a tour de force of authorship."

— *SHELF AWARENESS*

"A big-hearted novel chock full of memorable characters, a pleasure to read."
—DAVID RHODES, author of *Jewelweed*

"In prose that might have been chiseled from the magnificent landscape he describes, Charlie Quimby has written a great big American Novel. Full of pathos and humor and sadness, you won't reach the end of this book without feeling fuller and wiser."
— PETER GEYE, author of *Wintering*

"A book of confessions and connections, fear, forgiveness and, ultimately, the stirrings of redemption."
—*HIGH COUNTRY NEWS*

"The landscape and characters of *Monument Road* ring true."
—DAN O'BRIEN, author of *Stolen Horses*

INHABITED

A novel by

CHARLIE QUIMBY

TORREY HOUSE PRESS

SALT LAKE CITY • TORREY

Quimby

This is a work of fiction. All names, characters, places, and incidents are either the products of the author's imagination or are used fictitiously. No reference to any real person is intended or should be inferred.

First Torrey House Press Edition, October 2016
Copyright © 2016 by Charlie Quimby

Published by Torrey House Press
Salt Lake City, Utah
www.torreyhouse.org

International Standard Book Number: 978-1-937226-67-1
E-book ISBN: 978-1-937226-68-8
Library of Congress Control Number: 2016930117
Author photo by Susan Cushman
Cover art by Gayle Gerson
Cover design by Alisha Anderson

MIX
Paper from
responsible sources
FSC® C011935

To Emma, Jane and Susan,
who have granted me all I know of home.

INHABITED

And though one says that one is part of everything,
There is a conflict, there is a resistance involved.
—Wallace Stevens

An accident gradually gets accepted as the thing
that needed to happen.
—Rumi

Part One

~~

June – August

**Native landscaping costs less to maintain
than non-native plantings and turf grasses.**

—"Home" with Meg Mogrin, *Grand Junction Style*

She had been born here and so had to learn that eyes from wetter
climes saw brown as the color of failure. The dismay of northern-
ers weary of rain and snow should have been obvious from those
unhappy years in Denver when she looked toward the alien east
unstopped by the mountains. Farmtowns dustbowled out of existence. Cattle living in feedlot shit. A dachshund-colored haze
lapping the sky. The city clutching the skirt of the Front Range and
burying its face in snowcaps, granite and redrock. Though not so
apparent here, the west slope of the Rockies shared that arid reality
with the relentless high plains.

Homebuyers craved green. Green represented sanctuary, abundance, progress, fecundity, and until they encountered it in full
sufficiency, Meg Mogrin might as well have been showing them
burial plots. Her job was to guide the immigrants gently, since
surely they had hoped to find in these brown barrens their own
little patch of swampland.

She made sure retirees saw the orchards and vineyards and golf
courses. Families she drove past the sprinklered ball parks and the
waterslide at the pool, pointing out the gasflame-blue sky through
windows sealed against its swelter. And in season, the Botanical
Gardens. *In the west*, she would say, *towns thrive only because of water
and here we are at the junction of two grand rivers.* From drive-by
distance, the tamarisk remained a distant splurge of olive foliage and
pink feathery blooms, not a creeping riverbank strangler. Butterflies

1

shimmered among lavender blossoms, unmindful that the soil once hosted mill tailings and scrapyards.

On glorious mornings like this one, it was easy to forget how much of the town had settled atop ruin and reclamation.

Meg stopped to watch five made-up little girls strut across the parking lot toward the Discovery Castle. They looked like barhopping bridesmaids wearing leotards and leg warmers, saggy tees and pixie tutus layered in bright pastels, hair bunched by head scarves, wrists rattling with plastic bracelets. Their ten-year-old voices piped the chorus of "Hit Me With Your Best Shot." A watchful mother young enough to be Pat Benatar's daughter followed, no doubt conscious of how closely the Botanical Gardens bordered the river camps. Her gaze sought Meg's reassurance and solidarity. *What can we do?* she seemed to ask.

Meg could only shrug. She had given up shepherding children when she forsook the classroom for a profession that offered more finality. After she sold a house, she never once worried what would become of it.

She put her pickup back in gear, the company truck, a GMC three-on-the-column half-ton from the seventies. In the flush of her first upper-six-figure sale, she had purchased it already spiffed up with a tri-tone paint job and slapped on a High Country Living logo. It was impractical as an everyday ride. The idea was to leave it in the parking lot as a free billboard outside the RE/MAX second floor realty office. Then the recession hit and she had to dump the lease on her Escalade. With only the Jimmy to drive, she discovered how effortless it was to be noticed without being scrutinized, almost as if the pickup granted her temporary dispensation to be a man. If not exactly a classic, the truck was a survivor that could signify upmarket western Americana to prosperous retirees and let crusty ranchers know the fancy girl realtor could drive a stick. Now that business was back, a Buick served as her workhorse and she saved the truck for puttering around town on errands like this one. Real estate was mostly routine that arrived at unexpected intervals. What appeared to clients as urgent crises could often be eased away with a little timely effort. Redelivering this misdirected packet of fliers could be seen as a waste of her time or an opportunity to bank goodwill with the printer who had screwed up. Everyone bought or sold eventually, and when the printer needed a realtor, Meg Mogrin expected her name to occur to him like a favorite tune.

Across the lot, Zack Nicolai's rasta slouch cap flashed its stoplight colors next to a police SUV. Zack, a rabble-rousing member of the Homeless Coalition, had insisted on accompanying the literature drop to announce the tamarisk removal project to the encampments along the river. He leaned toward Amy Hostetter, one half of the police department's homeless outreach team. Meg knew her going back to their co-ed softball days when Amy's team had been perennial rec league champions. Her tall, Nordic-blond ambiguity exerted an attraction that was fundamentally physical, yet not precisely sexual. With varying degrees of intrigue and confusion, both men and women found her attractive. Meg had settled somewhere between being in awe and slightly intimidated.

Zack brightened when he saw a fellow member of the Homeless Coalition. "I'm glad somebody else decided to get their feet wet."

Meg wasn't tramping through any tamarisk thickets, not in suede flats and an Ann Taylor sheath. "Where's the River Alliance?"

"Apparently outreach is not their thing." He screwed up his face. "Unless it's ecology-related."

She had to credit Zack. He called himself an anarchist but he showed up on time.

He snatched the fliers and squinted at the printer's sample taped to the wrapper. "Oh, jeez. *Tamarisk Removal and River Restoration Project.* Nobody but kayakers and birdwatchers are going to wade through this beat-around-the-bush crap. Blah, blah, *non-native species*, blah, blah, *riparian habitat*. It should just say, hey, campers, we're getting rid of the invasive species—and you're it! Who wrote this crap? It's like we're dropping warning leaflets before the bombers come. They'll see Amy and Richard and think it's a police action. Nobody'll stick around to talk."

A trim Hispanic man in office-pressed Dickies workwear leaned against a Public Works truck nearby. Was Señor Dickies part of this? Where were the others? Meg had handed off the leaflets but she felt responsibility sticking to her fingers.

Señor Dickies checked his watch.

Ugh. She had to stop that. Snap-naming strangers had started as a game she invented to bug Brian, who was so adamantly against stereotyping. She'd give herself three seconds to come up with an original label based on first appearances, to see if she could make him laugh. It was supposed to be ironic, a commentary on his hyper-correctness. Now it was just a bad habit.

She introduced herself. Richard Diaz said he was along to estimate the pre-cleanup before the tamarisk removal could start. "Can't mix the waste streams," he said, looking doubtfully at her feet.

Zack steepled his hands and made a sad clown face. "Oh, please come along."

Such a poor showing. If citizens wanted the river cleaned up, they should do some of this dirty work. They should see the poor people being driven from their homes. The dignitaries would appear to dedicate a new park but where were they today? There was no one important, no one around she needed to impress. What the heck. She kept a ballcap for the sun and a pair of mud shoes in the truck, clodhoppers that would look ridiculous with this dress but perfect to complete the Village People tribute band assembled here in the parking lot.

They started down the nature trail through the cottonwoods and turned onto an unofficial footpath worn through the saltgrass.

Richard Diaz pointed out places he had played while growing up just across the parkway. The riverfront was much cleaner now but his neighborhood had scarcely changed. Two blocks of six-hundred-square-foot houses quartered by alleys and pinched by industrial lots was all that remained of Las Colonias, the settlement for workers at the old sugar beet mill. His grandparents had always pronounced Noland Avenue *No-Land*, he said, as if they were not certain it was theirs.

"I was born a spic, grew up a beaner, joined the Navy as a Mexican-American and came home Hispanic. Now my men call me boss…" He paused. It was clearly a line he'd used before. "To my face, anyway."

Some days the town seemed immovable. It was good to hear Richard's perspective and remember some changes took more than a lifetime.

They reached a sandy catch basin reinforced with tumbled and broken concrete slabs. A mired shopping cart pointed where the trail climbed the far bank and continued through hummocks lush with tall grass too fat to stand. This was the paradox of the valley's alluvial bottom: stretches of ground that looked suitable only for adobe bricks until water was applied. For decades, this floodplain had been trampled by industry. The introduction of tamarisk to stabilize the eroding riverbanks had seemed like an improvement. But the thirsty guest and its drinking buddy the Russian olive choked out the willows, cottonwoods and native grasses, leaving thorny thickets too dense even for nesting birds. But ideal for concealing campsites.

Barking set off as they cleared the other side. They waited to see if any dogs came out to challenge them. Meg spotted a flash of red, then a flutter of yellow. A woman draped in a striped bedspread stepped from a green dome tent tucked into the thatch. She glanced their way and then dipped out of sight. From this distance, the encampment looked serene but Meg couldn't help but think of cavalry descending on a sleeping village.

A massacre was called for, she supposed. With tamarisk it was all or nothing. Given a foothold, it bunched close as broccoli, withstood drought, fire and flood, sucked up two hundred gallons of water per plant per day, and excreted salt back into the soil so only sea grasses would grow. *Like Assyrians laying ruin to conquered lands.* The survivors had no choice but to leave their homes.

Amy Hostetter had walked quietly along with their little band. Now she squared her duty belt and clicked into full officer mode. "Here's the deal. We're going to be friendly and safe. Today's no different than walking up to somebody's front door. Say hello before you go in. If you see somebody's home, ask if you can approach. If they say no, tell them you got some information for them and ask where you can leave it. Nobody around, just stick it in plain sight and move on. Stay clear of the dogs. I'm here to head off trouble. If anything makes you uneasy, back off and give me a shout."

Two pit bulls lunged against their tethers, defending the clearing around the first tent. The striped bedspread Meg had glimpsed through the tamarisk now hung from a bicycle inner tube stretched between two sturdy Russian olives. If the woman who'd placed it there was still around, she did not respond to Zack's call. A lawn chair appeared to lie beyond the perimeter guarded by the dogs. As he approached it, Amy motioned him back.

"Look again," she said. The pits were tied to the ends of a rope threaded through a ring sunk into the ground. "If one attacks and the other one retreats, he's got the full length for a run at you."

Amy folded a flier into a paper airplane. She lofted it and the dogs followed her arm motion, then braked and looked around in confusion. The glider arced to its apex, wobbled and coasted to a landing near the tent. "Some police action, huh?"

Meg placed a leaflet under a rock atop a licorice-red sleeping bag, in the lattice of a camp chair, pinned one to a clothesline. Richard stopped to take pictures and make notes about location of the camps. As Zack had predicted, they worked for about twenty minutes without encountering anyone. They all met again where two trails converged on a stretch of beach. A kicked-over fire ring flashed the blackened teeth of a broken shipping pallet. A worn blue comforter spread on the rumpled sand. Fronds of tamarisk bobbed in the breeze. Someone had spent the night here under the moon listening to the river trickle over the gravel shallows.

"This is going to be a nice park someday," she said.

Zack scowled. "It already is nice for the people who are here. But they don't deserve it because somebody's decided they can make a buck on it."

What was he talking about? This was city land. Everything was evil capitalism with him, power politics versus the downtrodden. You'd think he'd never met a businessperson with a soul.

Zack showed her where a vet named Wesley Chambers had set up camp across the channel. A stripped white bicycle frame anchored a crude footing of submerged stones between the beach and a low island choked by more tamarisk. A beaten pair of desert tan boots faced the shore. Painted on the toe of the right boot: *NO*. On the left: *GO*.

"Wesley and a couple others live there. When the boots are pointed the other way, the heels say *OK*, which means visitors can cross."

"What if you don't know the code?" said Meg. She peered toward the island. Something about empty boots used as a warning. Or maybe it was the bike frame, like bones of the drowned. She was ready for this to be over.

"Wesley's okay. Just wade over and poke a flier in the boot," Amy said. "No need to disturb him."

"There's no need to disturb anyone," Zack snapped. "No one's hurting anything."

"Except for the ones with the loose dogs, open fires, trash.

Fighting, rape, drug abuse. Kids don't belong here. And you know it's unsanitary for everybody."

"So kick them off the river and make it illegal to camp anywhere else. If this town really cared, they'd have a place to go."

"I hear you, but why should taxpayers be deprived of enjoying their riverfront?" Amy said. "Nobody wants them to suffer, but there's a price tag for everything in life."

"Yeah, so many people in favor of doing the right thing. So many excuses not to do it."

"Our team's trying, just like you are. But not everybody wants our help. People like Wesley are down here for a reason."

"So am I," Zack said. "A *good* reason."

Up ahead a pale cottonwood towered fifty feet high, its bark in rags, limbs uplifted as if in surrender.

Stabilize the riverbanks and kill the trees. Reclaim the abandoned parkland and dislodge the poor. Offer helpful services and create dependence. Meg's business was so simple in comparison. Buyers and sellers brought contending interests to the table. They understood both sides had to be satisfied for a deal to work. The money was important but she helped find other ways to complete the transaction. The parties shook hands. Closure. In business, money was the lubricant that got things done, while in public matters, it was the reason to accept shameful outcomes.

Amy said, "This is your big night, right? If you need to leave, go ahead."

"It's okay. I've kind of stepped away from managing the event." It was flattering to know Amy knew.

Scholarship Night had been Meg's creation. In the first year it had been an achievement just to get scholarship recipients from the four district high schools to appear on one stage. The resulting shuffle of teens receiving a handshake from the superintendent was no one's idea of a fun night out, so Meg proposed a follies format for the second year, letting students demonstrate the talent they considered responsible for their scholarship. The staid ceremony turned into a variety show with musical performances and dramatic readings, dribbling exhibitions and blindfolded gymnasts on balance beams. One scholarship winner declaimed a sonnet celebrating the Tenth Amendment. A science nerd recited *pi* to one hundred places while juggling glass beakers. A kid dressed as a rodeo clown rode a mechanical bull from a defunct country and western club.

"Well, I hope the kids are still doing those crazy tricks," Amy said.

"Unfortunately, no. It was too much fun. The school administration squashed it. They made it into a reminder of why bright kids don't come back after college. Maybe we could slip in a guest appearance, though, if you have a trick you'd like to perform."

"I'm not that entertaining, really."

"My ex-husband called you a stud. He said you played ball as if you had superpowers."

"I wish."

"Okay, superpower granted. What would it be?"

Amy paused. Meg heard it, too, a low drift of voices. The disembodied murmur so close by chilled her. The sound came from a section they hadn't yet canvassed, near the dead cottonwood.

Amy noted the direction but showed no concern. "Okay, I'll take time travel, the power to give people do-overs. I'd return kids back to the day before they were abused, before they first shoplifted because their folks didn't feed them, before they tried booze or weed or meth. If I only had one shot, it would be Jimmy Johncock, the first guy from the river we finally got into rehab. Tony and I went when Jimmy graduated from a program in Denver. We were so proud. We were new to this outreach stuff and we'd thought we'd made a save. Three years later, Jimmy's right back here."

Richard and Zack appeared from a side path. Amy motioned to them to wait.

"Just to be safe, I want to check it out up there," she said.

Amy walked down the path and stopped where it made a turn toward the thick understory around the cottonwood. She fingered the radio mic clipped to her shoulder and spoke too quietly to understand. A dog started woofing, setting off the pit bull pair behind them.

"Anybody home?" Amy called. The barking intensified. Meg thought she heard muffled curses. "Grand Junction Police. Secure your dog and you're fine. We're just bringing by some information for you."

A hoarse voice called back, "Hang on, hang on, just a minute."

Amy raised a hand toward Meg and then disappeared around the bend.

The voices again, one high and one low, words impossible to sort out. Branches crackled and snapped. Meg thought she heard a car door thump closed. There was no road in here... No, it was more like a watermelon dropped on the ground. The dog quiet now. Scrambling sounds of retreat, then the commotion stopped.

Okay, she's letting them go.

Meg and Richard waited, expecting to hear the okay. Zack had a different notion.

"Amy!" he cried. "Amy!"

Amy. When they ran in her direction, it was toward the silence.

Home is where the memories are.

—"Home" with Meg Mogrin, *Grand Junction Style*

The Avalon Theater, built as an opera house just as vaudeville was expiring, had devolved into a movie theater before being abandoned by a bankrupt cinema chain. After community efforts had failed to revive the building as a performing arts center, the Avalon stood as a city-owned monument to stalemate, too treasured to level and too costly to renovate. In the lobby, the scholarship kids ignored their parents and dribbled salsa on the carpet. Teachers, out of habit, scanned for trouble. Businessmen thumped each other's backs, their accessory wives already in the auditorium, saving seats and clutching purses they dared not set on the gummy floor. Meg lingered under the marquee glow with the stragglers measuring their pre-event cigarettes. Eve Winslow had promised to meet her, but Meg understood that Eve might be playing mayor at the hospital tonight.

At least Meg had not seen the worst of it, only Amy on the ground and the rusty truck wheel above her quivering from a cable like some malevolent sputnik. Richard Diaz stopped Meg and told her to call 911. Zack and Richard worked to stabilize Amy, while she went out to direct the EMTs back to the scene. Amy was alive when they took her out. All Meg had heard since was a brief news report and angry accusations on talk radio.

This event was difficult enough, watching another girl accept her sister's memorial scholarship, celebrating one's potential while being reminded of another's loss. She wasn't going to be pathetic about being stood up. She'd give Eve a few more minutes before chancing a run past Senator Pinecone, camped at the entrance. The former state senator turned clean coal lobbyist had just snared a banker with a handshake only a check could uncouple.

Her phone vibrated, the call from Jay DeWitt, a hotshot hospital executive from back east. After viewing at least thirty homes, DeWitt and his wife decided to build. The lot they'd recently closed on posed some challenges but its view overlooking the city was stunning.

"Did you get my texts?"

"Just opening them now, Jay."

"Well, take a look. It's a travesty!"

A photo of four large dirt mounds. The second shot showed the piles from a different angle. Another offered a close-up.

"I'm not sure I see what's going on here." She didn't do dirt, she sold houses.

"It was supposed to be *clean fill*. The loads don't match—brown, putty-colored, tan. This last one they delivered is pinkish and chunky, like somebody shelled shrimp in a sand box."

"It obviously came from different sites around the valley. Clean means it's not polluted, that's all. It's just compaction fill. It doesn't have to match." She took a deep breath. *Jesus. Artisanal fill.* "What would you like me to do?"

"You sold us the lot. You found us the builder. You fix it."

At least DeWitt had called her instead of raining down on the contractor, whose relationship was more important to her long term. Imported jerks like DeWitt tended to depart suddenly with enemies and severance packages, and his new house might be on the market before too long. To keep the door open, Meg left him with assurances she hoped sounded more cheerful than they felt.

The morning's trauma had drained her reserves. No more multitasking. Though it went against her grain, she set her phone to Do Not Disturb and slipped it in her bag. She had meant to bring her brightest, most vivacious self here, but in the lobby glass she saw a gypsy woman exhausted after a long day of telling fortunes. Pairing jangly beaded earrings with a messy bun pulled up in a silk scarf wasn't such a festive disguise after all. Out in public, it took effort to maintain the super agent vibe when she disliked makeup and didn't look like Norah Jones to start with. Clients expected to meet the woman in the photo on her website, the one whose headshot leapt out of the real estate section filled with agents posing confidently in their big hair and statement necklaces. She had spent two hours getting ready for her first photoshoot and another two under the lights, only to look like someone she had never seen before, had never been. The agency ran with the shot until she went off on her own and replaced it with something more realistic, more Grand Junction and less Palm Beach, but still stylish and warm and energetic and savvy. Meg Mogrin reduced to a one-inch thumbnail. That picture was always in her head somewhere, the standard, the summation, the brand. But it was nowhere on her face tonight.

"You here solo?" a voice purred and an arm looped through hers. She turned into the piano-key grin of Donnie Barclay. Donnie glowed like someone half-famous, a second-rung character actor on his way to Telluride. Some moneyed people cultivated the blazer, boots and Levis look. Meg suspected Donnie merely lost interest in dressing up halfway down. Either way, it served his purpose. Without changing his costume, he could play the ranching patriarch with a little sideline gravel business or the prosperous entrepreneur who still clung to the old family homestead.

"I was supposed to meet Eve," said Meg. "Something must've come up."

"Oh, you know how that goes." Donnie knew how everything went. "Eve runs behind 'cause it filters out the weak and the impatient."

He squeezed her arm against his ribs and leaned in so close Meg could smell wintergreen on his breath. Donnie wasn't a flirt. He was interested in information. "Do you need to wait? I was hoping you could be my protector tonight."

"From Toby?" Toby Conifer, Senator Pinecone's proper name.

"From embarrassment. Toby's let the kooks get to him. Used to be you could count on him to support ranching and drilling and stay-out-of-my-wallet. Now he wants to be sheriff and thinks we should run the county like its own damn country. Which I guess you can, if you like living in the eighteenth century. I need to find me another Republican."

"Well, that shouldn't be hard around here," she said.

Donnie flicked his chaw into a waste bin. "He's just started to tell a dirty joke. Let's dive in while we have an opening." They slipped through the entry, leaving the senator to wave a futile limb. "Now we gotta get past the lady from the history farm. Look at me like you're fascinated as hell."

He had cheered her up already. "Maybe you should've brought Terri with you if you need protection so badly."

"Oh, Terri hates this shit. People who want to kiss my ass are always kissing hers just in case. The history farm wants Barclay Paving to buy some old Gilsonite mining cars for an *interpretive asphalt exhibit*, whatever the hell that is. I think it's just a way to get a choo-choo train for the school kids."

"Kids need to learn about our agricultural heritage."

"I'm sure. But I already spend a ton to preserve it"—he winked—"every year I hang onto the ranch. You coming up this year?"

"I don't know. Maybe."

"You can't work all the time. You gotta have some fun, too."

"The real estate market's coming back. I have some years to make up for."

"Yup, I know." He released her arm and turned to face her full on. "You gonna be okay tonight? You look a tad frazzled."

Donnie, bless him, thought he knew what weighed on her. More than two decades since Helen fell off Cold Shivers Point and Neulan Kornhauer came briefly under suspicion. Nearly a dozen years since Neulan's role in other women's deaths came to light. His flight and disappearance. Eight years ago, Meg took over funding the scholarship from her parents.

"Who's your girl this year?"

"You can't miss her. She'll be the one with the purple streak in her hair. She sings in a band, plays piano and bass guitar, and her name's Pandora Cox. How could I not pick her?"

"Sounds like a handful," he said.

"That's sort of the point."

"Is it a single-year deal or do you keep four scholarships going at a time?"

She could see him doing the math in his head. "Depends. Some are two-year community college grants. Not all the kids finish." Some who graduated had opted for marriage over career or assumed a bland adulthood. A few disappeared entirely. None had achieved the trajectory Meg had imagined for Helen.

"I didn't exactly know your sister." Donnie's gaze flicked out of the theater and came back to Meg. "But I feel your loss. I'm sure it's not easy with that Kornhauer sonofabitch still out there."

"I put him out of my mind long ago," she said.

"Well, let's hope he's gone for good, and that it was a slow, nasty trip."

The scholarship winners trooped onstage. A boy led the audience in the Pledge of Allegiance and then a young woman stepped to a keyboard set up behind a microphone stand. In all black, she had a classical singer's fullness and bearing, except for an amber wave through her purple hair. Pandora Cox rippled some opening chords. When her fingers reached the tonic, she rounded her lips into an 0 as if to say, *you're right, this is not going to be "The Star Spangled Banner."*

In an earthy alto she sang "America the Beautiful," drawing the nostalgia from the first verse's spacious skies and fruited plain. After a quiet shedding of grace, she marched the next verse in a more military cadence past the alabaster cities. This time the refrain slipped into a minor key. Were others hearing this lamentation? A vision of America with gleaming cities walled away from human suffering. Where goodness and brotherhood dwindled into shining seas.

"Well, that was different," Donnie said.

The daytime newscaster emcee asked a moment of silence from the already hushed audience *for the quick recovery of our fallen police officer*, then moved to his script, projecting a big-screen baby picture before summoning each award winner. The gimmick brought hoots from friends and family members but fell short of the loopy celebration Scholarship Night once had been. Not all of them were performers. Perhaps most kids preferred a more solemn event, appropriate to the idea their lives were about to change course. They could learn later that teachers could end up selling real estate, that poets made coffee for commuters, that engineers got laid off and lost their houses.

This is their show now, not yours. Not even Helen's.

When Pandora collected her parchment, Donnie squeezed Meg's shoulder. She turned, she thought, in appreciation, but her face must have told him it was time to go. He took her hand and ducked up the aisle.

Refreshed by their spontaneous flight and the cool outside air, Meg wasn't ready to go home. Donnie seemed to see that and headed her to the corner of Seventh where B.B. King's "The Thrill is Gone" tramped and tumbled over the patio bar. A glass of the Entrada Cabernet would be nice, maybe two. She just had to make sure Donnie didn't order a bottle because it would be all hers.

As they waited for their drinks, she entertained him with an account of her conversation with Jay DeWitt. Normally, she would never discuss a client by name, but Donnie was in the excavation business and would have figured it out based on how few houses were going up right now. He chuckled at her idea of supplying high-grade fill to picky customers, once she explained what *artisanal* meant. Oh, it was lovely to laugh after this hard day! She started to ease out of her heels and stopped. The relief in her feet told her she might not get them back on.

Donnie sipped his Windsor and Seven. "It's been pouring out-of-town geniuses lately. I hear the mayor's got you roped in with some corporate bigwig."

Where had he heard that? Eve had asked her to put together some ideas for an executive home tour and hinted that the related business might be substantial. But Meg didn't even know the name of the man's company yet.

"All Eve's told me is that he's divorced."

This bit of non-news appeared to please Donnie. "Yeah, I thought the city was in on it. Everybody's being so damn coy. At the Chamber meetings, Dan McCallam's about to pee his pants with excitement but he's keeping the news to himself. And Vince Foyer's not as subtle as he thinks. He's been poking around looking at good-sized parcels that are off the market. It's hard for a developer to take a crap in this county without me at least smelling it."

It had been a long dry spell for Donnie's gravel and paving businesses. Any development would be good news. He held plenty of commercial/industrial property around town, too.

"It's killing you not to know, isn't it?"

He bared his lower teeth and patted his wallet pocket. "Yeah, my tender little ego." They laughed. "You're looking perkier now."

There was no point withholding it. "Did you hear about the mess with Amy Hostetter this morning? I was down there when it happened."

"Are you okay? And here I been talking nothing but business."

He could be so sweet. Father sweet.

"Your company's been just what I needed. Listen, what if this tour I'm working on turns out to be related to your deal? Do you think Terri would let me show your summer house?"

"It's not for sale," he said.

"Just as an example. Glade Park should be on any tour of exclusive places to live. And for the full cultural experience, a ranch owner could show him around."

"I'll check with the boss." Donnie took her hand and wrapped it in both of his. "I'm glad you didn't get hurt. They can't clean up that shit hole fast enough to suit me."

As soon as Donnie left Meg at her car, she pulled off her heels and pitched them across the seat. Her third pair of shoes today—no, the fourth, counting the mudders. She had repackaged every part of herself at least twice for the day's events and was now ready for a robe and that third glass of wine she'd turned down at the bar. But instead of heading straight home, she looped south toward the river where her morning began.

Las Colonias Park wasn't on anyone's way, and that was its attraction to the homeless population. The feds had poured millions into clearing the ground of uranium tailings and the city had spent millions more to relocate junkyards and build a parkway to skirt the south edge of downtown. But the park itself had remained perpetually on the drawing board. Except for the Botanical Gardens, Las Colonias Park was only a barren river flats hemmed by a scraggle of tamarisk and split by a bike path.

She pulled over near the last remnant of the old uranium mill across from the park and peered through the streetlamp flare. No one about. No lights coming from the camps. It was as if night had already absorbed the day's horror into the bleak history of the place. There was nothing specific about such darkness. It could contain any dreadfulness, including the worst mistake of her life. The memory came back like a poorly fixed Polaroid, a bright white blank with smudges and shadows creeping to the foreground.

Right over there. About this time of night.

There was no Botanical Gardens building then. The junkyard had been off to the right and some shacks straight ahead where the hardpan was glazed in ghostly alkali blotched with crankcase oil. They had abandoned the Jeep there with the keys in the ignition, counting on some derelict to cover the vehicle with fingerprints. Their impulse turned out better than they had imagined. The Jeep ended up trashed near the Amtrak station in Salt Lake City, where everyone assumed Neulan Kornhauer had left it, after eluding the authorities closing in on him. Back in Grand Junction, security camera footage had showed the Choirmaster Killer fueling his vehicle and filling a reserve gas can on the day he disappeared. Then no more charge card transactions. No sightings. A decade later, investigators still combed coroner's reports on young women who had fallen from high places, keen to pick up Neulan's trail. Only Meg and Brian could tell them they should be searching instead for his bones.

The lights of a police cruiser illuminated her car's interior with the sad blue cast of a failing nightspot. Although she was driving barefoot, she hadn't done anything obviously illegal. He'd see she was respectable. She watched in the mirror as he got out of the squad car and hitched himself in three places before beginning the slow walk to her side.

"Everything all right, ma'am?"

She'd had only two glasses of wine but wasn't eager to pronounce the fact, and she was careful not to fumble the retrieval of her registration. He looked at her license, looked at her, then back to the picture, then to her, each time pausing a trifle longer.

"You heading home now, Ms. Mogrin?"

She nodded, thankful he hadn't asked her to step out for a roadside exam.

"Just because there's no traffic doesn't make it okay to stop here. It's posted."

"I'm sorry. I was here this morning when Officer Hostetter got hurt. I came back to... offer a prayer."

"I'm sure she'd appreciate your concern." He tapped the license on the window rim. "So you know this's not a good area to be stopping this time of night."

"It's on the way up, though, don't you think? Someday, the city will come back to the river." She couldn't help it. Maybe that's all her prayer was intended to be: something hopeful spoken over this bloodied soil.

"I care about what happens tonight," he said, returning her papers. "You drive home safe and leave the riverside to us."

She pulled away carefully and watched to be sure the officer didn't follow. She couldn't go home yet. That wasn't a good place for forgetting, either.

She headed for the Interstate, dropped her windows so the crosswinds buffeted the interior and pushed to a practically legal eighty. At the Palisade exit she circled back, desert scrub to her right, orchards and vineyards on the left, the city ahead glowing like a radium dial.

It was Neulan's fault. He had phoned her on his way out of town, for reasons she could only guess. It was her fault. Instead of hanging up, she agreed to meet him and chose the place. It was Brian's fault. Playing the protector, his adrenaline-washed reflexes. It was their fault. The two of them each half-thinking and relying on the other. They should have simply walked away. Or called the police, admitted they were idiots and told an approximation of the truth before their mistakes became compounded by cover-up. But in their moment of panic, they could not arrange their acts into a plausible narrative of how Neulan had died.

In truth, she was gratified to have trapped a dazed Neulan

at the cliff edge and to prod his faith, question his rectitude and accuse him of murders he refused to neither admit nor deny. Neulan pitching off Cold Shivers Point meant there would be no similar, self-justifying public forum. His anonymous end seemed just retribution for having reduced young women like Helen to a few lines in a memorial scholarship.

Brian, though, spiraled down into an anguish he could not quell. While she slumbered, he jolted up out of sleep, gasping, clawing back time. He was so keen to repair the world's wounds and assume its burdens. That had always been the difference between them—and the attraction. She observed wrongs and he went forth to right them. It was as if she wielded his healing power.

One manic night, tossed by visions of flash floods and floating corpses, Brian riveted her with a question: *What if it's found?*

It—the body, Neulan kept nameless. Their encounter had become the incident; Neulan's fall, the mishap; their cover-up was resolution. Abstraction was best to deal with such worries. But bones were most stubborn things.

A click and a rustling told her Brian had returned. He was undressing in the dark by their apartment's front door. So as not to wake her? He should have known her blood would be thundering, her senses alert to the faintest sound. Floorboards muttered his approach. His weight pressed a sigh from the mattress. She rolled to face him and was shocked to meet a foul marinade of sweat, gasoline and smoke.

Both of them stared at the four-o'clock ceiling.

"Is everything okay?" she whispered.

After a deep breath and long exhale to stop his voice from quaking, he said, "No, of course it's not." A moment later, he corrected himself. "I've never done this before, so how would I know?"

He was shivering. She sought his hand and found it over his sternum, cradling a fist. "I'm sorry you had to do this," she said.

"Let's not keep going over it," he said. "It's done."

It was. But they could not resolve what it meant. Brian wanted to confess without implicating her. She refused to allow his sacrifice for what she believed was a proper outcome. They finally agreed they would come forth together or not at all. Their trust, which had always offset their differences, now cemented their conspiracy, and they continued to live in this suspended state of disagreement until the impasse devolved into a numbness that made them inaccessible to each other.

To atone, Brian chose to live according to his convictions; he jumped back into teaching. Meg fled the classroom, no longer willing to present herself as a moral figure; her solution was to reinvent herself. The effects of their split passed for its cause. Brian's new job on a Hopi Indian reservation was incompatible with Meg's new career in real estate. Her friends, who had weathered their own family decisions, thought they understood.

You've been a busy girl.

I wondered when you'd show up tonight.

I wouldn't miss it. The scholarship's in my honor, after all. But despite that, it's been hard to get a thought in edgewise.

Is that what our conversations are—thoughts?

I think it's best if we don't get too analytical here. I thought I detected a whiff of him tonight. You know he's not welcome.

Sorry. It was involuntary.

No kidding. Let's talk about the girl.

What did you think of her?

If only Mom and Dad had named me something cool like Pandora!

You didn't need the help.

I will take that as a compliment.

Do. I miss you, Hel.

You have made that plain, Madge, and I appreciate the effort.

So you approve.

Yes. She's the best one so far.

But not the best ever.

No. That would take a miracle.

An unknown number from AZ, USA, sat in Meg's missed calls the next morning. No message. A robocall or an out-of-state prospect? She sensed it was neither. She only knew one person in the 928 area code. Reaching out and retreating was about the only way she ever heard from Brian. His last actual words had come postmarked from Tuba City two years ago. No salutation, signature or return address. Nothing precisely personal in the eighteen lines of semi-erotic free verse that fell out of the envelope. She granted him the occasional bout of longing. On the chance his call on the day of Helen's remembrance was something more than a coincidence, she called the number.

A woman answered—*Food Mart*—in what sounded like a Native American lilt. What sort of tale had Brian told so he could use the phone? He wasn't a charmer, exactly, but he was trustworthy, definitely the type a woman would let behind the counter.

"I'd like to leave a message for Brian Mogrin if he comes in. Do you know him?"

"Maybe."

"Then please write this down. Ready?"

"Go ahead."

"No message is still a message."

"That's it?"

It was not. She wanted to say: Do you think you're the only one with yearnings? If Brian had tired of his exile, she understood. Penance should have an end. But he must do better than no-return-address poetry and convenience store cryptograms.

"He'll know the rest."

Do you have any problems concentrating and/or remembering things?

—Vulnerability Index Prescreen for Single Adults

A shrill buzzing rose and fell, approached and departed, chattered as it slowed and then screamed away again. Two circuits. Three. Then quiet. Not a weed whacker; they burned weeds out here. He checked the sky. The sheriff's drone flew as high as four hundred feet so it might be hard to spot. Shouldn't surveillance be silent? If the point was sowing intimidation, though, it was working. His noise-infected thoughts circled the idea of retreat.

Same reason he'd left the river. To choose a camp you had to understand who was there as well as who had been there the longest or who was strongest, because they set the rules and vetted the campers. Then you had to know who was allowed to ignore the rules, because there were always exceptions and hidden power struggles, and watch the watchers, looking for something to steal. The worst was all those voices worse for wear: pointless quarrels, selfish complaints, the ignorant things people said. The call and response of sleepers yelping at the drunks to *shut up!* and the drunks bellowing at the sleepers to *go to hell!*

At the first sign of Lord of the Flies, it was time to get out.

The *zeeeeEEEEEEEEE* started up again like line spooling from a hot reel. He saw three of them now, too big to be playing in the road with a radio-controlled car, drinking from what looked like tennis ball cans. They didn't seem that dangerous but danger didn't always look like itself. He checked the sheath in his sock, just in case. He hated carrying a knife but he didn't want to be someone who died for disregarding the wisdom of the pack. *Isaac was that fool who got robbed clubbed stabbed choked kicked to death in his camp because he didn't listen, because he made himself too easy to take.* So he listened and slept with Jake's knife beneath his pad where he could find it. And each night its cold point edged a little closer to his heart.

Way too much sugar. Sometimes the bagel shop gave Isaac a day-old freebie if he'd take his coffee to go. None today but he took his order outside anyway. Always too much of this or not enough of that, a buzz in his head or a rumble in his gut. He didn't starve or pig out but he had no routine, either. Non-refrigerateds, pull-top cans, cereal out of the box, denteds and expireds. Peanut butter, canned meats and beans for protein. Salted snacks, energy bars, pepperoni, Little Debbie cakes can't go bad. Pickles had vitamins but no calories. He wasn't a fan of fruit; if it was free, it was already too ripe. Cabbage was okay, just peel off the bad leaves. Brick cheese, scrape off the mold. Priced-for-Quick-Sale baskets, BOGO, Manager's Special, Tuesday Tacos. Five-Dollar-Friday whole roasted chicken, too much to eat by himself so share it with somebody who shared back. Soup kitchen closed on weekends, so today it's church-basement Wonder Bread sandwiches served with blessings at Whitman Park. Filling, but who puts margarine on a cheese sandwich? Some guys speed-bus the tables at the food court, but he had strict standards. Nobody's leftovers for him. Creamer, sugar and ketchup packs only—but no more sugar today! No shoplifting and stay out of dumpsters, too. Isaac left that to the ones who couldn't do any better. A pride thing. It saved money to live rentless but it cost you years, sniffles, soggy clothes, lost belongings, shrinkage of yourself. Living small made you seem smaller, less significant. Not many fat people living on the river. No master bedrooms or two-car garages. They had nothing but that wasn't what put people like Isaac in a tent. It was having too much of something. Thoughts, panics, blues, smoke, drink, drugs, attitude. Like the sugar shakes he had right now. Maybe if he biked hard back to camp he could burn it off before he crashed.

Isaac Samson's camp was almost perfect. Miles from the river and even further from the aimless flutter around the Bermuda Triangle of the shelter, Walmart and the mental health clinic. It was concealed in a thicket of ditchwater trees next to a leased hay field back from a stub road that ran between an office park and the Goodwill, where they didn't care if he used the restroom. The Express Suites had a free breakfast where half the guests looked like they came from a shelter with their flannel pants and blank eyes. It was good to grab a banana, honey and some hard-boiled eggs, but he didn't overdo it. The nearby mall was depressing in a bus-station-the-day-after-Christmas way and Security stink-eyed anyone with a backpack, but he could keep cool in the summer if he dressed clean, carried a book and stayed out of the stores.

Across the road were a few dozen vinyl-clad townhouses built right before the crash. The owners not foreclosed were too stunned from being underwater to do much of anything but work and watch TV with the blinds closed. Next door, a scatter of outbuildings behind a small house farmer-built with no particular style, now occupied by renters who either turned over quickly or whose appearance changed drastically according to the meth supply. On the face of it, maybe not a premier set-up but Isaac had a notarized letter from the landowner informing To Whom It May Concern that Isaac Samson had Barry Lester's permission to camp there.

Barry collected rent off the books from the rough clan next door while waiting for the housing market to resume its northward march across his property. Isaac camped at the edge of the field in exchange for a couple hours a day at Freedom City, where Barry signed the paychecks. Well, not paychecks; Barry paid only in cash and only for special jobs like rigging a flagpole or setting up a bounce castle for a party.

Barry started out as Flag City, selling specialty flags via what they used to call mail order, mostly to customers who bought Made in America. His best products were U.S. military standards and POW-MIA flags, the fringed guidons used by color guards and in government buildings, school and custom rodeo banners sewed by relatives Barry's Internet bride Mai brought over from Vietnam. The walk-in store stocked flags of all nations and denominations for patriots and party animals alike. The Confederate battle flag, Jolly Rogers, lapel pin flags and bunting, Broncos car pennants, boat flags with martini glasses and Playboy Bunnies, peace symbols, rainbows, Yin-Yang and Tibetan prayer flags, Catholic flags, Episcopalian flags. Just about anything except a Muslim flag or hammer and sickle. Swastikas were available but strictly behind the counter for collectors only.

Flag City's glory time came post-9/11, but even an enthusiastic repeat flag customer only shows up about once a decade. Meanwhile Barry's Chinese suppliers had figured out patriotism had certain price points and started selling below him, direct over the Internet. Compete, grow or die, that was capitalism, and Barry couldn't afford to die. Some of his best Stars and Stripes and Don't Tread On Me customers were into survivalism. One day Barry watched a prepper webinar that convinced him he wasn't in the flag business, he was in the Preserving Our Way of Life business, which would kick into high gear once the central government and its fiat currency went bankrupt. He renamed the store Freedom City and stocked up on prepper specialty items. Unfortunately, the sales of home generators, water purifiers, hand-cranked radios and macaroni in ten-gallon tubs peaked without black helicopters and global collapse. So why not celebrate in the meantime with patriotic and holiday yard decorations? Get someone to go for Frosty the Snowman one winter, he might think about an Easter Bunny or a Jack-o-Lantern for next time the grandkids came over. Inflatables were an impulse buy. Nobody went shopping for a Hansel and Gretel popping from an oven. Barry's customers had to see them full-size and in action so to speak, to be aware they could choose from Santas in all kinds of situations, even one coming out of an outhouse—add the laughing elf for twenty bucks more. The next Christmas they could add a Lamb of God Jesus or a blow-up nativity scene, although in Isaac's opinion, the Mary and Joseph in that one looked too much like Cabbage Patch Kids.

Placed outdoors, the displays attracted attention from the heavy mall-bound traffic but also from kids who liked to shoot Rudolph the Red-Nosed Reindeer with a pellet gun or relocate Frankenstein to a neighbor's swimming pool. Since Barry was a desk potato and Mai weighed about as much as two of the sandbags used to anchor the displays, neither was keen about the daily set-up and tear-down required. They needed someone who'd work an hour in the morning and another at night, for next to nothing and no chance of advancement. Who better than the guy they caught mining cardboard in the Freedom City dumpster? A satisfactory arrangement all around.

Isaac's time was constrained by his open-and-close, seven-day-a-week bargain with Barry. He had to fill the empty hours without his head overflowing. Moving, waiting, thinking, always thinking. Thoughts ballooned, threatening to carry him away. Or they snagged high in the trees. The voices he sometimes heard came from his own mind, he knew, at least now when they were silent. But somewhere real words were being formed by real lips and they gathered in unwaveable clouds of gnats and bats and wasps whose sting he could not reason away. He always carried a book as if it were a device to arrest his mind's fibrillation. He'd find a story, trace a line at a time, turn the pages and lose himself in the flow. A book was *coverpaperinkletterwordphrasesentenceparagraphpagechaptertheend.* So few things were so finely connected like that.

He unrolled his yoga mat and settled against a bale filched from the hay field. He was half into a good story about a cowboy being squeezed off his land by a greater power. The same old story, really. The horse was going to die, but Isaac looked forward to that part, knowing his heart would be broken. He cried for whatever could turn out no other way than it always did. He cried for the good horses more than the good men because they were faithful, without any notion of their fate.

A line struck him. He unwrapped the crucifix of thick rubber bands around his notebook. He'd bought the entire stock of red and black cloth-bound volumes from a Barnes and Noble bargain table. In the reds he recorded passages from his reading, random observations, overheard conversations and rants. On visits to his storage unit, he copied the chronological entries into black books organized by categories: *Coincidence, Wrong, Puzzle, Structure and Systems, Findings, Edison/Reagan* and *Elements of Control.*

Isaac read until the evening passed into a grey that turned the letters runic. He watched the fading words form lines, then blocks, then merge into a black page. The transition reminded him of drifting into sleep, but also of Barry slowly going out of business, of the decline of empires, of death descending. Every fading of the light is our preview of the end, he thought, and when the end doesn't come, we start to believe the movie is never-ending.

Somewhere near, a shush, foam and fizzle. A gush of sparks arose, flowered green and descended as if broadcast from a king-size lawn sprinkler. A rattlesnake of firecrackers. A red thunderbolt shot above the trees, chased by a whistle and a sonic boom. Sporadic explosions, as if drunks on a firing range had vowed to shoot until they each hit a target. To the sound of ripping canvas, a multistage rocket spilled yellow, blue, white and red seed over the hayfield. A concussion seemed to slap the leaves above his head—and then silence. Cardboard flakes drifted down in a scorched cloud smelling of gunpowder, iron filings and burnt toast. Abruptly, a pair of light bars converged from opposite directions, flashing red, white and blue. Pounding feet. The dampened voices of feral types who for the rest of their lives would be hearing: *You have the right to remain silent.*

One squad nosed into the yard next door, while the other crept along the road, its spotlight licking the row of townhouses. The right-hand spot found the double-track into the hayfield and zeroed in on the trees. Isaac's hideaway was nearly invisible in full sunlight but the bright sideways shaft might pick up a shiny grommet or mosquito net sheen that would betray him.

As the car crawled closer, Isaac heard the big police pursuit engine panting.

"Police," a robot voice barked.

No shit.

He knew the routine and wasn't about to make a mistake. He showed his hands first, rose slowly and groped toward the light, stopped when commanded. Waited until the cop asked for his ID. Slipped the rubber band from the stack in his wallet: bus card, clinic card, library card, identity card. Inserted his finger to maintain its place while the cop passed his Maglite beam over the card and then Isaac's face.

"This address is downtown. What're you doing camped way out here?" The address was the Catholic Outreach Day Center mail drop and Isaac was sure the cop knew it.

"I have permission from the owner, a notarized letter says I can be on the property."

The officer shined his flashlight over Isaac's setup. He didn't ask to see the letter. "Trespassing isn't going to be your problem. You know the people next door?"

"Not really."

"You see who was shooting off those fireworks?"

"No," Isaac said. "I was here keeping to my own business."

The cop stepped into the camp and checked the view toward

the road. The brush that provided cover for Isaac worked both ways. Satisfied, he said, "There's a ban on. The drought, the fires on the Front Range, that's everybody's business. Your neighbors don't give a damn so until we get some rain, you'd be wise to sleep somewhere else."

The patrol car backed down the path. At one of the townhouses, a front light clicked off and all its windows went dark. Now they knew where he was. Isaac had been warned and outed all at once. He'd thought of Barry's permission as protection but when did a piece of paper ever stand between him and hurt? He should have learned from the last time never to believe in a letter.

If you weren't in a shelter,
where did you sleep last night?

—*Point-in-Time Homeless Survey*

July third. Last day of *America's Big Blowout Birthday Sale!* at Freedom City. Isaac had tried to get Barry to simplify the banner to *Big 4th of July Sale!* but Barry wasn't interested in advice from a set-up man, not even one with a degree in Library Science. Isaac plugged in the blower and the Air Dancer shimmied upward, its green Elastic Man arms grasping for motorist attention, then he checked the anchors on the fat talons of a twelve-foot-tall, starred-and-striped Bald Eagle. Uncle Sam, straddling a rocket like Slim Pickens in *Dr. Strangelove*, took aim at the Endoscopy Center across the road. A squeeze of the Patriotic Elephant's trunk (Barry didn't stock a Patriotic Donkey) confirmed it had achieved full inflation. High above the parking lot tableau, the store's signature, a quarter-acre Old Glory, idly curled and uncurled like a bullwhip about to slap some sense into a small country. Passersby might keep passing by, but none could escape noticing something big was going on at Freedom City.

After installing the patriotic figures, Isaac turned to the birthday cake. It was so out of sync conceptually and categorically. America celebrated with fireworks and corn on the cob, not cake and candles. Besides, the pastel yellow, pink and blue frosting clashed with the primary colors in the rest of the display. His opinion wasn't welcome on that either.

Isaac unpacked the cake, shipped in a carton so flimsy the cardboard seemed not worth recycling. Its beaten fibers imparted a faint odor of the ocean and off-gassing PVC. He set aside the patch kit and rudimentary instructions smudged onto paper thin enough to roll cigarettes. So what if the cake leaked? You didn't leave a birthday cake up for weeks like you did a Frosty the Snowman. As he pumped the cheap plastic foot bellows that completed the package, the cake stirred and swelled like a drunk trying to get up from the pavement. Isaac wondered what the makers in Guangdong thought about the country receiving these garish totems. Were they mystified that Americans expended their wealth this way? Did they even understand what a lawn was?

Isaac hurried through setting up the hot dog cooker and table so he could be gone before Mai appeared. She barked at him under normal circumstances and so far the big blowout had been a bust. Who was going to buy a flag or an Uncle Sam the day before the holiday? She was hard on Barry, too. Failure and disappointment confirmed her fatalism; today should give her great satisfaction.

"The cops came by last night. They said they're canceling the fireworks," Isaac said to Barry. Barry might know if the police had arrested his neighbors.

Barry didn't look up from his computer where he constantly price-checked competitors he insisted were false fronts for the foreign manufacturers. "The sheriff has another drone—for wildfires or search and rescue, *they say*."

On the screen, a deputy prepared to hurl into the air what looked like an oversized hobby aircraft. "*National Geographic* did that story a year ago," Isaac said.

"We don't get *National Geographic*." Barry thought it was global warming propaganda from Washington.

Barry didn't get the paper, either. He only read to confirm his fears. He acquired his news from prepper newsletters and websites that linked to patriot groups who were anti-everything, from immigrants, vaccines and solar power to Obama, taxes and the Federal Reserve. Isaac shared Barry's distrust of the government but his unease had nothing to do with politics; it was rooted in everyday experience. Barry was convinced he was on a watch list; Isaac had actually been interviewed by Secret Service agents at the Reagan Library. Funny how flag-wavers were more afraid of their own government than Isaac was. He should write that down.

"Instead of a drone, they call it an *unmanned aerial vehicle*," Isaac said. "They say they can search for the color of a lost hiker's shirt or detect his heat signature through the brush."

"Yeah, right," said Barry. "Why did this county get cleared so early to fly them? They got that Bearcat armored vehicle, too. And then they flaunt it. It's a warning shot!"

Barry thought everything was a warning shot. He obsessed about border-crossing terrorists and military troops on domestic maneuvers, the NSA listening to his conversations and the IRS taking his money. He had Mai's undocumented relatives sewing the Made in USA custom products in the back room and he rented the farm to tweakers because they paid in cash and didn't complain about conditions, so Barry had some legitimate worries, but when Freedom City was shut down, it would be by Google spies, FedEx planes and brown-shirted UPS drivers knocking at every door.

Isaac had spent his afternoon failing to locate Wesley Chambers. With Wesley's bike trailer, he could move his camp in one trip. Now that he'd been discovered, Isaac was anxious to clear out, even if it meant going back to the turmoil along the river, something he could consider only because of Wesley's company, and then only until he found something off by himself. Isaac didn't mind living alone. Loneliness only sank in when he was around people.

He returned to camp and packed up with the idea he might talk Barry into hauling his gear to town after the shop closed. Of course Mai would object. She didn't like Isaac and she figured their little under-the-table empire was better off including only family. It was too early to head for Freedom City so he sat and read for a while. Mike, the hero of the book, had made a dangerous plan to evade pursuing lawmen by jumping bareback and naked into a wild river cauldron that would suck them underground and maybe spit them out again. Either way, dead or alive, Mike would become free. Isaac knew something sad was about to happen to Potatoes the horse but he kept reading. The horse began to swim against the current until Mike turned his head downriver. *The horse knew.* Or maybe he didn't, but he was faithful to Mike. The adventure had distracted Isaac but now sorrow overwhelmed him. He wanted the trackers on the ridge to see Mike and capture him before it was too late but they were only visible to each other for one second and what if the trackers looked away just then? Isaac could feel the pages thin in his right hand but he had to stop reading. Mike was selfish. He thought he and Potatoes were one, that the horse cared about his philosophy. The trackers only saw the river and the river didn't care if they drowned or surfaced again. Isaac cried for the horse and wept for himself and how life was only one second on the river.

Car doors slammed. Isaac couldn't see them but he knew from the scrabbling in the street the kids with the remote car were back. He couldn't read now with his brain listening for the whine to start up.

He didn't want trouble so he tried to wait them out before departing to work. As the shop's closing time approached, he made his usual preparations to leave camp. A sliver of grass across his duffel's zipper; a pebble on the cooler lid; the camp stove leaned against a tree at a forty-five-degree angle. Then he marked the relative positions of everything with twigs. At least he'd know if anything had been disturbed. Now it was getting late. He'd have to go. He dropped his bike into low gear and waited for a break in the noise. When it came, he burst out of the trees hunched over and pedaling hard. One boy fingered the controller while the other two crouched over a black car with batwing fenders. Just as Isaac hit the pavement, he heard that revving dentist drill sound as the car reared on two wheels.

"Watch out hobo!" one of them yelled.

"Did you say hobo or homo?" another laughed.

The thing screamed past Isaac's tires and cut abruptly in front of him, but turning too fast, it rolled with a hard plastic clatter and flipped into the gravel at the road's edge. Isaac cranked away without looking back. If the car was broken, it would be his fault.

Isaac raced the back way to Freedom City, jumping the curbs and landscape barriers that separated the parking lots. The inflatables stood like sentinels protecting the store against invasion. Barry had already taken in the hot dog stand. Mai must have melted in front of those windows reflecting heat like a solar cooker. Another grievance she could hold against Barry, who'd insisted the free food would be a big draw, as if people couldn't wait to get a jump on eating their fill of Fourth of July hot dogs. The giant flag, which never came down because it required six to fold it, snapped overhead, the only sound in the empty parking lot. Inside, the display lights were off; only security lamps illuminated the shelves. *Shit.* He wasn't that late. The door resisted his pull. They'd probably locked up against stragglers while they finished in back.

He cut the power to the bald eagle and the air dancer. The eagle began to sag and Elastic Man immediately collapsed. Isaac ripped loose the Velcro skirt attaching the nylon sleeve to the blower and removed Elastic Man's telescoping support pole. By the time he'd finished breaking down the dancer, the eagle lay on its side. Isaac walked the air pockets flat so he could fold the bird. The dolly for moving the displays was still inside. He pounded the heavy glass with both fists. No response. He went around to the receiving door and tried the buzzer. Nothing. Barry's red Silverado wasn't in its usual parking place. The possibility of murder-suicide simmered in the store some days, the only question being which spouse would be which. But dead men didn't drive and neither did Mai. More likely, they were unwilling to witness further the travesty of *America's Big Blowout Birthday Event*. What did they expect him to do with the doors locked—abandon his responsibility? Where was the respect? People always looked through him, walked past him, talked over his head as if he were ignorant. They assumed the worst. Barry, at least, should know better. He depended on Isaac morning and night, took him along to customers' houses. He trusted him on the farm property and put his approval in writing. Isaac had fulfilled their deal to the letter and the day! And now Barry had blown him off without even a note. No *Sorry, Isaac. Had an emergency. Back soon.* No *Key's under the sand-bag—have a Happy Fourth!* He heard Mai saying to Barry—*Nobody going to buy. Just leave in parking lot. Melt. Kids take. Who care?*

Nobody cares. They didn't need him. His agreement with Barry would unravel the second he moved his camp. Mai wanted his job for one of her nephews. She would attack and Barry would fold. Like the innocent horse in the river, Isaac was about to be drowned by his master's folly. The six-foot-tall birthday cake mocked him. *Happy,* the second layer said. Isaac was not happy but then it was not his birthday. He unsheathed Jake's knife and tried to slash off the top of the candles. They simply flattened and bounced back up. He braced the cake with his foot and free hand and thrust into its *Happy* middle, releasing a fart of vulcanized air. He slit the elephant's trunk. It slumped to its knees and blubbered until Isaac unplugged the blower. Stabbing Uncle Sam seemed semi-treasonous, so he attacked the rocket he rode. With a sigh, they expired as one.

Isaac awakened to the *sit-sit-sit* of lawn sprinklers. Probing for an uncompressed inch of cardboard between his elbow and the river cobble, he remembered where he was, near the entrance to an office park under a low umbrella of yews that provided its only park-like touch. He was totally fucked now. Barry had only gone for takeout and left Mai locked in the store so she wouldn't have to deal with Isaac. From behind the dumpster, he'd heard them fight over the carnage outside. They started by blaming each other, but eventually they would figure out it was him. For the first time in months he could sleep in. Nobody in the office park was coming to work on Independence Day.

Isaac didn't require Wesley's bike trailer to move his camp after all. His Coleman stove and cooler were missing, along with the tarp; clothes from his duffel scattered in bushes and hung from branches; the slashed tent, crumpled on bent poles, was spray-painted NØHØBØZ; tent stakes were stabbed through the yoga mat. He found his sleeping bag sopping in the ditch. He apologized for dragging Wesley out here.

"Come back to the island with us," Wesley said. "We don't let this shit happen down there."

What Wesley meant was that he didn't let it happen. Wesley stood a shade above six feet, one-quarter of which seemed to be his close-cropped head, a skull as wide as a cinderblock with a jaw that seemed to predate civilization. His face had fleshed out and his arms lacked their old definition but his bulk still promised the capacity to do serious damage. It was well known on the river that in the military Wesley had acquired serious survival skills that went far beyond what berries to eat in the wilderness. Isaac regarded him as a peacekeeper, someone like the president who you'd trust to murder on your behalf.

But having Wesley on the island didn't guarantee peace on the river. The banks curdled with defeated tribes declaring war on each other—hard partiers, domestic disturbers, raving anchorites, angst bearers, mental-case poets. Loud was how they fought, expressed ecstasy and pain, showed strength, attracted witnesses, alerted allies, cleared space. Volume was an unarmed man's weapon, a lone woman's bodyguard, a weakling's last hope.

Isaac figured he might last there a week.

The group waiting for the Day Center to open looked the same to Isaac as every weekday. Men and women cupping cigarettes and clutching sacks of laundry. People locking their bikes and chaining their dogs. The bleary-eyed and red-faced ready for a breakfast of sugar and powdered creamer laced with weak coffee. Women seeking a safe place to sit out the morning. The jobless who needed a routine as badly as a paycheck.

Inside or out, waiting was the main activity at the Day Center. Waiting for a washing machine or a shower. Waiting for the phone or to sign in for a storage bin. Waiting for the mail to arrive or for somebody to finish with the newspaper. Waiting for the crapper—that was the worst. And when the Day Center closed at noon you went off to wait somewhere else—the soup kitchen, the park, the library or the bus stop. If you didn't like waiting, you could walk—the two reasons Americans bought cars as soon as they could.

Isaac waited outside Sylvia's office. Sylvia Tell was the Day Center director. Toward all her fallen guests she was skeptical and stern but ultimately forgiving, the way Isaac hoped God would turn out to be. When it was his turn, she gave him *the look*. Everybody knew it—one-third smile, one-third sour, one-third *oh, come on now*.

"I haven't seen you here for a while," she said. Her eyebrow stayed suspended and she folded her arms, turning the statement into a question. It was a trick of hers, like shining a bright light into your eyes. You were supposed to say something to make it go away.

"I lost my job and my camp over the Fourth," he said.

"Check over at Outreach."

"I'm looking for a place, not a case worker."

"Well, forget anywhere on the river. It's not like it was. The Point's gone. Las Colonias is next and they'll keep on going. You can't drift along any more. You have to make a plan, and I don't mean one of them Isaac Samson connect-the-dot-fate-of-the-universe plans. I mean for your own life. You've got to listen to others sometimes."

"I hear others plenty." That was a big part of the problem.

Sylvia did not care to hear from her guests about the system, bad chemistry, misfortune, poor upbringing or a lousy economy. She listened to a loving and all-knowing God. That made her world simple and the solution to other people's problems plain. She didn't have to deal with a flypaper brain, everything sticking where it landed. She heard a Bible verse and made it mean what she wanted. When Isaac walked down the street, he might hear a stop sign, Ronald Reagan and a stranger's dog speaking at once. How was he supposed to make plans when he knew that radio station was still plugged into his head? The world already thought he was a loser. How many failed plans before he proved worthless to himself?

Sylvia was speaking to him about being grateful for each day he was given. He was grateful for a day he did not explode. "I'm stating the facts of my situation."

"What you *believe* are the facts. Your belief in a fact does not make your belief factual."

He could feel Sylvia about to Sylvia him, tie him in knots with his own rope. Sometimes he liked trying to escape but today he was not in the mood. Today he just wanted to find a safe place to sleep.

"So you still plan to go it alone?" she said. Sylvia had earned a doctorate in bullshit from years of bartending and she could read his mind about eighty percent of the time. "Then talk to Rudy Hefner. Him and his new girlfriend were in yesterday. They found a two-bedroom in Vegas, nine hundred square feet, only four hundred a month—and she's paying half."

Sylvia's expression remained neutral, but it was not hard to imagine what she thought of that plan. Hefner was a big-bearded blowhard. His appearance at the Day Center meant his Gold's Gym Groupon had expired and he needed a shower. He claimed to live off a trust account he'd set up with his earnings from an Alaskan fishing boat. It paid him enough never to work again, provided he found a woman with low self-esteem who would put him up when the weather turned cold. Spring through fall he retired to a box canyon hideout that everyone except Hefner called The Mansion. The Mansion was concealed amid rock fall on Park Service land and had somehow evaded detection by the rangers, which Hefner took as confirmation of his superiority and the general incompetence of the feds.

Isaac said he would think about it. He would rather find the place on his own.

He checked his mail on the way out. A Social Security form letter. A fundraising appeal from the hospital foundation. A cable company promotional mailing. A standard postcard stamped in red: *Please Forward. If undeliverable or unclaimed after 60 days, return to sender.* His mother had actually made a stamp so the forwarding looked official. Her handwritten message on the other side was invariably the same: *Pray you are well. M*

He signed for each piece and dropped them in the trash.

**Despite so many homes on the market,
buyers can't find what they want.**

— "Home" with Meg Mogrin, *Grand Junction Style*

A text buzzed in from Eve Winslow:
    So sorry to stand you up. Coffee? Stop by shop at 10AM.

Meg arrived at ten knowing the shop might not yet be open.
Mariposa, like everything in Eve's life except the start of City
Council meetings, operated on Winslow Standard Time. She would
say, *I'm a bird not a plane.* In other words, clock time was an imposi-
tion upon natural forces like Eve Winslow.

Meg waited on an outdoor bench for the bird to land. The
morning was pleasant, the street too quiet for shopkeeper comfort.
A fountain splashed on the corner, and the trees along the prom-
enade rippled with a promising breeze. A man with a covered cup of
coffee came out of the bagel shop across Main and circled the patio,
testing the metal chairs for stability, adjusting the umbrellas, sitting,
rising, moving from table to table, finally selecting a seat. Slim and
tan, with slicked-back hair tucked behind his ears, he might have
passed as a beach bum if he were not so overdressed in a wool shirt,
lined windbreaker and topcoat. He extracted a book from his day-
pack and dropped a fistful of sugar packets on the table.

Eve burst out with a bright blue Mariposa shopping bag in
hand. Pressing fifty, Eve shared the high end of a decade with Meg
but passed for a woman of the next generation. Too plump to dress
from her own shop, she wore its finer accessories. Her short feathered and frosted hair made grey seem her lifelong color.

"God, I heard you were down there. You must be out of your mind! Amy Hostetter's in a coma. The best I can say is, the police have two suspects. It doesn't matter who they are. The headline's *Woman cop assaulted by bums in city park*. My voicemail is already full of calls screaming bloody murder, demanding we drag every vagrant out of town or shoot them on the spot. How's the house tour coming?"

They crossed the street to the bagel shop and passed the beach-comber, who was marking pages in a thick red notebook with empty sugar packets. A blue yoga mat jutted from the pack between his feet, which were clad in immaculate white leather sneakers that seemed sizes too large for his thin frame. His eyes, striking against his mahogany skin, were nearly the same Caribbean color as the mat. Catching Meg looking, Eve rolled her eyes.

"What have you got against Yoga Man?" Meg asked when they were inside.

"Yoga? Honey, please tell me you're kidding. You've been on the Homeless Coalition for months."

Yes, and she was in sales, after all, supposed to be able to read people, but she had been practicing trying not to judge.

The bagel shop had absorbed adjoining buildings as its success grew, while it retained features from previous incarnations. Furniture was mismatched, the walls decorated with a combination of local art, antique kitchen utensils and unplayable stringed instruments. It felt like a place where patrons could donate a beloved but runaway houseplant, and it hummed with the prospect of running into someone you knew.

Eve chose a table in the corner with a clear view of the entry. "Where do I even start? This attack came at a very bad time. The town is already up in arms about the parks being taken over. I've got council members who believe parks themselves are a drain on the city—property permanently off the tax rolls, ongoing maintenance costs, serving only a handful of citizens, most of them hippies and derelicts."

"Hippies?"

"Not my word. Anyone who hangs out, throws a Frisbee. You know, people who like to walk. Anyway, it's not as if our long-range plan for Las Colonias has gone anywhere. The city'll spend dribs and drabs, but not enough. Funding to make it a true community asset has to come from outside—state gaming funds, tourism grants, environmental dollars—none of which goes to projects people are fighting over."

Eve snapped a biscotti and dunked a half in her Americano. "Zack Nicolai was with you yesterday, wasn't he?"

"Zack was fine. A big help, actually."

"All he cares about is attention. The very last thing we need right now is to become mired in poverty politics with protests and lawsuits over squatters' rights. The Betterment project is not going to look favorably at a city with an intractable vagrancy problem."

"Betterment?" It sounded like a company run by the Quakers.

Eve lowered her voice. "You know we have interest from a company about relocating here, yes? It's time you knew the rest. A Michigan company called Betterment Health is looking for a new headquarters site, but they have even bigger plans. I'm not going into it all here, and you should keep this to yourself until we announce. This is for you." She took the Mariposa bag from the chair next to her and set it on the table.

"This town is stuck between the people who think economic development is putting out milk and cookies for Santa and the ones with long memories. Some never learn and others never forget. Remember how Sundstrand was going to revitalize the economy with its aerospace manufacturing? We've still got a damn street at the airport with their name on it ten years after they pulled out! But we can't let naysayers stop us. Betterment's project will be the biggest chance in our lifetimes to make a difference. I'm talking about you and me, homegirl, people with some vision. I've got enough trouble with the Tea Partiers. I don't want to have to fight through commie piss ants like Zack Nicolai, too."

Meg's coffee tasted scorched. Had they given her the dark roast by mistake? "I can't be your spy on Zack."

"Who said anything about that? I just want to make sure he appreciates the importance of business and economic growth. How the hell does he think we pay for affordable housing? We have enough people working on behalf of the poor in this town. Now we need some momentum behind job creation, building the tax base, increasing prosperity for everybody. You can talk about this stuff from a business perspective without all of that Chamber of Commerce chest-beating that turns off the liberals. Plus, you stand for home. I need the coalition's support. Tell them they don't have ten years to end homelessness. Our future is now."

Eve replaced the lid on her cup, noted the berry-red print and applied a fresh gloss for the trip back to the shop. "Oh, and the tour. Lew's from Michigan so nothing too deserty. You know how our summer can be a shock to those lake people. Sorry for all the paper but I don't want emails in the system. We land Betterment and school children will sing our names after we're gone."

The mayor swept out, misting the cafe with waves of regret that she had no time to chat. Eve wasn't heartless. She played a toughie because the good old boys always tried to discount her as a matron who ran a bead shop. Eve tended to spew emotive bullet points but Meg had never seen her this hyper. She peeped inside the Mariposa bag and riffled through the top layer of paper. An analyst report on healthcare IT services; business stories about Rochester, Minnesota's plans to raise its profile as a destination medical city; a plastic-bound presentation from the local economic development board; and printouts from Betterment Health's website. She looked for something about the exec who was coming out for the home tour. The corporate leadership page offered only short bios and no photos.

Chairman and CEO: *Lew Hungerman?* Meg pictured a dwarf-ish Edward Gorey character in an ankle-length fur coat, clutching a mutton leg—the sort of man who existed only in black and white. Of course he was single. What a fun day that was going to be.

She stepped onto the sidewalk with her homework in hand. A miniature forest of folded sugar packets sprouted from the grate of Yoga Man's vacant table.

On the other side of the iron gate, a million-plus foreclosure loomed like a cruise ship run aground on a sandbar. Former owner Kip Reiner had also lost his car dealership, a coke dealership and his passport. Now he was in home detention in his girlfriend's house, with the feds, the builder, two banks, the automakers and possibly a Colombian cartel after his hide. Everything about this place was off-kilter. Tuscan towers with red tile roofs flanked a Versailles staircase leading to a second-floor entry framed by a Corinthian-columned portico. A luxury builder's greatest hits on steroids, not remotely marketable in this state. Trailered boats, storage containers and construction dumpsters accentuated its state of abandonment.

The remote wasn't working. Meg pressed the button, waited, pressed again, waited, hoping the electronics were only slumbering and would eventually come back to life. Somewhere a software developer had surely targeted the real estate industry with a mobile app that would automate market studies, deliver virtual home showings and handle the ponderous paperwork. Managing repetition was easy. That's why real estate was such a popular second career. But selling houses was still about appealing to emotions and irrational judgments and dealing with unpredictable little failures like this one before they sent the entire deal off the rails.

She located the security code.

"Let's try the touch pad," Meg said to Vaughn Hobart. She'd brought him along to help her spot any issues with the construction. Vaughn had worked with her enough to know *let's* meant him. He unscrewed himself from the passenger seat, a move that required an extra rotation due to the long-ago collision that had fused his spine a quarter turn to the left.

The gate slid open. They entered through the triple garage in back. The rest of the windowless ground level consisted of concrete compartments intended as a home theater and a wine cellar with a walk-in humidor. Upstairs, custom kitchen cabinets awaited exotic wood doors that would never come. Fixtures had not been installed in the exposed electrical boxes. Blobs of plaster, nails and wire clippings littered the subflooring. The imprint of a table saw could still be seen in the sawdust where it had trimmed a stack of finish boards. Color samples had been dabbed on walls. None had been painted.

Meg snapped photos and jotted notes as Vaughn pointed out problems she didn't see. They made an odd team, smooth and rough, detailed and sketchy, long view and one day at a time. She'd found him when she needed a property man to mow lawns, clean pools and spruce up dinged corners and peeling paint. At the interview, he shuffled like a man on a ledge afraid to take his eyes off his feet. A *jackass of all trades*, he called himself, a self-deprecating joke wrung of its originality in too many AA meetings. She was looking for someone younger, but Vaughn had a new-found and palpable thirst to make more of himself and she took the chance. His indifference to fine details sometimes collided with her insistence on perfection, but he showed up, did what she asked and made steady progress. As he rose closer to her expectations, she doled out symbols of her growing trust: a company cellphone, the keys to the pickup, the code to her lockboxes.

The housing market turned suddenly. Meg asked Vaughn to wait for his final paycheck. He not only waited, he came by to wash her truck and noticed things about her house she'd been meaning to repair. He penciled out a punch list in his grade school hand and insisted on working it down. *I want to keep busy*, he said, *now that I know how good busy can feel.* With her encouragement, he studied his way through guidebooks on home inspection. She helped him compose a company sell sheet, the bulletpoints summarizing his qualities punctuated with tears.

The bank would not like her report. Reiner's property was too far along to knock down and would not sell as-is. People with manor-house money wanted to put their own imprint on a home, even if their taste was worse than a cokehead car dealer's.

After completing a circuit outside, Vaughn came hitching over, his expression grave. She considered the owner's ruined reputation. Surely Reiner wouldn't have buried bodies here.

"Looks like scroungers," Vaughn said.

He led her to two boat trailers parked at the back of the lot. One was empty and the other held a Lake Powell-sized power cruiser. On the ground between them a rumpled blue tarp appeared to have blown off the boat. Vaughn tugged on a rope threaded through one trailer's side guard. The tarp drew up and formed a tent-like peak, its edges weighed and staked at the corners. He threw a knot to secure the rope. She leaned in. Light leaked through worn patches in the sun-struck fabric onto a brown and orange sleeping bag. She reeled from the musk of foot, rotted vegetation and overheated air.

"What's this doing here?" she said.

Vaughn let the tarp drop. "Probably lookin' for copper and such on the scrap pile. It's been picked through. I expect they read the paper about Reiner, came by and saw the work stopped, decided to squat while they shopped."

"They're trespassing," she said. "The bank doesn't want any more trouble over this house."

Vaughn studied the western sky as if it held vital information. He rolled his head from one shoulder to the other. She heard his neck bones grind. "Look at them starlings up there."

The flock swirled and folded upon itself, transmuting from granular to solid and back again. A hillside of fluttering aspen leaves became a ribbon tying itself in a slipknot.

"It's called a murmuration." The beautiful word felt strange on her lips. Starlings were aliens here, like the tamarisk, like the white man.

Vaughn grunted, as if she'd offered him a tea cake. "There's a big raven in the cloud. You can see it when they divide."

The larger bird beat a slow circle through the maelstrom, disappearing and emerging, neither on the attack nor very intent on escape. The starlings at times seemed to tease it, ignore it and swallow it. Finally, the raven broke from the veil and as it lazed away, a small escort took turns dive bombing it from above.

"He's pissed but he's leaving," Vaughn said. "Squatters don't want trouble either. I'll take care of this here."

Meg killed a thousand screensaver starlings with a keystroke and called up a browser to fly her southwest. She found the highway that ran through the Hopi reservation and tracked it to the town where Brian's school was one of the main industries. No sign of pueblos or ancient plazas, but newer compounds stood in bright geometric clusters that might have passed for a lunar space station: a sewage treatment plant, tribal police and business offices, government housing inside a security fence. On the school grounds, the empty parking lot was crisply lined like a circuit board awaiting components. Netless red and green tennis courts languished under whorls of dust that had also airbrushed one curve of the running track. It circled an artificial-turf football field with end zone markings and yard lines legible from space. She wondered if Brian still ran, and whether he circled this field or struck out across the desert. Around and around or point-to-point, he'd be pushing against that unbroken wind. She clicked back the zoom and watched the BIA roads disappear, then the specks of green, the names of the villages, the line marking the state highway and finally, the sacred mesas, reduced to sand-colored smudges on a green planet.

Light and dark provide cues vital to wellbeing. Make your bedroom a sanctuary where you control their influence.

— "Home" with Meg Mogrin, *Grand Junction Style*

The moment belonged in light and she had always kept the photograph where the sun could find it. Her sister's soaring exuberance and Meg's bemused distraction overlapping and forever fused into a third, inscrutable presence. The image and her memory also flew into each other. Both were fading now.

A sand-footed retaining wall charcoals a flat horizon against a dull grey sky. A lie told in black and white; the sky was a cloudless sapphire. The shoeless lookalikes in winter-hued summer dresses scrawl their crisp shadows across the concrete—one galloping, the other poised, heron-like. Helen flies at the camera, hanging in midair, arms spread, chest thrust forward, bared legs coiled, an exploding halo of trailing hair, while Margaret (Meg came later) perches with one hand locked in an Indian grip with her sister, her other hand anchored atop the wall.

Margaret's wariness seems self-preserving rather than protective of her younger sister. Her knees are pressed together, her right foot probing and her left planted, as if she intended to slither down the five feet to the ground. Their father's camera had beautifully captured Helen's blissful leap and foretold Meg's unmooring, yet it was a deceptive photograph. Meg was certain she had laughed, too, as they tumbled into the sand.

On the winter day she discovered her house, this sunlit room had been a selling point. July sun, however, was brutal and the gates of hell yawned in August. To reduce the bleaching, perhaps she should let the photo summer on the bookcase away from the windows. Clearing a new place, she discovered a dust jacket spine had been bleached green from its original brown. The mauve cover next to it ripened to bright blue when she slid out the book. To her dismay, the chair, the carpet, everything had suffered sun damage. Moving Helen into the kitchen's northern exposure would safeguard her image but make a point about domesticity she didn't care to press. Her bedroom? Unwise to seed her dreams with a glimpse of the fallen.

A tubular-bell gong in the hallway broke her from indecision. She'd long meant to install a more cheerful timbre, but the reminder came so rarely. She stood in shadow where she could judge the visitor's silhouette through the door's frosted glass. A woman. Meg placed the photograph on the entry table and opened the door.

Pandora Cox, her amber streak now a bluish-black. Minus her stage presence, too. Hands joined primly over her belly, she planted one foot, the other toed, her thighs pressed together.

"Pandora! Come in. What a surprise."

Pandora turned back toward the street and waved to the driver in a white pickup with a cab-over camper.

"I thought it was best to thank you in person," she said, stepping just inside the door. She peered around as if in search of the powder room. "I knew you'd have a beautiful home—oh, for cute! Is this you?"

"My sister and me."

Pandora lingered over the image. "Which is which?"

"I'm the…pensive one."

"I knew it!"

Process of elimination, no doubt.

"I loved your 'America the Beautiful.' I'm sorry I missed you at the event."

"Me, too." Pandora bit her lower lip, released it. Despite the scholarship between them, they were still strangers. "I was wondering if there was any way I could get some of the money now."

Meg looked out at the truck, its running lights on and the diesel clattering. She closed the door.

"It doesn't quite work like that. The money goes to the school directly. CU-Denver will get the payment when you enroll."

"Oh." Pandora twisted the bottom of her t-shirt. "Well, I'm not going there, it turns out."

It turns out? This might be the fastest washout yet.

"So where would you go instead?"

"Williston. Cody's getting a job on a rig in North Dakota and I'm going with."

"I meant college. The money's for school, you know."

"Oh, I know. There's a college there—Williston State. The cash would just be for gas and get-started money. I can pay you back once he gets his paycheck."

"Have you thought about where you'll stay? Winter in that camper won't be much fun." According to a recent news story, a one-bedroom apartment in Williston averaged close to twenty-five-hundred a month if one could be found.

Pandora's smile was a sly one. She squeezed the fingers of her left hand. A band with a minuscule chip of something shiny. "Cody thought of that already. I applied for family housing at the college. It's only seven-fifteen a month. If we don't get a student apartment, I'll get a dorm room. It's perfect!"

Well, at least it was clever.

"He told me I was crazy to ask for the money now, but I said you believed in girls following their passion."

Yes, if the girl knows where it leads.

"You'll be following him to a small town overrun with oil workers. And if Cody's working and you're in school, you won't see much of each other. Does Williston have the music program you wanted? It won't be like in Denver with all its opportunities. You have something to offer the world but talent has to be developed. You should go where you can learn and connect with other musicians."

"Whatever talent I've got, I'll still have it in two years."

"This is about more than the next two years. The choices you make now can affect the rest of your life—that's all I'm trying to say."

"Oh, I get what you're saying." She turned toward the door. "But you don't even know us. Cody's smart but he can't just go off to college. He helps support his mom. There's no jobs here that pay even close to the oil patch. Up north, he can still send her money and get his own start. And he *loves* me. He'll take care of me if I ever need him to, which I won't. We were just asking for some temporary help, that's all. A little bit to get us started. I really thought you'd understand."

Oh, the days when love mattered more than anything, when immortality seemed more likely than failure. "No. I'm sorry, but no. The money is for college, not…"

There was no reason to complete the homily. Meg's big sister act had rarely worked, and now she was sounding like a mother. The girl was right. Meg did not know her, certainly not from the application process, her color-shifting hair or the venturesome rendition of one song. Who was she to say how Pandora should pursue her dream? Even good decisions contained a kernel of risk. Pandora was approaching the age when she had a right to choose badly. This choice didn't necessarily mean abandoning music, but Meg didn't have to endorse it.

Pandora retreated down the walk. The girl's shape shrank in the cloudy glass of the closing front door, warping and then dissolving. The truck's door slammed and its headlight haloes lurched away.

Meg rediscovered the picture in her hands. Her house was too full of things coupled to other lives, including the one she no longer led. When she sold it, she would winnow the books, read and unread, sweep out the plants and sell the furnishings. Vestiges of current ownership were almost always a negative, even a source of mirth. Prospective buyers didn't respond to houses that remembered. They needed to project themselves onto an idealized blankness. They were Pandora on the road to Williston.

She brought the leaping sisters back into the living room. The end table bore a darker, ghosted smudge where the frame had sheltered the sun-blasted finish. She replaced the picture exactly. Everything fades, she thought. It's the price of being in the light.

**It's easy to form a bad impression
of a good neighborhood.**

— "Home" with Meg Mogrin, *Grand Junction Style*

Promoting the potential of spaces, the beauty of landscapes and the vitality of communities was Meg's livelihood. Homelessness didn't exactly fit her brand. It didn't fit anyone's brand, unless you were Catholic Outreach. But Eve had told her, *You'll be fine.* For a time, she had been. Not a cause she would have chosen except as a favor for a friend, the Homeless Coalition was just another civic duty that might someday pay her back. Oh, she felt sorry for the people who had to scramble for shelter and food each day. She was proud of the town's efforts to help them find housing. But the coalition's charge was to end homelessness in ten years. End it here in Grand Junction, as if no tentacles of hardship could ever again penetrate this happy valley once the magic spell had been cast. Ten years was a lifetime in the business cycle. Even presidents weren't expected to serve that long. New construction had showed its cracks by then. In that span, newlyweds went searching for bigger houses and first graders started driving to school. It was foolhardy to believe thousands of lives would change for the better and none would change for the worse.

But the unreachable goal was not what burdened Meg's climb to the second-floor conference room. The sight of Amy Hostetter on the ground in the tamarisk had rendered suspect her instincts about familiar places. Her hometown's darker fringes became foreground. If squatters could appear at the Reiner house, where else might they lurk? A week ago, Yoga Man's sugar packet forest would have enchanted her; now it struck her as a symptom of downtown littering. Meg had even sensed something sinister about Pandora's boyfriend waiting for her in his truck. This was not how she wanted to think or feel about her town.

The coalition met in a former church cinder-blocked and subdivided into a hive for secular do-gooders. The groups listed in the office directory were homegrown and locally funded, at levels ranging from a bootstrap to a shoestring. Their building served as neutral territory, away from the outsized authority of city politics, government human services agencies and the Catholic Church—although not beyond the influence of Sister Rose Lavelle, director of Catholic Outreach and chair of the coalition.

Sister Rose appeared, sparrow-like, next to Meg as if alighting from some higher branch. Her eyes were bright and penetrating. "I always enjoy your articles in the magazine. What will you be writing about next?"

Her close-cropped grey head inclined toward the answer.

It had never occurred to Meg that Sister might read her "Home" column. *Grand Junction Style* did not target those who'd taken a vow of poverty.

"It's about ways to expand your home without major remodeling—multiuse rooms, taking advantage of outdoor spaces, that less-is-more kind of thing." It sounded so trivial when she said it to a nun. Maybe she should add a few lines about being content with what you have.

"I look forward to it." A half bow and Sister Rose resumed her glide of inquiry around the room.

Not a bird, Meg thought, a queen who had renounced her crown.

Sister Rose settled in a chair at the large conference table. As if a bell had rung, the pre-meeting shuffling halted and Meg joined the committee members finding their places: mental health and social case workers, social justice advocates, shelter and housing officials, representatives from the library, the school district, the hospitals, legal services and veterans affairs. No members of the City Council's Vagrancy Committee appeared this time, and Meg sensed a growing void between them and the rest of the coalition. Two visitors, neither of whom Meg recognized, occupied the outer ring of chairs against the wall. Meg felt a new affinity with Zack Nicolai after their experience on the river, and she took a seat between him and Tony Martin, Amy Hostetter's partner on the police outreach team. Sister Rose unclasped her hands, and without further declaration, the meeting came to order.

Tony Martin offered a brief update on his partner's condition. Amy was ready to go home, he said, still annoyed at herself for missing the tripwire and eager to start rehab. So mild and considerate, he scarely seemed like a cop, even in uniform. He would make an excellent undercover officer, should the department ever have to investigate an accounting firm or a ring of flight attendants.

Sister Rose introduced one of the guests, co-founder of a group called Rescue Our Parks. Jennifer Barnes appeared capable of rescuing parks all on her own. Probably a business major who'd aced her courses, found the right man and planned to resume playing professional beach volleyball after her kids started school. When Jennifer stepped to the front of the room she seemed to Meg prepared to spike something.

Jennifer began by acknowledging that the Rescue Our Parks Facebook page featuring a fake homeless man and his bottle sprawled next to a playground reinforced an unfair stereotype, and she promised to take down the image. "Our group is *not* anti-homeless. The name Rescue Our Parks is meant to provoke discussion about objectionable activities in the parks."

"Great!" Zack Nicolai didn't speak for the coalition but the others at the table were happy to let him take the lead here. "Let's start with a discussion about this statement: *Our parks are being used as personal living rooms by people who scorn society.* You realize that people who live in a shelter don't have personal living rooms—so they sort of have to do their *personal living* in public."

Jennifer retained her cool. "I get that this is a tough, multidimensional issue. We have nothing against those who are homeless through no fault of their own. My heart breaks for people who don't deserve to be in that situation."

"That's wonderful. My question is how you can tell the difference between a person who scorns society and a person society scorns? Or does your ability to detect undeserving homeless people only work in the park?"

"Excuse me?"

"If I get laid off and lose my apartment, it sounds like I'm a deserving homeless person. What if I'm drinking because I got laid off and lost my apartment?"

"All right, Zack, you've made your point," Sister Rose said.

"The last time I took my daughter to the playground at Hawthorne Park, a woman was asleep wedged in the bottom of the slide tube. When I asked her to leave the play area, she became belligerent. This is only one in a string of threatening experiences in the parks and on river trails—people relieving themselves, unleashed dogs, demands for money. People shouldn't be afraid to use public places or take their trash into their alley. We love our neighborhood because it's near a park but it's gotten so we're about ready to move."

Liz, the shelter manager, scrunched her face as if seized by a toothache. "I believe you're sincere when you say you're not anti-homeless. At the shelter we enforce rules against drinking and throw people out based on their behavior. But as a community we don't judge whose suffering is most worthy. We should recognize why people need the park, for good or bad reasons. Exclude them and the issues just surface somewhere else. Help people in crisis and maybe the parks won't need rescuing."

"I wonder if some of the fear comes from criminalizing more of the poor's turf," said Eric from legal services. "Once you define

resting in public as loitering, the public's more likely to regard someone who's tired as being dangerous. It's perception."

Meg was only beginning to learn the continuum between discomfort, perceived threat and actual danger. She knew from Officer
Martin's reports that the outreach team spent most of its day dealing with homeless people in distress, disorderly conduct that caused
alarm in others and petty theft. Actual crimes against the general
public were very low, compared to the cases where the homeless
were victims, often of each other. She understood how Jennifer
Barnes felt; she'd been in the same place only a few months ago, and
as a woman, would never be able to fully let down her guard.

Sister Rose made the clasping gesture again and addressed
Jennifer. "Your family is rightly your first priority. And your love for
them naturally provides all kinds of nurturing and support beyond
food and shelter. If only everyone had loving and intact family ties.
To help the dispossessed of the community, we must enlarge the
boundaries of kinship."

Jennifer Barnes's eyes flashed. "If you're saying the solution is
for my family to form relationships with alcoholics and mentally
unstable individuals, I must tell you that is not going to fly."

Meg felt embarrassed for everyone. Jennifer had come with
concerns about protecting her children only to be lectured for her
insensitivity. It seemed a potential ally was about to slip away, perhaps to join more extreme adversaries. Meg caught Jennifer at the
door.

"We should talk later. Maybe I can help."

Jennifer looked at the card Meg had thrust in her hand, shook
her head and kept walking.

"Communities can get tired of dysfunction the way families do,"
said Sally, a mental health caseworker. "That's when you start to see
support for more severe measures. Some pressure's good for nudging
the hard cases but making them criminals doesn't produce change."

Tony Martin bristled. "That's not what we're doing."

Zack held up his hands. "We don't mean you, Tony. But the police department's outreach team used to be three and now it's just you. I don't see the city's commitment there anymore."

"We're short-staffed. The department's holding Amy's slot open."

"See how it works? Every turn of the dial has a rationale. Not filling the outreach position is a budget and headcount problem. Crack down on panhandling—it's all about traffic safety. Tear out the camping habitat—river beautification. And now the library, for cripes sake!"

"Banning backpacks was *not* my idea," said the library's representative.

Zack crossed his arms and rolled his eyes heavenward. "Right, it's never anyone. Nobody's anti-homeless. The library isn't banning people. It's only banning the backpacks holding the valuable stuff carried by people who have no safe place to leave it! Look at the big picture. More and more resources are going from helping people to pushing them around and nobody wants to call it oppression."

This was where Meg was supposed to speak up and back Zack down, tell him that if he wanted more resources, he should stop treating the business community like robber barons and browbeating mothers worried about their kids. It was like no one was allowed to pursue their own interests as long as Zack perceived injustice. Everyone at the table was there because they believed the town could be better. He didn't have a monopoly on virtue.

As if drawing a curtain closed, Sister Rose lifted her hands and pressed them together. "Some of you have met Wesley Chambers. He has proposed establishing an official, sanctioned tent city as an alternative to the current situation. He's here to give a progress report."

Wesley Chambers stood and tucked in the tail of his blue cotton check dress shirt. He had likely found it in the free store and didn't know that it originally cost at least a hundred dollars. The two men in town who had shared that shirt had no awareness of each other, Meg thought, and I might know both of them.

Stepping before the room's chalkboard, Wesley crossed his thick arms and adopted the glower of a football coach about to conduct a health class for indifferent teens.

"This town thinks it has a problem with transients. I wish that lady had stuck around so I could say this: Please don't call me a transient. Everything is transient. Everyone is. Some of us know it sooner than others."

Meg noted Wesley's lace-up boots, not so different from the pair she had seen on the island. Amy Hostetter had said Wesley was on the river for a reason but not what had happened to him. Maybe she didn't know. At some point the reasons for things didn't matter any more.

"You all know what a weed is. A weed is a plant that pops up where it's not wanted, like a camper is a person, like a person becomes this transient." He enunciated the word with an arched brow. "Now, if the City considers me a weed, they're going to chop me down and mulch my butt. Naturally, that tends to make me less enthusiastic about participating in your community affairs. But I do care about where I live. I have friends here. I enjoy the natural surroundings. How I live is not who I am. Living in a tent doesn't make me a scumbag."

And living in a big house didn't make someone a model citizen. Meg knew that but she had never heard the other side put so plainly.

"Sorry. You know that stuff. The town's solution to its camping problem is to get rid of the so-called transients. My solution is a lot simpler—allow it. Treat camping as a form of self-reliance instead of a crime. Don't make it illegal to consume less."

He took a half step back and thrust his hands into his pockets.

"A tent city won't solve the law's problems with troublemakers, but it will stop making troublemakers out of people who don't cause problems. The camp I'm calling Thistletown will offer some security and dignity to folks who need a break, who don't have money and don't like walls, who want to set their own rules and act like adults. So where do we start?"

He scanned the chalkboard tray. "Looks like somebody stole your chalk."

Wesley clapped an eraser on the green surface, creating a dusting of yellow. With his finger, he traced three words. *Land. Location. Legal.*

"Land's the obvious requirement. An acre is about minimum. Some communities like this are on five acres or more, but if you get too big it starts to be a crowd. I don't think you want to go more than about twenty tents or thirty people per camp, so everybody knows each other. The ideal would be a place with utilities, sewer and water access where you were allowed to put a finished ten-by-ten structure on the tent platform. Do we own, lease or occupy with owner permission? That's a whole topic in itself.

"Location matters, too. For the most part, our work and services are in town, where residents and merchants don't want us. Locating out in the country makes it harder for us to get around without transportation. That's why the river worked so good—out of sight and close by. It doesn't have to be parkland. We could do okay in a semi-industrial area.

"Legal. Right now it's illegal to live in non-permanent structures within the city. Even if we got a camping permit of some kind, under the ordinance we'd still have to move periodically. So we need a change that allows a tent city to stay put. Then there's zoning, health regulations, liability. I'm kind of sorry I even turned over that rock. Zack, you want to take it?"

Zack said, "I researched how other tent cities do the self-management. Most of them have a non-profit sponsor—the city, a church, a veterans' organization that assumes liability and fiscal administration. The residents raise the money and run the place."

Zack had to know it wasn't that simple. This was all about the politics and organizing community support. Maybe that's why he was involved.

"You know she's going to ask you to help," Zack said after the meeting adjourned.

Meg looked over her shoulder for Sister Rose. "Oh, don't encourage her."

"See anyone else here who could do it?"

"It's not a winner, Zack."

"It's better than what's happening now. People are going to die this winter."

"Wesley's ideas might make sense in these meetings, but not to the rest of the community. You think Jennifer Barnes is going to say, *oh goodie, a tent city?*"

"Oh, man, I feel bad about beating up on her. She should be able to take her kids to the park. I probably know the woman she was afraid of. I should've given Jennifer my number and told her I'd come down there next time to help work out any misunderstanding."

Zack held open the front door and Meg stepped through. "You seem like an agitator and then suddenly you don't," she said.

"I can't yell all the time. People get tired of *the world's on fire!* shit. But it is. Maybe not their house, but it is somewhere, and they only notice the fire when I'm obnoxious. I tried toning it down with the City Council and being factual and respectful. You know, to show I was a serious person. Then they'd thank me and go on with their same-old, same-old. Facts and reason don't produce action. They barely produce new thoughts. Discomfort is the only thing that moves authority. So I provoke."

"Right. You and Jennifer Barnes."

"But she aims it at the powerless. Her interest is her own comfort and to hell with everybody else."

Meg couldn't let Zack get away with it. "Her interest is her kids. She's a mother, not a hater. The coalition needs the support of people like her."

"My interest is the downtrodden, not the coalition members and their business dealings." He looked in the direction of Hawthorne Park, two blocks away, then turned back to Meg. "You chased down Jennifer Barnes like you couldn't wait for a shot at selling her house."

That was so wrong and unfair! A burning rose from her gut into her chest, then shot down the veins to her wrists and flushed her face. Jennifer must have thought the same thing. Mortification at the unjust impression loomed over the rest of her day, but she knew it was half true. Everything Meg Mogrin touched was perfumed with an artful trace of promotion.

Do you have enough money to meet all of your expenses?

—Vulnerability Index Prescreen for Single Adults

A mallard green BMW with two passengers backed out of a garage. The double door rolled down and kissed the concrete with a sigh. Isaac lowered his head and pedaled slowly until the throaty V8 faded away. He found a place to drop his bicycle out of sight from the road and circled back. He dodged up the driveway of the BMW house and located a spigot in back. If he did take over The Mansion he'd need a reliable water supply close to the canyon trail. Six gallons, enough for four summer days, weighed fifty pounds, and there was no way Rudy Hefner had packed that much in when he lived there. He wished now he had sought out the insufferable Hefner for some pointers.

The wash cut through the uplift that formed the Colorado National Monument. Unscalable cliffs on the left, a less severe hill rose to the west. He followed the dry stream bed for half a mile until a twenty-foot granite wall stopped him. He backtracked, alert for Hefner's departure point. This time he found the faint trail, which had been screened by a pair of juniper when approached from below. He leaned into the steep slope and imagined his pack full of provisions. After climbing five hundred feet, he paused on a sandstone slab and took measure of his solitude. From this vantage, the houses could not be seen. The valley visible in the distance seemed greener than the one he'd left. His water was warm already. Civilization settled downstream for a reason.

The trail topped out and then dropped down to the main canyon, which sat atop the bedrock blockade. The canyon floor widened. Piñon and broom crawled to the base of sheer sandstone walls. Monumental wedges had sheared from the west face. They slumped against the cliff or had shattered into boulders, boulders into rocks, rocks to pebbles, pebbles to sand—a continuous scatter of broken time. From what he had heard, The Mansion had to be concealed somewhere amid that rock fall.

Isaac homed toward the wall, eventually stumbling across the trail where Hefner had stopped scrubbing out his tracks. He would have to adopt that trick if he stayed. It made no sense to conceal a camp and then beat a path to it. The tracks made a high approach above the rocks and circled back past a split boulder. A sandy flat the width of a single bed lay between the halves—a fist aimed at an opposing palm—forming a stone cocoon. The rock would absorb sun's warmth, release it into the night and then provide a cool respite for part of the day. A nice spot to sleep, but a disappointment if this were all of The Mansion. Moving on, he saw how two slabs the size of tennis courts had jackknifed over a third chunk of sandstone forming a giant A divided into two rooms. The larger room was tall enough to stand upright in and tapered to a window-like opening at the back. The other, the size and shape of a deep understairs closet with room for one hardy human to sleep.

He unwound from his pack and made a slow turn in the entrance. A tan tarp rolled onto a pole could be unfurled like an awning or pulled over the opening when the weather turned bad. In the corner where a smoke-blackened crevice opened to the sky, a kettle sat atop a rocket stove cut from a Coors Light mini-keg. Nearby, a bean pot and a sand-scoured iron skillet. A quartet of plastic milk cases served as a larder and bookshelf. Provisions and paperbacks commingled. Canned peaches. McMurtry. Wieners and beans. Flynn. A mouse-raided cracker box. Sandford. A quarter jar of peanut butter. Hillerman. Two packets of Taster's Choice. Burke.

A seven-dollar canvas camp chair lay on its back in the middle of the room, its beverage pocket in shreds. An army surplus duffle packed with crumpled clothes. Flattened cans in a plastic bag. A trenching tool and a hatchet. A coil of sisal rope. In the berth-like second room, a sleeping bag and a Bugler tobacco can half filled with sand. The leavings reflected no generosity on Hefner's part. He had packed in The Mansion's furnishings a few items at a time and would have had to take them out the same laborious way.

Isaac found a plastic trash barrel buried downhill of the shelter, fed by a flagstone-lined channel to collect runoff, its cover weighted by a cracked bowling ball with *Steve* engraved above the finger holes. The empty inside was mineral-encrusted but otherwise clean. Until now, The Mansion's mocking name had seemed fitting for a blusterer like Hefner. But in this orderly canyon abode, Isaac heard the contented roar of a free man.

Sheltered from the wind, he did not sense the rain's approach until too late. Dark clouds rolled overhead. The narrow view of the sky between the canyon rims allowed no way to gauge the storm's extent. Desert storms often promised moisture they couldn't deliver, sending patchy clouds to drop fly swarms of virga that evaporated before reaching the ground. The air throbbed with an ominous overtone and a train wreck of thunder burst over him. Foolish to make a break now. If a monsoon followed, runoff from the acres of bare sandstone above the rim would funnel to the vee at the top of the canyon and spew a sudden, chest-high torrent down the granite slot. Not many drowned in the desert but when they did, it happened fast in places like this. The sky turned even blacker. He unrolled the tarp curtain, tucked himself in the camp chair and waited. A rapid-fire buzz whipped over the tarp and then paused as if the wind needed to regain its breath. A sundering blast threatened to unzip the heavens, then the downpour. The dirt outside boiled into rust-colored slurry. Runlets babbled past, gathering momentum over the slickrock. Down the wash, he heard the clack of stampeding stones. The air seemed carbonated. He stripped off his clothes, let the mist kiss his skin with breaking bubbles.

Isaac woke to the flush embrace of parched earth and rain. A solitary bird called chu-*wee*, chu-*wee*, ruhruhruh, and then answered itself. He stepped past the curtain. A thin cascade spouted at the canyon's head and dropped to a grey-green welcome at the bottom. The cistern barrel was full now, the water settled and clear. He could not see the wash, but he heard its flow, cheerful after last night's roil. This minute, Isaac liked living here. He liked it very much.

A wind-chime tinkle of faraway voices. He fixed the source, two ant-people daring each other on the canyon's opposite rim. Something flew apart from them and settled into a long glide. Not a drone—a yellow Frisbee heading his way. He swallowed his shout of protest. Sound had located them; they might spy him. His solitude was an illusion, his effort wasted. He had come this far only to find another place where he did not belong.

The approach he'd taken over the hill would be treacherously slick and his mud-clogged boots would leave an indelible trail. He could wait a day or two for the ground to dry, or try the shorter course down the wash now that the flow had subsided. He explored as far as the first drop. Twelve feet or so with an uneven landing. Rugged but doable. But suppose he encountered completely impassible stretches further down. Could he climb back out or would he be stranded? Not a risk he was prepared to take. He turned uphill, resigned to wait for the mud to dry, and spied the crafty boatman's solution. Snagged in a piñon, a length of line secured to the trunk, a casting weight on its free end. With the aid of the rope, Hefner could go straight up and down the shortcut.

Isaac appraised The Mansion a final time. He might be the last visitor to know who had lived here. A hundred years from now bits of Hefner's stash could turn up like arrow points or shards of grey ware. He checked the date on the canned peaches, popped the ring, peeled back the lid and sniffed. Still good. He raised the can to Hefner before drinking off the sweet syrup.

Down the wash he encountered sections scrubbed clean, brown sugar sand and pebbles packed into former potholes, crevices jammed with gravel, mud and twists of grass. Cottonwood saplings bent sideways, latticed with sticks and branches and clots of roots dangling like Druid ornaments. One chute required butt scooting in the stream to fit through a slot. He dragged his pack behind. Where the wash met solid granite, the declivities sharpened and became less forgiving. Twice more, Isaac used lines Hefner had anchored in the bedrock.

A shining quarter moon glinted in the sandy bottom. He kicked away enough overburden to identify a chrome headlight ring. Maybe an entire car lay buried there. He moved downstream, alert to other newly exposed prizes. A flash of milky quartz winked from a packed bed of fine gravel. Its thumb-shaped contour seemed too polished to have been tumbled in the stream. Perhaps a broken dish or chunk of kitchen sink. He dug away the binding crust and pried under its concave back. The palette-shaped fragment flipped free, revealing a grey-green circle with an obsidian center. He bent to make certain.

He'd always pictured glass eyes as marbles.

Isaac cupped the eye in his palm and stroked the smooth curvature. Fine red vessels threaded the white. The iris feathered into grey and yellow vanes that plunged into the pupil's dark crater. He met its blind stare with a gaze of wonder. What use was another eye? He saw too much already.

Fun has always been part of our hardworking western heritage.

— "Home" with Meg Mogrin, *Grand Junction Style*

Years had passed since Meg last attended the Barclay's annual bar-beque at the Crown B. A party that once celebrated the end of spring branding, it had been nudged into July for warmer evenings and in recognition that most of the partiers no longer came from the branding crew. Their ranch skills inclined more toward drink-ing, dancing and shooting fireworks. Since the winding drive back to town challenged even the sober, all were welcome to stay over-night in one of the houses, the barn or the meadow, thus averting one danger with another.

Meg had come early under the pretext of helping Terri Barclay prepare the feast, which also gave her the option of departing before things got too wild. There was not much to do since the food was catered by a chuckwagon outfit run by a Barclay neighbor. Donnie asked the caterer if he would be serving Donnie's own beef, since a few head were missing last fall. Meg sensed some tension behind the joke since neither party treated it as very funny. The alleged rustling could have happened fifty years ago. Change came slowly in Glade Park, and its history was sometimes indistinguishable from its grudges.

Terri herself looked out of time but at home under a broad-brimmed hat, her long Emmylou Harris hair pulled back in horsewoman's tresses. She bore her grey not as an erasure but as an underscore. Women in Terri's family, which had been around as long as the Barclays, had never been expected to rein themselves in and even when she met Donnie at seventeen, it was too late for him to try. Her name was on half the Barclay property, fifty-one percent in the case of Barclay Enterprises because it gave the company woman-owned status for bidding on government contracts. Donnie was pragmatic. While he didn't want a woman or the Feds telling him how to run his business, he was willing to listen—especially when the government suggested easier ways to take its money.

Terri eyed Meg's black pegged jeans and embroidered corral boots. "You want to go for a ride before it gets too crazy?" she said. "I haven't got Roamer out all day." Donnie had named Terri's gelding Roamer after a former Democratic governor. He had not intended it as a compliment.

Meg enjoyed Terri's company but the boots were for show and she did not consider a rocking saddle five feet off the ground to be a relief. "Thanks. It's enough just to get back up in this clean air."

They moved instead to the kitchen where they mixed punch and cut key limes for the moonlighting school teacher who would be tending bar. He wanted to practice his cocktails and they agreed to be his judges. Before long they were happy, chattering guinea pigs.

"Donnie said you needed a break. What's going on?"

"A bunch of different things. It's a busy time."

"He's got a big soft spot for you." Terri's frown seemed to be working out the reason. Meg wasn't sure how she had earned his attention. It was as if one day Donnie had walked up and introduced himself as a long-lost uncle.

God, Terri didn't think something was going on...

A lime rolled under Meg's paring knife. The blade snicked the pad of her thumb, drawing blood.

"This is probably enough limes." Terri examined the wound. She wetted a tea towel for Meg and went in search of a bandage.

Meg dropped the knife into the sink and put pressure on the cut. A dull summer house knife meets a round fruit in a tipsy moment. Now the hand holding the towel reacquaints itself with the bloodied one. Easy to blame the neglected blade or the tough rind, but her wound resulted from losing awareness. Was that the purpose of pain, to bring us back to ourselves? Was the purpose of inattention to escape our pain?

The kitchen clock read twelve forty. It had to be later. The second hand ticked against the seventeen and did not advance. She heard its faint buzz now, like a fly tapping the windowpane. She ran cold water over her thumb. The cut didn't hurt any more but the idea of the laceration opening its tiny mouth turned her stomach.

Terri returned with a Band-Aid tin. "Let's see. Good and clean. All I found for disinfectant was horse liniment so we'll forget that."

Meg dabbed away the trace of blood. Terri sized the dressing and peeled the tabs back from the adhesive. The sudden discomfort Meg had sensed in Terri couldn't be about Meg's relationship with Donnie. It had to be about Helen. People were still apologizing to her for holding back years ago. Others offered belated sympathy only to probe for the awful details or to recount their own painful stories. Terri secured the strip and allowed her touch to linger. She had no reason to feel embarrassed. Meg had always figured Donnie's sympathy was fifty-one percent Terri's.

"You can say it. It's been a long time now. It's okay."

Terri patted Meg's hand before releasing it. "Why do we hesitate to say the most important things?" She rinsed the cutting boards and left the towel to soak.

"I've kept this to myself because I didn't feel I should be the one to tell you. Donnie volunteered on the county search and rescue team when he was younger. He was in the thick of it—mounted, technical and water patrol—almost every week. Most of the time they'd find a lost person or save some fool who was in over his head. Even when somebody didn't make it, there was this moment of hope going out the door. But knowing you're on a retrieval, that's hard."

A car pulled up in the yard. From the voices and the dog's excited yips, the Barclay son Chase's family. Terri's eyes moved to the window. "Hard knowing they were young and full of whatever got them in dutch. One summer he'd pulled two kids out of the cauldron at Black Rocks, one at the Potholes, and then in October he got the call to Cold Shivers. Are you sure this is okay?"

Meg squeezed herself. This was headed beyond what she had expected. She nodded.

"Donnie was belaying the team going down into the canyon. Helen came up in the sling to him and he lifted her out by himself. He told me, *she felt so light, as if she was part of the air, and if I didn't hang on she'd keep on floating up.* Imagine, her body rising out of his arms. He felt something he can't describe in any way that makes sense to him. So he passes it on to you. Peace or protection or whatever it is, I'm sure that's what he wants you to feel."

And Helen. This is what Helen wants me to know.

Conversations around the bonfire had drifted into well-worn territory. Meg was toeing the happy edge of inebriation. They all were when Chase Barclay announced a demonstration of his new spud cannon. He'd built a more high-tech version of the one he and Donnie had made together years ago. *A shoot-off!* shouted one of his buddies—all like Chase, young men who were mulled versions of their fathers. Meg had never seen a potato launched, so she joined their festive stroll to the bluff above the barn. The stars had reasserted cool dominion over the post-fireworks sky. Simultaneously close and untouchable, they made earth's gravity seem a giddy accident. A shower of potato projectiles from this happy place seemed a necessary and proper counterweight to the cosmos. *Yes, we know we're nothing, but watch—this'll be cool.*

Donnie stayed behind.

Chase showed off his design to appreciative huffs and anticipatory gurgles from the boys. Forward observers were dispatched to measure the landings. They marched off into the field counting their steps aloud and dropping crushed beer cans as markers.

Unsteady flashlight beams played over the irregular ground, carving silhouettes that vanished and reappeared. Voices yipped and mixed with laughter. Finally, signals of readiness wagged from the target zone. Chase filled the original gun's combustion chamber with hair spray. He raised the barrel and a confederate recorded its elevation by angling his arm in parallel. An orange flame chuffed from the muzzle. Cries from the barn were picked up in the field as the spotters ran to the point of impact and called out the distance. After the beams wavered back to show the target range boundaries, Chase aligned the new gun to his friend's mock-Nazi salute. A stun gun spark ignited the metered propane. This time Meg was ready for the concussion. A much louder bang slapped the air. Judging by lights jittering away from them, it sent the projectile half again as far. The profane cries of discovery confirmed it. Chase invited his pals to fire the new launcher and after the first round was completed, he offered the women a turn. The older model, with its shorter range and hair spray propellant, now qualified as the girl gun.

Meg stepped forward and seized the longer tube. Murmurs of male approval. One of Chase's buddies stepped forward, a lean cowboy-type she'd noticed at the lower party. Smarter than he dared let on in this company, she thought. *Justin.*

"Let me do your spud," he said, and forced it into the tube. Curls of brown peel stripped and fell at her feet.

On her shoulder the apparatus felt lighter than she expected, the plastic warm, the propane bottle cool. She found the trigger button and contemplated a new target. Only a man would build a weapon and then devote his creativity to making it more lethal. More and more and more. She swung the barrel upward and found Venus. Was it necessary to aim? The recoil made her lose track of the tuber's flight. It didn't matter. The joke was between her and the planet.

"Nice shot." Justin said it so only she heard. Or maybe so he could put his warm breath in her ear.

The manboys tired of going for distance and went for velocity at impact. A sheet of plywood splintered. Full beer cans exploded. The ice-filled styrofoam cooler blew to bits. They were setting up a discarded microwave oven when Meg decided to slip away. Justin offered to walk her back through the dark. His fingers rested on the curve of her spine, lightly, as if he were mentally composing a message before typing it. Or perhaps this was how cowboys judged a woman's age.

"I know the way," she said, pointing to the house strung with chili pepper Christmas lights. "Straight downhill."

"It's not the direction, it's the footing," he said. "I'm a certified cattle trail guide, get you down with no cowpie action, guaranteed."

He grinned and awaited her reply, his thumbs hooked behind a belt with a rodeo buckle the size of a cheese grater. Justin hadn't yet said enough to get through her filters but she took his arm. "Chase seemed quite pleased with himself," she said.

"Oh, he's pumped." Justin's tone left a *but* unspoken.

"They seem to play it as a friendly competition."

"I've known Chase and his dad my whole life." Justin steered her around a brown pat in the grass. "I bet Donnie has a load of PVC pipe delivered tomorrow—along with a tank of hydrogen or something. At some point the old bulls have to let it go."

They were halfway down the hill. Justin inclined her toward the meadow. It had been a while, as in years. Not that there weren't opportunities. Her abstinent state was less a commitment than a reluctance. She'd had her fill of life turning in an instant.

"Did you win that buckle or did you buy it?" she said.

He stopped to judge whether it was a kiss-off or a come-on. The grin again. "That's for me to know and you to find out."

The New-Year-like euphoria of the night. The stars. Waking to frost on the grass. A terrible idea and yet she might fall for it if she stayed any longer.

"My car's over that way," she said and moved away from the edge.

Is this what Brian was reaching for with that last damn poem from Tuba City?

> *Would it be wrong for me to miss you*
> *Your heartbeat on my chest*
> *Just one and once*
> *Just once and one?*
> *Or draw a sandy line and then*
> *Erase it with our hands*
> *Just one and once*
> *Just once and one?*
> *And trace again the path, the edge, the leaking sun*
> *The chance that comes*
> *Just one and once*
> *Just once and done?*

She had thought *Erase it with our hands* was about sex or regret, but maybe he was asking about a different *it*. There were so many from that night.

It was the tryst at Cold Shivers Point.

It was Brian's instinctive swing, surprising them all when Neulan tried to charge through the gap between him and the edge.

It was a dazed Neulan kneeling, his shoulder dipped, his left hand curled like a question mark, his right groping for his glasses.

It was Meg's gratification at Neulan's blood trickling from one nostril and streaming from his crown, around his ear and soaking his shirt collar dark crimson.

It was both men heaving as if trying to recover from a sprint. Breathing, breathing slower, her breath joining in a triangle of stress. All three of them waiting for some way to resolve this impasse. For heads to clear. For the breath to form words.

And now as she drove closer to Cold Shivers Point, *it* became the forever disturbance of the place. She pulled over, she told herself, to make certain she was sober for the twisting drive down Monument Road. Just to take in the air. But she got out of the car and walked the short path to the overlook.

She had only imagined Helen falling. Now Donnie's story brought back another time, when Neulan was the one who had expected to rise.

〰

"*Scheisse*! That hurt," Neulan said, his glasses replaced cockeyed.

She wanted to laugh. At his bewilderment. That a killer wouldn't say *shit* in front of a woman.

"We didn't come to hurt you," she said. "We came for the truth." True enough, but now that she saw his blood she could not deny her satisfaction.

Neulan stared as if he hadn't heard. He fastened on the path to the parking lot past Brian, who crouched with the bat cocked for another swing.

She pressed: "You asked me to forgive your silence about Helen. All right, if you want forgiveness, now's the time to confess."

Neulan straightened his glasses. His head panned slowly as if on a swivel. His gaze passed over Meg and fixed on the distant valley floor, glowing like an aquarium in a darkened room.

"Here we are, on the pinnacle above the holy city," he said.

"Cut the crap," Brian said. "Did you push her?"

Neulan said, "Push who?"

Still denying and deflecting. She bored in. "I want to know what happened with Helen that day."

"I told you, she was daring me. Skipping, dancing on the rim." He mimicked her moves awkwardly.

"You think this is a joke?" Brian said. "I could bunt you into eternity right now."

Neulan's mouth twisted. "I'm fairly certain a bunt is not called for in this situation." He brushed his arms, wiped an X across his chest and pulled his unbloodied ear in an exaggerated manner. "That's the sign for go ahead and try it and see what happens."

Brian was an athlete, not an overmatched girl. Yet Meg saw that even one-handed, Neulan had a tall man's reach and leverage, a zealot's certainty. The cliff edge trapped him, but it could be used to his advantage, too. His piety and performer's craft masked his arrogance and cunning.

"That's how it worked, didn't it? Never the same place twice but you always brought them to the brink somewhere."

"To Him. I led them to God."

"You used God and music to win their trust so you could seduce them." Neulan had always chosen his victims carefully. Getting what he desired confirmed his glory and invincibility. Under the guise of accepting souls, he took lives as if they had been offered to him.

He shook his head violently. "They were pure and I left them pure. They were *ready*!"

His later victims were churchly but Helen wasn't pure. She had no interest in being saved. She had only larked through the motions with Neulan's church youth group, hoping for the inspiration to capture a Joan of Arc audition. Helen's faith was in herself, her passion was living, her soul was a creative force. He must have found her intensity bewildering as well as seductive.

"What about you, Neulan. Are *you* ready to meet your maker?" Brian's grip on the bat handle tightened, his knuckles, rows of tiny white skulls.

"He can't be," Meg said. "He's a murderer."

Neulan spit in disgust. "Their lives were not taken. They were returned to the Creator." His long arms swept the space around him. He lifted his face and tracked across the sky. "Those who accept his forgiveness shall have everlasting life."

"If it's so great up there, why are you waiting down here?" Meg said.

Neulan's fierce gaze swept over her, then his eyes rolled back and he began to sing in round, bursting notes: "Spirit of the living God, fall a-fresh on me."

She had never been in the presence of such a voice, enormous yet beseeching. The sound swelled as from the bottom of an ancient well.

Spirit of the living God, fall a-fresh on me.

Melt me, mold me, fill me, use me.

Me-me-me-me-me. The canyon reverberated with Neulan's voice doubling and redoubling, an antiphon of reinforcements.

"Listen to the angels," he said.

"It's an echo, asshole," Brian said.

Meg pressed him. "You aren't ready. The truth is, you're afraid God isn't there for you—that He'll forsake you because of what you've done."

Neulan bowed his head and brought his hands to his chest, one fisted, one clawed and broken. Then he straightened, his good hand opened and he raised it above his head and spoke in an exaggerated, movie-God voice. "Away from me, Satan, with your false citations."

She moved as close as she dared. "We're still here, still waiting. Scripture doesn't work for you now, does it? No verse to comfort you."

Melt me, mold me...

"No path to salvation..."

fill me, use me.

"...for the unrepentant murderer."

Neulan closed his eyes. He crossed his arms over his chest and began to tilt toward the canyon. Meg had done that pose in teacher training. The trust exercise—the *me* turning the self over to unseen arms.

Spirit of the living God, fall a-fresh on me.

Neulan leaned back and back and back, his body a question mark poised between fear and gravity, life and its end. The three of them on the rock bound by the interrogative. A thundering in her ears as she too experienced the ecstasy of his release.

〜

Headlights swept through her car, just as they had that night when Meg and Brian's panic and indecision suddenly resolved into action. If Neulan's vehicle was found in the parking area, they thought, his body would soon be found, and, hearing the news, that driver might recall a red Jetta also there. Neulan had left the keys in the Jeep's ignition, his preparation for a fast escape. Brian ripped open the door, wiped the bat on his shirt and flung it across the front seat. *Follow me*, he said, and she compounded their mistake into a conspiracy. The two cars snaked down Monument Road, bearing Meg and Brian toward their eventual uncoupling.

She always felt Neulan here more than Helen. His wickedness sent shockwaves through time and space. Her grave reverberated with the bass of this evil. Good's treble could hardly be heard.

Do you have any friends, family or other people in your life out of convenience or necessity, but you do not like their company?

—Vulnerability Index Prescreen for Single Adults

Wesley's camp sat on a wooded island reachable from Las Colonias by hopscotching across a shallow ford. A pair of worn jungle boots marked a path that led through an irrigated vegetable garden to a concealed clearing. Five campsites tucked around its rim. Two contained dome tents; another had a homemade tipi fashioned from tarps, duct tape and bubble wrap. Wesley had framed a rectangular hut with shipping pallets sheathed in salvaged doors and plywood. The spot next to Wesley was open. Long extension cords snaked around the clearing, supplying power from a liquid propane generator. A central fire pit had been fashioned from rock and car bumpers with a legless Weber and a steel catwalk step used for a cooking grate. Deeper into the brush, a patio chair with a plastic bucket underneath the cut-out seat served as a latrine. Isaac had visited other camps that had the feel of semi-permanent settlements, but nothing as neat or organized as this. Wesley's little village was just over a mile from downtown.

"Peace and quiet. Clean camp. That includes substances, too. Don't steal. That's it as far as rules go." Wesley pointed around the circle. "Meet the family. John's recovering from heroin, relapsed, got kicked out of his halfway house, now he's trying to get back in the program. Don't worry about those purple puncture marks. It's Russian olive arm. He's doubled up with Gravy. That kid's a little testy, but he killed his best friend drunk driving, so who wouldn't be? Doug got laid off as a seismic shooter for Halliburton. Don't mind if he ignores you, he's half-deaf. Terrell's got the tipi. He's happy he just got off probation. We're all getting over something."

Isaac tapped his chest by way of belonging. "Nerves," he said, as simple as he could state it. He knew something about each of them, too; by sight, by story, by the place from which they'd fallen. John had been a hotel banquet manager. Gravy spent a lot of time after a shower getting his curls right. Isaac had seen the teardrop tattooed on his cheek but hadn't known what it signified. Doug came to the library daily, dressed like he was preparing for an office job interview. Terrell sometimes played the Day Center's guitar on the smoking patio and sang in a high, sweet voice. His pecan color was not welcome everywhere and in some places on the river it was dangerous to be a black man. A white icicle scar rose up Wesley's spine to his hairline. Isaac had seen more when they were in the shower room. A swath of his back wrinkled and brown like beef jerky.

"Where will you go after they tear out the tamarisk?"

"Not far. There's a plan. Once you go rentless, you got to be relentless."

Isaac had heard that line from Wesley before and thought it was true. Living unsheltered never truly let you relax. Even when it seemed you were doing nothing, your mind was churning. Living on the river brought the freedom of being undomesticated. Like a deer or a bird or a field mouse, you were free to have a shorter life.

Terrell plucked a browned ear of corn from the grill. He peeled back a portion of the husk and watched the steam escape, then pulled all the leaves down to the shank so the cob had a handle.

"Fresh Olathe sweet corn. Off the truck today. Plenty for y'all."

"That crate must've fallen off the truck when they weren't looking," said Gravy.

Terrell shook his head. "Nah, they gave me one for helping unload."

"Is that all they paid you?" said Gravy. "That's only worth about twelve bucks and you can't buy anything with it."

"See, here's what you white boys don't understand. They paid me some, but I also got to spend my afternoon in a ice-packed truck and a grocery store cooler, while you were out scooping dog shit in a hundred degrees."

Gravy scowled. "I'm not doing that any more. That job was just temporary."

"Well maybe you could get on full-time now. I hear the Poo Patrol's business is picking up."

Everybody laughed but Doug, who sat outside the circle reading.

Terrell handed over the ear to Gravy. "Hey, no disrespect, man. We all scooping shit down here."

"Not me," said John, a rangy, pale man who moved around camp with the caution of an old lady on ice. "This methadone, I only get to grunt about once a week."

Wait, Wesley had said no substances. Wasn't methadone a drug? Or was it a medicine if it was prescribed? Isaac took medications sometimes. Would he and John have to turn them in like they did at the shelter? Wesley's rules couldn't be as simple as he'd said.

"You need fiber!" Terrell said. "Come here, have some of this. It's fresh."

Isaac explained how Olathe corn tasted better because it was handpicked, packed in ice so the sugars didn't break down and shipped the same day.

"You work in produce?" Terrell said.

"Not for a while. I'm between positions right now."

"I hear you. We all somewhere between get up off your ass and bend over." Terrell peeled another ear, passed it to Wesley and took one for himself. "M-m-m-m. You heard the man. It's the best, sweetest corn there is. You don't even need butter. This corn's half syrup, half whiskey."

"I'm surprised you didn't stick with that vacuum cleaner deal," Wesley said. "You sure got a patter."

"Yeah, I can talk slick right off the okra." Terrell tempered his smile. "Wasted two months dragging around a vacuum, dressed like a Witness and chattering like a tweaker."

"Selling's not for everyone," John said.

"Wasn't selling. It was scamming. I scammed people, the company scammed me."

"You shoulda known a vacuum cleaner job had to suck," Wesley said.

Isaac wished he talked more their way—the words slow and slathered in their own juices, the jokes striking fast and easy.

Terrell said, "It seemed okay at first. They train you and tell you how great the product is. You'll get five hundred bucks for doing fifteen demos in a week, plus commission on sales, and you can win trips and prizes. You think hey, let's go make some money! Then they give you maybe ten crappy leads and if you can't prove you did fifteen demos, you get zip. Where'm I gonna find five extra people a week who want to try a twelve-hundred-dollar vacuum?"

"Who you know wants a vacuum, period?" said Wesley.

Terrell brandished a stripped corncob. "You just give me an idea of what to do with this." Then he tossed it on the fire.

"They do suck you in. Once you figure out there's no money in the demos, and you've already put two months in, you'll do anything for a sale. You try every trick they taught you. Never let the customer get you out of their house until they're in their PJs turnin' out the lights. Then the supervisor says, now you're a big boy, an independent contractor, and we're not driving you to appointments any more."

Terrell flexed his fingers and raised his chin, a gymnast readying for the leap to grab a horizontal bar. "Then it's like, how'm I gonna get all that shit to my sales calls?" He threw up his hands. "A brother with a fancy new vacuum cleaner biking through Grand Junction at night. *On my way to an appointment, officer.* Oh, yeah, that'll go down."

"Did you ever sell any?" Isaac asked.

"One time. Old lady bought one on payments, hundred and fifty off, with her Electrolux in trade. Trade. We take it to the dump so the customer won't have a vacuum if they try to cancel. Her son stops payment anyway. I didn't get dollar one. You think that company's giving you a shot, taking a chance on a felon. Damn, that's one reason I busted my ass. They don't think I'm a loser. But then you realize, no, it's because they think you *are* a loser who'll do anything. That you got no morals." He stepped back for his third ear of corn. "I be shittin' gold nuggets tomorrow."

"You know who owns that company?" Doug had put down his book. He must have turned up his hearing aids. "Warren Buffett—richest man in the world, give or take. Those guys who hired you were a distributor, I bet, and you're an independent contractor. And then there's another business that owns the brand but doesn't really make the vacuum cleaners, they just sell products to distributors, and somewhere buried in a holding company inside Berkshire Hathaway, Warren Buffett owns everything. He collects the profits and thinks he never cheated an old lady in his life."

Doug seemed like someone Isaac could talk to. Somebody like Herbert Hoover, who would understand about how Edison and GE and RCA and NBC created the depression, nukes, Ronald Reagan, capital credit and everything since.

Wesley sat apart from the fire. He said, "That's why we need Thistletown."

"What's Thistletown?" Isaac said.

"Wesley thinks he's Braveheart," said John. "Don't get him started."

"It's a self-governed camp. I've seen them out west. I hear it worked here on The Point," Wesley said.

"You may hear that," said John, "but you wouldn't have liked it."

"We'll be respectable, with support from the Homeless Coalition. Us here had nothing to do with Dexter's meth lab. We start small, with our own little city where they can't kick us off. We show it works and build up from there. Do the things shelters won't do. Couples can stay together. You can be home in the daytime. No religion pushed on you. Keep your pet. Get rid of the bullshit. Let people live in dignity the way they choose. I know a building we can fix up. Put in a workshop with shared tools to build furniture, fix bikes. Bring in services, so our people don't spend the whole day walking around to get what they need."

"Good idea," said Gravy. "Let's start with a test lab. Free condoms with every UA."

"I'm serious."

"Dude, maybe you like all that structure because you got it in the Army, not prison. I've had my fill of hoops for a lifetime."

"There's no hoops in this camp," said Wesley.

Not that anyone saw. But the system was everywhere and Wesley couldn't keep it out. It didn't ask permission or even announce itself. It was on you like the soft water that left Isaac feeling slimy after his shower, trying to get the soapy feeling off his skin. You can't control it or choose it. The system has no knob to adjust the hardness, just this bargain: If you want to be clean, you have to slime yourself. And the funny thing? The water softener system was not there for the guy in the shower. It was for the one who owned the building. It took out the iron and the minerals that plugged pipes and stained the porcelain. It made Isaac feel like a kidney bean out of the can just so the man's toilet bowl stayed white.

Isaac spread a blanket over a piece of carpet on the sand. The night was sultry and he didn't mind sleeping uncovered. He stripped down and put on a pair of sleep-soft sweatpants. A breeze snuffled through the tamarisk and brought fresh riffles of sound. Wesley and Terrell's lowered voices like birds crossing the water. The long zip of a sleeping bag. A downshifting semi's deep chuckle as it hit the business loop. He could see the sky through the brushy crown above his head but the constellations were washed out by the city lights.

Thistletown, named for the Scottish national symbol, Wesley said. He wanted to declare independence without saying it, without promising too much. Every camp had its settlers and transients, leaders and followers, dogs running wild and coyotes going tame. All thinking they were free and wise, the ones beating the system. Then something always came up to ruin things—the weather, the law, a bad element, paranoia, power games. But just wait, Wesley said. We won't ask for too much, won't take the bad seeds or the easy riders. Thistletown'll be good people like you and me.

Something shook the tamarisk. A quavering *Knock, knock.*

And Wesley: *Who's there?*

JJ.

Ah, buddy, you're lost.

Isaac crept to the opening of his pad. A figure just inside the clearing, planted like a tree swaying in the wind. The man's head rocked back, showing eyes puffed to purple slots, and he staggered a step to keep from toppling. Jimmy Johncock. A quack came from his swollen lips and he twisted to the ground. Wesley and Terrell moved toward him. Jimmy braced himself with one arm and tried to get his legs under him. Halfway up he fell back and rolled onto his shoulder. He gathered himself in slow motion. His head rolled up toward Wesley but kept going until it reached the end of its travel, snapped forward and eventually fixed on the men's knees.

"You still with us, Jimmy?" Wesley said. Jimmy raised his hand as if he knew the answer. Wesley grasped above his wrist and leaned back while Terrell stood braced with arms wide. Jimmy wrapped around himself like a washer load of wet sheets and came up to slump against Terrell.

"He looks beat up," said Terrell. "You think he needs detox?"

"Everybody's sick of him. They might just tell him to crawl there," said Wesley. "Let's get him to bed."

The two men wobble-stepped Jimmy away. Seeing Jimmy this way was sad, in the way inevitable things were. From the time Isaac knew him in middle school, an invisible force had been winching Jimmy out the door. He would get his footing but could never seem to keep it. A sweet boy from a feeble family with a mother who believed the cure for alcoholism was drinking at home. Everyone had tried with Jimmy. Teachers. Cops. Sister Rose. They'd chipped in to send him to his last rehab in Denver and brought him back to a job with a carpet cleaning business. He did okay. But now his old drinking buddies knew somebody with money and before long Jimmy had returned to doing at least half a gallon of vodka a day with his friends.

Wesley and Terrell talked softly for a while after they returned and put the cookfire to bed. Isaac could hear only snatches about how if an uninvited drunk walked into your house, you could shoot him and get off free. That was state law. But if one came in your camp and you clubbed him with a piece of firewood, you'd be the one in jail. After they settled, he listened to the long lapping breath of the Colorado and thought of all the machine keepers who had never heard the earth's night shift at work, who slumbered through its rotations of sound and temperature and light, and missed the nocturnal critters punching out and passing the morning to the sentinel birds, and heard instead the clock's crow that released a lemming surge of tires to hum on distant highways.

He woke to a disturbance in the brush, reached for his hunter knife and listened, hearing only Wesley's regular pin-prick wheeze. That's right, he was in Thistletown now. New Jerusalem. Salt Lake City on the river, where everybody's water's not too hard and not too soft. He burrowed the knife back under the carpet and returned to sleep.

Someone yanking his arm. *Come on!* Confusion. Cauteries of light. Stinking smoke. Wesley yelling, Isaac fumbling. Backpack? Where are my jeans? *Leave it! Let's go. Go-go-go.* Bike locked. *Fiii-errr!* Cursing, splashing, people stumbling in all directions. *Move!* On bare feet. Sirens. Shadows flattened by searchlights carving the black air.

Are TRO infestations, dry conditions, human-caused fires and/or altered disturbance regimes responsible for the increased frequency of fires in riparian areas?

— Colorado River Basin Tamarisk and Russian olive (TRO) Assessment

From across the parkway, Isaac and Wesley watched red flames gulp the thickets pinched between the river and the park's hardpan. Black-backed billows lazed to and fro, a fire beast lacking the strength to escape its cage. The firemen watched, too, their hoses aimed to stop the advance rather than extinguish the flames. When it became clear the fire was controlled, the refugees straggled to Whitman Park to wait out the remains of the night.

The police ignored the curfew and let them sit trading tales of escape and theories of the fire. It was kids, it was drunks, it was a careless smoker. It was revenge by the cops for Amy Hostetter. It was the same ones who firebombed the Day Center years ago. Some said it was too hot for campfires that night and others swore there were some. Irene proclaimed it the devil's work and Edward argued everything was God's will.

Thurman Trowbridge was the first to filter in from the south camp further downriver. Every TV station had Thurman "Trow" Trowbridge on tape for when they needed two seconds to illustrate *the plight of the homeless*: his eyes sunken deep; greasy hair Medusa-like; his beard a tumbleweed scrawl over a golf ball complexion. His teeth had long ago left the gums to fend for themselves. Grime, wood smoke and glass pipe burns tattooed his cracked hands. The county had lots of his pictures on file as well; Trow and law enforcement were on a nickname basis. His legal infractions mainly involved having the wrong things in his pockets and his bloodstream, and being in the wrong places doing the wrong things with the wrong attitude. Trow had the tweaker's unpredictability but little of the anger. He had renounced driving because he didn't want to be a menace. Now, he was simply a caravan of trouble no one wanted to park close by.

"This is it," said Trow, "this is it. Sylvia's been telling me the time was coming and I had to get ready."

Trow pivoted in a complete circle, face upturned, reaching to the sky. "She says: *What about it, Thurman? You can't live outside forever. Getting your own place is the road to independence.* But I'm already independent. She said, this time, they're serious. If I don't accept help…it's the Koran or the sword. Off to the concentration camp with you. Bus ticket to Pueblo, your last rodeo. Or—I can still be saved!" He counted the steps, little finger to thumb. "All I got to do is go for a mental health assessment, then do treatment, go to meetings, pass a million UAs and I can get on the VA housing list. Wooohooo! Can you see me living in *housing*? Some little *efficiency*? I was in the army for four years and I never saw one place I wanted to live in. I haven't lived in a house since I was fourteen. Indoors, okay—barracks, apartments, motels, shelters, abandoned places, jail—but it never worked out. Because every indoors is a box and the box comes with rules. The VA apartments, you sign a contract, give up all your friends, your blessed sacraments, even the mushrooms. Put me inside, I wouldn't be Trow any more. I'd be this little dried-up vet named Thurman with his VA teeth washing dishes at Starvin' Arvin's, taking a job away from some poor Mexican trying to feed his family. With a *caaal*endar. Going to *meeee*tings. Efficiency!"

Trow snorted and a rope of snot rapunzeled to his chin. He was laughing at himself but his choices had a certain integrity. It mattered to him that he had not sunken to the bottom of the barrel. He had dived in and swum there all by himself.

"There's only one home I want." Trow seized the army surplus web belt around his waist and shook it with both hands. "This is what you need when the clouds part and God says *who's coming with me?* Everybody's jumping around—*Take me! Take me!*—but if you got one of these, He'll go for you first 'cause it's easier to grab you right up to heaven." He inspected Isaac's sagging sweat pants. "You need to get you one."

Trow rummaged in his pack and tossed Isaac a pair of Crocs. "That's my problem right here." He pulled out a fist-sized chunk of what looked like melted metal. "Ever seen a meteorite? Feel it. Heavy. That's why you can float in outer space. All the matter's sucked into the meteors. You ever find one, people'll say, that's no meteorite! You know why? Because a meteor is like gold and diamonds from space—and they don't want you to own it just for picking it up off the ground. They tell you it's worthless so they can talk you out of it. Or they tell you it's too valuable for a guy like you to keep care of it."

Isaac didn't say anything. He hadn't told anyone about the eye he found in the canyon. People would want to see it. At least a meteor wasn't like a glass eye. The comet wasn't going to want it back. He didn't think it was valuable but they might try to take it anyway if they thought a glass eye was magic. Some guys with no luck had funny ideas about how to get some. Now it was lost again. Probably burned up with his stuff left behind last night, the beautiful colors melted into a blob.

Trow stuffed the meteorite back into his pack, not lightening his load after all. "Only way I'm handing over this puppy is if they promise to put it in a museum—because meteors belong to all mankind."

The fire had burned from the footbridge at the east end of the park and petered out when it reached the river flats to the west. Within the burn stood a dead cottonwood, two limbs raised as if in surrender and blackened up to the armpits. The thicket below, where Screech and Dexter had set up their shake and bake lab, was now reduced to a charcoal scrawl. Elsewhere, charred matchsticks reared from nuclear white mounds of powdered ash. Ghostly stilts of smoke rose and dissipated like steam from hidden hot springs. A man with a long-handled shovel moved slowly over the ground, probing and occasionally turning something over.

"Doesn't look good," said Wesley. "It crossed to the island."

The fire had swept through the camp settling for ruin rather than consumption, going for the plastics and artificial fabrics. Isaac and Wesley found their bicycles padlocked together with the trailer, the tires stinking, the grips, cable sheaths and derailleur components melted to the metal, the paint scorched, leaving the steel frames a powdery orange. Terrell's corn steamed through the damp crate's slats, giving off a roasted, sugary smell. The two tents were reduced to poles splayed over ash and lumps of carbon. Terrell's camp now revealed the smoldering frame of a legless couch and a scorched flat screen TV draped with the bubbled black streamers left by his plastic-wrapped tipi. Indoors, they all might have died, overcome and suffocated by the chemical cloud.

"My generator's toast," Wesley growled. Except for the rotted boards, his wooden hut had burned to nails and old door hinges. He kicked still-warm coals. "Shit's been moved. I think somebody's already been through here."

Isaac had so little to burn. The laces had disappeared from his shoes, their white leather turned blackened and hard. No sign of his jeans with his wallet and keys. His backpack was a stinking bundle, its straps missing, the plastic zippers fused. Jake's bone-handled knife had survived and he used it to cut open the pack. He rooted for the metal Band-Aid box where he kept the glass eye and found it unharmed, still wrapped in a rag. What did it mean that his luck kept getting worse while the eye survived? The devil withstood the flames around him, too. Wishes granted by magic lamps only brought misfortune to the finders. Isaac hoped it wasn't too late to locate the eye's rightful owner and restore his equilibrium.

From what had been a place of shelter last night, he could see clear across the park. He watched Trow pick a jagged path toward the man with the shovel. Taking turns kneeling to examine the ground, the two might have been descendants searching for grown-over gravestones.

Wesley headed their way. "Finding anything?" he said to the shovel man.

"Just checking it out. You live down here?"

"We did."

"Were you around last light?"

"Are you a cop?" Wesley asked. No cop would go dressed in work Dickies, Isaac thought.

"Public Works, Richard Diaz. My crew gets to clean up this mess. Sorry if you got burned out. We'll be here in a few days with a brush hog, so if you've got anything to salvage do it now."

"What's the rush?" Wesley said.

Diaz shrugged. "People upstairs don't want it looking like this."

"Not like it was pretty before," said Wesley.

"At least it was green," said Isaac. "Tamarisk was better than this. Better than before."

Diaz looked at him. "You remember."

Isaac nodded. For decades, free tailings from the uranium mill had gone into road base, concrete, sandboxes and gardens. You'd get more radiation from the sun, from a watch dial, they said, but the government removed millions of tons of the material. The house next door to his family's had to have its foundation re-excavated. Two kids in Isaac's class died from thyroid cancer in their twenties. Now the worst had been removed, they said. But they couldn't take back what was in the town's bones.

Diaz swept his hand across the parkway toward the little houses. "Every day my mother wiped tailings dust off our dinner table. Some people think they can improve this place. I want it returned to nature."

Isaac said, "We'll never get nature back. A third of the river gets diverted across the mountains to Denver. This used to be the bottom of a sea."

Diaz stared at Isaac, expecting more.

"Welcome to the club," said Wesley.

Trow waved them over to the east end of the park, beyond the dead cottonwood. He toed a white clinker that looked like a cigar left to burn all the way down. He crumbled the brittle residue and sniffed his fingers. "Smells like sulphur."

"A fusee," said Wesley. He looked back to where the camps had been. A short dash away, the bike trail cut through to a road screened by Russian olive. A good place to start a fire and leave unseen. "They burn like hell and bright. That explains the light we saw."

"There's two more over this way." Trow walked the edge of the burn. At the next spot, he uncovered the stub of a charred, red paper tube with a plastic cap stuck on the end.

Wesley's slow head roll spoke his disgust. "No firebug sticks the striker cap on the butt of a flare after he lights it. This town got what it's wanted ever since Amy Hostetter got hurt."

"Long before that," said Trow.

Sylvia stood in the Day Center kitchen watching the big room through the two-way mirror.

"I lost my storage unit key. All my keys," Isaac said. Most of them keys to locks changed, to padlocks cut, to whole buildings gone. "I need my duplicate."

She swept *the look* over him. "What were you doing down on the river? I thought you were gonna go full hermit up at Hefner's place."

"I'm on hiatus from househunting," he said.

Sylvia yanked open a stuck drawer in her desk and retrieved a metal file box. She unlocked it with a little silver key from a jar of paperclips and began sifting through the assortment of keys inside. Some were labeled with chains or paper tags attached with string; others had names taped to the head; one old-fashioned door key hung from a rabbit's foot. All jumbled together like spare change.

"Remind me what yours looks like."

That was disappointing. He'd marked his with a brass Samsonite tag he'd pried off a crushed suitcase found by the railroad tracks. "*Samson*-ite. You really should put them in little envelopes and file the names alphabetically. They'd be easier to find," he said.

Sylvia shook her head. "This makes it easier to forget who hasn't come back."

Isaac approached the storage facility gate with his usual trepidation. He knew he looked suspicious entering on foot, so he came after the manager left and before night fell. He imagined his image moving from one monitor to another as the security cameras picked up his passage. He slipped under the metal door of his unit before it had completely crawled up on its rollers and drew it down again. The light in the ten-foot cube didn't work. He felt for the box of tent candles, lit one and set the can on the floor.

He could have navigated the whole space in the dark. One side of the unit stored things he might sell someday: picture frames, a birding scope, an imitation Persian carpet, brass door hardware, LP records, antique crocks and flower pots, a stained glass window, a French horn, dog clippers, a fox stole, baseball cards, rusty but serviceable tools, hammock chairs, children's books, a skateboard, stuffed animals. All thrown off the back of the speeding consumer express. On the other side, his archives and keepsakes stored in plastic tubs: his books and notebooks, extra clothes and camping gear, clips of his published letters to the editor, and his documentation of Thomas Edison's plan to rule America. At the back was a lozenge-yellow Raleigh Record, the bike his brother Joe had bought for him at a yard sale. The old road bike was impractical for carrying cargo or navigating rough ground. He'd almost turned it down. He didn't want his family's well-meaning concern. It made him feel too responsible for their happiness.

Joe's bike would have to serve. He pumped the tires. In the morning he'd find out if the tubes were any good.

Isaac unrolled a sleeping bag in the narrow pathway between the shelves. The concrete was cool, the air sweltering. He extinguished the candle, raised the door a crack and propped it open with a coffee can full of glass doorknobs. If caught sleeping here he'd be evicted. He had already lost years of archives, what his father had called *a trash heap*. No potentate can bear libraries. If their contents agree with him, they are redundant. If they fail to mention him, they are outdated. And if they oppose him, they must be destroyed. Just like Isaac, tyrants want to reorder the world's too-muchness. But burning was so much simpler.

The Clarion ran a picture of smoke rolling through the park, with the fire crew standing watch. The caption treated it as a brush fire with no mention of the cause. The newly displaced moved to other camps, abandoned buildings and loading docks, brushy areas near bike trails, boat launches and railroad tracks, even the old city cemetery. A silent game of musical chairs played out daily as rousted campers were forced to move on. With the surge, the churches activated their emergency program designed to handle the winter influx at the shelter. Borrowed cots and bedding were set up in gyms or classrooms. Volunteers from the host church stayed overnight as monitors. Isaac had sampled overflow in years past but could not bear the close communion of snorers, farters, sighers and insomniacs. Hoping to join Wesley, Isaac tried without success to find where he had gone. Sleeping in staggers, he spent more uneasy nights in his unit, awaiting the rough hands that would mean the end of everything.

Talk at the Day Center speculated about Jimmy Johncock's whereabouts. Word on the street was the cops wanted to talk to him about the fire, so JJ's disappearance made sense, but there were no secrets here, only half-truths, lies and misinformation. Someone always knew something and would spill it in trade for harm, advantage or plain old drama. By the time an arrest showed up officially in the Blotter, known here as the Friends and Family section of the newspaper, the subject was often back on the street. JJ hadn't appeared either place, but he seemed to be off the hook when the Blotter ran a short update on the fire investigation:

> *Investigators attributed last Tuesday's Las Colonias fire to careless handling of fusee-style flares used by vagrants to ignite damp firewood. Since no property damage resulted, officials said no charges were likely.*

Damp firewood? No property damage? No charges? No wonder so many people believed in intrigue. The truth wasn't ever sorted out in the newspaper.

Isaac watched Gravy fly a new sign on the corner of Fifth by Whitman Park. He held a spiral notebook sideways and flipped over one page at a time so the message changed like a digital billboard:

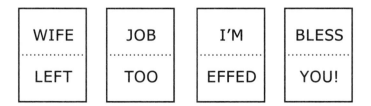

"Actions speak louder than words, bro," Gravy said. "Gotta keep things moving and changing."

A cop pulled up to say Gravy was disrupting traffic with aggressive solicitation.

What about the Two-Dollar Tacos guy dancing in a chicken suit outside El Pollo Loco or the Lady Liberty outside the tax office? Gravy wasn't asking for money. What about the Spiderman guy hyping cell phones? It was a good question, Isaac thought.

"Stay out of this," said the cop. "That's commercial speech. Spidey's selling, not panhandling. Besides, *effed* is profanity."

Gravy kicked the argument up a notch, protesting that he wasn't soliciting. He was a street entertainer creating awareness of social issues. "Furthermore, *effed* is only a rhyme and a rhyme is not a crime and you have a dirty mind."

At this point the clash became one of principle, which meant nobody was budging and the cop was going to win. At least he could write a ticket Gravy wouldn't pay and then a warrant would be issued. It was like a Get Into Jail Free card the cop could slap on Gravy whenever he wanted. Or, Gravy could argue himself right into the squad car and shorten the process considerably. Gravy closed his notebook and moved to a park bench.

The cop pointed to the curb and said, "Don't let me see you here again." But he knew he would.

Isaac asked Gravy if he'd seen Wesley. The kid was still amped up, jab-combing his fingers alongside his head, as if the cop had messed with his hair.

"If I see him, I'll tell him you're looking for him."

Isaac wasn't sure he was. He was really looking for peace and quiet and hoping Wesley would know where to find it.

〜〜

JAYzus!

Isaac's father Carl loosens his chokehold on the steering wheel and slaps a palm twice on the dash. *JAYzus CHRIST!*

Isaac cowers in the back seat on the passenger side. Joe is safe in the middle, Jake untouchable behind their father.

Keeee—the air crackles as Carl raises his hand to grasp the lightning bolt—*RRRRIST!*

The dashboard compass lurches hard NE to SW and back, then quivers, unable to escape Hurricane Carl.

Isaac, go get your mother!

Isaac has to go, last in, first out. That's why the boys race for the back seat on Sunday.

We're going to be late for GOD-whump!-*DAMN*-whump!-*CHURCH!* - whump!

Three whumps against the cloth headliner, the roof of the Dodge like a bass drum. She must be able to hear from the kitchen.

Isaac pushes the front seat forward and hunches out. He thinks he might throw up. His shoulders stay bent as he crosses the carport to the kitchen door. He slides sideways through the smallest opening to keep dust from blowing into the house.

His mother is on her knees in her church dress, scrubbing a brown spot where the linoleum pattern has been worn away in front of the stove.

Come on, Mom, it's time to go.

She looks up sharply. Isaac knows to wait. His father knows not to come in.

We'll get there. We always do.

She draws the stiff brush back and forth across the floor three more times, then swills it in the pail and raps it against the rim. When she stands to put the brush under the sink, her knees are marked with two rosy hearts.

WOMPWOMPWOMPF. *Let's GO-O-O!*

Joseph! Your baby brother can't do a simple task. Not one goddam thing I ask him to do.

BAP BAP BAAAAAP.

Isaac tries to take her hand.

Please...

I have to put on my hose, sweetie.

He watches her to the bedroom door. He scans the kitchen, notices the Fat Chef cookie jar's torso is askew and he sets it right. A car door slams. The kitchen door rattles open.

Thanks a lot.

I tried. You know how she is.

Joe mock-harelips it back to him. *I tried. You know how she is. You wimp. Where is she?*

Changing. Putting on her nylons.

Great. If she's not out in ten seconds, you have to go get her.

I can't. She's getting dressed!

BAP-BAAAAP!

She could be back there sewing on buttons!

She doesn't do it on purpose.

Ten...nine...

It's not my fault.

Eight...seven...

The bedroom door opens. His mother steps into the kitchen wearing the same indigo dress, now with white pumps and a white straw hat that matches the wicker handbag draped on her wrist.

Are we ready?

As Isaac and Joe hesitate, she stoops to pick up the pail of water.

Let's go, your father's waiting.

Isaac scurries ahead and Joe follows Marian, herding so he'll earn the credit for extracting her. Jacob sits in back with arms crossed, above everything.

It's a miracle, their father roars.

He cranks the Dodge, then revs the engine loudly. Marian crosses the carport with her pail, to where a clematis climbs one of the corner posts. She slowly trickles the clear water around its roots.

FAUGH! MARIAN!

A forearm slams against the tilted back of the front seat. It rebounds upright against the broken catch and returns to the folded position.

Remind me to bring that pail into the kitchen when we get back, Carl. I don't think I have time to put it away now.

No one but Carl speaks on the ride to church. His flaming words decry drivers and pedestrians who impede him, unneeded stop signs, unresponsive traffic lights, illogical speed limits, the decision to build the new church in a distant location, thus forcing him to break the law—points he accentuates with brake-stomping stops and smoking accelerations.

Well practiced, Marian and the boys brace against whiplash as Carl screeches to the church entrance. They emerge and he peels off to find *the last damn parking spot!*

A row at the front remains open to the last minute. The Samson pew.

As the priest enters from the vestry, Carl thumps triumphantly in his seat. Marian half turns so the boys see her tight-lipped smile.

Each parent seems to say: *What did I tell you?*

Moderate winters, affordable home prices and easy access to the outdoors make this valley an attractive retirement destination.

— "Home" with Meg Mogrin, *Grand Junction Style*

"Lew Hungerman's coming in a *jet*?" Meg said.

Eve Winslow paused on the other end of the line. "Isn't that what you say when you meet someone at the airport?"

"I say meet his flight. His plane. You said his jet."

The mayor huffed. "Okay, word girl. He's landing at the charter hangar. I don't know if it's a jet. Maybe it has propellers. Or it's the company flying saucer. Anyway, Dan, Vince and I are picking him up at five-thirty. Come."

"Gawd, you'll need a limo." Meg imagined the delegation holding up a placard for MR. HUNGERMAN. "You don't want to look desperate."

"Hon, we *are* desperate—just not that desperate. Meet us at No Coast, then. Jules has the table."

No Coast was a bit informal for entertaining a visiting dignitary. Perhaps Hungerman had been over-subjected to the country club by now. If he couldn't appreciate a sushi bistro in a strip mall next to an aquarium shop, he wasn't going to do very well in this town.

Panhandlers harvested the traffic at the intersection where Meg waited for the light. At her corner, a young woman with a pit bull in a red bandana flashed a cardboard appeal: *I'M OK BUT MY DOG WON'T EAT RAMEN.* Meg smiled enough to show she liked the line but not enough to invite the woman off the curb. On the cross street, a beaming regular waved a peace sign to passing cars while his dreadlocks shouted at drivers not to stop. A third panhandler on the diagonal corner strolled along the queue, dropping large white cards one at a time. He faced away from Meg and she couldn't read the message but when her lane started to move, he turned and walked back to gather the cards from the ground. Yoga Man.

Jules Lodge had already arrived in the back room and commanded the corner furthest from the door. She threw off a striking but aloof confidence. The aura had no doubt served her in business school and so far in her banking career. Meg didn't expect Jules to stick around forever. She was too feline for a dog town.

Two tables were pushed together and set for six. Meg took the end next to Jules. "I see you wiggled out of the welcoming party, too," Meg said.

Jules didn't like pointless displays and was much better than Meg at letting people know it. "Once was enough. I went with Vince Foyer—you know how he loves to ferry people in his Jaguar." It was a double dig. Vince was a deeply closeted commercial broker. "Lew Hungerman shows up in this linen jacket over a stretch tee you know has to be dry cleaned, and he sets down his gorgeous Paul Smith flight bag. I thought about lugging it out to the car just so I could caress the lambskin, but Vince beat me to it."

"I feel like I'm way behind on this," Meg said. "Eve's already sending me vibes I'm supposed to marry him."

"You should. That would help a lot. He's a little too anchor-manish for my taste." Jules, dark and intelligent, was more foreign correspondentish herself. She made a motion of pushing away a plate and Meg couldn't help envisioning it covered with men's bones.

"What's wrong with that?" Meg asked.

"It's not the looks and the nice clothes. It's that underlayer. You know, is he sincere or reading from a script? Does he go for me or does he just like me looking at him? But I can see why Eve thinks you might be attracted."

"Meaning what?"

"That you have such discerning standards—and you're so good at dealing with mixed messages."

How could I be your friend if I wasn't? It was nice to know that was the impression she gave. "Everyone seems to have heard something about his project but nobody's willing to share."

"How would you stay in business if everyone knew everything?" Jules allowed her martini to tilt close to the rim before righting the glass. "So what have you heard?"

She had read Eve's bag of documents, conveyed as if it were a diplomatic pouch, but most of the contents were background. Enough to see the Betterment Health headquarters would mean hundreds of new jobs and potential contracts for local support businesses and could possibly attract associated development. Meg assumed Jules, who chaired the downtown development authority, knew all that and more.

"From what I can tell, Betterment Health's a glorified collections agency with some special software for hospitals. It seems to be a legitimate six-hundred-million company, but I can't see how it needs more than an office building here. Eve's talking about this being the city's biggest land deal ever. It's hard to connect the two."

Jules nodded. "It's easier to find Hungerman's triathlon times than his record as a developer. He's been working through consultants here and locking up people with confidentiality agreements, so if we want the whole scoop we may have to get him loaded tonight and steal his laptop." A Cheshire smile. "I hear you're showing him some houses."

"He might rent a place for a month. Eve says he wants to get a sense of the community for his family."

Jules rolled her eyes. "Spare me divorced fathers pandering to their kids. Nobody uproots a company that size for his personal life. Look for the story he isn't telling, because there has to be one."

As if Meg didn't know. Every deal she'd ever done involved a dance of concealment. Rodents, leaks, mold, loud neighbors, failing appliances, bad septic, phantom partners, dodgy income. It seemed her whole life was about looking for the rot.

"It sounds as though you don't care for him."

Jules raised an eyebrow, nipped at her olive and resubmerged it. "A sushi place is nowhere to go for a decent martini." She lasered a brilliant smile toward the doorway. "Oh, here they come."

Dan McCallam could be counted upon to be at the elbow of any visiting business dignitaries but it was Eve who ushered in Lew Hungerman. Perhaps the sharp-dressing Chamber of Commerce director sensed how off-the-rack he appeared next to a man whose cashmere jacket draped as if it were his own pelt. Hungerman radiated warmth from his blazing smile and cool from ice blue anchorman eyes that were not network but definitely major market. He zeroed in on Jules as men invariably did, with the lingering appreciation of a car show shopper regretting his full garage. Then he turned to Meg and took possession of her hand as if he'd intended to save the best for last.

"So you're going to be my guide," he said. "I hope we'll have time for more than a parade of homes." His eyes flashed an invitation to read between the lines—or perhaps go for a swim. His ease was disconcerting and he knew it. Oh, God, did he know it.

"Is there anything special you'd like to see?" *What a stupid thing to say.*

"I've heard about your amazing mountain bike trails. I'd love to get out on Tabeguache—is that how you say it?"

It was and it threw her. Brian had a touch of the same quality: the laid-back swagger of outdoorsy men with indoor jobs who couldn't be blamed for disappearing at any moment because something—the sun, the trail, the river, the snow—was always calling them out the door for an afternoon. Or forever. This man's version was more exquisitely rendered than Patagonia—a boutique label you might find, say, in Aspen, in a shop called Hungerman.

"I could line up somebody to take you out there," Meg said.

"Meg's more the literary type," said Jules.

All right, so she didn't bike. It seemed more explanation than necessary. Eve and Dan McCallam were still standing, waiting to see where Hungerman would sit. When he took the chair against the wall next to Jules, Eve quickly moved to the end next to him, leaving McCallam with his back to the room.

Vince Foyer appeared, beaming. In his trademark black and white, bow tie and austere wireframe glasses, he'd always seemed to Meg a giddy amalgam of Italian architect and Orville Redenbacher.

"Success?" Hungerman asked him.

"He wouldn't part with the big placards," said Vince, "but he was handing out these." He fanned three hand-lettered index cards.

"Was he a preacher or a panhandler?" Hungerman said.

"Hard to say," said Vince. "He said he was creating awareness. I offered him a twenty and he accepted it."

"That's still soliciting without a license," said Dan McCallam. "Or is it religious freedom?" The new panhandling ordinance had everyone confused.

Eve made a sour face. "We're supposed to be selling Lew the *high*lights of our city."

Hungerman studied the cards. "Oh, this was, seeing the guy do the Bob Dylan bit. *Don't Look Back*, right?"

"Of course!" Meg said. They were talking about Yoga Man. "'Subterranean Homesick Blues.'" Dylan dropping the cards: *basement, medicine, pavement, government*. The song did seem about being strung out and homeless.

"Lew collects street memorabilia," said Vince.

Jules covered her mouth and bugged her eyes in Meg's direction. Vince could be a prig but Meg wasn't about to mock him.

Hungerman held up one card. "Okay, literary type: 'Do not listen for something you have heard before.' Is that Dylan?"

"I suppose it could be," Meg said.

"Sounds like a fortune cookie—or a greeting card," said Vince. "Look at number two."

Hungerman read, "'It is not enough turning bread into dung.'"

"Oh, that'll make a nice greeting card," said Jules.

"Here's the one we saw when we drove by: 'You must ask for what you really want.'"

Impossible! Hearing the line now pierced Meg as when she'd first read it, copied in Helen's hand. It sounded wrong in Hungerman's voice. Her fingers flew to her temple, as if to adjust the reception.

"It's from a Rumi poem," she murmured.

"You see?" said Jules to Hungerman, toasting Meg with her replenished glass.

"The poem's not his to sell," Meg said.

Hungerman considered the point. "I would assume even a panhandler would know poetry doesn't sell. Maybe it is just about awareness, like he said. So how do we interpret it? 'You must ask for what you really *want*' or 'You must ask for what you *really* want'?"

"Or 'You must *ask* for what you really want'!" said Vince, who was always closing.

Meg had rolled the line through all those interpretations, searching for some insight into Helen's state of mind during her last days. The entire verse was about being aware of how close this life was to another world of the spirit. Why had Yoga Man picked it? Was he turning the tables, reminding us of the times *we* passively want something and fail to make it known? Why should we look down on a beggar holding his sign if we stumble through life without expressing our own deepest needs?

"That's not what I get out of it," said Dan. "He's a transient mooching with lines that sound like something out of the Bible."

And what if the transients wear tailored clothes and have eyes like melting glaciers?

Dan McCallam dropped the last edamame pod into the bowl and folded his hands at the edge of the table. He leaned forward slightly, as if he were about to deliver a confidential stock tip.

"Last year, the city's economic development office did not bring one new job to town. There's been little outside commercial investment here for years before that. Half of Main Street's for lease. The reality is, oil and gas bring in jobs but it costs us when it's here and costs more when it leaves."

Meg felt Jules's toe nudge her foot. Yes, hearing Dan follow "the reality is" with a statement about actual reality was mildly shocking. Dan never expressed doubt about the energy industry. He'd blamed state environmental regulations instead of global prices for oil's fickle relationship with the area. Dan had also led the cheer squad welcoming big box retailers who'd put some of his members out of business.

He continued. "This is not just an issue for the business community. It's a community-wide leadership issue."

Meg looked to Eve, expecting daggers. How could it not be a criticism of her? Dan McCallam's real focus was not attracting new businesses; it was packing the council with business-friendly members to benefit the good old boys. The mayor presented an unreadable front. As unthinkable as it was, perhaps Dan was also talking about himself.

"We have pursued an all-of-the-above economic development strategy and it has brought us nada. We have too many competing interests cancelling each other out. Our message is…" Dan groped for the word.

"Unfocused," suggested Hungerman.

Dan nodded. "I'm excited by Lew's proposal. The scale of his vision takes getting used to, but that's because it represents such a giant leap forward. The Chamber Board's committed, and we need the council behind this, too."

Meg caught Eve looking at her. An inscrutable, one-eyebrow commentary. Dan's speech did seem a bit overblown. This wasn't a meeting of his local powerbrokers. Vince was the local contact on the site search and Jules represented the downtown development authority, which had little actual power except what the council granted. Certainly, the City would be on board and Eve was already fired up. *And who am I, the tour guide?*

Lew Hungerman accepted a fresh tonic and watched the waiter leave the room before he began.

"Let me start with the big picture and why I'm here. I'm new to the west but I've come to understand why prosperity is moving to the Rockies. Aspen, Telluride, Steamboat, Park City. These towns've tried to maintain a link to the past, but they aren't mining and ranching towns anymore. I understand why people may like their hometown the way it was, but the world has moved on. The economy has. I'm from Detroit where we can't escape that reality. You can't, either.

"Eve, merchants like you ensure your town is not like every place else and local ownership keeps more dollars in the local economy. That's important. But a community truly prospers when it attracts wealth from elsewhere. I'm not talking about corporate franchises or tour buses. I'm talking serious money that can define your whole community for better or worse. Do you want to be a Gillette or a Jackson?"

Energy boomtown or retirement mecca. Bars full of rough-necks or a ski resort in a valley where it snowed money. Was that even a question? But those were much smaller communities. Grand Junction was too big to be defined by one thing and too small to pretend it was like Denver.

Hungerman paused to gauge his effect. Dan McCallam and Vince Foyer nodding, Eve impassive, Jules drawing her bow.

"I'm sure you're not trying to insult us," Jules said, "but maybe you could not try a little harder."

Hungerman accepted the zinger with a nod. "I'm sorry if that sounded arrogant. My point is, decide what you *really* want to be, not just how many jobs you want. If you're willing, together we can draw this community's assets together in a far more compelling and ultimately rewarding way."

He picked up a rolled towel and methodically cleansed his fingers. So far he had not said anything Meg hadn't heard said by consultants or progressive town leaders like Eve, who seemed especially intent on Hungerman's hands as they caressed each other.

"Baby Boomers, the wealthiest and most self-indulgent generation in human history, are retiring with little intention of surrendering their youth. They constitute a large proportion of the forty million elective medical procedures performed each year in the U.S. Sure, if they have serious medical problems, they'll go with the name brands—Mayo, M.C. Anderson and the Cleveland Clinic—but who wants to hang around a bunch of really sick old people when your goal is enhancing your quality of life? Have you been to Houston in the summer? Minnesota in the winter? Mayo's added campuses in Florida and Arizona, which is great for the golf cart crowd. But what if your lifestyle tends more to hiking and biking, outdoor photography, maybe some less intense skiing, wineries and—let's say it—recreational marijuana? There's a niche you can fill very nicely. Grand Junction is already a regional medical center. You've developed your own accountable health care model that has driven down costs and improved patient outcomes. You've got abundant sunshine and world-class access to public lands for recreation. In my view, your sweet spot's there—a place to visit or retire where there's good medical, natural assets and a livable-scale community."

She'd read the article about Mayo and other renowned medical clinics in Eve's document dump. But those were big players, well-established where they were. This was Grand Junction.

"I've transformed my company once before by anticipating opportunity and it is gratifying personally to help something tired become robust again. But what I'm proposing here goes beyond my organization and beyond myself. It will take an entire community's buy-in to realize the whole thing, and the entire community will benefit if we tackle this together. Our headquarters and a hotel partner will anchor the Betterment Longevity Institute, dedicated to holistic rejuvenation of body, mind and spirit for active individuals who seek more out of life." Hungerman smiled to himself. He had probably just quoted from the prospectus. "And as you can guess, we are very interested in partnering with a community eager and able to rejuvenate itself. Our team has met privately with many here who love that our positioning puts health and outdoor recreation in the spotlight, which fits with your city's emerging aspirations. The market is out there and we know how to reach them. All the Betterment Longevity Institute needs is to find the right home for our brand."

He dropped the towel in his plate, leaving a mounded, snow-capped peak. Was the ascent he described Mt. Elbert easy or treacherous like Crestone Peak? Dan McCallam wore an expression he could have carried straight into heaven. Vince Foyer adjusted his tie and appeared about to propose marriage. Jules tapped a ruby nail into the tabletop and the mayor delivered a penetrating look in Meg's direction.

Her father liked to tell a story about a field trip when he was an insurance company trainee. His boss was considering whether to invest in land surrounding a new ski hill in a narrow mountain corridor. The boss was not impressed and her father wondered who would drive there from Denver to ski when Loveland, Arapaho Basin and Winter Park were closer. Aspen was already renowned as an international destination. There was nothing year-round in Vail, never had been, not even in the gold rush days. The boss shook his head in disbelief all the way back to Glenwood Springs, which had scarcely grown since its boom as a resort town in the 1890s. Nothing big ever grew on the west side of the divide, he said.

Meg took that to mean ambition had to leave town, and certainly she acquired her own experiences to support the assumption. But here was a successful man from a major city ready to invest in Grand Junction. Maybe the vision to make something great had to come riding in from out of town, blind to the past.

She asked the obvious question. "Where are you going to put this?"

Hungerman's eyes made a quick sweep of the table and came back to her. "Let's pull back a bit. The proposed headquarters site is still confidential. There's nothing binding the land yet."

Jules mimed zipping her lip. Eve said, "Everyone knows except her, Lew."

Hungerman leaned toward Meg. "In broad terms we want about six hundred acres to link downtown to the river."

In broad terms, it was breathtaking. Meg had sold a few ranches and had an idea of the scale but it was difficult to imagine where he would find that much land in the city.

It was about equal to the size of the original town plat. And between downtown and the Colorado were rail lines and major thoroughfares, a mishmash of land uses and property owners, brownfields and homes, plus Las Colonias Park.

"It's finally time for a River Renaissance," said Dan. "Thirty years since the clean-up along the river started and there's still nothing there. The City hasn't even grown grass." McCallam ignored Eve's glare. He rubbed his hands together as if placing them under a restroom drier. "We can poke along forever with an unfunded park improvement plan that'll do squat for economic development or support Lew's roadmap to do something truly transformative."

Transformative was not a Dan McCallam word and Meg doubted he could spell Renaissance but he seemed truly pleased to have used both. Hungerman rewarded him with a smile before he turned to Meg.

"Since Las Colonias will be in Betterment's front yard, we'd like the opportunity to, uh, guide its evolution toward discouraging incompatible uses."

Eve broke in. "For cripes sake. You're not going to hurt any feelings here. Just say it in plain English."

Hungerman adjusted his Viking-raider blues to the sincerity setting. "Grand Junction is a bit rough around the edges. It's encouraging to see you've begun to address vagrancy more assertively."

"We have a reputation," said Vince.

"As a generous, altruistic community," Eve shot back.

"But we are still in need of some comprehensive housecleaning," said Dan.

Hungerman reached across the table and placed his hand flat in front of Meg, as if he expected her to cover it with hers. "That's why your involvement will be so critical."

My involvement.

"Our investors won't go forward in a contentious environment. This proposal can't be seen as a direct move to seize control of the park or to extirpate a particular group of people—even if they're derelicts."

Extirpate. What an odd word to use in conversation. It distanced everyone at the table from what he was suggesting. He withdrew his hand, picked up his towel and began folding it. "Betterment stands for progress. Uplift. Longevity. We are so very fortunate to have you and the Homeless Coalition out front on this, Meg."

Hungerman didn't understand how the coalition worked. She looked for someone to correct him, but everyone was studying her, awaiting her reaction—everyone except Eve, who watched Hungerman square the white cloth, his fingers working around the edges.

Then it struck her—the nausea and the realization at once. The meeting was over. This meeting they had staged for her.

**We will not regret the past nor wish
to shut the door on it.**

—The Promises, The Big Book

Vaughn Hobart was a grown man mowing lawns in the desert, not
exactly the wave of the future, when Meg Mogrin said she needed
a handyman. He didn't know the word for what he needed. He'd
barely begun to see through his own bullshit after being stuck in
the center of himself—not a bad man or even a selfish one but too
damn aggravating and him too dumb to see it. One by one, good
people tired of his slipshoddity and moved on with their own business. It had seemed they'd abandoned him, but he saw it differently
now. Thirty years was a long time for a man to come around to
knowing himself. You couldn't make up for that much lost time.
You could only start where you found yourself and make amends
where possible. A few opened their arms. Others were content to let
then be then. No one slammed the door in his face. He wondered if
he ever was quite as worthless as he'd thought.

One day Meg gave him the keys to her truck. Later she handed
him keys to other people's houses. The day she told him his last
check would be late and he should think about going out on his
own, he thought he was being fired. He almost went out and took a
drink. Instead, he went home to feel sorry for himself. He realized as
he walked through the door: sonofabitch, *she* was the one in trouble.
Right then he began to believe he was finally on the right path.

Vaughn pulled through the gate at Reiner's half-finished mansion,
not bothering to cut his lights. He hadn't been able to surprise the

squatters before and one time, for sure, they'd slipped away into the brush as he drove up. No way he was going to chase them down in the dark. No more warnings and deadlines. He'd sucked up plenty of patience in his time so he felt qualified to judge when enough was enough. He'd cut them some slack because of the kid and because they were keeping a clean camp and leaving the house alone. He had no desire to make their lives worse, but he told Meg he'd take care of it and now he had to follow through.

His flashlight searched for the notice he'd left duct-taped to the trailer. Like the others, it was gone, and as before, their crap was still under the tarp. Vaughn cut the ropes securing the tarp and spread it to receive the squatters' leavings. Probably Kip Reiner's boat cover, but what the hell. No telling what might be in that rat's nest after this much time. With a manure fork, he lifted a sleeping bag and a snarl of blankets. A sea duffle heavy with clothing. He scooped a couch cushion, rubber bathmat and tube socks rolled into balls and made shish-kabobs of food wrappers and Walmart bags. He speared an almost empty Kessler bottle, releasing a vapor he hadn't tasted in seven years.

Something fluttered over his head. He turned just in time to catch the next dirt clod with his chest.

"Who's that?"

A third projectile sailed wide right and plinked off his truck. It gave him a fix on the thrower's position in the brush. He raised the fork in that direction and said, "You're done trespassing. You want to leave in the sheriff's car, keep it up. If you care about any of this stuff, you better act more peaceable."

A man's head emerged turtlelike from around the stern of the boat.

"Peace, then, brother," the man drawled, squinting from the pouched eyes and thickened brow of a boxer. No, more like a face real boxers had practiced on long and hard. The man made a peace sign with one hand but kept the boat between them.

Vaughn held the pitchfork ready across his chest. "Who's got the arm on him out there?"

"Sorry about that. The boy don't mind."

"Wonder where he learned that from? You saw the postings. I gave you plenty of time to move out."

The man rubbed his head, the crown shaved to the same black stubble that covered his face. "What postings?"

"I stuck 'em right here."

"Never saw nothin'—but okay. Don't call the cops. Looks like you got us half moved already. Glen Leary." Leary's horseshoe-hard grip said he'd been working. A half-smile exposed a tiny brownish Florida, his broken right incisor representing the panhandle and the rotted left standing in for the peninsula. "Figured this'd be temporary, but temporary's gettin' to be my permanent condition."

Vaughn had an idea what he meant. "Didn't see any woman's things. Is it just you and the kid?"

"Kids," said Leary, holding up two fingers again. "Hidin' in the brush. I'd as soon they didn't hear this. I'm tryin' to sell this as a campin' trip but they want to know why they're sleepin' under a boat. I was supposed to floor on this job here, then it never got started. Drove up from Cortez. I figured there might be more work around here. We went to the Walmart but they don't allow overnights here, I guess. The truck broke down and we got towed. They wouldn't let me get my tools out of the impound unless I paid the ticket and storage. Story of my life. Figured this bastard owed me something."

"He owes a lotta people," Vaughn said. "This place belongs to the bank now."

Leary cast his squint toward Vaughn's truck. "Hobart Home Inspections. I'll work. I just finished pullin' down a barn. Ten bucks an hour and free lockjaw. I don't 'spose you got anything better?"

"Only help I need right now is takin' a load to the dump, unless you got a better idea."

"I might. Let me think for a sec. You ever married?"

Vaughn could tell a question from a preamble, so he motioned to Leary to get the story off his chest.

"Never marry a woman with the same name as her mother— that's my advice," Leary said. "We lived with Alice, the mother, starting out. Any time she wanted something out of you, she'd say, *am I gonna have to start charging rent?* It got old. You'd wake up and some strange guy'd be havin' coffee in the kitchen and Alice'd say, *oh, he's just here to fix the car.* She had three cars that never ran and three men that never stuck around. Shoulda been my first clue.

"So I get this flooring job down in Pagosa and I tell Alice, my wife, we both need to get away from your mother, so why don't you come with. We get back after a few weeks and my Alice says, *hey, where's my car?* And her mother says, *I drove it and it got stolen,* and there's this big fight about how could you let my car get stolen. Now we're set back because Alice wasn't covered for theft. One day we're on North Avenue and Alice screams, *there's my car!* And it was—same bumper stickers and everything—so we follow it to this parking lot, and the woman who gets out says *I bought this car* and Alice says *well you bought it from the guy who stole it from me* and the woman says, *no I didn't, I got the title transfer right here.* And sure as shit, it said Alice Jones. Her mom up and sold it, no questions asked."

Vaughn dropped the tailgate with a bang. Leary took the hint. He said, "I pulled some copper off that scrap pile. Mind if I bring that? I didn't touch nothin' else."

It wasn't much. Vaughn couldn't see the bank hauling it down to the steel and salvage. They threw it on the tarp and folded the edges over. The bundle sagged as they hoisted it into the bed. Like a body, he thought, Leary's life reduced to one load of dead weight.

"Remember Hurricane Irene?" Leary said. "I'd heard about the good money after Katrina, so I headed out east replacin' carpet and such. I come back, and my Alice's run off, kids dumped at her mom's. The trailer's stripped out, I mean even the appliances were gone, with two months rent owing. My motorcycle, nothing left.

It'd just took a while for her own Alice Jones to come out."

Leary pressed the gate closed and leaned against it. "After Alice, I should be big on honesty. But I can't tell the kids we're fucked. Everybody says lies only make things worse, but when the truth sucks, how much worse can a lie make it? What if makin' shit up is all you can make? What if lies are all you got left to spend?"

Leary seemed the type who expected credit for admitting failures, who considered *I owe you* as good as paying you back. Vaughn knew exactly how that worked.

"You should be able to find some help with the kids," Vaughn said.

"Yeah, foster care. The county frowns on single daddies who live under tarps. Let's get this shit show on the road."

Leary called out. Two pale children emerged from the brush. The boy wore a long-sleeve t-shirt and camo drawstring pants with bulging pockets, his feet running over the backs of dirty canvas shoes. The girl wore a pink hoodie over an otherwise identical outfit. Vaughn figured them twins, about six or seven. They had matching grey smudges under their eyes and identical brown pixie cuts. Even their ears stuck out the same, with tips slightly flattened as if they'd grown under the press of oversized hats.

Leary placed his hand on one head, then the other: "This's Gina... Gene, say you're sorry."

Gene looked up at his father. "It was only a dirt clod."

Leary, his hand still clamped on the boy's head, directed Gene's face toward Vaughn.

"Sorry," the kid said. "I was just trying to scare you off."

"Well, that's funny because I was trying to scare your dad off. Did you take down the papers I hung up?" Vaughn said.

"They said to get out. Where would we go?"

The kid could read. Maybe they were small for their age.

Leary moved his hand down to his son's shoulder. "This man came to give us a ride there."

Vaughn pushed up the center console and the kids scrambled into the cab. Leary fished out the belt and buckled in Gene, setting Gina on his lap.

"Where to?" Vaughn said.

"Not far. You hit the county road and I'll show you."

Gene watched Vaughn steer the truck toward the gate. "Why do you sit crooked when you drive?"

Leary tried to shush him but Vaughn didn't mind. "A truck hit me, knocked me crooked," he said.

"We're supposed to look both ways before we cross," said Gina.

"And you should. I wasn't careful. I thought somebody'd stop for me, but he slid on the gravel." He had been flagging down a ride to the liquor store.

"I bet that hurt," Gene said.

"More than a dirt clod, for sure, but I don't feel it any more." Never even thought about it. For a long time the cant of his spine had been an excuse, and Vaughn had given up excuses.

"But now you're stuck that way forever?"

"Yeah," Vaughn said. The rest was for Leary. "But there's worse kinds of bein' stuck. Like when you see trouble coming and you're scared to move."

Leary pointed to a dirt road that disappeared behind a screen of trees. A full moon had risen over the mesa and the night was brighter than in the earlier hour.

"This land's posted, too," Vaughn said. The road ran to a gravel pit on the river. At best, they might get a day or two if they stayed out of sight from the hauling trucks.

"I know what I'm doin'," Leary said. "Just stop right up there."

Vaughn was about good-deeded out and ready to head home. Leary told the twins to stay put in the truck. Vaughn dropped the tailgate. The long load would've been easier to wrestle with both of them pulling from the ground but Leary had already climbed in to push.

The bundle began to sag when it was about halfway off and Leary hollered, "Hold on for a sec."

Vaughn held up his end, waiting for Leary to take a share of the weight. Two faces watched through the back window, a matched set, right down to their concentration on the pitchfork in Leary's hands.

Funny how in the moment Vaughn's mind crawled after the wrong things. The four eyes in the back window growing wide. Wondering whether Leary was going to stick him in his foot or through his gut. How germy the tines must be. But he also thought how men advertised their troubles, admitted their sins and drew on their former badassness so they didn't have to show how scared shitless they were.

Vaughn put up his hands and let the blue-shrouded remains of Leary's miserable estate droop between them. "Can you paint?"

"What?" Leary jerked up the fork as if to fend off the question.

"You can rob me or you can help me," he said, hoping *rob* would nudge Leary's mind away from murder. "Which example you gonna show those kids?"

Leary glanced over his shoulder at the window. When he turned back his ferocity seemed forced. "My family's none a your business!"

"You put 'em in this mess. I coulda called the law. I coulda junked your whole caboodle long ago. But I chose different because of your family. So—can you paint or not?"

Leary's face squeezed between hurt and relief. "That's why I do flooring. Every knucklehead says he can paint."

"Then surely you're qualified."

The pitchfork chanked into the hard earth and threw up sparks. Leary stood still, his fists clenched around the handle, his eyes pinched tight. "Where at?" he croaked.

"North of town. Mask, paint and clean up. It'll be a full day's work."

Leary turned and stared into the coppice. "Take a truck with the owner's name on the side. Quite the plan, wasn't it?"

"So you didn't mean to stay here," Vaughn said.

Leary's slow shake of the head showed Vaughn a man ashamed of attempted robbery. He resolved then to put a week at a motel on his credit card and have Leary pay it off in labor.

"Well, if you're ready to think straight for a change, get back in the truck."

He figured Leary would try to soften things up but this was work now and Vaughn let him know he didn't care to get deeper into it. Though he'd run his own tale through plenty of meetings, he didn't know of any business arrangement improved by hearing the other person's sob story.

He'd been cut loose when he was eleven. It probably didn't work that way any more now that Child Protection was spelled with capital letters. Even if there was a child welfare system then, Vaughn's family was more likely to run into the Department of Wildlife than a social worker. His mother had squirted out her babies by different miserable men in spread-out places across multiple counties, abandoning them all in similar fashion. It had looked like luck when Abner Self took him in and put him in a bunkhouse with Abner's nephew Leonard, who was older and didn't much care for having a stranger kid to share it with. Work was part of the room and board deal. Abner didn't accept that a boy Vaughn's age was better at some things than others. The ranch wasn't slavery, but neither was it the Ponderosa with Uncle Ben. Vaughn learned a little about a lot of things from Abner, the chief lesson being that hard work made you sour and inflexible.

Alcohol was the first thing that ever made him happy. Tasting Abner's brandy opened warm flower buds under his skin. He was young and craved a companion for the long party ahead and booze offered to drive, then took him home and tucked him into a bed of unconsciousness. He was never one of those morose, toilet-bowl-gripping drunks who made life miserable for others. Or so he thought until the day it finally dawned on him there were no others around for him to disconcert.

Vaughn had been wintering in the shadow of the Broadway bridge on a strip of bank nobody else wanted. He didn't even have a tent and it was not a camp, just a flat ledge barely concealed by some scrub and so narrow that if he rolled over he'd tumble all the way to the river. With lined coveralls over layers of polar fleece, triple socks, wool mittens inside insulated choppers, and a balaclava, the mummy bag kept Vaughn from frost bite and hypothermia. The key was not going to sleep damp or too drunk.

One frigid night, small feet pressed across the nylon, moving tentatively toward the opening cinched around his face. Zipped in with arms pinned at his sides, he held still and slitted open his eyes, expecting a stray cat, not the skunk whose whiskers now brushed his skin. A long few minutes passed as the skunk sniffed at his alcohol breath and pawed the hood's ice-encrusted aperture before moving on. A night later it came back, curling up for a short stay. After a week or so of this routine, he named her Lucinda. If he was going to sleep with a skunk, it seemed better that it not be a male. There was something thrilling about submitting his face to a creature with the power to blind him, and a sense of intimacy developed that he dared not mention to the men who drank with him before stumbling off to their lonely camps. Lucinda's pong was mild, no worse than campfire clothes, and he began to accept it as her body's natural perfume, a wild pungency that stirred feelings he hesitated to categorize. She was not a pet. He had considered taming her with nuts and dried apricots, but feared the treats would change the careful balance of their relationship. No begging and no obedience; their warmth and snuffling and trust felt three-quarters like love.

He drank a bit less to stay alert for the faint crimp of her paws across fresh snow, for her light scuff through the brush. She arrived without regard for time, stayed as long as it suited her, left for no apparent reason, yet her steady attendance seemed deeply faithful. Perhaps she was only guided by the weather. One day Lucinda stopped coming. What a sick fuck he was. Dumped by a skunk. After three nights without her he made a ruckus in the park, punched the wrong wino and ended up in detox.

Word in the tank was the liquor store on the far side of the river had a close-out bourbon that in Vaughn's more discriminating days had been his favorite. Crossing the bridge meant heading from booze territory to meth land where there were people he preferred not to encounter. He had once been robbed in the bridge's concrete-chute walk as night traffic rolled by and the river passed underneath. But it was daylight now and he counted out the change for his trip. He climbed the pedestrian path to where it looped back over the bridge and had walked almost to the river's edge when he caught a familiar scent. He stood right above his hidden camp and hadn't detected Lucinda down there. Had she just come by?

A dump truck hurled past, slapping a wall of engine heat against him but it was the perfume that swelled in his head. He scanned the traffic lanes and saw impossibility. A concrete barrier. Noise. An impassible gap between the divided spans. His skunk followed a friendly, well-traveled corridor beneath the bridge. Yet his heart knew. He breathed deeply and looked again. Black tires pounding black fur into black pavement, the dark rectangle so flat and indistinct the cars no longer bothered to avoid it. How many nights had he listened to the hum and thump over expansion joints above his head without catching the fading tang of Lucinda's death?

He gulped the bittersweet air, leaned over the barrier and drew a long blast from a passing horn. There was no way to tell if it was her. There had to be other skunks, less clever, less wary, less his. He waited for the light at the crossroad to slow the onslaught and stepped out waving his arms. He had been hit before and wasn't afraid. The cars would have to move over because he would not give up this ground. He hadn't counted on her being frozen and sealed to the deck. He stripped off his gloves and dug with bare fingers to find an edge free of ice. His breathing came fast and a drip formed at the end of his nose. His blackened nails turned red but he felt nothing except the cold of his tears.

A truck side mirror nearly clipped him. Heads and fists shook. The coal-rolling diesel engulfed the lane in a foul black cloud. Hopeless. Vaughn bellied back over the barrier, his throat thickening until he thought he might strangle. From the walkway he saw his ground cover with the bag wrapped in it, mashed in the snow with concealing branches pulled over, leaving the bare brown spot, so obvious from above, the imprint of the invisible man. He took a deep diver's breath, as much as he could contain, and headed for town, over the viaduct that crossed the tracks and past his regular liquor store and past another. He held everything inside but couldn't stop his breathing. Had he exhaled the last of his friend or was some of her still coursing in his bloodstream? The thought made him cry for Lucinda and then he was crying for himself and when he reached the Salvation Army he was crying for the whole friendless and faithless world. They took him in and when he refused to wash his hands, they told him he might get an infection and they couldn't have blood around the others. He wanted to tell the lady in the blue gloves they could have the blood if he could keep Lucinda's smell on his fingers. Instead he covered his face, whispered the only prayer he knew and accepted the bar of motel soap the woman dropped in his hand like a quarter.

Every day before his next meeting, he walked the mile to the bridge to declare he hadn't added any booze breath to the air and to take in Lucinda's fading essence. It lasted as long as he needed it. The world stank but Lucinda taught him it only reeked in warning. A skunk's spray was its last resort.

Inappropriate or illegal use of computers may result in loss of computer privileges and/or loss of library privileges.

—Library Code of Conduct

Isaac explained to the young woman at the Information Desk that he had lost his library card. He hated how irresponsible that made him sound.

Kristin responded with the smile of someone not yet resigned to explaining simple things over and over. "We can issue a new one today. You just need a picture ID."

"I lost that, too—in a fire." He should have said that before. It would have made her more sympathetic. And that he had a library sciences degree. He told her a funny story from his library internship days about patrons always scanning the ISBN barcode instead of the CIP barcode. She seemed puzzled. He shouldn't have mumbled.

"Perhaps another patron can vouch for you," she suggested.

He didn't see anyone. Usually the library was full of people he knew. Other staff would recognize his face, he was certain, but would they vouch for him? He dropped the name of the public services manager. His many job applications surely had lodged him somewhere in their system. Linda Cornish had even interviewed him once.

Kristin's expression made clear she wasn't going to bother a manager over a lost library card. She searched the screen for a solution. "I could look up your record, and give you a guest pass just for today. What's your address?"

He gave her the Day Center's mailing address. Would the fact that he shared it with a hundred other library users throw up a red flag?

Kristin leaned forward. "I'm sorry, that's not coming up with your name. Do you have anything that could confirm your current address—a recent utility bill or a rent receipt?"

He tried to laugh. "Who comes to the library with a rent receipt?"

"Do you happen to know your library card number?"

An even more ridiculous question. He was probably the only person in history who could answer it and when he did, she didn't even notice. Two clacks punctuated a string of rattles. Were all government computers equipped with amplified keys?

After the screen refreshed, she said, "I'm showing your name at a different address." She waited for his answer, fingers poised.

His mother's house. He'd never changed it. That had been another time, another life when he still imagined himself working in a library far better than this one. He gave her the address.

She nodded, clicked once and peered at the screen. Her friendly manner turned opaque. "I'm sorry, Mr. Samson, but your library privileges have been suspended."

"On what grounds?" he blurted, too much like a lawyer. He switched to sounding baffled, like the innocent man he was. "It must be a mistake."

She made a fine adjustment to her keyboard's position as if resetting her patience. "I can't answer that. I'm afraid you have to leave."

It *had* to be a mistake. His record was clear of fines. He'd always observed the rules of comportment. To be humiliated in his home library! He couldn't let this stand and he let Kristin know it.

She lifted the telephone receiver and cupped her hand over her mouth.

Good. Call a manager. Linda Cornish could settle it and he could start his search for information about the lost eye. He knew every infraction that could lead to suspension, and he was innocent of all twenty-two. He had damaged nothing, maintained good hygiene and harassed no one. Had brandished neither weapon nor indecent body parts nor left packages unattended. Neither smoked, chewed tobacco nor eaten in an unauthorized place. Not played loud music, tampered with software or solicited signatures, or sold any products, including illegal drugs. And never brought in a bicycle, skateboard, animals, alcoholic beverages, shopping cart or other oversized objects.

Linda Cornish emerged from a back room, formidable as a thunderhead in a black and purple sweater shot through with silver. If there were an ugly Big Bang sweater contest, she would definitely be in the running.

"Why am I suspended?" he demanded.

She blinked at him as if he were an extra in a police lineup.

"Inappropriate use of a computer," she said.

"Impossible. What's the evidence?"

"The letter went out yesterday." Linda Cornish presented a copy, a little too smugly, he thought.

"Well, I haven't looked at porn, sent spam—whatever this means—ever."

"It doesn't matter. Your card was used. You can establish another person did this without your knowledge or consent or you can request readmission in six months. Those are the options."

Those were not the only options. What about taking his word for it? He couldn't go six months without access. The library was his oasis, his *vocation*. They wouldn't ban his brother if he lost his card. They'd believe a soccer mom. His outraged arguments only stiffened Linda Cornish's posture.

Sam the security officer appeared at his elbow. A retired cop, Sam now relied on his white fringe and mellow manner to keep the peace. And a taser. When did Sam start carrying a taser?

"I lost my pants in a fire. Someone must've found them and took my wallet."

"That sounds far-fetched," Linda said.

Not on the river. He should've just said he lost his wallet.

"So why didn't you report it?" Sam asked.

"Who reports their library card's missing when they lose their wallet? You wait until you need it!" He was trying to be reasonable but couldn't help shouting.

Sam had heard a million lies and crazy excuses, maybe even *I thought it burned up in my pants but I guess a guy stole it.* He tilted his head toward the exit.

It was humiliating. Being treated like a child pornographer instead of a colleague! When had any bureaucracy ever moved this fast? It had to be a plot. They thought he was reading subversive materials. He was a threat to the other librarians. When had the Library of Congress recruited any of them? They were waiting for this chance! Sam had a grip on his arm now. They passed the long face-out rows of new releases. The books judged him as beneath their interest, their titles chattering. *Being Mortal. Demon Camp. Capital. Little Failure. World Order. This Changes Everything.* He stiffened his free arm and raked clear three yards of shelf before Sam pulled him away. Isaac let the momentum pitch him into the Friends of the Library sale table. More books scattered. Four hands on him now. Pushed into the parking lot. The heat hit him hard. Doors closed. Laughter. He looked around, didn't see anyone. Oh, no, not the voices. They had been so quiet. Quiet so they could listen. Listening until they heard the thing that would hurt him the most.

In the old days, the voices gave him very bad advice. They convinced him to order extra-large, triple pepperoni pizzas for breakfast. They told him anything with Michael Jackson's picture would be valuable some day. At their urging he stole single socks from the college laundry room, filled them with sand and slung them on rooftops. They whispered that the saplings in a neighbor's yard would grow into hanging trees, so he snapped them off.

Now a voice said he needed a computer. Finally, a voice that knew what it was talking about.

But he had to be careful. A computer would demand electricity, Internet access, software, a place to sit, shelter from the elements, safety from thieves. A computer needed a house more than he did. And then the house required its own things: furniture to arrange and appliances to feed and cookware for every eventuality and pictures to display and treasures to lock up and TVs to drive away loneliness. Silverware drawers and dish cabinets and spice racks and pantry shelves to organize. Patio furniture for sitting outside. A garage to hold band saws and compressors and lawnmowers and artificial Christmas trees and kayak paddles and snow tires. A room for each activity, a niche for every knick-knack. Shoes paired, socks matched. Clothes assigned to closets, hangers and drawers, arranged by color and function, season and wearer, clean and dirty. Exhausting!

If he wasn't careful, this could start something.

Calling Shelly was like talking to the bank. His sister-in-law served as his payee when he was drawing Supplemental Security Income. He used his SSI funds sparingly to accumulate a cushion for when he was no longer considered incompetent. Not that he was now.

"Computers always get you in trouble," she said.

"I got my degree on a computer," he said.

"You know what I mean. You get immersed in the craziness on the web and you don't come out. That whole thing with the Library of Congress guy."

"Garrison."

"If you'd stayed off the computer, you'd never have tied the library internship to the NSA."

"They're both located at Fort Meade!"

"And you'd never have tried to track down Garrison at the Reagan Library, which convinced you he was involved in the whole Edison thing."

"That whole thing with Edison was *real*," he said. "General Electric had light bulbs and radios and clocks in every house in America. They were about to take over the country and when Herbert Hoover figured it out and tried to stop them…"

"You wouldn't have taken the Winnebago to California and then your dad wouldn't have pressed charges."

"…they crashed the stock market so the country was already in a panic and Hoover was afraid to make it worse, so he broke up the company into GE and NBC and RCA. Then RCA invented TV, and NBC controlled the programs, and GE brainwashed Ronald Reagan and groomed him to be their President of the United States. You can look it up." There was a lot more to it, of course. *A lot more.*

Shelly sighed much louder than necessary. "Nobody cares about that. My point is, it all goes back to the computer. You need to stay grounded. The Internet is too much like your brain. It makes things seem connected in ways they really aren't. Are you taking your medications?"

Technically, it was none of her business. "I've been feeling better without them."

"Isaac…stopping your meds because you started feeling better is not the best plan. Neither is buying a computer just to research a lost glass eye."

"I'm banned from the library. I'm doomed without books or a computer. Are you going to help me or not?" Silence. "Please, I'm trying to do a good deed. I'll buy something cheap. Don't make me beg for my own money."

"Can we meet at Best Buy? I don't think I can bear Walmart."

"Or you could just send me the cash," he said.

Shelly paused. She may have been considering how much easier it would be. "No, Isaac," she said, "I don't think I can do that."

Isaac locked his bike near the store entrance. The greeter chirped a welcome and eyed his backpack. Shelly waited by the Samsung display, aiming her assistant principal stare at him as if he'd been running in the aisle.

"What?" He hadn't done anything. With Shelly he was still working off the backlog of his offenses.

"Let's just do this," she said. "I'm glad to see you're okay."

Isaac cared nothing about distinctions among the models. All computers started out as cute kittens and soon fattened into demanding yet unresponsive cats. He found a notebook computer at a price that satisfied Shelly and disappointed the salesperson, who nevertheless mentioned the extended warranty. To Shelly. The offers continued at the checkout: credit cards, discounts, loyalty points and protection plans.

Isaac didn't want the box. It would advertise he'd gotten a new computer.

"You should keep everything in case you need to make a return," the clerk said.

"If it's a piece of crap, why do you need the box?"

The clerk looked at Shelly. She turned her head toward Isaac.

"Uh, you can return it if you're dissatisfied with your purchase for any reason," the clerk recited.

"I won't be dissatisfied if it works. And if it doesn't work, you can't put it back on the shelf. What if I'm dissatisfied with wasteful packaging?"

"Let's go," Shelly said, snatching the box and the receipt and striding away. But Isaac didn't leave.

"Sir, you can return it if you're dissatisfied with the packaging. But we ask that you bring all the contents and packaging, your proof of purchase and a photo ID. Otherwise, there may be a missing item deduction."

"Why would you need my ID if I have the receipt?"

"It's company policy. So we can track returns and exchanges. This helps prevent losses and keeps our prices low."

"But it's not a loss if I'm bringing back something I paid for."

"Sir, I have to help this next person in line. If you have more questions, I could get a manager..." The customer behind him nudged her purchases forward. The clerk reached for the phone.

Isaac's second call for a manager today! Why did people call the manager instead of thinking for themselves? Why did he need their permission to leave their packaging?

The greeter edged over to Isaac. "Hi, do you mind if we look in your backpack, sir?"

"I do mind. I didn't take anything. You watched me go through the check out."

"Nothing personal." The attendant smiled. "Have a nice day then and thank you for shopping."

Isaac slapped the door as he went out. Shelly thrust the package to him. "Why must you make everything so difficult?" she said.

"Because everything *is* difficult. You just don't see it. That guy's job is to welcome people like you and profile people like me. You get the red carpet. I get the stop sign."

"Oh, come on."

"Did he ask to check your receipt?"

"No, but so what if he did? It's nothing."

"For you it's nothing." He removed the computer and slipped it in his backpack, then stomped the cardboard flat. "For you, it's one speck, a grain of sand. What's wrong with a little grit? Try rubbing your nose against sandpaper all day."

Inside the vestibule were receptacles for recycling batteries, toner cartridges, plastic bags and cables. Nothing for cardboard. He thrust the packaging at the greeter.

"Recycling."

"Ah, we only recycle products and components." His have-a-nice-dayness seemed about to expire.

Isaac dropped the bundle at the greeter's feet. "All right, call it trash. You do have trash cans, right?"

He'd expected Shelly to be gone when he came out, but she

stood where he'd left her.

"Okay, are you happy now that you've antagonized everyone?"

She didn't understand he'd burn out the brakes if he applied them every time he met an obstacle. Still, he knew he'd been a jerk to her. He told her he was sorry.

She said, "I know where you can rent a place for three-ninety-five."

"So do I. But I don't want to be around people who pay three-ninety-five."

"Are you working?"

"I'm fine. I'll look for work after I finish my research. Maybe I can get a job mistreating shoplifters. At least I could do it without insulting innocent people. But first I need an ID. Tell Mom I need my birth certificate."

"Why don't you tell her?" she said. "What's wrong with this picture? You don't have a place to live but you're paying rent for a storage unit full of crap. You've got a copy of Thomas Edison's proposal to move off the gold standard and you don't even have a copy of your own birth certificate."

He was impressed that Shelly remembered about Edison's currency plan. "Pardon my insufficient planning. I didn't think to grab my birth certificate before Mom kicked me out of the house."

"You ran out. You left it in shambles."

"One room was all."

"Like our kitchen."

"I'm sorry. I thought there were transmitters."

"Isaac, that's not even what I'm talking about. Of course you need your ID. But you can't be fighting this imaginary system all the time."

Shelly was a good person but she didn't understand the essence of a system was its invisibility. Her life was seamless. When she woke up, her wallet was still in her purse. It never occurred to her that Isaac didn't need an ID for the reasons she did. He needed it to show the cops.

The police labeled the yellow workman's cottage the Anarchist House. Everyone else knew it as Zack's house. Street people found it by word of mouth and the front porch with a couch too broken down even for an anarchist's living room. The entry was a gantlet of warning and welcome: a long, fist-shaking manifesto signed by the Whitman Collective railed against oligarchs, oppressors and their informants; flowerpots sprouted with cigarette butts; a lending library spilled 'zines and remnants from college reading lists. The papered-over glass in the front door declared:

> *Behold I do not give lectures or a little charity,*
> *When I give I give myself.*
> —Walt Whitman

How could people like Zack Nicolai be anarchists? They had too strong an urge to fix things. Isaac had looked up *anarchist* and discovered it didn't mean bomb-thrower. It meant they wanted voluntary, self-governed communities. Anarchists were more like Wesley than anything. They didn't want the world to fall into chaos; they just wanted an end to the GE version of the world.

The front room was set up as an office and lounge area. Its lone occupant was reading a comic book. He lived in a back room and spent his days reading, sniffing for narcs and keeping unauthorized visitors from wandering through the rest of the house. His right eye trailed off to the side while the left sized up Isaac. Yes, the house of anarchy had a bouncer—Steve, like the bowling ball launched into the canyon. Steve had been the town's most literate electrician until a fall from a ladder put him on disability. Now he read mostly comics and graphic novels because they were easier on his vision.

Isaac usually went to the Day Center, because he felt less comfortable among the wanderpunks, anti-war vets, queer power activists, runaways, buskers, artists, taggers and dopers that hung out at Zack's house. Walk-ins at both places could read a newspaper, grab a book, find a ride on a bulletin board, learn where to get a meal or score a voucher, pick over free stuff or leave things they didn't need. The main difference: fewer people at Zack's house likely to snatch his laptop if he turned his back.

"What's your password?" Isaac asked.

"It's *yawp420*, all lower case, all one word." Steve watched Isaac type and then raised a thumb when he saw him connect. "A lotta guys can't spell yawp," he said.

Isaac submitted his keystrokes to be searched by bots and algorithms and whatever agency monitored the Whitman Collective. His fingers darted like minnows high in a mountain stream. How amazing he could stir the ocean from here.

For hours he wandered a pandemonium of false leads and irrelevancies—taxidermy and doll parts, vintage fishing lures and decoys, crafts and jewelry. A press release about unclaimed glass eyes in the Disney World lost and found had inspired local writers around the country to turn up detached eyes in local airports, buses, police stations, amusement parks, beer halls, rental cars and hotels. Newspaper accounts through the ages named one-eyed loggers, sailors, adventurers, football players and children. He liked the story about Prince Metternich, who had hidden his artificial eye until a portrait painter noticed that the prince's gaze was unaffected by bright sunlight on that side. Blue-eyed animals were glass-eyed, according to cowboys and dog breeders. He found glass eyes for sale on eBay, demonstration videos on YouTube, references in films, pulp fiction, children's books and TV shows. He studied how ocular prostheses were made and fitted. He located a national directory of oculists and discovered the process for getting a replacement at a VA hospital. A clinic's gallery of faces challenged him to identify which eye was artificial.

Steve looked up from his reading. "No porno, right? You seem pretty intense there."

Isaac told him what he'd found.

"Some people think I have one but my eye's just lazy—like Ronald Reagan's. Of course, they covered it up like Roosevelt's polio."

Ronald Reagan had a lazy eye? He could start a new research file on his laptop. *Lazy Eye Mafia.* The thought of moving to this new subject excited and terrified him.

"You got it on you?" Steve asked.

Isaac dug it out. "People assume they're like marbles. They're not glass, either."

"You ever heard that song, 'Glass Eye'? The band, I forget. They started out in Colorado."

In ten seconds, Isaac found it. The song barely made sense. The lyrics didn't even mention a glass eye but some of the words seemed to be about him:

> *Surrounded by clutter you call a collection*
> *A forest that's nothing but trees*
> *Searching the earth for some long-lost connection*
> *You won't find it down on your knees*
> > *A one-eyed man is not half-blind*
> > *Don't need tongue to speak his mind*
> > *Don't need hands to feel unkind*
> > *Don't need eyes to cry*
> > *Don't need eyes to cry*

"Do you believe in connection or coincidence?" Isaac asked Steve.

"Neither. I believe in we don't know shit."

"Exactly. Most of the world operates beyond our awareness. We only get these little glimpses of what's really going on."

"Like quantum mechanics."

"More like, are you a bowler?"

"I used to be—before my accident."

"What happened to your balls?"

Steve glared at Isaac. A Jack Elam bad cowboy face.

"I mean, I might've found one of your bowling balls."

"Why do you think it's mine?" Steve said.

"It has *Steve* engraved on it."

"Dude, my name's Scott."

When your life is in flux, renting may be a better option than buying.

— "Home" with Meg Mogrin, *Grand Junction Style*

Sister Rose invited Meg to meet with Wesley Chambers at Grand Valley By-Products. She asked if Meg needed the address. After a moment to recollect the name, she knew immediately where it was.

For Meg and many locals, the glue factory represented more than a metaphor for the end. The local animal rendering plant represented an indelible place. A century ago it had situated next to the old sugar beet mill, where feedlot cattle fattened on the factory waste. After the mill and the stockyards closed, it held on for another seventy-five years, processing animal carcasses and spoiled meat into lard, tallow and other byproducts, the most prominent of which was stench. The miasma loomed over the river, where rafters and tubers had to pass. Parents warned children if they didn't study, they'd end up working in the glue factory for the rest of their lives. Meg and generations of city high school students, insulated from the blunt realities of farm life, had been sent there by a biology teacher to obtain bacteria samples from the intestines of dead livestock. Whether this constituted science or sadism was a perennial subject of debate.

As a transplant, Wesley Chambers bore none of those memories, and if he knew anything of the abandoned property's dismal history he likely considered it a plus for his tent city. Meg imagined him waiting there, a horror movie's optimistic out-of-towner who'd just bought the haunted house. If that were all, Wesley might manage it. But there were political realities surrounding this place, newly intensified.

Scarcely seeming to ask, Sister Rose had managed to move a community on behalf of the poor, aligning Catholics and Mormons, Baptists and atheists, power brokers and anarchists, Democrats and Republicans. Though her selfless spirit and clear sense of justice were rooted in her faith, her authority magnified when she emerged from behind the veil of her church. She projected integrity rather than saintliness, which inspired a like response. The word *no* vaporized in Sister's presence.

So Meg was stuck. There was no point resisting Sister Rose's expectation. Yet there was no way she could imagine Wesley succeeding. Not with Betterment Health in the wings. And certainly not at the edge of Las Colonias Park.

Sister Rose, in a blue business suit and white Reeboks, waited with Wesley outside a barbed-wire-topped cyclone fence. Behind it sat a concrete block warehouse, its blank walls blotted with flesh-colored rectangles overpainted with new graffiti. The front door bowed from periodic break-ins. Weeds sprouted from crumbling pavement and trash trees had taken root in foundation cracks. Closer to the river, storage tanks and a few less substantial structures remained. Most of the parcel had been graded to bare dirt. The warehouse itself appeared solid. The air carried the sweet perfume of flowering Russian olives.

"Wesley really wanted you to see this. I told him we can't go in without permission, so the tour will be rather brief," said Sister Rose.

"Sister, nobody'd dare arrest us with you along," Wesley said.

He produced a map from the County Assessor's website showing the area surrounding the warehouse and factory lots. In the empty east quarter south of the warehouse, he had penciled neat rows of rectangles.

"This shows what fits. But you need to see the whole thing to get an idea how perfect this place would be."

Perfect. Wesley had to be the first person since the Utes to see it that way.

The property was isolated on all four sides. Across the road was Sandstrom Trucking, which, as Wesley could tell from the Assessor information, had acquired the land for a bargain price and then idled its depot with the downturn in the natural gas market. A mere fifty yards east of the warehouse, the DNR owned a triangle of woods that ran to the river, which bounded the south edge. An overgrowth of Russian olive trees shielded the western view toward the park a quarter mile away.

"We can start small on this end without buying the other lot. The neighbors are either light industrial or small farms beyond the woods. All anybody will see of the camp is a few patches of color. The one drawback is we're about two miles from a bus stop, but that's nothing for someone to walk—at least for us."

Meg looked from the map back to the barren ground and tried to picture the cheerful tent city Wesley had in mind. It was no less real than Hungerman's enterprise and far less intrusive. Yet Wesley's modest vision was the one that seemed unachievable.

He turned his attention to the warehouse. "I've been inside there. It's nasty right now, but the building's solid. We've got men experienced in the trades who could do renovation. Nothing fancy at first—running water and sewer for showers and restrooms, a secure room for storage, an office for admissions and security." His animation grew. "Later, we could heat the whole building, add a laundry, a coffee room and kitchen, a workshop, a place to kennel animals."

While Meg couldn't disclose the conflict with the Betterment proposal, she could at least offer some market realism.

"Even if Sandstrom's not using the property now, they'll want it back when the drilling slump ends. And why would they lease it out if the camp brings all this pedestrian traffic around their truck terminal across the street? Best case, suppose Sandstrom agrees to sell. They've invested a lot in clean up. It won't be the bargain it was before. And nobody I know is writing that mortgage, so you'll have to come up with the cash somehow."

Wesley pointed north toward the rail yard. "What do they care about being on the river? The City does land swaps, right? There's plenty of flat land around here to park trucks. Nobody's done squat with this place except pollute it. Thistletown will get people off the streets, and it'll be an improvement over what's here. The City should want to kick in."

The City had passed on acquiring this land when it was cheap and expanding the park was uncontroversial. Why provoke controversy now by prying it away from a well-connected business owner? Some would accuse Sandstrom of making a killing at public expense and others would object to government intervention in the marketplace. Eve on her best day would be reluctant to carry it forward.

"Those swaps are to expand parkland or keep businesses in town," she said. "Even in a perfect world, the City isn't going to hand over land without conditions. You'll have to abide by a lease and health regulations. Even rent-free, you'd have utilities and trash hauling."

Wesley waved away her point. "You think people without money don't know what things cost? I figure it's sixty thousand a year to operate. That's fifty occupants paying a little over three dollars a day, less than to stay at the Mission."

The shelters also served food for their four dollars, but she let it go. "All right, you've got the money side covered. What about the politics? Not just with the City; within your community. Self-governance is a beautiful concept, but I deal with homeowners' associations. The disputes and drama can be brutal."

Wesley rolled his eyes. "You ever lived in a shelter, lady? Been in jail? How about an army barracks? Girl Scout camp doesn't count."

Meg stiffened and drew back half a step. She had dealt with plenty of male condescension, but no man had ever spoken to her with such scorn.

Sister Rose cocked her head and raised an eyebrow. "Meg's on your side, Wesley," she said softly.

He snatched his pack from the ground and spun away. "Then she should know I don't need a lecture on how to live with assholes."

He stalked toward the park, slamming the fence with a series of hard forearms. *Chang-chang-chang.* The chain link resounded his frustration.

Sister Rose sighed. "Understand, Wesley's a warrior. He sees the barriers just fine. He needs someone to tell him he's not crazy, his objective's worthwhile, and that if he takes charge of this, he'll find support."

"Some support, yes, but he'll never sell it to the City. The shelter's already struggling to stay open because it can't get funding. A tent city's even more controversial."

"But there may still be a place for it. A shelter doesn't work for all."

Yes, shelters worked for people trying to recover their former life or move on to a new one. And some were born and raised in them, so shelters felt familiar. Working the welfare system was like going into the family business. Wesley's objection was that shelters were neither a home nor a temporary stop. They were another form of incarceration. But even if society bore some blame for the condition of homelessness, and camping was simply a rejection of conventional life, it was the wrong message to send. To have any chance, Wesley had to sell his vision as a redemption story. He had a higher nature, a free will and a sense of responsibility like everyone else. He was a veteran who'd never accept being treated as other than a full human being. Enough local citizens might get behind this version of Thistletown. Otherwise, they'd only see tents and a bunch of vagrants getting a free ride.

Wesley had stopped where the property fence met the path into the park. He paced back and forth, clenching and unclenching his fists. Beyond him, Meg could see the crown of the dead cottonwood where Amy Hostetter had been struck down. It stood now as a visible warning of the park's danger and depravity. The island where she'd seen Wesley's boots was only a few hundred yards from there. *Before the fire, this was his neighborhood.* He saw its neglect and its potential, but not how much had gone into reclaiming it before his arrival. His good intentions for this patch of river put him in opposition to growth, opportunity and transformation for the entire town. Meg could explain the reasons why he would never be allowed to sink roots here, but she couldn't advise him on how to achieve what he wanted. She had already chosen the side of progress.

"I'm sorry for driving him off. I know you counted on me to help."

"You still can." Sister Rose looked at Meg with the bright expression of an adult encouraging a toddler to speak. "He's deciding whether he should come back and apologize. Let's give him a few minutes."

"He can't do this on intensity alone. I don't see anyone else lining up behind him."

"It's possible Wesley overestimates our population of orderly loners. So many insist they prefer to camp. Why would they say otherwise when there's no dignified alternative? Like him, they have pride. Being on the river allows them to hang onto their personal sense of agency—and also their crutches and their demons. But offer them a realistic option to live independently and most will accept the keys. Perhaps even Wesley will come out of the woods someday. It would not be the worst outcome if this proposal failed without destroying Wesley's confidence in himself. He might learn and emerge as a leader when he's more ready."

"Why is he out here?"

"All he's told me is that he's a firefighter who's afraid of fire."

Meg turned toward the park. Wesley was gone. No apology, then. The compassion she'd felt was already receding. Pain and dislocation were everywhere. The world had too many dying cottonwoods, empty warehouses, men with backpacks bearing crutches and demons.

"Oh, Sister, this reality's so dark and far from mine. I'm afraid I can't do the work justice."

"Yes, we've all thought that. The problem's too big. I'm only one person, my skills aren't right, nothing I do can possibly make a difference. It must be difficult for successful people like you to associate with an issue you don't believe can be resolved. But God doesn't put more in your heart than you can manage. Don't measure yourself against saints. Don't fret about ending homelessness in ten years. Homelessness ends when it ends for one person. And then you do it again."

Sister Rose brought her fingertips together. After a moment, she patted them in silent applause. "At the end of my life, the Lord isn't going to ask me how many people I put in apartments. His question will be the one he asks everybody: *How did you love?*"

Somehow Wesley had gotten inside the fence. He crossed the open space briskly, disappeared behind the warehouse and emerged again on the east end of the property skirting the tree line toward the river.

He forgot his maps! They were still on the hood of Sister's car. Meg raised her hand and called out. Wesley slipped sideways into the woods without looking back.

Sister Rose said, "He brought the maps for you."

Out-of-state homebuyers are sometimes shocked to discover there's more to Colorado than Denver and Aspen.

— "Home" with Meg Mogrin, *Grand Junction Style*

You must ask for what you really want. The line sounded both grounded and mystical, aimed at beggars and dreamers alike. Perhaps Rumi was telling them all: when you ask for what you really want, you become revealed for what you really are.

Lew Hungerman lodged at the Entrada, an intimate, demi-Tuscan hostelry attached to a winery west of town. A favorite setting for graduation photos and second wedding ceremonies with beautiful views and a sense of monastic exclusivity, the Entrada had more character than Grand Junction's downtown hotels.

Approaching on the long drive through the Entrada vineyard, she could see Lew Hungerman waiting under a portico. He waved and came out to meet her, half-ducking, as if the sky were about to bang him in the forehead. His layers of outdoorsy technical fabric seemed more about projecting energy than actually expending it, reminding her she had heard nothing more about his interest in mountain bike adventures. The pebbled black messenger bag slung over his shoulder had to be the fabled Hungerman lambskin.

He declined a bagel but accepted the coffee in a stainless steel travel mug, tasting the still-steaming coffee with a careful sip. (French Roast, black. She'd checked with his office.)

He opened the bag on his lap and said, "I don't expect your services to be on spec."

"This is just a tour. I'll send you an agency agreement if your plans move forward and you want to work with me."

"Fine, please do. Meanwhile, I have an NDA I'd like you to sign. We touched sensitive territory the other night. There are a lot of moving parts with this deal, things you may need to know in order to help me, details not ready for prime time. It's better to have something in place now."

The non-disclosure looked to be a standard one-way agreement to keep confidential specific properties under consideration for purchase; no keeping copies or sharing contracts, plans, drawings, financial information; and making no oral or written descriptions of the proposed projects. She made a show of ticking off the points and passed it back, confident that Hungerman had quickly intuited her value. Now she would demonstrate it by putting him in front of Donnie Barclay.

He handed over an envelope labeled *Mogrin NDA*, then swung the bag into the rear seat, releasing a zest of grapefruit and seaweed cologne. "Don't let me forget this." As he twisted forward, his hand strayed to her shoulder. "I appreciate working with people who are detail-oriented. The house picks you sent were fine but I'm not doing four stops. Let's cut to the chase and pick one. Your turf, your call."

She suppressed her irritation. She'd worked hard to give him a good overview, and lining up the viewings in a single morning had not been easy. Was he simply trimming his schedule or checking her strategic judgment? The wooded Crestview neighborhood was the most midwest-like. The historic mansion on Seventh had gravitas and was closest to his project. The Redlands Mesa golf course property was impressively finished and Hungerman would fit in nicely with the valley's leading egos. The Crown B was rustic, with a long commute. But she had promised Donnie. *What the hell.*

"The Crown B," she said. "It's a taste of the Glade Park experience, which is different from the valley. If you like it up there I could work on finding something less ranchy and closer in."

"Will it also give me a taste of Donnie Barclay?"

He wasn't supposed to know who the property owners were.

"I thought it would be good for you two to be acquainted. I was surprised you hadn't met already," she said.

Hungerman unwrapped the bagel she brought, enough to see it dressed with chive and pimento cream cheese. He fixed his eyes upon her with anchorman soulfulness, as if no script were scrolling between them. It was a talent.

"They were right about you," he said. "Let's go. I want to be back by ten-thirty."

So she was on the team now. She made the cancellation calls as she drove, feeling reckless and in control.

Driving first-timers up the three serpentine miles of Monument Road to the Glade Park turnoff always revealed something about her passengers. Did they marvel at the views or quiver at the exposures? Were they interested in the story of the road's construction or the geological layers it cut through? Hungerman minded his window with the desultory attention of a frequent flier. He inquired about Meg instead.

She assumed his questions were meant to ingratiate, and she stuck to businesslike responses. She breezed over her switch from teaching to real estate and from married to divorced, leaving out the complex substrata of Helen and Brian. Business was great. She loved what she did. After so many repetitions, this distilled account had begun to seem like the true story.

"Not to be rude, but isn't real estate usually the last refuge—the backup plan or sideline that ends up becoming a career?"

"Yeah, it's like waitressing, only with better tips." She was careful to say it lightly. She had not yet decoded his pattern of give and take.

"I mean you seem like a woman with a lot of options, someone who dreamed of doing something else."

Where was he leading her? She made a show of concentrating on the road. "It was more wishfulness than a dream. I wanted to write poetry because I loved it—and loved the idea of being Emily Dickinson, only with boyfriends."

"And you still write?"

"I do a sort of lifestyle real estate column. I've gotten away from poetry—even reading it. Why be reminded of that foolish lust for immortality?"

"Jules called you literary. You recognized that Rumi line."

"A coincidence." She didn't want to go there.

"All three were Rumi, you know."

The curve ahead kept her from looking over in surprise. "How do you know that?"

"I googled them. I thought you'd be interested."

Why did he care what interested her? The possibilities were disquieting. Move the subject to his project. "We should talk about Donnie Barclay."

"He's been a hard man to get a hold of."

"How did you know the ranch house on the list was his?"

"I ran the addresses past Vince Foyer. He was impressed you'd thought of it. It made me think you knew about our Las Colonias plan before I told you about it."

Meg hesitated. Residential real estate clients were relatively easy to fathom. A project like this one had so many crosscurrents.

"Not about Las Colonias specifically."

"But you figured out we were interested in meeting Barclay." He said it as if it weren't that important.

"Actually, he was interested in you. The first time I heard something big was in the air, it came from Donnie. He gave me the impression he was feeling left out. I thought I'd be doing you both a favor by getting you together."

"Is Barclay a client of yours?"

"A friend."

"A friend you can tell me about?"

"Where should I start? You seem to know about him already."

"Oh, we're well aware he's in ranching and construction materials, which are both ways of saying he's in the land business. He owns a key piece of property between the river and downtown. With him and what's city-owned, we'd have the scale to commit. The rest is a checkerboard, not worth messing with those owners unless he's in. He seems to know that, too."

Meg hesitated. Donnie surely knew more than he had told her. In fact, she was beginning to wonder if Donnie had used her to arrange for a meeting with Hungerman. "Donnie knows a lot of people. He's generous with information and he gets a lot in return. I can't say what he knows or thinks about your project. He may look only half-groomed and seem a bit scattered, but do not go in there thinking he's a rube."

"Respect. Got it. So how should I come at him—besides money, of course—jobs, civic spirit, legacy?"

"You'll have to read him. But I'd say all three."

"Vince tells me Donnie likes you."

"Donnie won't make a deal with you just because he likes me."

"If I were Donnie, I'd do anything you asked. Can we pull over?"

They had reached the top of the rimrock where the road flattened before climbing again to Glade Park. He'd seen the sign marking the turnout. An enticing name, Cold Shivers Point.

Meg had made it this far without her heartbeat quickening. She didn't slow. "Let's do it on the way back." Returning, Cold Shivers would be on her side of the car. If she didn't make a thing of it, Hungerman might forget. "Do you really collect homeless people's signs?"

Hungerman laughed and clapped his hands. "You are good! No, that was an impulse. We saw the guy on the way in and I thought his signs might make a useful prop. It was a bonus to see you get fired up about it."

Was she? She couldn't stop the flush rising in her face. "Do you honestly expect us to just make them disappear? It feels like you posed it as a test—practically an ultimatum."

"Do you homeless advocates think I should commit investor money to a town that can't clean itself up? Yeah, it's a test. Politicians prefer words. I'm a big fan of action."

You homeless advocates. Is that what he thought she was? Wesley probably didn't. "And what's our test for you?"

He seemed amused by the question. "I'll do my part with the development to create jobs and pay taxes that fund schools and city services."

Someday pay taxes. There were abatements and credits and other gimmicks between now and the day Betterment paid any taxes.

"I meant something in advance, like you want from us. What if you made a donation right now to expand the shelter? Or you pledge to include affordable housing units somewhere in your project. Or when you're negotiating for the property on the river, you do a swap." Land for a tent city would be stretching it, but Wesley had planted the seed. "You buy a parcel to trade that just happens to be well away from the Betterment campus and convey it to the City earmarked for veterans or transitional housing."

Hungerman didn't answer at first. Was he stunned by her audacity or actually thinking it over?

"I like your thinking but it's still my money that's being spent here. I have to stay focused on the business outcome, not good intentions. And right now, to get approval, I need to lead with shiny objects, not promises about low-income housing."

Had she overstepped? Of course this deal wasn't as simple as planting a Walmart next to the highway. It would probably take a decade or more of local commitment before the riverfront began to look anything like Hungerman's vision. As she started the drive down to the beautiful green ranchland of Glade Park, she shifted into tour guide mode and told the story of the Coates Creek school. An odd similarity struck her: the historic log schoolhouse had been hauled to its present site by a powerful rancher who wanted it closer to his children. Too bad for the others. The school board approved the relocation after the fact rather than fight to get it moved back.

"Gotta love the good old days," he said.

From the road, nothing much stood out about the ranch. Rail fencing flanked a plain wooden gate, an iron Crown B hanging from the crosspiece. Corrals, but no livestock in evidence. Sheds with their boards and shingles battened down. Barn tucked back against a bluff as if the composition demanded it there. A low, white-chinked settler's cabin in a nimbus of lilac bushes. Further along the creek, the former ranch house under a fountain of cottonwoods. The summer retreat Donnie and Terri had built two decades ago seemed both to respect and repudiate these ancestral structures.

A border collie mix met the car and herded it to Donnie, who emerged from the porch with his hand raised against the brilliant morning sun. The dog circled his legs until it received his approval and then dropped to await the next moving object. Donnie's tracking of their approach was no less alert. Meg knew his act well enough to see he had dressed to play either gentleman rancher or shit-kicker. His crisp, rose-embroidered white shirt looked fresh off the hanger, his work jeans puckered at the knees and showed brown rub marks on the thighs. Donnie met her with a handshake, an arm clasp and a wink, then rocked onto his toes for the introduction to Hungerman. His animation worried her. She'd told him to be charming but he had some funny ideas about what that meant.

"Heard you were important," said Donnie. "Now I know it. Queenie didn't bark and Meg brought you in her nice car. She only lets me set in her pickup."

Oh, boy. Donnie was trotting out his cowpoke grammar.

"Then I'm twice flattered," said Hungerman, giving Meg a sidelong look. "Thanks for having me. She told me a little about the ranch. I sort of expected to see cows."

"The cattle're out on my lease. You innerested in ranching?"

"To be honest, not really."

"Good, that'll save us all some time."

Okay, then.

They entered the house through the rag-rugged screened porch where the Barclays took the sunrise over Piñon Mesa. A white coffee mug cooled on a scarred blue table. Meg pictured Hungerman sunk into one of the deep-cushioned wicker chairs that crackled and wheezed at any movement. How many mornings of this solitude could he endure? The house tour was proving to be a sham and everyone must know it.

The house was built well, its articulated spaces and vernacular materials suggesting an architect might have been involved before surrendering it to the Barclay clan. Now it was imprinted with hunting trophies, ranch relics and furnishings orphaned by Terri's in-town redecorating. In the great room, a stuffed mountain lion stalked a near-complete taxonomy of North American ungulates. A bulky, hair-on cowhide couch grazed on a storm pattern Navajo rug under a flatscreen TV the size of a dinner table. Expensive stuff but well-used in the sort of place where friends left their shoes on, sloshed drinks and plopped down knowing whatever was breakable had already been broken. Hungerman took in the display, deadpan, and drifted to a large sepia photograph depicting Donnie's great grandfather and a Ute chieftain holding up clutches of dead rabbits by the ears.

"You hunt?" Donnie inquired.

Hungerman shook his head.

"I hear you got boys. All I got for grandkids is girls. Madison. Taylor. Whitney. Last names for first. What kind of girl names are those?"

Meg jumped in. "You named their father Chase. What did you expect?"

"Chase isn't a last name—it's a verb! Anyway, I love 'em but they prefer to ride. Boys like to shoot." Donnie picked a lever-action carbine off its pegs and offered it to Hungerman, who accepted it with the guarded interest of a man presented a tray of engagement rings. "You bring 'em in October, we'll take 'em out to the dynamite shoot. They won't have to kill anything."

Hungerman handed back the rifle. "They'll be in school in October."

"Okay, s'pose not. They'd have to show a safe hunter card, anyway."

"I don't think Lew is in Grand Junction to learn how easy it is for everybody to discharge explosives," said Meg.

"I like to start with the best stuff and work my way down." Donnie had waited for a meeting as far from Hungerman's comfort zone as possible and now the developer was about to get the full treatment. "I get she didn't drive you up here to test the mattress. I've checked out your company. Looks to me like you know how to squeeze insurance nickels into dimes, and I now hear you got some big development on the burner. I grow beef, patch roads and move a little dirt around. And we both seem to have an interest in longevity."

Hungerman cast a glance at Meg. She'd told Donnie nothing and hoped her expression said so.

"Where you staying now?" Donnie said.

"The Entrada."

"*La Entrada!* I spent a night there once. Had this brown oatmeal shampoo you squeezed out of a tube. Wasn't sure whether to put it on my hair or spread it on the toast."

"Donnie's kidding," Meg said.

"Yes, appearances can be deceiving," Hungerman said.

They had just moved to the table when Hungerman asked her to retrieve his bag from the car. "I have an NDA for Donnie in there." Seeing Donnie's raised eyebrows, he translated: "Non-disclosure agreement."

Donnie raised his hand as Meg stood up. He said, "I know what it is. If you bring back a piece of paper for me, I'm not going to sign it, so save yourself the trip."

"It's standard," said Hungerman.

"Not with me. I'm not going to blab or steal your damn secrets, and I hate paying lawyers. So let's just agree to be straight and not screw each other, all right?" He extended his hand to Hungerman, who took it. The wrestling match had begun.

Hungerman quickly sketched the Betterment Longevity Institute plan. Meg had no idea what Donnie knew, but she'd seen enough of him to know his blunt *let's all get our cards on the table* style was the way he concealed the card kept in reserve. Hungerman had been coy about his interests, too. He would lose negotiating leverage once Donnie knew he had settled on Las Colonias. The men talked about the construction business and the new infrastructure a Betterment campus would require, never quite getting to the subject that interested them both—the properties near the riverfront. At one point, Meg caught Donnie watching her as Hungerman spoke. *Of course.* Donnie couldn't read Hungerman, but he might pick up something from her reactions. She wondered what she'd already given him.

"Most of the out-of-town boys I know come here to spend their money, not to make any. The richest one of all's built himself a whole frontier town. At least he owns a coal mine down the road but it hardly covers the overhead. Then there's Devin Magruder, the cowboy actor. Nice guy, family man, my ex-neighbor. He built him up a nice *el rancho*, but it's hard to flip a twenty-five-million anything around here. We got a fancy resort over south where you can stay in a *casita*, ride a horse, take a helicopter spin and gawk at the owner's classic cars collection. I hear you can also get in touch with your inner self. Personally, I'd be distracted by the fifteen-hundred-a-day it cost me. Honestly, how can that make any money? What I'm saying is, all those were vanity projects. We're simple folk, diggers, growers and builders. So when you start talking about the money in destination healthcare, my head gets a bit scratchy."

"Let me know if you need a translation," Meg said.

"No, I'm good," Hungerman said. "I appreciate the candor. I'm not here to become one of Donnie's beautiful spendthrift stories. I'm here for advice."

"Well my advice is, if you put up a headquarters and hotel, build a parking ramp. Cars here turn into a toaster oven after an hour, and you don't want all that pavement around your resort so it looks like a shopping mall. Anyway, we didn't clean up the junk-yards just to park cars on the river."

So Donnie knew somehow.

Hungerman looked at Donnie, then Meg, then back to Donnie. "You people are something," he said.

"Thank you," said Donnie. "Would you like any other advice?"

"Sure."

"Parking ramp construction is a specialty deal."

"And I suppose you know a local contractor who could build one."

"You could probably sell the City on events parking. If they kick in, they'd have to bid it out, but yeah, I do," Donnie deadpanned. "Just a thought."

"And if we were interested in property down there owned by DTB, LLC and Claybar Investments, I suppose you could put us in touch with the principals."

Terri Barclay let the screen door bang to announce her arrival. "I hope I left you enough time," said Terri. "If Donnie hasn't made his pavement-is-civilization speech yet, I'll come back later."

"No, we're good," Hungerman said. "Freedom needs freeways. Farm to market. Factory to store. Ambulance to hospital. Kids to Gramma's house."

"You're a quick study," Terri said.

"Well, he did repeat himself."

"For emphasis!" said Donnie. "You all laugh. Roads built empires, all the way back to the damn Romans."

"Capital flows build empires now," Hungerman said. "Servers and fiber optics. Bandwidth. Information."

"Yeah, well, next time your airplane comes down out of the clouds, try to land on bandwidth," said Donnie. "Take away pavement and the Grand Valley'd be Mexico without the limes."

They were scarcely back on the road before Hungerman said, "You were right to set this up. I need him whether I want him or not."

"He sounds on board."

"You think so." It was a statement, not a question. "He's played hard-to-get for months and suddenly he's all ready to build me a parking ramp? I'm waiting for the other cowboy boot to drop."

"I think you handled him fine. I'm sure Donnie would love to see this go through. We all would."

"I know he's your buddy but you have to be with me on this. I need an advocate with Barclay and a back channel to the mayor. Plus the homeless factor. If a retainer makes it cleaner for you, let me know."

Now was the time to mention Wesley Chambers. But she knew better than to present clients with problems or surprises. She would make this tent city thing go away. Sister Rose had told her it wouldn't be the worst thing. A call to Eve. Some feedback to the coalition. A courtesy call to Lyle Sandstrom. It would be all for the best.

"No," she said. "No retainer. I'm doing this for the town."

Hungerman reached across the seat and placed a hand on her arm. Meg didn't look over. The road was dangerous and so were blue eyes that oozed sincerity on demand.

"I see why Eve and Dan like you, too."

That was funny, since Eve and Dan barely tolerated each other.

"Has either of them talked to you about running?"

Running? She hadn't run in years.

"They tell me the city council doesn't have a clear majority to support the proposal. Some could go bonkers over any Las Colonias privatization. And those pinch-penny, one-year-a-time guys. We need to redraw the lines in the spring election, elect a progressive businessperson who'll also be palatable to the enviros and bleeding hearts. I think you'd be a factor. Really dynamite, in fact."

Oh, you don't know me. The prospect of public office made her carsick. Not campaigning or the grinding, petty details of running the city. Not the droning meetings with their proclamations and obligatory ceremonies. Not even the infighting and public abuse. Everyone postured. It came with the job. It came with *her* job. But underneath, leaders were supposed to be uncorrupted. Not just act better—be better. Knowing where the bodies were buried was supposed to be only a metaphor.

Trips to Glade Park always took Meg back in time. It was a decade earlier there, maybe more. The present was still closer and more attached to the past than to the future. The old-time ranchers like the Barclays had survived and built their wealth in a land that didn't easily give up abundance. They were like the juniper, willing to let a limb die if it meant they could hang on, and they were suspicious of people whose families had not suffered in kind, preferably for three generations. In the valley, affairs aimed more toward the future, which came down to the pursuit of money and hope.

Hungerman was absorbed in a call with Vince Foyer. He didn't notice when they passed Cold Shivers Point.

They were halfway down the face of the Monument when Hungerman broke it off and said, "I have half an hour. Show me the one thing I should absolutely know about you."

"About me?" she said, startled.

"You, the town. I've already gotten the message that you, the woman, aren't interested." He said it carefully, as if setting down something where he could find it again.

What did someone like Hungerman see? Did he even notice the ancient and contradictory walls of the valley? Did he care about caverns that coughed up dinosaurs, junipers dating to the crucifixon, the river that had carved the Grand Canyon? He seemed more interested in the works of man. She could show the plucky Main Street, the hospital's hilltop kingdom, the university's burgeoning campus, the teeming acres of malls and industrial parks, but those had likely all been rolled up in the initial site survey. Development, she'd heard someone say, was based half upon facts and half on hope, but always going forward. How much could he know of the town's real life if he was always going forward?

She parked along the Riverside Parkway beside the old mill. Hungerman took in the massive masonry structure with its metal roof and bricked-over windows. Across the park, a ragged crew of Community Service workers tossed sticks on brushpiles scraped from the remains of the tamarisk fire.

"An empty field and an abandoned, fenced-in building. Are you trying to make me feel at home?" Hungerman seemed amused.

"I was hoping you'd know where we are."

"This is Las Colonias," he said. "What's left to show? I've been all over this place."

"You've seen the landscape, the maps and the soil reports. But have you seen the past?"

He moved to open the door.

"This isn't a walking tour," she said. "This is about what's gone. Like the Utes. They were too nomadic to be farmers, but they did grow corn along the river. The tribes signed a treaty that let them keep the western third of the state. No white men wanted this arid valley, but after the silver boom, they wanted the whole state. Three treaties and an uprising later, the Utes were removed to Utah. About two minutes later, Grand Junction's founders put up over five thousand city lots for sale." She smiled. "We were a creation of speculators from the very start."

"Nothing wrong with that," he said.

"Small farmers were lured by stories of abundant orchards springing from the desert. The mining towns paid boomtown prices for fresh fruit, but after the Panic of '93, silver prices collapsed. The fruit growers who didn't go under had to farm at a more corporate scale and ship to distant markets. Then along came the Spanish-American War. It cut off trade with Cuba, the country's main sugar supplier. Investors convinced the county government to kick in money to build the state's first sugar beet factory."

"Let's hear it for wars of opportunity!" Hungerman said.

"Farmers here weren't so keen on the hard field work a beet crop required. The brand new factory went broke within a year. Later, Holly Sugar took over, imported Mexican labor, built company housing and made a go of it until the Depression. That's when the stockyard closed, too. In those days, a man grew flowers on the island. He sold out to a junkyard. Are you with me so far? Indian corn, fruit, sugar, beef, flowers and then junk." She pulled away from the curb, as if to emphasize the shift she was about to make, and headed for the Entrada.

"After the Second World War, that old plant was converted to process uranium. The Bomb created a market and Atoms for Peace inspired a boom. Uranium prospecting went crazy. By the time the Feds shut the mill down in 1970, it had produced two million tons of radioactive waste and provided free tailings used as fill all over town, around homes, roads and sewer lines galore. In the mid-90s they finally finished the cleanup. Not a great chapter in our history. Bombs, pollution, cancer and Federal cleanup. Twenty years later, there's nothing here, except the Botanical Gardens, a burned out homeless camp and a historic building nobody would touch until you came to town."

"You must've been a good teacher," he said. "The history doesn't worry me. Or are you telling me Las Colonias is cursed?"

"Not cursed. Sort of laden. Inhabited by the ghost of everything that's ever happened." Everything. The junked cars and Neulan's Jeep. Amy Hostetter's blood added to the polluted soil. The glue factory and Wesley's doomed plans for independence. The tamarisk roots that would rise again. "It's like there's this glimmer of radiation from past mistakes, not strong enough to kill you, just to remind you there's no such thing as a clean slate."

"I don't think I want you to write my leasing brochure," he said, "but I might have a marketing job for you after the election."

He either expected her to lose or to be okay with a massive conflict of interest.

"We do believe in the future. And the proof is, we've believed in it again and again and again. We've followed socialists and libertarians, Rotarians and Klan members, Republicans and Democrats, utopian dreamers and hardheaded businessmen, enviros and polluters. So please don't come here with pretty promises you can't keep—because we will believe you."

Meg stopped at the Entrada's portico. Hungerman sat for a moment. Was he reflecting on her account or simply composing himself before his next meeting? Finally he said, "Good job today with Barclay. You have ideas. You speak your mind. People respect you. I think there's so much we can do for each other. Let's get together for a drink before I leave." He gave her arm a light squeeze and was out of the car before she remembered.

"Your bag!"

He continued toward the lobby. Meg stepped out and called again. He turned and thumped his temple with the heel of his hand, grinning, playing the charming idiot. But he didn't come back for the bag. *God, what it must be like to be waited upon for everything!* Jules was right. The leather was spectacular, a thousand-dollar whimsy. No working messenger owned a bag like this. She handed it over. He reached through the strap, shouldered it and circled her wrist as he drew back his arm, stepping toward the entrance as if it were all one dance move. When she did not follow, he stopped with his thumb resting over her pulse point.

"I'm trying to figure you out," he said.

"I sell houses, Lew." It was the first time she'd used his first name. Once out, it felt too intimate.

"That's not what I meant," he said.

She was afraid of that. "This really isn't the place…"

"Then let's find a better one. In a few days, I fly to Idaho Falls, and I could use a realtor's advice."

Did he really think she'd fly off with him? Based on what? *Make it light.* "I'm only licensed in Colorado," she said.

"No need for a license. I'm just looking, and you already have a good idea of what I'm after. Think about it. I'll be in touch."

He released her wrist but his eyes stayed locked on hers, his smile still trying to draw her his way. *If not now, later.* She felt the flush rising in her face and she broke for the car, hoping it didn't show.

Was this how timesaving executives handled assignations? Surely a man so practiced at pitching to strangers should know his *we don't need a license* innuendo was atrocious. Had he shortened the house tour so he'd have some free time with her back at the inn?

Can I ask you a question?

May I.

How much experience with boys did you actually have when you were advising me?

Some.

Could you quantify, say, in total bases reached? Because I'm beginning to doubt your credentials. In fact, maybe I should be the one giving advice, and I'm still a virgin!

I've always wondered.

Don't you find this Lew Hungerman just a tiny bit creepy? He practically groped you.

This is business. We're adults. You don't have experience in either one.

I have a hard-earned education in the subject of manipulative behavior, though, and I've been watching this guy.

He's nothing like Neulan.

Oh, like they only come in one flavor.

So what have you seen that's so revealing?

The same things you have.

Have you ever been treated for drug or alcohol problems and returned to drinking or using drugs?

—Vulnerability Index Prescreen for Single Adults

Kayakers found Jimmy Johncock well downriver from Las Colonias, speared on a river snag. From the burns on his arms and legs, the coroner figured he'd tried to beat out flames before he stumbled into the water and drowned. It seemed like Jimmy—fighting fire to the last breath, being brave and fucking up. He wasn't afraid of a fight but he was never any good at it. Sober, drunk or hung over, Jimmy went down pretty easily. He was always a good loser, though, someone said. *A real good loser.*

Sylvia Tell identified Jimmy. The police knew they could go to her because she didn't want any of her Day Center guests to end up in the potter's field by the police gun range having to listen to target practice for eternity. Someone came up with the idea of sprinkling a little of Jimmy in every cop car in the city. The project seemed doable and quickly attracted volunteers although any of them holding a baggie of ashes would never get it as far as the back seat. But in the end, everyone agreed Jimmy's proper resting place was in the river, and The Point, where Jimmy had lived off and on, was the best location for the farewell service. That it would require all the mourners to trespass did not enter anyone's mind.

Since he was among the last to see Jimmy alive, Isaac felt obligated to attend and maybe Wesley would, too. It stung that he'd lost track of Wesley after the fire. Isaac had thought they were better friends. The street word was that Wesley had been the one who tipped the police about Screech and Dexter for setting the booby trap that hurt the officer. That certain druggies were looking to get back at him. Wesley could handle himself, but maybe he'd chosen not to fight and left town instead.

Disappearance was a simple fact of life, a strategy everyone used at some time on the river. You hid because you lacked the fortifications against trouble. You fled warrants and avoided paying debts. You holed up when you were sick or depressed. Sure, people looked out for each other. But no one wondered why you hadn't been out to mow your lawn. No one missed hearing your stereo or your heels clacking on the floorboards overhead. No one called to ask why you'd missed work. It wasn't unusual to see a car parked somewhere for too long. Your mail could go uncollected for weeks. And sometimes when people did notice they thought, *good riddance.*

Standing on the steep bluff above The Point, Isaac could see the entire wooded triangle formed by the railroad tracks and junction of the Colorado and Gunnison rivers. Isolated by the water and the bluff, The Point had been left untouched by the original claimants and ignored by their heirs. More than a century later, the title remained in the names of long-dead men, the land unvalued and untaxed. It might as well have been the moon or a new volcanic island. It was ripe for colonization. Sheltered from view and close to downtown, it had attracted squatters who established a community that ebbed and flowed with the weather, grudges and police raids. In a given season, it could be dangerous or peaceful, closed or welcoming, and ranging from half a dozen inhabitants to several score.

After decades of tolerance, the railroad declared The Point a safety hazard and announced plans to cut off access. Maybe the company was truly concerned. Maybe it was just part of the general war on vagrancy. The Homeless Coalition negotiated the camp's departure and a hundred volunteers helped the occupants move and clean up the site. The railroad had leveled a shielding berm and put up a fence. The Point was uninhabitable now. Like the entire riverfront was becoming.

From above, Isaac could see the outlines left by the winter roundhouse, the fire pits and the individual tents. Steps carved in the bluff by the former inhabitants had begun to erode. He descended, prepared to arrive on his ass.

Trow acted as greeter and guide around the end of the fence. Already the gathering included a mix of Jimmy's drinking buddies, recovery friends, two of his caseworkers and assorted others, maybe twenty-five in all. An aluminum fishing boat beat upriver toward The Point, and when they saw Sylvia in the bow three men went down to pull it onto the beach. Sylvia disembarked clutching a cardboard box. She introduced Jimmy's mother. Mrs. Johncock's long, homemade dress and sun-dazed expression made her look like one of the re-enactors at the History Farm, here and living in a different reality. The third passenger, Sister Rose, surprised everyone with her disguise of a broad-brimmed yellow hat, cornflower blue culottes and green rubber gardening boots.

The assembly formed a circle in the sand. Sister Rose began by saying that despite the tragedies of his life Jimmy had known God's love. Everyone here had been an expression of it. Sylvia talked about Jimmy's gentle soul, how he'd never hurt a flea, then corrected herself. Half the audience knew fleas first-hand. Tony Martin, a cop from the outreach team, said he had learned from Jimmy the difference between helping and saving someone; that serving was necessary because protecting wasn't always possible. Trow said JJ used to occupy a tent next to him. He drew a white stone from his pocket and laid it on the spot under a tree. *And now he lives in the place where everything is new,* Trow said solemnly, as if he were quoting the Bible.

Jimmy's friend Casey produced a vodka flask and sloshed a bit over the same ground, then he waded out onto a shoal and let the rest of it drizzle into the line where the green Gunnison met the brown Colorado. Isaac suspected then Casey had used water instead of vodka. Sylvia brought out the ashes and Tony Martin escorted Jimmy's mother into the shallows. Mrs. Johncock, Sylvia and Tony took turns casting crumbles of Jimmy to the two rivers, the bits hitting the water like roils of water skippers. Then Sylvia invited others to join in if they wanted. Some did, taking their pinches and strewing them. Isaac stayed on the beach, not wanting to deprive someone who had loved Jimmy better. Casey stuffed some kernels of bone into the bottle, replaced the cap and launched it. Everyone watched until it floated out of sight, then Jimmy's mother shook out the plastic bag that had contained the ashes and stuffed it back inside the box. She wiped her hands on her dress, which was soaked well above the hem. The others brushed their palms in unison as if they had reached agreement, that it was all right, finally, for them to give up on Jimmy Johncock.

Trends always become outdated.
Dwell in the present and be true to yourself.

— "Home" with Meg Mogrin, *Grand Junction Style*

Whenever Meg opened the door of a property she was showing, it seemed the home took in an expectant breath. But of course the hopefulness belonged to her, her client and the seller, all asking: *Is this going to be the one?* Such alignment was rare in life—all the parties wanting the same thing, even for a moment. Usually, the moment did not last.

During the drive with Hungerman, Meg's mood had shifted away from that simplistic, anticipatory state. Now she saw the complications. She had started out as a local ambassador, steering Hungerman from the grittier sides of town, introducing him to more of the right people, rooting for a deal to go through. Nothing official; for the time being she was just Eve's girl on the spot. Then how quickly he had drawn her over to his side. She had too blithely signed the non-disclosure. Remembering Donnie's refusal, she hoped it wasn't a mistake. Now, before she asked Eve if there were any other sites in the running, she had to check if her agreement applied to Idaho.

While Ashley retrieved the form, Meg looked up Idaho Falls. Same elevation and similar population. A market hub serving two states. A downtown greenbelt along a manicured river. Irrigated agriculture. Remnants of the Atomic Energy Commission and its residue there, also. Proud of its homegrown culture. *100 Best Adventure Towns* with minor league baseball. Some differences, too. Colder and wetter, a very small branch of the state university, far more religious, less of a medical center. Still, too similar to be a coincidence.

Ashley presented a folder, which contained the agreement and its envelope. Oh well. Meg *had* handed over the envelope from Hungerman and told her to file it. Ashley Cassel was sweet and willing, but it was taxing trying to bring along an employee who was never going to measure up. She would remain ensconced at reception until some nice Mormon boy decided she was Temple-worthy.

"You don't have to save the envelopes, Ashley."

The girl bit her lower lip. "But I didn't know what else to do with the rest."

The rest? A white index card lettered in two different hands:

YOU MUST ASK FOR WHAT YOU REALLY WANT.
I think this line was meant for both of us.
    –Lew

Even without paperwork, all relationships had elements of confidentiality and concealment. Normally, she'd tell Eve about an invitation to fly away for the weekend. She'd name the man or not. It would become a joke or a secret between them. Big deal or no big deal, she could trust her friend. But here there were millions at stake for the city and layers of intrigue she had only begun to fathom. She had not asked for this breach from business into her personal life. What were her obligations to a man once their relationship was on paper?

From the sound on the line, Donnie Barclay was busy turning gasoline into noise. One of his ATVs or some giant machine was shaking the earth on his behalf. He rarely got his hands dirty any more but he still enjoyed raising dust. He could talk if she came by the gravel pit, he said. She confirmed its location, a few miles from her house, beyond the mall on the opposite side of the river, shielded from the highway by prairie dog lots filled with RVs for sale and disassembled oil rigs huddled together like abandoned city blocks. Dump loads of fill lined the road to the gravel pit. From their stages of erosion, a decade or more of deposits awaited the reckoning blade that would level them into something more salable.

Donnie met her at the gate in a utility vehicle with bug-eyed headlights. He handed her a hardhat and safety glasses, neither of which he wore, and extended a pair of blue earplugs, which she declined. She'd come to hear what he had to say.

"Put 'em in," he said, rolling a tip to show how it was done. "No sense going deaf before you have to."

The gravel pit mined an ancient floodplain terrace left when the river changed course. At its bottom four stories down, a mantis-like machine gulped scoops of sand and river rock fed from a beeping loader. The material was conveyed on belts and rollers and agitated through heavy screens. Rocks the size of footballs hopped toward relentless crushers that hammered them and then trundled over their remains. The machine's splayed arms disgorged graded pyramids of sand and aggregate. Donnie zoomed down into the bedlam, shouting over the ruckus. They might as well have been conversing on a freight train under heavy machine-gun fire. He drove out again and parked under a stressed and lonely cottonwood knuckled into the lip of the pit.

He extracted his earplugs and Meg followed his example. The quiet here was relative. Nearby a pump chugged, sucking water from the floor of the mine and discharging it to a channel that gushed down to the river.

She unfolded her jumble of excitement and misgivings. Almost everything.

"Whoa. If I'd known all that, I'd've met you for a cocktail," he said.

"Nothing's totally bad in itself. It just feels like everything's colliding."

"It's tough to do good by everybody. Sometimes you just have to hash out who you're going to disappoint," he said.

"But I care about everybody. There's the community's stake, too."

"We do like to tell ourselves that, don't we? Love thy neighbor and all. You got to look at it different. Not make it personal. Think about who you'd rather piss off."

Or who she can trust. She didn't know if Wesley was a champion for homeless people about to pull off something great or a deluded vet with PTSD who just wanted to be left alone. Hungerman's project seemed the town's best hope to turn things around, but when she got in close, alarm bells went off. Both of them wanted something from her to a disturbing degree. She asked Donnie what he expected out of this, because he didn't seem motivated by the money.

"Maybe not. I'll still pull over for a big sack of cash on the side of the road, though. And you bet I'd get twitchy writing a check with more than one comma. I'm only rich like Cowboy Bob is a poet—not the same thing as the full deal."

Meg wondered if Donnie knew any full-deal poets. He spit just off the floorboards of his ATV and wiped his mouth with the back of his hand.

"See, the more money enters in, the harder it is to see people straight. Hard even to sort out for yourself. Being able to ride across my land is worth more to me than a six-million-dollar road job. But if I trade the paving contract for a ride on a horse, I'm a fool, so I take both. It's not that the goodness of something turns to greed when it gets big. In my book, greed is buying your Cadillac with the widow's investment funds. It's cheating on your taxes. Greed is screwing the people who work for you as if you were God on a bad day. Greed is an ugly little thing. It's about loving yourself too much, and money has very little to do with it.

"So Lew has a big idea that he says will benefit a lot of people. If it doesn't, he'll look like a crook. If it succeeds and he makes a pile, he'll still probably be called a crook because of the toes he stepped on or the people he squeezed out. So what? Point is, you don't get to decide what other people think of you. Nobody's ever punished for all their wrongdoing or rewarded for all their goodness. In fact, sins often prove most profitable. And being too damn righteous can get you killed. I try to be a little bit of both and let God do the math."

"So does that mean you're behind Lew?"

"I'm not in front or behind him. Right now I'm where I can keep an eye on him. At this point in my life, I've got no great need to build that parking ramp. But somebody is going to do it, and I'd rather it was me. We'll do a good job, but I never know when I'm pouring the concrete how things'll turn out in the greater scheme. Look at damn Las Colonias—who knew about radiation back then? We thought nukes would make the Russians behave, give us watches that glowed in the dark! You think you've done good and then you find out otherwise. Or maybe you thought you made a mess and it turns out okay.

"This crater here may look like hell right now, but those connected lakes up-river? Those quiet potholes all the way to Palisade where you've got your bike trails and your bird habitat and your fishing holes? Fifty, a hundred years ago, they were gravel mines and now they're amenities. And meanwhile, there's a city with jobs and houses and an airport and a college that wouldn't have been here on this crappy, salt-encrusted dirt if those old boys hadn't dug out the river bottoms for a living. Where were we?"

"Hungerman. Greed. Progress."

Donnie started up the ATV and bumped down the track of the discharge hose to the bike trail where motorized vehicles were prohibited. Meg braced herself as he gunned along the path.

"Look here. This dinky little stretch of the river's posted for hunting. The bikers freak out. Well, guess what? Us hunters love this river, too, and we'll know a hell of a lot sooner when the habitat's got problems than some fat-tire tourist blowing through on his way to the brewpub. I'm paying tax money right now so they can grind out all this tamarisk, which was originally put in by the Army Corps of Engineers to shore up the riverbanks. More folks from out of town come to do what was good for us."

Donnie turned a sharp radius and sped back, ignoring the glares from a pair of approaching cyclists. "Look now," he said. "From an angle, the baffles in this fence screen off my operation. Moving like this, you can hardly see through it. But if you stop at the right angle, you can. There we are, offending gentle sensibilities. What I'm saying is, progress and doing good is always part fuck-up, excuse my French. You can't always predict which part."

The ATV bucked up the hill and followed the fence around to where Meg had parked. He stepped off the machine and opened his arms. A hug and his usual fractured platitudes. Donnie knew how to deliver comfort. Yes, the fate of mankind didn't depend on Meg Mogrin.

"I can't tell you what's in Hungerman's soul," Donnie said as he released her. "It's hard enough to know what's in mine. Don't worry about Sister Rose. Yeah, who wants to let down a nun? But your chances are pretty good that she'll forgive you. City Council? You'd be good and I'd vote for you but you wouldn't like it. I'd have to drive you around the gravel pit once a month to keep you sane. That Chambers fellow may be trying to do good, but Jesus, nobody wants that camp around them. They're getting too bold, if you ask me. We had one up in our neighborhood this week, sticking fliers in the mailboxes—about some glass eye he found in Columbus Canyon. That's illegal, you know. According to the cops, he's tacked up posters around town, too. That's illegal posting. He's lucky they didn't charge him."

"What was he doing way out by your house?"

"The canyon's behind us in the Monument. He thought the neighbors might know something."

"I thought you were by Red Canyon."

"There's two canyons. This one's hard to get to and there's no signs to mark it, so people don't think of it. But everybody knows it." Donnie pinched his lower lip. "It's that canyon you see below Cold Shivers Point."

Cold Shivers. It had been nothing but the rim of an empty bowl filled with air and heartbreak. But of course the bowl was a canyon and the canyon had a bottom and the bottom collected whatever was thrown into the air. A girl. A man. A glass eye. Brian had said he'd taken care of it. God, to think there might be some other *it.*

She drove through town, not knowing exactly why she was looking. *We Buy Ugly Houses. Lost. Work at Home.* No one would notice that poster in all this clutter. Perhaps they all had been taken down. Anyway, no one besides her would connect a glass eye found in Columbus Canyon to Neulan Kornhauer—unless Neulan had a glass eye...and Donnie had called the police! *Calm yourself.* She turned north toward her office. Then she saw it, on a light stanchion near a boarded-up Travelodge where a man squatted on the pavement wiping sticks with a rag. The abridged motel sign above his head read: *AVE O GE.* She circled the block, parked in the grocery store lot nearby and crossed the street. The man looked up hopefully. She could smell the varnish and see that he'd set up a folk art crucifix assembly line. No thank you.

The white cardstock sign featured a marker-drawn illustration of an eye shaped like an artist palette. She snapped a quick picture with her phone. At the corner, a flashing orange hand and robot voice counseled her to *wait...wait...wait.* She crossed and skulked back toward the car.

Neulan had been dead to her. And now, until she could be sure about what this eye meant, he was alive again. Brian did say that he'd taken care of the body. But he had kept the details close and she had never wanted to know. There'd been a fire, she thought, a burial. But there had been a violent landing and weeks had passed. It had been night and Brian might not have thought to search the ground. Was a glass eye like a fingerprint? Could it be traced? Did Neulan have any friends who would know? Too many questions. She had to be careful. Seeking information only increased the danger that this would rise again.

She looked at the image in her phone. *Leave a message for Isaac S.* Did that mean he wouldn't answer? Maybe she could glean some information from the voicemail or whoever answered. She wouldn't have to leave her name.

A woman answered without identifying herself. Was this the right number? "I'm calling for Isaac S...how do you spell his last name?"

"Samson, no p, just like it sounds. Let me check." The woman's voice moved away from the receiver. Meg heard it set down with a clunk, then the squawk of a tired chair released of its burden. A dampened hum of voices.

Isaac Samson? Besides Joe and Shelly, how many Samsons were there in town? It seemed unlikely they'd have a homeless relative. Shelly was in her book club. She'd never said anything. And Joe— beyond hellos, they'd really only talked once, years ago. About him knowing Helen...and Neulan and... *She had told him about seeing Neulan at Cold Shivers!* Nothing incriminating, just two sad people on a street outside a bar offering each other small comfort. But now anything said seemed too much. These were only dots, far apart in time, that inclined toward each other only in her mind. They might not connect at all. But Isaac Samson had edged them all closer.

A pencil rattled out of a cup. "He's not here right now. Do you want to leave a message?"

Part Two

≈

September – October

Homes are time capsules—some waiting to be filled, others sealed long ago.

— "Home" with Meg Mogrin, *Grand Junction Style*

They had been such successful conspirators. No confederates or confidants. No letters or emails, no incriminating messages, no conversations that could be recorded and related back to the crime. Not even phone records, since Brian didn't have a phone. Meg and Brian had developed no code words for the condition of fallen bodies, the whereabouts of glass eyes or the finer points of *habeas corpus*, so her only recourse was meeting in person. Brian would be surprised to see her, of course, and she accepted that he might surprise her. But for all their years of silence and separation, she trusted him more than anyone. If she had reason to worry, he would tell her. If she had screwed up, he would help her think through what to do. They were forever joined by Neulan, the way good divorced parents stayed responsible for their children even after they left the nest.

She would have to tell Brian about her fateful first meeting with Joe Samson, drinking beer in a pizza place, his hair triple-mohawked from his bike helmet. She had kept it to herself for so long, it almost felt as if she had cheated. Joe's story of riding Monument Road, the reason for his vigilance and his hope of saving the day. Super Samaritan in spandex. Joe remarked on her resemblance to Helen as if it had come as a revelation, as if he had been waiting half his life for this chance to confess and didn't care that he was standing in front of a biker bar with the smokers outside making fun of his butt. He thought he had inadvertently helped Neulan escape justice, and nothing less than Meg's forgiveness could soothe his anguish. What else could she do but reassure him, never imagining how her falsified tale of meeting Neulan at Cold Shivers might someday prove her own undoing. Or maybe not. *Maybe not, maybe not,* her mantra for the long drive.

How the settlements stood apart from each other out here. In the country she was leaving, the mountains had the first say about where towns could be but here the towns were declared by the prophets, and the prophecy was only fulfilled by water. Each mile she drove seemed a further retreat into Biblical times. Crossing the state line, from the tortilla brown of *Colorful Colorado* descending to badland Utah's *Life Elevated*. The first four exits with No Services. The old rail stop of Thompson Springs, where an abandoned Fifties diner and motel swap alien abduction tales. The garish curio shop colors at Crescent Junction obscuring the uranium tailings disposal cell behind it. Then turn onto forty miles of Thelma and Louise highway that ends where earth movers chip away at the Atlas Mill tailings pile on the bank of the river, a welcome so much more dramatic than the sideways entrance to Arches National Park. Into blasé Moab, an oft-reinvented town throbbing with jeeps, mountain bikes and beer—and boxy new motels by Marriott topped with reddish prestressed concrete arches. Eventually Monticello arises in a thickening of trees that surrenders on the far end of town. Blanding repeats the miracle. If trees didn't exist in these desert impoundments, Mormons would have to implant them. The only shade offered in the Navajo towns of Chinle and Kayenta is under gas station canopies and in canyons too remote for franchises or highway engineers to venture. Desert peoples everywhere believe themselves chosen. Why else live in such a godforsaken landscape?

Barren places can be beautiful when encountered without expectation. Ruins retain a dignity that a living place does not. A single tree can outshine a forest. But everywhere Meg looked on this drive, she saw desolation.

Meg's and Brian's last road trip together had been along a blue highway like this one, plotted by Brian to be a healing journey. It might have worked right after their rupture began with her decision to quit the classroom and move back to Grand Junction, but post-Neulan, the outing seemed a good-faith formality, the sort of thing done by partners who wanted to remain friends. The road to Taos followed a long, gradual descent across a sagebrush steppe. Abruptly, a six-hundred-foot chasm split the land. What a surprise it must have been for the first travelers to find their route changed when the Rio Grande Gorge revealed itself. So opposite the dread the westward wagoneers must have felt trudging out of Nebraska with the Front Range of the Rockies towering ahead for days.

Brian stopped the car next to some Navajos hawking trinkets from blanket-covered tailgates. The sellers huddled with their backs to the wind, ignoring the tourists creeping onto the narrow bridge for a look at the gorge. One daredevil leaned over the railing, flailing his arms in mock distress. A sixteen-wheeler approached from the east and blasted its horn as it crossed. Howls and whoops flew up in its wake. A woman plopped down on the walkway and planted both hands on the deck. Her companions failed to coax her up and finally two men lifted her to her feet and assisted her slow shuffle back to land.

"I bet you can feel the bridge vibrate when the cars go across," Brian said.

"Be my guest." Meg understood the woman's fear. Not that the bridge would collapse from the traffic but that her perch forced her to acknowledge the earth's deep indifference to her life. Somehow, the proposition excited Brian.

"I'll bring back some shots for you," he said. "At least get out of the car so you can see into the gorge."

The wind pressed hard against Brian's door and he had to force it open. The gusts were telling Meg to stay inside, but since they were still trying to please each other, she let herself be blown out. She stayed in the lee of the car while Brian worked his way with the camera to the mid-point of the bridge. He was the only person she knew still shooting slide film. He wielded a manual camera as if he were striking a blow for freedom of expression. He called and waved her to stand at the end of the walkway with her hand on the railing. In the wind-chilled air, the sun-stroked steel's warmth surprised her.

Brian clicked his way back to her. His breath was quick. "Amazing! One part of your brain is saying, *this is so cooool* and the other is shouting *fuuuuuck, get me out of here!*"

He started the engine. Meg's belt buckle clicked with such finality she released it to ensure she could free herself. *In case I'm still alive after the car hits the river.* Brian sensed her discomfort and without a word dug a map from the door pocket and shook it open over the steering wheel.

"Okay. Maybe we don't have to go over this bridge," he said.

Brian was always so careful not to judge her, a quality that had elevated him above other men and ultimately swept her into his arms. But rather than asking what she wanted to do here, he was assuming, which made his sensitivity almost condescending. The far rim waited a few hundred yards away. Maybe she could suppress her fear for that long; he should know to offer her the choice.

Brian stepped out of the car and the map tried to take flight. He turned, arms outstretched, so it plastered against his chest. The Indian vendors, amused, looked at their feet as the kite man blew toward them. They helped him pin the map in the bed of a pickup, pointed downstream and then at the map. Brian, fighting the wind on the way back, thrust the map through the car door in a crumple and then spread it on the dash. His finger traced an invisible line parallel to the river.

"They say a county road follows the gorge down to a crossing at grade. It's only a few miles out of the way and not as hairy. Then we can double back to Taos."

They took the detour. At the time she was irritated by Brian's fixation on the fluttering map. Now she was struck by how hard he had been trying to hold them together.

Long after—after the trip, the marriage—she found a coffee can of slides he had taken that day. Tiny in their paper mounts, the shots from the bridge did not capture the tectonic terror. The river seemed distant and unthreatening; the gorge, a lush interruption in the parched land. The quaking bridge, a trustworthy engineering marvel. Meg hunched at the termination of the railing with one fist buried in her jacket and her face obscured by sunglasses. She provided a focal point to the composition without being the point of Brian's photograph. That was the story of their relationship. They were together in perfect orientation to the world but slightly at odds with each other. Meg perceived him at a distance, while his lens brought her close. Where she sought a ford, Brian imagined a bridge.

The Food Mart looked exactly as it had on Google Street View, generic red letters on a whitewashed cinderblock wall penetrated by a window for watching the gas pumps. The interior had the same snack-food-and-cigarette stock of every quick stop in America, minus the beer, plus kachinas. Meg foraged for something with which to purchase information. She bore a box of rock-like raisins and a jar of dry-roasted peanuts to the clerk, who had so far not acknowledged Meg's presence. Chosposi, by her name tag, her cheeks plump and starting to crowd the beauty in her eyes.

An indirect query seemed the right approach.

Chosposi gave no sign she'd heard of any teacher named Brian Mogrin. Or that she'd even heard the question. She surveyed the purchases and Meg's credit card. "Any gas?"

Meg shook her head.

Chosposi pointed to the sign by the register:

Min. $10 purchase on credit cards. EBT OK. —The Mgmt.

Meg handed over cash. "Is he still around?"

Chosposi presented the change without counting it out, coins sliding off the bills. She said, "Anglo teachers come and go. Pretty much all the same."

Meg could only imagine the shock of reservation life for the idealistic first-timers. "Brian's older—not old, my age—and he's been here for years."

Chosposi stared off at a spot above Meg's head. "Oh, him." Her eyes came back to the counter but not to Meg. She shrugged, maybe because she didn't know anything more. Maybe because she did.

"We used to be married," Meg tried.

An eyebrow inched two millimeters. "No messeege is a messeege," Chosposi said. Her face suggested a smile beyond capture. "Oh, that was a good one."

Meg followed Chosposi's directions through the village, a cluster of blocks hidden from the highway in a side canyon. She drove along a creek past a cloudy green reservoir and continued on a dirt reservation road. Fainter tracks branched and disappeared, marks on the land but not landmarks to her eye. Scrawny dogs beyond breed trotted down drives from unseen houses, confirming to her she was still on the through-road. The compass display on her rear view mirror confirmed her western heading but it seemed she had traveled too far. In such a featureless landscape, how could she have missed the rock-marked turn Chosposi had described? Perhaps she'd misunderstood. Perhaps a trickster had turned the rock into a cactus. Perhaps she was lost.

Her GPS offered no assistance. An intermittent blue dot pulsed what she presumed was her location on a blank tan background but the display labored as though the servers had never been tasked with rendering this sector of the earth. She considered that Chosposi had sent her wandering as the butt of some inscrutable Hopi joke: *No place is still a place.* She continued until reaching a rocky flat that marked the boundary of her hopefulness. Now, if only she could replicate her mistakes in reverse.

Turning, she sensed a movement—the first sign of life since she'd left dog country. A lean runner inscribed a fluid, looping line along a high bench. He bounded down an invisible trail, his arms floating for balance. For an instant, she thought it was Brian.

She'd given up running, blaming lack of time, the Grand Junction heat and a surfeit of knee pain, but in truth the cause was losing his easy, inspiring company. Brian's feet barely licked the ground, his fingers relaxed as if dispensing mints, his conversation might have been prerecorded, so little breath it required. Unlike shuffling joggers or overstriders beating out imaginary throws to first, Brian drew the distance to him, reminding her it was only air between them and their destination. Meg had trained hard to match his graceful lope and effortless mindset, but once she left Brian's slipstream she stopped feeling so free and untamed. Her running, like everything else, required too much effort and calculation. Once she lost her conditioning, she gave up ever returning to form.

The runner was a Native boy, shirtless and sinewy, movement distilled. He shifted to a lower gear and then dropped into a stroll as she overtook him. He seemed amused yet too shy to speak. She explained her quest and he nodded, turned and motioned her to follow.

"Let me drive you," she said before he trotted off.

Over his shoulder he said, "Then I won't know the way."

He resumed his former pace, and Meg matched her speed to his. They seemed to be traveling on different planes. He changed his gait over dips and rocky irregularities without slowing while she had the sensation of groping around furniture in a dark room. They arrived at a fork where the boy jabbed his finger in one direction and then waved her to proceed down the other branch. She understood the first way led back to town. This was where she had missed the junction rock in Chosposi's directions. There it was, the color of the soil, the size of an ice chest. The boy led her to a doubletrack that climbed a small rise. A slow circling dogtrot brought him around to face her. He bent his head and lifted a hand as he passed, disappearing over the last hump in the road before her dust cloud had entirely settled upon it.

Meg had dampened her expectations when Chosposi told her Brian lived in a trailer during the summer. But not to this level. She had imagined something like Jim Rockford's tacky single-wide, a shambles redeemed by its splendid setting and its gentle owner. But this was not Malibu, which was why the Hopis still had it. She had hoped for Brian to have something better than bare dirt. Better than the red Jetta he'd driven from Grand Junction, now beaten and faded to lichen orange. Better than this breadloaf-shaped *campito,* a sheepherder's trailer that belonged in a roadside museum. Perhaps this was why Brian had stayed at arm's length even when he reached out. He didn't want her to know how far he had fallen.

Her mission suddenly felt cruel and intrusive. What an idiot she had been, working herself into this paranoid state and now about to drag Brian into it. He had moved on. He apparently valued solitude and frugality. Why would he care to be reminded of her bustling and comfortable life? An ex-wife made frantic by her emotional isolation. Ugh. Get over it. She put the car in reverse.

The Dutch door at the end of the *campito* split. A head ducked out. The hair was still dark but cropped shorter, the face still angular, pressing toward gaunt, the eyes tracking but not quite registering. Brian-Not-Brian. He might not be able to see her inside the car. She should just go. She should floor it and get back to the highway before dark. But she had come all this way on her foolish errand. Why not stay a fool for a little while more?

His expression changed. Not recognition, more like hope. He unlatched the bottom of the door, dropped to the ground and came crow-hopping in bare feet toward the car. She hadn't planned how to start this. Certainly not by waiting as if she'd pulled up to a drive-through window. She opened the door. Frying bacon injected the afternoon air with a fresh sense of awakening. Brian wore a faded t-shirt, the name of the long-ago race almost illegible: *Loveland Classic*. She used to sleep in hers. *Say something.*

"Remember me?"

"Margaret Vavoris, isn't it?" He opened his arms in mock wonder and edged around the car as if she had brought it for his inspection. "Doing well, it looks like."

"And you, still economizing."

He smiled, dropped the act.

"It's a surprise to see you, Meg. A nice surprise."

He escaped into the trailer while she waited outside in a lawn chair slung with disintegrating nylon webbing. He emerged with reassuringly cold Diet Cokes, a box of Triscuits and six strips of bacon on a paper towel. He set the spread on a wooden cable spool and perched on the platform built over the trailer's tongue.

"I hope this wasn't going to be your dinner," she said.

"I usually just graze. I have some eggs, though, if you're hungry."

"I grabbed something to eat in town."

"Really?" He seemed to know it was a fib. He broke up the bacon, placed it on crackers and offered her one. "How did you track me down out here?"

"I asked around about any crazy white guys in the neighbor-hood."

"And?"

"Apparently you have no competition."

Small talk had never seemed smaller. She had planned on tell-ing him straight out what she was after and instead blathered local news Brian cared nothing about—until she told him about Amy Hostetter.

"It's not fair," he said. "She was a good one."

"There's a lot of good cops. You just had a crush on her."

He smiled. "Maybe I never told you this. I used to wonder about her. She was the only woman in the co-ed league who wasn't there because of a man. I mean, she belonged in women's fast pitch and I know they wanted her. It seemed like such a waste of talent. She obviously loved to compete. She was our school liaison officer and one day I asked her. She said that team demanded more commitment than she could give. Like what? The fast-pitch teams traveled sometimes but Amy didn't work shifts. She just shrugged.

"I finally asked a guy on her team if he knew. You know what it was? Amy took calls from families when she was off duty. Even during games. She'd leave play to go pick up a kid who was stranded or freaking out somewhere. Talk about commitment."

Brian was that way, too. She told him about her rescue by the young runner, how she had glimpsed something of Brian in his stride.

"That kid could be great if he wanted to be," Brian said. "He'll run all day but he finds the idea of training comical. In races, he'll leave everyone behind but not by as much as he can. He doesn't like to show people up. He could compete in Division-I but he wouldn't like it."

"And how do you know all this?"she asked. "Doesn't he get to choose his own future?"

"Sure, he gets a choice, even without the running. An Indian student in the top five percent of his class earns a full ride at ASU. The Hopi value learning as a way to benefit the tribe, but they also value home. Phoenix is too big and foreign. The team isn't your family."

"What's the future then—for him and for girls like Chosposi?"

He smiled at the mention of her name. "Do you know what Chosposi means? Bluebird Eyes. Her grandmother gave her that name. She's of the Badger clan. Her Anglo name is Grace."

"Those are pretty names," Meg said, "one ancient and one

old-fashioned."

"Not many Britneys and Tiffanies out here. Don't judge her by what you see at the quick stop. She lives in two worlds. Grace is more the one selling toilet paper and beef jerky, while Chosposi's protecting the spiritual center of the earth for all humankind."

He smashed his Coke can and methodically flattened it. "Everything out here has multiple forms. Not just what we see. For the Hopi everything that ever happened still is. Now, always—those are the choices the language gives—not was. There was a big debate among linguists over whether Hopi has a future tense. You'd think the Hopis would be more help in the matter, but I suspect for them the answer's irrelevant—like soccer fans listening to arguments about the Packers versus the Cowboys. From what I understand, they measure their distance from events by intensity or significance, not time."

The day she learned about Helen. The night on Cold Shivers. When Brian left. Intense. Close. Always.

"This seems a little above third-graders," she said.

"It makes my head hurt, but it's already embedded in them. I think all kids start out Hopi. They don't separate the real from the pretend, the living from the dead, the essence from its many forms. They see a fluidity to dogness: a rez dog, Clifford the cartoon dog, a stuffed dog, a boy barking like a dog, a hot dog. You ruin it once a teacher says, no, that's wrong, that's a canine and that's food."

She saw what he was saying. The sunset had smeared a gold and purple glaze across the sky. A bowl and not a bowl.

"Chosposi said you spend your summer months out here," she said. "It must feel like one long vacation."

"I don't usually have guests," he said, as if there were some question. "Do you want a tour?"

The *campito* dated to early twentieth century but up close she could see the blue paint was fresh, the galvanized metal roof seams were fitted and sealed. Knotty cedar boards ran horizontally above painted hoops supporting the arched ceiling, creating the effect of a wood-lined culvert with an octagonal window at the end. To her right, a camp stove sat atop an old cast-iron wood stove, zinc compartments with sliding doors tucked around it. A single place setting stood upright behind a rail on a narrow shelf. A metal washbasin attached to the wall filled from a water can and drained through a rubber hose to the outside. Midway, benches faced each other. One served as his bookshelf. Brian lifted the other seat to reveal a compartment that held a butane-powered refrigerator chest. At the rear a full-sized bed filled the wagon's width. It was raised on a stack of built-in drawers, from which a small table projected. When he pressed it, the table disappeared into a slot. Everything was battened down as if the wagon had to be ready to roll at any moment.

"It's beautiful," she said. "Crazy beautiful, like a space capsule or a submarine."

"Except here, you can step outside and still breathe," he said. He hopped on the bed and let his legs dangle.

Yes, she reminded herself, *breathe*. She took a seat on the bench. "How did you find it?"

"An elder gave me the wagon and a place to put it."

"Quite a gift."

"Oh, he didn't want it. The Navajo are the sheepherders, not the Hopi. It was a semi-wreck. I think he wanted me to stay but didn't want to ask. He figured giving me this to fix up would keep me around a while."

"I had this picture of you as a monk. I wasn't too far off."

"I'm just trying to learn, to fit in with others without losing my own ways." He clapped his hands on his thighs as a sort of declaration, the way a man plants his shovel when the hole reaches bottom. "Visitors don't just show up here. This is a government town, there's nothing for you to do, nowhere to stay. It's like an electric substation, all this infrastructure just forwarding juice that's generated somewhere else."

"I'm sorry if I'm disturbing your peace."

"No, it's okay," he said. "Just tell me why you're here."

"I needed to talk to you and to talk I had to see you. I couldn't just leave a message." All true and incomplete. Why was she still tiptoeing?

The single light in the room went out. Through the window above the bed she noted the gathering darkness.

Brian said, "Ah, it's on a timer and the motion sensor doesn't quite reach this far in. If you want light, wave your arms. Or not."

Everything in the wagon, it seemed, had some invisible aspect or secondary purpose. The mattress atop the cabinet, for example. An hour ago it was a divan. Did Brian's extended hand just turn it into a bed? She settled next to him, sensing his wary expectation. They had been classmates, colleagues, lovers, husband and wife, now bonded by the experience that had split them. She did not summon the light. What she was about to tell him belonged in gloom.

She explained how the town was still obsessed with Neulan's crimes. Its shame over allowing the killer's escape begged for resolution. People might have recollections kindled by a glass eye found in the canyon. Imagine the renewed furor if it were Neulan's. She wanted to know if he'd had one but didn't dare associate herself with the question.

As he listened, his shoulders slumped. His gaze dropped to his hands. His tone went flat. "That's all that brought you?"

Meg had thought of the eye as her problem for Brian to solve. Now she grasped her misjudgment.

He spoke in careful starts and stops, as if walking a candle down a breezy path. "I hiked in with what I could carry...shovel, a camp saw, some gasoline. The way into the canyon was rougher than I expected. I worried about locating the body in the dark but it was hard to miss. Never mind. You care about the eyes."

Brian blew out a breath that left the conversation, went through the half-open door and found the *always* of their past. His fist ground into the mattress. The arm bracing him seemed to bear more than his own weight. Meg touched his shoulder and felt the muscles knotted across his back. She let her fingertips rest on his thigh, birds on a wire poised for flight.

"The sockets—there were no eyes at all. I figured it was the ravens. I'm sorry."

"Don't be sorry," she said.

"I fractured his skull!"

"You don't know that. He was still upright and conscious."

"He wasn't acting right."

"How can you tell what's right with someone like him?"

"We have been so fucking through all this."

"We helped rid the world of a monster. Neulan made his choice."

"Did he? You act like you've forgotten."

"Forgotten what?"

"What he said when we had him cornered at the edge."

"He was singing," she said.

Brian dropped to his feet. "Before he started singing. You told him we'd called the sheriff. That they were blocking the roads off the Monument. I saw him flinch. He was considering what it meant— that he wasn't getting away. I thought, good, he isn't going to fight us. Then you started boring into him, calling him a murderer, questioning his faith. That's when he started singing."

She had forgotten her lie about the sheriff's blockade. Her overwhelming memory of the night was Neulan's sickening certainty. Her realization that Helen was nothing to him but a sign from God that Neulan was special.

"You kept going after him. Taunting him. Saying God wouldn't have him because there was no forgiveness for murderers. That's when he said, *Now you're a murderer, too.*"

"He didn't!" She would remember; it was practically the confession she had come for. Brian had always thought Neulan wasn't thinking clearly after the blow to his head. But Neulan was cold and rational to the end, taunting, enjoying her pain.

"No way. That's just your guilt at work," she said. "You have nothing to atone for."

"It's your guilt suppressing. Now this glass eye pops up and makes you all paranoid."

Their differences exposed all over again. It was as if Neulan had sensed their vulnerability that night, found the crack between them and cleaved it into a chasm. Perhaps the great manipulator had managed a blameless distance from his victims' fates. Perhaps he did believe his leap of faith would save him. But she was certain of his final, controlling intent. He had left them to become witnesses to his legend or suspects in his death.

"It's not just paranoia," she said. "There's one more thing." Or two. Joe Samson and Isaac. The brothers each held fragments of Meg's secret. She explained how she had told Joe about meeting Neulan at Cold Shivers. If somehow he and Isaac connected the rim and the canyon and Meg's passing mention...

"I get why you wallowed in your mutual connection to Kornhauer. But Jesus, you *told* him we were there at Cold Shivers?"

"He was sharing something very painful and private. It seemed right to reciprocate. I thought it would bring him closure, saying I was at peace with Neulan getting away. I was in the now. I didn't think of it as an *always*."

Brian's weight shifted toward her. "Listen to me. What's done is done. We screwed up and agreed to disagree about turning ourselves in. Nothing happened. And after all this time, the chances are even more remote—into the stratosphere. Even if Neulan did have a glass eye and Joe knows it *and* he remembers your conversation *and* he puts everything together, that doesn't mean he'll reveal it."

"I don't know," she said. "He's a reporter."

"I thought you two had a little thing."

"A passing commiseration. We burned Neulan in effigy and

watched his ashes blow down the street."

"Well, if he's any kind of friend, he'll keep it to himself. What he knows isn't the fundamental problem here. It's that we went too far."

"Neulan chose to go over. I don't feel guilty."

"Then why are you here? You don't feel guilty but you don't want the truth to come out. You want reassurance but you're afraid to ask anyone who can actually tell you what you want to know. Why is that—because screwing up and hiding it doesn't fit your image?"

Brian had nothing to risk. He didn't appreciate what she had, the life she had built, her business, her place in the community. He was living alone in the desert, dealing with third graders from a culture that would never accept him. Feeling holy.

Brian waved his arm to turn on the light. "Sorry, that was mean. Maybe you should go to a lawyer if you want advice."

"I did. Years ago."

His voice registered the blow. "And what did she say?"

"*He.* You don't have to be PC with me."

"I thought it might be one of your lawyer friends."

"They don't do criminal law. Anyway, I didn't want to complicate any friendships with this."

"You're here complicating things. What does that make me?"

"Oh, I'm sure it's different for men, with your deep and nuanced relationships. What time are your buddies coming over for the drum circle?" She was pissed and wanted him to know it. It must be nice to be so pure and laid back and above it all. "He advised me not to come forward, but if I absolutely felt I had to clear my conscience, the best course was to *drop the dime on the ex*, as he put it."

"Well, it sounds like you got competent counsel," Brian said quietly. "Look, the lawyer presented you exactly the alternatives you and I were debating at the time. You got the advice you wanted, to let it go. Follow that. I'm through thinking about what happened."

He moved closer. Another step and he would be against her knees. "We have this tiny opening between us and suddenly a torrent is trying to blast through. You, at least, could prepare for it. I'm still trying to figure out what's going on. I was hoping you drove all this way for more than to ask about a fucking glass eye."

He had taken the risks. He had been willing to sacrifice himself for her. What had she done for him? And what was he asking for?

"Why did you call me?" she said.

He puffed his cheeks. "Look around. I've been here longer than if I'd pled to manslaughter."

"But coming here was your choice."

"It was a consequence of our choices."

"I didn't choose your hang-up calls and mysterygrams."

A weak smile. "I've been informed no message is a message," he said.

"But a confusing one, Brian. Your reaching out felt like a tease. So if there was a different message, explain it to me. Keep it simple. Pretend I'm one of your third graders."

He straightened some books slumping on their bindings and then sat on the edge of the bench, leaning forward, elbows on knees, looking at the floor.

"When I left you, I was leaving the arguments and the tension and the guilt that had ruined us. I gave up on having you—but couldn't shake wanting you. Is that simple enough? I thought I'd forget once I was beyond range of your voice and your flesh and the sight of you walking through a room. But I couldn't let go of the thought of you, the essence, the rightness of you. I couldn't analyze the feeling. I wouldn't even call it hope. It was like trying to understand why chocolate instead of vanilla. I guess I had to replenish that feeling once in a while, to reassure myself you were still real. And without laying myself out there all the way, I wanted to remain real, too. If you didn't feel the same way, I'd never know since you couldn't respond."

It was so much more than she expected.

"Did you know you called the day Amy was hurt? Did I tell you where it happened? I went back to Las Colonias that night, after the scholarship event. So much was colliding. I was a mess. I would have talked to you."

He shook his head. "I had no idea, just like when you drove up."

"I almost turned around."

"Yeah, I'm used to it. I guess this place can be pretty shocking. Well, I'm glad we had this little talk. So nice we could both clear everything up." It was only two steps to the door and he took them.

The *campito* somehow shrank with his departure. She saw how Brian had pared everything down: a plate, a bowl and a cup; a knife, a fork and a spoon; one extra pair of shoes. The only sign of indulgence, his little library on the bench. Waters. Campbell. Frame. Erdrich. Maslow. Pirsig. Keenan. Cleaver. Myth, mind and captivity. And there, between *The Beet Queen* and *Soul on Ice*, a gold metal edge, a drugstore picture frame slipped sideways, a color print from the Taos trip she'd never seen. Her younger self was still anchored at the end of the bridge, but this time in closeup without her sunglasses. Her eyes shimmered and streamers of her hair blazed with backlight. His directions came back to her: *Relax. Forget the wind and feel the sun...pretend you're happy on a warm beach.* And she did pretend. She had never known how beautifully.

The half-door framed him, splayed in the lawn chair outside, his hands clasped behind his head, looking up at the night sky. Of course he saw things the way he did, living where life was unchanging, where he didn't belong, where his hard work produced so little, where the culture accepted privation and the land swallowed failure. It was sad to have arrived in a place where numbness felt like freedom. So very sad for them both.

She stepped onto the trailer hitch above him and said, "I think

I should go."

He leaned back. His upside-down face was hard to read. "Go where? The night drive is a head-on crash waiting to happen. The closest motel is forty-five miles away on the Navajo rez, and it's tourist season. You can spend the night at my place in town if you want."

"Or I could call and see if they have a vacancy," she said.

"Or you could stay here—and I could go to town."

Or.

He climbed out of the chair, waiting for an answer she wasn't ready to give. She should at least call the motel first.

"Is it even possible to get a cell phone signal around here?" she said.

He shrugged. "I know a high point where you could probably pull a bar or two."

"How far a drive?"

"It's shorter to hike there."

"It's dark out."

"Don't worry. After it's cooled off, the snakes go to bed."

Does anybody force or trick you to do things that you do not want to do?

—Vulnerability Index Prescreen for Single Adults

Mishner and Ford sat opposite each other in the Day Center vestibule. They were not allowed inside when they were hard-over drunk, which was most of the time, but their less toasted buddies would bring out coffee for them. Mishner's rosary bead eyes rose from the steaming cup to fix on Isaac. Ford didn't look up. He glumly peeled the plastic from a cold quick-stop burrito as if it were his last meal.

Mishner and Ford. Isaac didn't know their first names, so he was surprised to hear Mishner call him. "Hey, Isaac, where you hanging these days?"

Isaac was out of the storage unit now, living in a tiny rental house across the tracks from downtown. This was not information he shared because when word got around about a place the wrong people always showed up. In exchange for attending a Stage IV lunger in his dwindling days, Isaac got to use the kitchen and sleep on the couch. Because of all his pain medications, Ron Gudmunson needed a housemate who was reliable and drug-free. Ron's caseworker had talked to Sylvia and Sylvia told Isaac.

"You still looking for Wesley Chambers?" Mishner said.

"Has Wesley been here?" Isaac asked.

"He was looking for you. I hear he's taken over that old glue factory." Mishner looked to Ford for confirmation. Ford watched strands of limp factory lettuce sprinkle the floor.

Nice to know where Wesley was. The situation with Ron Gudmunson wouldn't last forever. The glue factory seemed like a genius move. Who would care if anyone took over that rotten place? Maybe Wesley was trying to regroup the guys from the island to help start Thistletown. For the first time in months, Isaac felt as though something good could happen.

The computer had not gotten him into the trouble that Shelly had predicted, but it did lead into tunnels of distraction. He looked up Reagan's lazy eye and discovered that Lincoln and Kennedy also had similar conditions. Three popular presidents who had all been shot. That sent Isaac after William McKinley, who reportedly had a direct, piercing gaze. Before long, Isaac was reading about how Edison had sent an x-ray machine to locate a stray bullet in McKinley's body, and the McKinley-Edison trajectory turned up *Edison's Conquest of Mars*, a science fantasy in which the president and Congress select Edison to direct earth's war against the Martians.

> *"Give me carte blanche," replied Mr. Edison, "and I believe I can have a hundred electric ships and three thousand disintegrators ready within six months."*
>
> *"Your powers are unlimited," said the President, "draw on the fund for as much money as you need," whereupon the Treasurer of the United States was made the disbursing officer of the fund, and the meeting adjourned.*

Once Isaac would have been excited by that ridiculous passage but now it made him sad. Industrialists controlling the treasury was not a revelation; it was an American tradition. He thought of all his work assembling the evidence node-by-node and page-by-page to portray the great General Electric plot. The tape holding his master diagram together had yellowed and crackled. Unfolding it and layering in his meticulous footnote cards for display would require a gymnasium floor. Even if he could scan all the material, it would be incomprehensible at the scale of a computer screen.

None of his newer projects had gone anywhere, either. His poetry cards, the idea he had lifted from Gravy, had confused drivers already buried in text messages. His glass eye posters drew a warning from the cops and those not torn down had disappeared under notices from housepainters and owners of lost cats. He'd received no queries at the Day Center and heard nothing from his Craigslist ad. Local eye clinics would not share patient information and his emails to oculists were never answered. Joe brushed off the idea of a newspaper story. *The finder keeper needs the loser weeper*, his brother said. *Get back to me if you find him.*

Ron spent his days in his bedroom. The room was small and made smaller by the sounds of Ron's television and the miasma from Ron's labored breaths. Isaac carried in a chair when Ron wanted to visit and carried it out again when their time together was over for the day. Ron had been a parts and warehouse man, steady in a job that called for steadiness. He had received and unpacked shipments, moved pallets, stacked boxes and found them again, made deliveries, tracked paperwork and filed it. It was not a life history that gave him much to talk about, so when he heard Isaac was a librarian, he was happy to have the company. Ron thought they had their work in common, moving rectangular packets in and out of storage, and Isaac did not disabuse him.

Ron claimed he had an almost photographic memory. He could call up part numbers and lines on waybills, pinpoint boxes and skids from his desk and route shipments anywhere in the country without looking at a map. An entire warehouse in his head. After he got laid off and before he got sick, he worked at Home Depot, sending customers to the precise locations of the products they sought. Isaac understood. When he had trouble sleeping, he still wandered the aisles at Safeway.

"We thought computers'd make our jobs easier. Hah! The simpler work became, the worse it got. Brains and memory didn't matter any more. We were arms and legs. The computer peckers in the office didn't just track the parts, they tracked us. Go fetch, chop-chop! Scan a sticker. Run it over there. If you did it fast, they wanted it faster."

Ron wanted company while he watched *The Cannonball Run*, a screwball comedy about an outlaw cross-country road rally. Isaac had never sat through the whole thing. Ron had seen it many times and knew all the lines, so he had suppressed the volume. He watched listlessly except when Farrah Fawcett appeared. Walleyed Jack Elam played the doctor who kept her drugged in the back of the ambulance driven by Burt Reynolds and Dom DeLuise. Sammy Davis Jr. drove up with Dean Martin in a red Lamborghini. Isaac remarked how it was strange they'd cast Elam and the glass-eyed Davis in the same movie.

Ron knew about his search. He said, "That's 'cause glass eyes are funny. You take it too seriously. Dean Martin did this long prank to buy a drink with a glass eye in *The Sons of Katie Elder*. You seen that one?"

He hadn't. He hadn't researched any movies because they weren't real. Maybe there was a whole other layer of this he had missed.

"It's probably on YouTube," Ron said.

Ron didn't have Internet. Isaac thought he might look for it later. After a time, Ron drowsed. Isaac stirred to leave and Ron pinned Isaac's arm to the bed. He pointed at the screen and smiled. All the racers joined in a brawl with a biker gang led by Peter Fonda. Like the rest of the film, the scene was a broad parody of movie cliches—bodies flying through windows, impossible kung fu leaps, invincible noggins, accidental knockouts, clobbering your own man and last-second reversals. Ron watched to the end of the fight. Then his head tilted again.

Isaac sat a while longer, half watching the cartoonish action and half listening to the respirator tap at the end of each breath. All the driving teams were stereotyped odd couples—blonds and brunettes;

black and white; masculine and effeminate; fat and skinny; sane and crazy; drunk and sober. Having a buddy was all that mattered on the race to the finish.

Ron knew he was done for. He didn't need a roommate to bring him pills or run errands. He wanted a *compadre* who had his back, who knew his pain wasn't just from the cancer. Even if it was too late for his co-pilot to hurtle in at the last second and clonk Death over the head, Ron deserved that guy. Everybody did.

Isaac took out the chair and left the television on in case Ron awakened while he was gone. Then he shouldered his backpack and locked the front door behind him. He told himself he'd grab some wi-fi and cheer himself up with that Dean Martin clip, but instead he kept walking.

Since the warehouse was the most solid building at the rendering plant, Isaac began looking for Wesley there. Someone had clearly been inside recently. The plywood over the front entry had been pried back. Isaac fixed his headlamp and stepped inside. The interior had the peculiar odor of abandonment—urine and smoke composted with newspapers and wool. The floor was littered with broken beer bottles and miscellaneous party trash. Graffiti ran wild over the walls. The office divider walls had been torn out for firewood. Plumbing and electrical wiring had been stripped.

He thought he heard footsteps and voices deep inside the warehouse. "Wesley?"

No answer. Why would there be? No one was supposed to be in here. He stepped deeper inside. Past the offices, the interior opened up to a cavernous space. He called again. "It's Isaac."

This time, a voice. *Back here.* A flashlight illuminated a far wall, silhouetting a figure seated on an overturned bucket.

"Wesley?" He passed a stack of barrels, a few knocked from formation and rolled on their sides. Broken glass crunched underfoot. He bore carefully over the debris, nudging a path with his headlamp.

Something flew at him and fluttered overhead. Bats. He hunched along. He sensed something snatch at his head and as he ducked, his headlamp lifted. A bright swirl as the light went out. The flashlight in the distance switched off, too. His blood coursed in his ears, his scalp primed to leap off his skull.

"What did you bring us?" That was definitely not Wesley's voice.

The blackout was seamless. Two men in here, maybe more. No reason yet to think them unfriendly. He'd surprised them. "I don't have much—some cheese and crackers."

The first man rose from his seat. A rattle and squawk as the bucket scraped the floor. A painfully bright pinpoint beam approached. With his hand, Isaac blocked the light from the tactical flashlight and turned to locate the other man. The light had burned an afterimage in his retinas.

"Crackers? We were hoping for an Apple." The invisible men cackled.

His computer. It had to be Mishner and Ford. They must have seen him with it.

"It's just a Toshiba."

"Better than nothing," said the voice behind him. Ford.

Mishner aimed his light at the floor. "Drop the pack."

Isaac carefully laid down the pack. Besides the computer, it contained his key with the Samsonite tag, which they probably wouldn't figure out went to his storage unit. His notebook and pencils. A windbreaker. Socks. Vending machine crackers. Nothing major. Ford slid the pack across the floor with his foot.

"You said Wesley was here."

"Your darling Wesley. He talks like he's king of the river but he's a chicken shit. He ratted out Screech and Dexter for hurting that cop. But when Dexter's buddies torched him out, he ran like a bitch."

Isaac took the news in his gut. Is that what happened? The fire was set to get Wesley? Mishner might be making that up, too.

"Now pockets."

He had nothing but five dollars and the key to Ron Gudmunson's house. He held out the bill in one hand and dropped the key on his foot so it wouldn't make a sound when it hit. It pinged away somewhere on the floor.

"Where's your wallet?"

"Don't have one."

"Fuck, Samson, what's wrong with you?"

Ford put hands on him. *Jake's knife*, Isaac thought. He started down for the sheath in his boot. Shit—he'd left it on a side table next to the couch. Ford's knee hit him in the face, then something else across the back of his neck. A kick in the ribs and another close to his kidneys.

"You asked for it, fucker. Stay down or I'll stick you."

The lights retreated toward the door. A copper penny taste in his mouth. He groped around for the pack but it was gone.

"You never saw nothing."

They were right. He blindly patted the floor for Ron's key, finding only glass and nails and bits of the unknown. He gave up searching before he lost track of where he'd seen the lights disappear. Reaching outside, he vomited against the building. He could already feel swelling over his cheekbone; he'd have to wait and see about the ribs. The police station was on the way to Ron's house but what would they do? Some trespassing vagrants got in a fight. What else is new? Mishner and Ford would say he was mistaken. Or he started it. Crazy Isaac. They never saw a computer. Two against one. Their word against his.

The doors to the house were locked. The only light, a blue flicker from the bedroom window. Isaac peered in. A slight lift to the sheets, Ron's open mouth a dark circle. The play of colors from the unseen screen. Isaac imagined Ron in a morphine fog wandering his fading warehouse, where work blended into obsolescence, dreams into computers, Dean Martin buying a drink with Sammy Davis's eye, *Cannonball Run* meets *Katie Elder*. Ron's photographic memory soon to be unrecoverable. Isaac had been stupid. A loser like him had no right to rouse his frail host. He found a tarp stuffed in the rafters of the empty carport. He rolled himself up in it and lay against the bottom of the back door as if he might stop a draft from seeping through the crack into Ron's house.

Home is your life's grandest display and the first place you go to hide.

— "Home" with Meg Mogrin, *Grand Junction Style*

An expanse of dark and undefined scrub lay between the *campito* and the alleged cellular hotspot. Brian carried an elbow-shaped metal flashlight that might have served in World War II. Its dim yellow ray was close to expiring, more turn signal than headlight, but it could still do damage in hand-to-hand combat.

He led her into a web of trails that seemed to have grown out of the land rather than been worn into it. The one he chose, scarcely a foot wide and crossed by quail runs, seemed well-traveled.

"I thought you were alone out here," she said.

"It doesn't take much traffic to lay down a trail on this ground. Coyotes find routes. I follow the coyotes."

"How do you know where you are?" she said. "I got lost in broad daylight."

"You learn," he said. "All these paths connect to something else, so eventually I can get anywhere on foot."

"Even across Hopi land?"

"If we were Navajo grazing sheep here, it'd be a different story, but we're away from the closed areas."

She risked one of Brian's discourses to ask, "Why is it all tribes claim their land is sacred?"

"Because it is, no matter how harsh. Being there makes it the center of the world. They take care of it because the homeland sustains them and vice versa. If they spoil what they have, they're forced to wander. The tribe next door doesn't want their company and the spirits of their ancestors will be pissed if they leave. Staying in place makes so much sense. They call home sacred and populate the other regions with ghosts and monsters. Then there's even less reason to stray."

He described what he called the white man's version of the Hopi emergence legend: lost people found their way from a failed world to the next one. They chose hard work and humility and accepted the job of holding the world together. With their sacrifice, the human journey was supposed to turn out better this time.

"This center of the world stuff isn't just about putting earth's well being above everything. It's about individuals taking seriously their responsibility for where they dwell. If you live selfishly, you destroy your home. The white man has this only figured out half-way. To satisfy our desires, we surround ourselves in luxury and destroy other places instead."

She had missed Brian. Her Grand Junction friends were sensitive and well-read, but they were more absorbed in work and family. Brian uncoupled from his work without neglecting it, making her wish she could, too. Around him, she felt connected to ancient wisdom without the flightiness of the homeospiritual crowd. Did he know the effect he had on her? How he made her want to be better than she was?

They had been climbing gradually. He stopped at an outcrop above a series of rocky switchbacks that dropped to a long incline. Two water tanks squatted in the distance, backlit by a glow from the town tucked below them.

Brian said, "I should've asked about your life instead of blabbing all the way. Try your phone here. You'll find some motels in Chinle."

Meg had passed through a roundabout at Chinle. She imagined returning, pulling in late and alone; the motel's generic lobby with an appliqué of Native symbols; the smell of bleach in the cold sheets; the senior citizens waiting for the morning bus tour blinking at powdered eggs and fry bread for breakfast. Unbearable. Booking a decent room before she left was such an obvious precaution. Now here she was, splayed like an open suitcase in the middle of Brian's retreat. He had a right to be confused. And it was only going to get more complicated. There was nowhere else she wanted to spend the night.

The promised two bars appeared and her phone displayed the missed calls that had come while her phone sat in the car. Eve. A client mulling a counter-offer. Lew Hungerman. And a fourth number that wasn't in her caller ID. She asked Brian for fifteen minutes, enough time to call around to motels—and deal with this business. He handed her the flashlight, checked his Casio and trotted down the trail.

He doesn't even know my phone's a hundred-times better light.

The clients had made up their minds about the house; they simply needed reassurance they weren't suckers if they agreed to pay a few thousand dollars more. Meg left instructions at her office to prepare the offer sheet so it could be sent in the morning. She moved on to Eve's message.

Meg. We haven't talked since your tour with Lew. How did it go? Listen, have you heard anything about Betterment courting other cities? The Chamber swears we're it, but I smell something. I just don't want to be blind-sided. Okay, call me.

So Meg wasn't the only one. *Courting other cities* sounded like Idaho Falls. She thought she'd better check Hungerman's message before returning Eve's call.

Hi. It's Lew. Just wondering if you've given more thought to my invitation. I'm scheduled for a fly-in on Thursday, exact return TBD, but I could have you back Saturday or Sunday. No pressure. Separate rooms, of course, if that's what you're concerned about. I might've come across as too...I don't know, eager in some respect. If not, I understand. It's short notice. Anyway, I'm not giving up on getting you involved. So...let me know.

She ran the message through again, to see if she felt any less fondled. She heard Hungerman testing her probity, easing her mind toward his bidding. He'd made it sound as if sleeping with him were her idea! She had to talk to Eve before she told him to buzz off. Something was weird.

She hoped the unknown number would be something straightforward.

Hello. This is Joe Samson from The Clarion.

She stabbed the pause button. Was every loose end in her life converging? Had Isaac talked to him and somehow... No way she was calling Joe back tonight. Maybe she should forget all three calls, pretend they got lost in the ozone. She looked for a sign of Brian returning. Nothing moved. An ominous flash in the far western sky. And then, the vibration from an incoming call. Eve.

"Meg. Where are you? You sound like you're on an ice floe in the Arctic. Listen, a couple of Lew's people had a sitdown with city planning staff today. Mostly presubmission formalities, explaining the drawings package, blah, blah, planner stuff. And one of our guys noticed the renderings they presented seemed...generic. Not at all site-specific. Anyway, it was just a vibe he got. He mentioned it to the Betterment crew and they said, oh, yeah, those concept drawings were done before they'd narrowed down the locations. That's what he said, *locations*—plural. Are you there, hon? I know I'm blathering."

"I'm here," Meg said. *So it was possible.*

"Then I call Lew, *do not tell me you're still considering other cities for this!* And he got all cute and said of course there was a downselect process or some b.s., and then he says, *and I'm sure you'll put together your most attractive package no matter what.* No-matter-what what? How is there a *most* attractive if it isn't a contest? Is he serious? Is he playing around? Tell me what the hell's going on."

"Um... I..."

"You're breaking up," Eve said. "I refuse to lose this. The stars will never align this way again. Fine, let's go all out. But I will not lay myself on the line to move the Council if he only intends to use us to negotiate a better deal somewhere else. McCallam will crucify me."

What could Meg say? She didn't know anything about Betterment's plans and couldn't say if she did. The flight to Idaho Falls might only inflame Eve's distrust—or worse, Eve might urge her to go with him.

Lights pulsed on the horizon. Suddenly, a burst of lightning strobed above the cloud scrim. It clarified into an uprooted forest of thrashing electric branches that obliterated the cowering quarter moon. A metallic zing suffused the air. And no sound. No thunder or wind. Just this great shaking, as if the earth had half-repressed its fury.

"Eve, you should see this. We're not being attacked are we?" Terrorists didn't have missiles, did they? That left the Russians. Aliens. God.

"See what? Where *are* you?"

"I'll try to text you a picture," Meg said.

"Don't change the subject. Whatever your deal is with Lew, I refuse to be duped. I have to live here when his game's over. I hope you feel the same way."

How strange to agonize over this disclosure, when Meg had once coolly concealed a man's death. Eve was her friend. She expected loyalty. Hungerman expected to get into her panties.

"He asked me to go on a trip with him."

"What kind of trip?"

"A trip out of state."

"I meant business or pleasure. I'll assume business," Eve said.

"He's been cagey about that, too."

"Are you going to tell me where—or do we have to play Twenty Questions?"

"I'll give you a hint. It starts with an *I*."

"Not Illinois."

"No."

"Idaho? What's in fricking Idaho? Boise? Coeur d'Alene?"

"Let's say it's a city roughly comparable to ours. When I checked it out, I didn't find anything in the news about Betterment."

"Of course until the last week, our paper would hardly be saying anything, either," Eve said. She sounded calmer. "He has us all nicely compartmentalized, doesn't he? So are you going?"

"Of course not."

"No, how could you? I thought I was doing you a favor with him. Instead, I put you in a pickle. I'm sorry. Maybe there is something going on. Or maybe he knew you'd turn him down and would tell me about it so I'd believe there is." Eve sighed. "God, politics has twisted my thinking about everybody. Shoot me that picture, okay?"

The call went dead. Meg pointed her phone's camera at the storm but the images disappointed. The blazing tributaries had blurred to smeared chalkboard sentence diagrams. She texted one image to Eve: *Armageddon loses something in translation.* The message appeared to go, but the strokes crazing the heavens might have wiped it out before it reached a satellite. The entire landscape jittered as if an old war newsreel were shuddering off its sprockets. Brian crossed under the tracers, running up the switchbacks. When he reached her his skin smelled clean as a surgeon's.

"We should get back. That storm's far away but anything can happen," he said. "Did you find a room?"

She thought her answer made his pace quicken.

On their return, she presented Brian a fuller *now* of her life—her business recovering, Vaughn's evolution, Pandora's record demise as her latest scholarship girl and her uncomfortable position with Wesley. She described her sense of being maneuvered by Eve and Hungerman and Sister Rose, how each fanned a different ember of her ego. And the surprising conversation about running for office. Yes, she had name awareness with her magazine column and advertising, and yes, the community needed progressive leadership to attract new business. But through Eve she had glimpsed the corrosive effects of public life. The constant negativity. Ready assumptions of corruption or incompetence.

"I was surprised you wanted to move back there," he said. "When we met you couldn't stand the place."

That wasn't quite right. She loved the place; it was home. She couldn't stand what staying there demanded of her—to be stable, dutiful and competent. To fit in. To achieve, but not too much, to fulfill her destiny as a smart girl who might think about doing something different with her hair. She had in mind a new self more expressive and exciting than a blond with brown roots and a banker husband. She wanted to create. The first step to her reinvention was a new environment, away from hometown assumptions and expectations. After college, like a patient receiving a Betterment Institute facelift, she could return to amazement and acclaim, fully transformed. Into what, exactly, she expected to discover.

Then Helen's bright flame was extinguished. In her daring and ambition, Helen had taken risks to win attention. To an artist, exposure meant the spotlight, a path to success, but in an uncaring landscape the word described harsh conditions, severe drops and fatal consequences. Caution that smothered also protected. In the aftermath of Helen's death, Meg recalibrated her life. She would inspire people from a more grounded position as a teacher.

And then a second shock. Instruction turned out to be much harder than she expected, the classroom more chaotic, students beyond her control—findings made more dispiriting by Brian's easy brilliance with children. He came home chattering about the sweetness and delight that poured from his kids while she sat in knots tied by her day's defiance and insurgencies. Why did they resist Robert Frost and Emily Dickinson; Huck Finn, Jane Eyre and Miss Jane Pittman? If her students were lethargic in the presence of greatness, the blame must lie with her teaching. *You are not who you think you are not who you think you are not who you think you are* was written behind her on the board a hundred times over.

Her failure in Denver cast no shadows on the other side of the mountains so she returned home, already authenticated as a high achiever—with a new name and a husband, some whispered, who seemed too good to be true. With her father's help, she launched herself again, this time into the receptive circle of real estate, never considering that she had also landed within the orbit of Neulan Kornhauer.

Brian read her silence and moved the topic to the present. "So you're writing a column. That's cool. Take some pictures of the *campito* while you're here. You could do one about living small."

"That's not just small, it's tiny. I'd be out of business if everyone lived like you."

"You were almost out of business when everyone lived in houses they couldn't afford. Why not write about the things that really matter? Write about *why* people live. About *how* to live together, instead of apart from each other and divorced from the land."

He wasn't so pure. He lived more apart than anyone she knew, but she was not in a mood to argue. "It's a home column, not a political column."

Or a relationships advice column.

The light show flashing behind him eclipsed his face. "It *is* a political column if you never say anything about the real costs of living the way we do," he said. "Money always makes a political statement—whether people have it or not, how they get it, where they spend it. And housing is where people spend the most on themselves. That has to inform how you write about home. Do you ever mention your work with the homeless?"

She didn't want to talk about that, either. Certainly not in *Grand Junction Style*. *Her work with the homeless* sounded so noble and selfless instead of what it really was—a sham display of social consciousness that might not help them at all. She had not meant her role to turn out this way. It was supposed to be a feel-good thing, a nice moral endeavor, not a compromise.

"It seems exploitative to write about," she said. "It feels like, look at me, the charitable businesswoman, the benign benefactor."

"Well, yours is not the story there, is it?"

The heavenly display gradually lost intensity on the way back. The darkness reasserted. A blister had developed on the back of her heel. Out-of-breath and out-of-place, Meg scrambled to catch a man completely at home.

Brian stopped just as the trailer's mushroom dome came into view. A light in the window.

"That shouldn't be on."

"I might've left it."

"The timer takes care of it."

"Trouble then?"

"Depends on your definition."

Then she saw the battered blue Mazda pickup, two bumperstickers on the tailgate: *Do what's right* and *Save what's left*. A mountain bike slung on its side in the bed. Not exactly the ride of a burglar.

"Alex!" he called.

The trailer door opened and the light cast a figure in full silhouette.

"What an epic night!" A woman's voice.

A shiver of lightning illuminated olive skin, a black bell-rope braid over her shoulder. Meg immediately thought Native American but Alex could have been Greek, Hispanic, Creole, all in one.

"A friend," Brian whispered. "We teach together."

Do you.

The friend—the young friend—stood above them on the step of the wagon. Her assertive crouch and cargo shorts projected a slight sense of military occupation. At Meg's nose level, a bicycle chain ring mark was visible on the inside of her right calf. Her nicely toned right calf.

"Hey," she said, "I brought you an apple pie."

Brian offered a breezy introduction to defuse his embarrassment. Or perhaps to prevent the feline Alex from delivering a neck-breaking pounce.

"Meg—as in *Meg*-Meg? I've heard so much about you." Alex waved and ducked back through the door, returning with a crisp, brown-latticed pie.

"That top crust—it looks like bacon," Meg said.

"Applewood smoked with maple sugar. I got inspired. Bri, I see you still have some of the *dulce leche*. That'll be an awesome combo."

Fit, offhand, confident, she had the ethnically ambiguous look so in demand with national advertisers: part mountain-biking brown she-devil and part apple-pie-baking paleface dolly next door. When did that girl combo become an option for real? If Alex ever delivered a pizza to her table, Meg would tip extra simply to express her appreciation for evolution, the melting pot, and the feminist brush-clearing that had given America this Eco-Babe.

Alex dropped lightly off the end of the trailer, gave Brian a hug and tossed a *nice meeting you* to Meg. The Mazda erupted tiny knocks as if about to produce popcorn. Neither headlight pointed where the truck was aimed to travel.

Campito life suddenly seemed so much less monkish. "She's lovely," Meg said.

"Uh-huh."

Alex's single tail light winked goodbye.

"She didn't have to leave. We're not married. I don't care."

"Are you still doing that snap-judgment thing, where you pre-label someone within three seconds?"

"Sort of. I'm trying to quit."

"And?"

"Eco-Babe."

Brian shrugged. "I know, I'm too old for her. The social circles are pretty limited out here. We see each other in the summer. It's too awkward during school. Such a tight little world—three different groups of Anglos who stick together and talk about the other two. The teachers. The BIA-BLMers. The Indian Health Service docs."

"I'm sorry if I got in the way. I'm glad you have a relationship." Not entirely glad. But it was good to see that he had a life beyond the classroom, his desert runs and this heartbreaking retreat.

"This is her last year. She's going to grad school and not coming back. That's the relationship." He made a point of studying the diminishing events in the northern sky. "And you?"

No fair. He had driven to the edge of nowhere and still found someone. Her life pulsed with people and challenge and activity, yet without men who wrote her poems. She'd come here to figure out a situation, not to catch his semi-girlfriend delivering late evening pies. And certainly not to acknowledge how adept she had become at living alone. But she hadn't expected a familiar t-shirt to knock her a little sideways or to enjoy hearing a whiteman's version of Hopi wisdom or to cross the drift of a scent she'd once loved. She hadn't imagined the old tension mellowing into something more like playing tag.

"Does your offer to put me up still stand?" she said.

"My government pad? I can't vouch for its state of housekeeping."

"I'd really prefer it out here."

"Mmkay." His head cocked as if trying to pinpoint the source of a faint sound. The storm shook one more fist of light and tucked in behind the clouds. "I don't know what that means."

"It means I'm not ready to leave right now, that's all." That wasn't all. It was just all she knew for sure.

A rumble and a wobble as if a semi had passed close, then a ticking that quickened to a snare drum rattle. The dry, silent storm, hovering like an omen, had warned of this. Gravel-loads of hail hammered the *campito's* metal roof, a full rocking assault. Her body hummed to vibration and the clean ozone smell. Her arm swept the mattress and found the far wall. *Right...* Not Brian, only his sheets and the shirt she slept in. He had curled in the back of her Enclave, either to stand guard or keep himself safe from her unspoken appeal. He did not understand why this moment was so necessary to her now. Their marriage was over but their custody of disquiet endured. Now, instead of talking they sprawled in each other's vehicles, going nowhere, awaiting another drumming. She considered sending a signal with her car's remote. A quick tap. *You're it!* But it was three-thirty now, too late for mixed messages. Too late, period.

Meg's breakfast pie was served plain with a fork on a salad plate and Brian's with a spoon and a blob of ice cream on a dinner plate. *The* dinner plate. *The* spoon. The little dog laughing. Meg wondered why the spoon ran away with the dish. Perhaps the fork had already found someone else.

"One of everything. You really don't entertain much, do you?"

Brian cupped his bowl of coffee in both hands. He blew across its black surface. "There's not much call for it, especially first thing in the morning."

What was he telling her? Meg cut into the pie. It seemed less formidable now that it had been sliced into wedges. At first bite, sweet and salty, the oily crunch of bacon made it not very pie-like. More a bed of apples topped with bacon. Interesting but not magnificent. Of course, the taste probably wasn't Eco-Babe's entire point.

"A life of pie for breakfast. I'd like that recipe," she said.

Brian's face reappeared from behind the bowl. "I could get it for you."

"The recipe for being Alex?"

His gaze fixed on the bowl. "I don't believe in recipes."

"Baking's different," she said. "You have to be precise."

Brian poked at the ice cream pooling around the bottom crust. "I'm sorry I can't be more helpful to you."

"It's pointless, I suppose, to dwell on the past after all this time—not even dwell—to go back there at all. Not much can be undone at this point."

"No, except maybe to bring some closure for others."

"Others?"

"For the people who still think Neulan's alive. Victims' families. Investigators. Even his family. This whole glass eye thing must have dredged them up in you."

They should have been, but no. You were.

He carved a chip of bacon and halved an apple slice, then apportioned a bit of crust and spooned it all up with a crescent of ice cream. He continued to clear his plate slowly and methodically, as if dividing an estate among a bevy of equal heirs.

"Tell me what you're thinking," she said.

"I'm thinking how I hate speeches that begin with, *If you want my advice...*"

"Go ahead. I'll tell you if I hate it after I hear it."

"Maybe later. We always said this thing was going to be a team deal." He waited for her affirmation. "A united front. No finger-pointing, no compromising, no one railroading the other into something. Not one person sacrificing themselves."

"But it happened anyway."

"Who are we talking about here?"

"I could never do this," she said.

"That was the idea."

They stepped outside to a meadowlark's trill. *Chee-chee-chittalo Chittalo-chow.* And an answer: *Chee-chee-chittalitta-chee.* All yesterday's dust was scrubbed from the air. The sage burst forth with the turpentine aroma of a painter's studio. Ruts in the road coddled precious water. They picked their way around mudslicks that already had started to dry and climbed a hogback that split into fingers pointed toward the far mesas. The view seemed featureless, worn shapes and muted colors, the same dull landscape she'd driven through the day before. Brian reached for her and found the tips of her fingers.

"We caused a man's death," he said quietly. "I did. You did. He did. However you slice it, however you choose to remember it, we were part of his end. The more time passes, you'd think it would be easier to erase, but I feel worse. I'm not talking about guilt, exactly—more a gathering awareness of something too complicated to tackle all at once. You may drill away at what a life means, but the fluency comes with time, the way a first language seeps in. You hear before you speak. You see before you read. Keep at it and you someday arrive at wisdom.

"We killed a man. I stopped him in his tracks and then his time ended. Call it manslaughter or reckless endangerment if you don't want to say murder. A man younger than me never got a chance to change, to repent, to face punishment, whatever was waiting for him. You say he was a monster. Okay, that night was the only time I saw him, but I spend a year with a new bunch of faces in my classroom and can still be wrong about them. When they leave at the end of the year, I think I can tell who'll be a star, who'll be trouble, who'll muddle through, who'll die drinking on the rocks. But I'm wrong sometimes. Somebody else gets through to the kid I didn't. Something I never saw coming deflects a girl from a bad path to a better one. It reminds me how long a life can be and how many chances it contains.

"So—every sunrise I think, here's one more day where we're all heading out for a new shot at life. We deserve a chance to make something better of it. Yeah, maybe Neulan would have done something bad with that chance. But I'm not God. I teach third and fourth graders. I'm supposed to hope. It's the only way I can do my job."

Poor Brian. Poor, poor Brian. By now he should have completed his atonement.

He clasped her hand in both of his. "My advice, Meg: if you were able to forget everything before the eye showed up, go back to forgetting. And if you can't, the source of this random object is not the problem you need to solve."

For all his great sensitivity and urging her toward her better self, Brian had never been able to see things from her side. She had tried and failed more than once and finally she had a decent life and a secure future. She was on the inside now, with a town counting on her to make a difference. Unaccepted and wasting his talents, he had nothing left to give up in his end-of-a-dirt-road life. He didn't appreciate what she still had to risk. He was the one who needed the advice.

"You should just follow Alex to grad school next year. Move on to something different. You deserve it."

"And you don't?"

It was not quite an embrace. He might have been a tree holding her aloft in his boughs. Suspended, she allowed herself to sway. The meadowlarks were calling out in the brush, locating each other, saying whatever birds say when there is no danger in view. Over his shoulder, the panorama reduced to earth and sky, like a great pair of hands cupping something small and precious. If Brian meant her to feel comforted, it was working, even though Meg knew she was being enveloped in a goodbye.

She waved her car's remote key fob under his nose. "I almost beeped you last night."

"Whoa, not another missed booty call."

He snatched it playfully and began pressing the buttons like a mad concertina player. The locks thunked and parking lights flashed. A kitchen timer chime came from the liftgate. The panic alarm flushed three quail.

"Now you see why I didn't."

"Definitely a mixed message," he said. "This button doesn't do anything." A circular arrow with the point coming back almost to the tail.

"Oh, that's the remote start. You have to hit the lock first and then hold it down."

"Seriously?" Brian weighed the device in his palm as if considering how far he could hurl it. "Since when are you too delicate to get in a cold car?"

She had never used it. The remote came with the car. She was tired of defending herself to him. Not everything in life came down to the choices he would make.

She drove all the way to the Lukachukai turnoff where the first stop sign suggested a different route home. She checked the GPS. The way east toward Shiprock looked paved all the way but the earth view images rendered the road in disconcerting fragments. Instead, she bore north, back the way she'd come, until the highway intersected with the road to Four Corners. She took it, then angled north at Teec Nos Pos, where two bleak trading posts stood apart from each other, as if to avoid catching what had killed the neighboring Chevron.

Long, dull vistas. Barely enough traffic for her to mind the stripes on the road. Ahead, a branch in her lane. A FedEx truck bearing from the other direction. Imperfect timing. The shoulder appeared dodgy. Oh, well, it's an SUV. Run over the stick. *Not a stick!* A thick bullsnake basking on the asphalt. *Too late.* Her mirror showed the snake flinging itself impossibly upright, tall as a man, an essing jump rope of outrage. When its strikes at the heavens lost height, it still flailed its body upward in quavering sideways loops. The writhing did not end until she returned her eyes to the road ahead.

As she drove, the image looped. Long ago tribes had followed this deer trail. White men made it a road. The state paved it. The sun warmed the earth and the reptile found the radiant comfort of the asphalt. A truck traveled this route in response to random orders. Meg chose a different way home. Her father, the insurance man, had taught her the danger of a sudden swerve. On this day these accidental influences produced something unexpected: a serpent discovers it can stand erect. What a revelation! Perhaps it looks across the desert and remembers the Garden.

As a girl, she had memorized the Golden Rule before she grasped its meaning. The words first sounded in her child's brain as a nonsense string of syllables, like the *ella-meno-pee* middle of the alphabet: *Undo unto others as you would have them undo unto you.* Eventually she untangled the language and understood that a good-for-good exchange reversed the compounded wrongs of the Old Testament tooth-for-tooth. But the Golden Rule failed to account for neighbors who were incapable of good or for men who believed everything should come unto them. Evil done to others demanded undoing.

**We will lose interest in selfish things
and gain interest in our fellows.**

—The Promises, The Big Book

Glen Leary's first painting job turned out all right. Vaughn fronted the money to get Leary's truck out of impoundment with the idea he'd continue to work off the loan. Back to living in his truck, Leary became more difficult to pin down. He picked up some work with a trailer flipper and claimed he was too busy to take on Vaughn's odd jobs. To Vaughn, the promises, excuses and evasions sounded familiar, and so did Leary's failure to keep up on his IOU. Bad times or good times, a drinking man could always find the reason he wanted to get high or slide downhill.

Leary had complained to Vaughn about a summons for a bullshit public urination charge. The municipal court docket was online now, much easier to look up court dates than in the old days. Vaughn had already kissed the money goodbye. He wanted to set eyes on the kids. He figured Leary would drag them to court, looking for sympathy. It had certainly worked on him.

Vaughn asked his friend Leonard to provide backup with his Old Testament scowl if Leary tried to weasel away. Leonard had eased out of ranching and now volunteered with a therapeutic riding program. Retarded, blind kids, crippled. Soldiers back with wounds and PTSD. The cop hurt in the summer was there now.

"Never loan money to a man who tried to pitchfork you," said Leonard.

"You've never loaned money to anyone."

"Guess I have it pretty much covered then."

At first glance Vaughn thought the Farmer's Market had moved to City Hall and filled all the parking spaces with tents, folding tables and banners. Then he noticed the lawn chairs and a portable basketball hoop. Rugs, blankets, wooden pallets and bedrolls covered the pavement. Each metered slot occupied and not one contained a car. People waved signs: *No Home is No Crime, Parks for All People* and *Homeless—not Worthless!* A cop tweeted and windmilled his arm to urge traffic past the barricaded spectacle. Car horns responded in short taps and long blares.

A woman pushed a baby stroller loaded with oranges, bagels and bottles of water. A man with a bloodhound face slashed at a dead-strung guitar, singing "This Land is Your Land" in a nasal imitation of Bob Dylan imitating Woody Guthrie. A fellow in a knit hat and vegetable-patch-colored scarf sat under a potted tree. He wore a Che Guevara t-shirt under a tweed sport coat. Vaughn scanned the crowd in case Leary was somewhere in the confusion.

Che stepped up onto two milk crates pulled from the foliage. He squeezed two siren whoops from a battery-powered megaphone, then looked to make sure the camera from Channel Eleven was recording.

"Welcome to our new people's park!" His amplified voice, flat and metallic, slapped the music store wall across the street. He put down the bullhorn and shouted in a hoarse voice, "Now, you might think this is a street..." he crooked his neck back and forth in an exaggerated manner "...but it looks like a park to me. How so? Because it's being taken over by *homeless people!*"

His expression of mock horror brought forth laughter, applause and whistles. "That's right, the City thinks you're taking over this whole valley! Taking over the parks, the downtown and the freeway exits. Hanging around ATMs, traffic lights and sidewalk cafes. Now here you are, stealing the good parking spaces—and most of us don't even have cars!"

He waited for the laugh. "Pavement makes a crappy park, so why are we here? Because for all the attention we get from the cops and City Council, we're invisible when it comes to housing. Because for all the laws they want us to follow, the City won't follow its own Ten-Year Plan to End Homelessness. Instead, they send the police to chase you out of the shelter you have. They've made The Point and Las Colonias uninhabitable. Fifty camps gone, at least, without adding one new unit of affordable housing or one new shelter bed. So today we're claiming this street to replace the ground that's been lost. We're not squatting. We're paying for these spaces—plugging the meters at ten cents an hour—and there's no law to say we can't sit here peacefully. So…" He signalled two men standing in a brick planter behind him. "We're calling this encampment *Winslowville* because the street is what passes for shelter in Mayor Eve Winslow's city."

The men unfurled a bed sheet declaring *Winslowville* in rainbow letters. A cheer went up and another man with the shoulders of a bouncer joined Che on the milk crates. His face was half forehead. The other half reminded Vaughn of his days hauling around a fifty-pound headache.

"We gotta get inside," he said.

At the court entrance, they emptied their pockets, raised their arms for the wand and regrouped in the back row of seats. Vaughn didn't recognize anyone but the place was as familiar as the offenses about to unfold: shoplifting, terroristic threats, driving under the influence and public urination. It was probably the old straight-arrow Len's first time in a courtroom.

He and Leonard had coincided at passing intervals, none that seemed momentous at the time. Two boys: one orphaned, the other unparented. Later, young men at odds: one looking to land where the other was barely hanging on. A litany of minor grievance ensued: selfishness earned an eviction, an offering became trouble, a condolence went unnoticed and a small favor turned into a lecture.

Leonard aired his thoughts with the frequency and duration of a lunar eclipse, but Vaughn believed his friend finally accepted how deeply they were twinned. Certain kinds of hurt were unreachable, no matter how much talk or drink you sent stumbling after it.

They sat together in silence on the hard seats. Leary didn't show.

The speeches outside were over. The occupiers lounged in their spaces. At the end of the block, a meter monitor pulled up in his three-wheeler and opened the back.

"You'll never see that money," Leonard said.

"I know it," said Vaughn.

"But that ain't all you were here about."

"Maybe not."

"Them kids're gone," Leonard said. "Maybe it'll work out for 'em. Look at us."

So says a failed cowboy who walks in circles with horses that have retards on their backs to a disowned drunk who'd managed to get semi-lucky. They were not what you'd call a scientific sample.

The meter monitor placed red hoods over the meters despite the arm-waving appeal of Che and the blockheaded bouncer man.

"Things're different now. Kids are, too," said Vaughn, although he hardly had any experience in that regard. His siblings were strangers, long scattered under different last names: Frank, Gerald, Vernon, Connie and the stillborn Lucinda.

Leonard had had a foster boy at the ranch for a while, which made him an authority in comparison. He said, "It's hard to sort out a mess you didn't make. You tend to spruce up the easy parts. With kids you can't just jump in and out."

Hanging with the program had not been Vaughn's strong suit, and some things could be neglected only for so long until they became too stuck to fix. His back might've straightened out if he'd done his rehab like he was supposed to. Now he'd been crooked longer than he'd been straight.

"I pity that lady cop, trapped on a saddle and listening to you point out her shortcomings," Vaughn said.

"Come out and watch sometime. It might change your opinion of my recuperative influence."

"So she's coming around?"

"Working on it. Amy's invited to throw the first pitch at a Rockies game next spring. She'd like to make the leather pop."

"People'll be happy just to see her out there."

"I guess throwing a ball's a balance deal. Right now she's still trying not to fall on her face."

"Like the rest of us," Vaughn said.

**What's the least-used space in your house?
For many, it's the guest room.**

— "Home" with Meg Mogrin, *Grand Junction Style*

Soon after she bought her house, Meg learned the limits of her tolerance for yard work. Gravel, cactus, clumps of native grasses and drought-resistant shrubs replaced the thirsty lawn, labor-intensive annuals and fussy beds of perennials. The only remaining evidence of the prior Eden was a rank of unruly snowberry and a grape arbor that framed her backyard view.

From the kitchen the Book Cliffs were just now surrendering their dusty rose to a bluing that foreshadowed nightfall. Her patio chairs had been pushed against the hedge. Perhaps the previous night's storm front had rolled through here. She glimpsed a figure standing in shadow beyond the jumble, now moving from the murk toward the house. A woman, clutching a lumpy white plastic bag between fists ready to fend off attack, her head bowed, cropped hair plastered as if she'd just emerged from underwater. Meg checked the lock on the sliding door and flicked on the outside spotlight. A sunburned face squinted toward the window.

Pandora!

Pandora shuffled forward with the weary step of someone queuing in a long, slow line. Her skin looked rubbed raw, her greenish blouse and grey shorts smudged and crumpled like well-traveled dollar bills.

"All the way I practiced what I'd say to you," Pandora said, her voice husky. "Now all I can think of is, may I have some water, please?"

"Of course." Meg looked for the boyfriend—what was his name? Maybe Pandora never left for North Dakota. No explanation for her appearance seemed promising.

"Are you all right?" Meg said.

"I'm not sure about the *all*."

Pandora closed her eyes and threw her head back in the cool kitchen air. She dropped her sack and unslung a small gym bag from her shoulder. In two long gulps she drained the water down to the ice cubes and then held the glass against her forehead.

How long had she been in the sun without a hat?

"Are you hungry?"

"Maybe later." Pandora extended the glass for a refill. This time she took measured swallows. Satisfied for the moment, she set down the glass. "You were right."

A thin, bright pink line where the ring had been. *Of course.*

"Oh, I'm so sorry," Meg said.

Pandora's eyes flicked in appreciation. "Nothing was working, almost from the day I last saw you. I left him four days ago, got here yesterday and slept in your yard last night. I'm sorry to dump my problems on you, but do you have any lotion?"

As she applied the skin cream, Pandora's story began to ease out of her.

"Cody failed his drug screen for the first job and we had to chill until he could test with a different company. Williston State said I'd applied too late for fall quarter and the dorms were full. Cody said it was my fault we both had to live in the camper, as if going there in the first place was my idea."

Pandora's face turned from red to white to rose. She put a drop on her fingertip and painted the scarlet rim of one ear.

"He got hired to drive a truck hauling sewage from the man camps to Dickinson. I didn't know anybody but him. It was crazy there, like you said it would be. Everything overpriced. An hour and a half just to get through checkout at Walmart. Men walking around day and night with too much money, drinking, fighting, acting stupid. Not all of them—the normal family guys would work their fourteen days and fly home for two weeks—but the town was not normal."

She drizzled a wavy line of lotion from wrist to elbow, wincing as she worked it up to her shoulder.

"I found a housekeeping job just so I'd have something to do. Seventeen dollars an hour—crazy! More like zookeeping, cleaning cages. That's where I found out the honeywagon drivers worked fourteen-and-fourteen. Cody was coming back at night like he'd been driving every day, but half the time he wasn't."

Her thighs were only slightly pink. She salved them with the excess from her hands and the underside of her forearms. The scorched tops of her feet sported fishbelly-white V's left by the straps of her flip-flops. She squirted a generous blob of lotion on each foot.

"I asked him and first he lied, then he said he'd taken a second job so we could get a house sooner, then he accused me of messing around when he was out. God, it had only been three months since we got engaged! I gave up my scholarship for him. Did he think that I'd just take up with some random roughneck? He started texting me at odd times, insisting I answer right away. When I didn't, he took my keys, called the housekeeping company and told them I didn't have his permission to drive his truck. They let me go because I was supposed to have my own transportation. Then he told me I had to watch the camper. People knew he was off working. He gave me a gun and took me out to learn how to shoot it. I was supposed to spend the day in the truck yard where we parked. I knew by then it was drugs. Cody was using and making deliveries on his route. He thought it was genius."

"So you left. That was brave."

Pandora shook her head. "I was scared. Not of Cody, exactly, but his decisions. He was so sure of himself. I couldn't think, couldn't breathe. I was more afraid of being suffocated or arrested than I was of getting raped on the road." She rubbed her palms back and forth until the last of the lotion was absorbed. "Now here I am with nothing but two bags and twenty dollars from pawning the ring."

That little chip of stone. A pawnbroker must have felt generous that day.

"I was such an idiot. Cody didn't need me there. He just wanted a nice, reliable lay while he made his money. I should've known. Who has brighter eyes than a cranked up liar?"

Pandora's bitter smile suggested she had wrung all the tears out of that subject. She capped the lotion bottle and set it on the kitchen table. Meg nudged it back to her.

"Keep it. And don't beat yourself up. You made a mistake but it's not irreversible." Surely she knew enough not to get pregnant. "What's your plan now?"

"I don't know. I'm waiting to see if he's followed me." Meg stiffened and Pandora noticed. "Not followed me to your house—to Junction. He'd never think I'd come here. We talked on the way north about how you were a complete bitch about the money."

"Well, that's reassuring."

"No lie. Anyway, he'd go straight to my parents' house, even though they told me I was not welcome back if I went off with Cody. He knows all my friends. If any of them knew where I was, he'd have some story that would get them to tell."

He knows where I live, too. The rumbling white truck and its blank-eyed headlights seemed more ominous now. What if this was a ruse by the two of them?

"Anyway, thanks for the water—and the use of your yard last night," Pandora said. She nudged the flip-flops into alignment and fitted them gingerly to her feet. She checked the tie on her bundle and hoisted the gym bag, flinching as the shoulder strap slipped up her arm. "I know there's a path that goes down to the river somewhere around here."

The kid could act. She was resourceful, too, but without resources. The river was nowhere for a girl to sleep. In summer clothes even an overnight fifty degrees would penetrate to the bone. And then tomorrow—hitchhiking, trying to read the drivers who stopped, looking over her shoulder for Cody. Turning redder by the day.

"Is that all you have for shoes?"

"Cody took my Nikes when he took back the truck keys."

A controlling, drug-dealing boyfriend was a matter for the police. There were community agencies equipped for these situations. Meg could use her connections to get Pandora in somewhere tonight.

"You need a safe place where Cody won't find you. I can help with that."

"Oh, thank you," Pandora said. She dropped her bags. "It'll only be temporary."

Temporary? Here? No. Meg ran through the options. Women's shelter. *Full.* Teen shelter. *She's eighteen.* Regular shelter. *Yuck.* Anyway, it was too late to get in tonight.

All right, she'd pay for a motel, some meals, a few days to let things settle down. That was the way to stay out of the drama and not worry about Pandora rifling the medicine cabinet.

"I knew from the scholarship you had to be a good person," Pandora said. "And I remember the last time I was here, seeing that picture of you and your sister. You called yourself the pensive one. I didn't really know what the word means, but you had this amazing calm. You looked like her guardian angel."

If only.

"This is the guest room." More accurately, perhaps, the spare bedroom, since no one before Pandora had used it, and its décor so out of character from the rest of the house, as if Helen had once lived here. Their parents sold the family home and moved to Arizona, where they had purchased a smaller container for their emptiness, leaving Meg to deal with Helen's things. After all, she had space that needed filling. *Too much house*, her mother had said after taking the tour. *What were you thinking?*

Helen's print of the leaping sisters photo topped the old dresser she had painted with Keith Haring-style figures in bright primaries. Yards of books, arranged by Helen in the order she had read them, the titles demarcating the epochs of her seventeen years: the E.B. White bedrock, the Judy Blume sequence, *The Outsiders* stratum, the *Johnny Got His Gun* formation, the Rumi-Stanislavski uplift. A mock-Soviet-style red, black and yellow poster from Duran Duran's "Strange Behaviour Tour," which Meg had taken down from its thumbtacks and had framed. A plush cat, its stuffing crushed nearly flat, the only Meg hand-me-down that Helen had ever accepted. A framed page from a Joan of Arc audition script, with yellow highlights and lavish underscoring. *Soft but _INTENSE!!_* inked in the margin.

"Cool. You were in theater?"

"Only a little bit—Elwood P. Dowd's sister kind of thing. These are all Helen's things. Were."

"Oh! I'm sorry for being so dense. Here I am all like, *I broke up with my boyfriend and got sunburned. Poor little me.* If you'd rather not have me in here..."

"No, it's fine. I'm glad to have you." It would be good to see footprints in the carpet, still furrowed from a months' ago vacuuming.

"One thing, just so there's no misunderstanding." Pandora opened the gym bag. "This is Cody's." She withdrew a green duck canvas case, a bulging trapezoid with a leather Cabela's tag.

"I can't have a gun in the house."

"You can bury it in the back yard if it gives you the creeps. I never wanted it. I only took it for the road."

The image of an armed Pandora ready to defend herself from horny truckers and pursuing boyfriends was both disturbing and reassuring.

"Is it loaded?"

"Always assume yes. I know that much."

"We'll turn it in to the police."

"No. They'll want to know where we got it. I don't want Cody madder at me than he already is."

"If you're afraid, you can get a protection order."

A slow shake of her head. "Cody sells drugs to roughnecks. He's decided he's the smartest guy in North Dakota. He would ninja a protection order just to show he could get away with it."

"But would he hurt you?"

"Do words count?"

Yes, words might as well be bullets, especially with a gun in the room. Then there was no question of who could speak, who had to listen and how things would be settled.

Meg had bought this Wyoming-sized mattress because it suited the master bedroom's scale, never considering how it would swallow her. She woke surprised to find herself flopped sideways in bed, not lost and alone at sea. She had been the mayor of a town that had suffered a mining disaster. Borne on a litter through blackened streets roiled with victims' stunned families, she reached out to their beseeching faces, but her arms shrank to flippers. She could only clap noiselessly over their heads. In shame, she dove into the sea on a lonely swim through fog and white-pillowed waves. Just as she became dangerously exhausted, a water-logged book the size of a steamer trunk drifted by. It sank when she tried to hitch aboard. A dream so transparent, it needed no interpretation.

Meg looked in on Pandora, arm crooked around a pillow, face down atop the bed, her brown-rimmed soles peeking from under the duvet. She had been too sunburned, she claimed, to endure a shower. It must not have occurred to her to take a bath.

Are you asking me?

Asking you what?

If she reminds me of me.

Seeing her in your room made me think of you.

It's not my room.

Right. It's just...Pandora hitchhiking with a handgun. You dancing on cliff edges. I always preferred my daring to be safe, like poetry.

More than safe. You wanted control.

Without control, how can you be sure?

You can't. I was on a boring church outing, remember? Life doesn't come with safety locks. Safe is not an objective condition. It's a feeling— mostly about shit that will never happen. And when the really bad shit does come, you won't be in control anyway. Meanwhile, look at your life. You're perched on the great white cloud of the local powers that be. So what if you don't control squat? Take the hint from that girl. She's here asleep because she feels safe in your house.

Do you remember that night I warned you about sneaking around with church boys? It was the last time I held you.

You had me pinned in the bed when I woke up. You told me not to be stupid...do you think I was?

No, I think you were probably too kind. Too kind and too brave.

I like that, killed by an overdose of kindness and braveness.

And because you thought you were in control.

**For every home there is a season.
A time to list and a time to buy.**

—"Home" with Meg Mogrin, *Grand Junction Style*

October weather was the town's reward for suffering through summer. After September's steady spread between highs and lows, the extremes began to compress until settling between room temperature and just above freezing. Needled with a fresh dose of this air, footballs revived and resumed their Friday night flights. Cottonwoods, lately beloved for their shade, drew fresh attention to themselves with cliddering flocks of golden leaves. The light angled noticeably; deep shadows came earlier where the sun dove behind the Monument; the Book Cliffs added new colors to their palette. These changes solemnized the month when Helen fell and Meg forever after called the season autumn.

Today might be the last warm Saturday before the tables left the sidewalk outside the Dream Café, a casual, buzzing place where she inevitably encountered people she knew among diners and passersby, an atmosphere in which a woman, cheered by, say, a Banana Strawberry Crepe and Peach Mimosa, might consider that her life was not a shambles after all. While not exactly viewing the world through Brian's Hopi-tinted lenses, she saw more plainly the virtues of staying close to home and had accepted that she should forget the past and not obsess about the future. She was doing some good simply by doing what she did well—connecting people, matching families with homes and representing the positive things about her town. In return, this year had been good to her. Beyond the bread and butter transactions, she had sold properties in Redlands Mesa and Quail Run to buyers who had traded their inflated California houses for Colorado luxury. She expected to move another expansive home in Sobre El Rio before the first snowflakes hit the vineyards. In anticipation of that jumbo mortgage, Jules was due from the bank to buy lunch.

"You're a hard person to get hold of."

Joe Samson plunked down at the table. Meg thought reporters were supposed to notice things, like the second menu, water glass and setting. A bubble of something warm and ether-like broke inside her, a half-pleasant twinge. Joe had been such a strong presence in her mind of late, it was a shock to see him in the flesh.

"Sorry. I've been swamped. Whatever the story, I figured you'd have no trouble finding another broker happy to see their name in the paper."

"This is related to some homeless stuff." He said it so offhandedly. Did he want her to sweat a bit before he mentioned Isaac?

"Sister Rose is the one to talk to."

"This is outside her realm, I think. You heard about the protest?"

Thank God. "I haven't read the paper for days." Joe's frown made further explanation seem necessary. "I was in Arizona."

"A group surrounded city hall to protest the homeless crackdown and lack of low-income apartments. They want an okay for a tent city to fill the housing gap. Until then, they've threatened to occupy downtown parking places with a roving camp that Zack Nicolai has named Winslowville."

Eve must be so pissed. Meg was surprised she hadn't heard the eruption. This was the sort of thing she was supposed to stay on top of for Eve.

"And, in typical fashion, the Council is rewriting the code to prohibit non-vehicles in parking spaces." Joe seemed happy about the protest. City Council meetings must be so boring for him most of the time.

"I don't see why you want to talk to me." But of course she did.

"I heard you were working on the tent city planning with the Homeless Coalition."

"I wouldn't say I was working on it. I've been asked to advise the planners."

"Do they have a location in mind?"

"Nothing official."

"So you must know Wesley Chambers. What's he like?"

"He's…this is not for publication, Joe. He's not political. Zack calling out Eve Winslow is definitely not going to help Wesley's cause."

"But the conflict's ironic, don't you think? The town's plowing up tamarisk, tinkering with ordinances and cracking down on panhandling, camping and loitering—all because transients won't take responsibility for their lives. Now here comes a guy who says they will, and he has a plan to do it."

"It's a dream, not a plan. It won't happen here, especially now."

"Now?" Joe arched an eyebrow and took out his notebook.

"I just meant…the economy. Wesley seems very determined, well-intentioned. He wants to do something positive but he doesn't have any kind of base in the community. He used to live on one of the islands before the fire."

Joe tapped a pen on the notebook's open page.

"Chambers was a firefighter in Beaverton, Oregon, injured when a burning gymnasium roof collapsed on him. He got a disability settlement, divorced, disappeared and then showed up here. The police say he's a vet, has no record, has even been helpful keeping peace on the river. I'd like to talk to him. He was at the demonstration but I can't locate him now. Zack Nicolai won't say. My brother knows Chambers, but not where he is. He just got beat up looking for the guy."

So Isaac *was* Joe's brother. His connection with Wesley was one more reason to extricate herself from riverbank politics.

"I'm sorry. I didn't know you had a brother in town. Shelly's never said anything."

"It's a sore topic. We love him, but at some point you have to protect your family and your sanity. Letting go still sucks."

He had to mean protecting Shelly and the kids. So Isaac was outside his family, which meant he might never tell Joe about finding the eye. Her relief mixed with sympathy for the brothers. For Isaac living outside what Sister Rose called the circle of kinship. Was being close to home and family comforting or did it estrange him even more? And for Joe, losing a brother and retaining a window on his suffering. Did he avoid Isaac when he saw him on the street or did he reach out, knowing it would make no difference? No wonder Wesley had left his Oregon hometown to wander unknown lands, where the ghosts and monsters posed more straightforward threats.

The server, assuming Joe was her lunch date, headed toward the table. Meg waved her off. Jules would be here any minute.

"I can't say anything, okay? Wesley already thinks I'm trying to torpedo his camp idea and Eve would like this whole thing to go away."

Joe stuck the pen in his pocket. "It's still a good story: *A disabled fireman's dream goes up in smoke.*"

For a moment, she wished Wesley Chambers had come to her before he got enmeshed with Zack Nicolai. She might have been able to redirect him toward a more realistic solution, to help him... No, her powers of redemption were not that great. Wesley was on the river for a reason. So many reasons.

Joe looked past her toward the middle of the block and Meg could tell from his concentration that Jules must be crossing Main Street. A woman accustomed to stopping traffic.

"What are you two plotting?" Jules demanded.

"Downtown revitalization," said Meg.

"Insurrection," Joe said.

"Oh, are you joining us?" Jules said.

He answered before Meg could. "Just going—but since I have you two... Our editorial board just met with a Michigan honcho who's close to announcing a big development project. He said all the right things about downtown, about how he's going to transform the local economy." Joe watched for a reaction and got nothing. "But come on—a medical destination? St. Mary's and Community are trying to nuke each other. Doctors aren't taking new patients. Big city companies don't invest to create jobs in the hinterlands, they come to where the talent is, and I doubt Betterment is looking for rock climbers and mountain bikers. If Lew Hungerman truly wants a nice environment for his kids, he can send them to Cranbrook. Anyone else think he's spreading pixie dust?"

"I can't help you," Meg said. "He's a client."

Jules said, "The bank never comments on specific companies."

Joe covered a mock yawn. "That's right, you both make your money up front. Commissions and fees. What does it matter if nothing gets built? But even if it does, let's be honest. He's promising way more than he can deliver."

The words from Jules dropped like ice cubes into a cocktail shaker. "*The Clarion*'s socialist business reporter...just described... most real estate ventures! Destination medical is a real trend and Betterment's niche makes sense in a recreational community like this."

"Granted. In fact, Hungerman's been looking at some other places like this: Idaho Falls, Spokane, St. George." He seemed pleased to note their surprise. "That's the great thing about private aircraft; I couldn't track him if he flew commercial. So what do you think? It's a free country. Is he playing us? My editor says we're not writing anything to derail this. Fine, let him unveil his project his way, but if we're up against other cities, we should know what's being peddled to them. Jules, I'm just a journalist, not a socialist. Think of me like the hometown guy covering the Broncos. I love them but I'm going to say what they're doing wrong. I do want private enterprise to win. I just don't want it to run up the score."

He passed the menu and place setting over to Jules. "Right now, for the benefit of this developer, the city is putting the squeeze on people who have nothing. We're petrified he might take his marbles somewhere else—but nobody wants to talk about the people he'll displace."

"There's a whole public hearing process," Jules said.

Joe snorted. "It'll all be decided by then. This isn't about some sidewalk cafe. Millions are going to change hands. There's been private politicking for months, good old boys making deals. They've convinced themselves. When some shit land turns to gold, who's going to care about the derelicts and crazies who thought it was theirs?" He tried to smile over the tremor in his voice.

Isaac's story was the one Joe wanted to write, but he couldn't. He was only the business reporter. His brother was on the wrong side of the deserving/undeserving homeless divide. The town needed to believe in itself, and Hungerman offered the validation it wanted so badly. Sacrifices had to be made, and Joe knew it as well as she did. There was no ram in the thicket to save this Isaac. Wesley's old boots, *No* and *Go*, mocked them all.

"Your editorial board—did Hungerman say where the project was going?"

Joe nodded.

"Then you should talk to Wesley Chambers and you should also warn him. He has no idea he's in the path. There's a triangle of woods east of the glue factory. Look for a trail close to the river."

"Joe can be such a prick," Jules said. "I should call Ian."

The Clarion's publisher. Jules had dated him until Ian got too serious.

"Don't. Joe already knows he's living in the wrong town if he wants to write exposés." Nothing was going to stop this unless some other city could top them—or the valley was truly cursed. Perhaps Wesley and Zack and Sister Rose spoke for deep human values, but this was economics, and it spoke for humanity, too.

Jules examined the menu. "I'm not worried about the homeless backlash, but privatizing the park could be a battle. It's a dealbreaker if the City doesn't give Betterment control. I can't begin to tell you the contortions Lew's going through with land swaps, layers of financing, reorg of his company. They don't service as much through call centers any more. Most staff locates where they have provider contracts. He's having trouble attracting executive talent to Detroit. His investors like the Betterment Institute venture but don't see it tied to the core business and don't see Lew running it. They're bringing in an exec from a luxury hotel brand. Once that happens, a Scottsdale bank is in. Meanwhile, Lew is pushing for the homerun land deal he can leverage to reinvent his company and change his life. His father and uncle own a chunk of Betterment Health. He's got vice presidents on the payroll, deadwood relatives from the old days, who used to repo cars. And let's not even talk about his ex."

"How do you know all this?"

"Lew's not as superficial as I thought he was. He just has to maintain this facade." Jules raised a finger to her lips. "I'm thinking the Red Bull Mimosa. It's Friday, and I'm flying to St. George tonight."

"You're not..."

"Don't worry, I'm a big girl."

Meg didn't worry about Jules. She wondered who Lew had invited to Spokane.

Where did you live prior to becoming homeless?

—Vulnerability Index Prescreen for Single Adults

Isaac didn't mind walking but he hated walking his bicycle, hated the cars passing too close to the shoulder, hated looking to drivers like someone who wouldn't plan ahead, didn't carry a spare tube and couldn't patch a flat, when he'd done nothing except fix flats since he'd started riding Joe's Raleigh. Done nothing except watch the air go out of everything. Ron Gudmunson dead, discovered locked alone in his house while Isaac was out looking for Wesley, who was gone or underground. A letter back from Rudy Hefner saying he had no idea how the glass eye got in the canyon. Trow facing a sentence of either another rehab or a psych stay. Irene and Edward, their Tercel packed above the seat tops, hoping to reach Durango before they ran out of gas. Everyone pressed by this invisible force to keep them moving, fearful and sleep-deprived— tortured for their own good until they lost it completely and came in for repairs. Or they ended up like Jimmy, surrendered to the river, his dazed mother wading back from his wrong-way baptism.

Isaac had tried being a good son, a diligent student, a reliable worker, a faithful Catholic, a grateful recipient, a compliant patient. He had consulted doctors, endured tests, ingested pills, tolerated counselors, attended groups, woven potholders and painted by numbers, hung dream catchers, let priests and preachers and crystal gazers lay hands on him, exercised, immobilized, cleansed and fortified his body, read and written, gone mute and screamed his lungs out, masturbated himself to sleep and movie-marathoned himself into a stupor. And still this clamor: *submit.* Submit and survive.

Walking with his back to traffic on this road, he was just asking for it. A citation, a beer can in the back of the head or a sudden swoosh in the gravel behind him. Real funny, going to get his birth certificate gets him killed and they can't identify the body because there's no ID.

Isaac had checked the pawnshops and found his computer with Ford's name on the ticket. Without a receipt he couldn't prove anything and he couldn't get a receipt without Shelly's help since her credit card made the purchase. Plus, he didn't want to hear *I told you so* this soon after she had told him so. Even with a receipt he'd still need an ID and a police theft report, which would mean admitting to the cops he was trespassing. The humiliation wasn't worth the price.

A voice out of nowhere startled him.

"Need some help?"

Isaac turned to face a fierce red beak with sculpted nostrils. A helmeted man hovered above him, limbs joined to a bicycle, his cheetah body standing tall on the pedals. Composed. A carbon fiber centaur in sport glasses.

"I'm okay," Isaac said.

The cyclist made minute adjustments with his front wheel and cleated feet to keep aloft without moving forward. He cocked his head at Isaac's fat cheek and purple eye and must have determined the injuries did not need attention. After a quick sweep over Isaac's bike (vintage but not sufficiently classic to be interesting) he turned his notice to the tire. "I've got a spare tube you can have."

Isaac didn't want the man's tube. He wanted his effortless balance, his power to float like that.

"I'm almost home," he said.

"Okay, man, your choice. Have a good one." The rider powered away, the bike wagging between his legs as he cranked over the hill.

Isaac had meant to say he was almost to his mother's house.

He could've walked the last hundred yards with his eyes closed. Marian had wanted a winding driveway but Carl had toted up the cost and run it straight as a landing strip aimed at the garage. Nothing looked much different. Trees grown taller. The pond dry, its liner showing. The Ramada Inn entry pillars, blistered by the southern exposure. A bird at the edge of the porch. A bead of its blood on the concrete, a smear on the beak, a clot of shit on one talon. He cupped it in his palm and pressed two fingers to the firm breast. A phoebe, he thought, the body warm, still capable of being alive. But the head lolled and under the ruff its neck was pliant as a blood vessel. He looked for a mark on the clerestory above the door where the glass reflected treetops under blue sky. Exactly the phoebe's sky, except impenetrable. As he laid it under a barberry, he felt its essence pass from air into his memory.

He knocked four times. Evenly. Not urgent, not slow and ominous, the restrained sound a son should make at his mother's door after some years away. He waited. Had she heard? Was she waiting, too? How long before trying again? Should he vary the pattern? Volume? Three knocks or five? Was he expectant or beseeching or simply awaiting a response? Perhaps she'd seen him approach and had taken him for a missionary. How many times did a missionary knock before giving up? Wait, the Mormons came in twos wearing CamelBaks and ties. The Witnesses drove cars and wore suits. He tried the doorbell. Didn't the police knock instead of ring? God, he should've rung first. He could hear the bell through the door. Maybe she wasn't home.

Maybe she was calling the police.

〰
〰

Marian Samson had let the halogeton live all summer but soon the weed's succulent green would wither to brittle, brown, seed-scattering skeletons. She straightened from her work in time to see the man with the yellow bicycle while he was still on the road. She recognized him the way she identified autumn's approach, sensing a familiar change before the details arrived, before the bicycle obeyed the hand rested on its seat and turned up the driveway. Marian stripped her sticky garden gloves and slipped in the back door, locking it behind her, then went straight to secure the front.

Marian had almost given up thoughts of Isaac's return. One can only live in anticipation for so long. She had hoped for an apology first, a letter filled with insight and regret, something rigorous like a college application essay. Better, they would conduct a prolonged correspondence, since Isaac could be focused and coherent in bursts. Even a phone call. But he had never grasped the importance of social attachment, so how could he master the etiquette of being a long-lost son? She used to think prodigal meant *peripatetic* until she tried to fit the eleven letters in her crossword. No, the correct answer was *spendthrift*. Isaac, the child most like her, had wandered but he was hardly a wastrel. He had squandered nothing except a life.

For the moment, she appreciated her unwelcoming front door, drawbridge-heavy and studded with hammered wrought iron clavos in the colonial Spanish style. The contractor had suggested installing a roller on the corner but the massive entry had been Carl's idea and he would not be questioned. Regular visitors knew to assist with a shoulder when Marian answered or they simply came to the back of the house. When the door fell out of plumb and had to be rehung, Carl blamed Marian for opening it wrong.

After Carl died, she called in a new contractor who told her replacing the door would involve reconstructing the entire entry. The price was shocking but the real deterrent was knowing that even if she repainted the interior, sold the outsized furniture and replaced the cowboy primitive light fixtures, the house would still reflect Carl's decisions about the location, layout, dimensions and internal systems. Everything she did within its space—looking out a window, walking to the bedroom, sitting on a toilet, leaving out-of-reach shelves unused or calling an electrician to change light bulbs in the ceiling—was a product of Carl's overbearing will. Erase his influence? It would be easier to redecorate an asteroid.

She knew there were twenty-eight clavos in the door and counted them anyway, adjusted the entry rug so it was square with the tiles and counted the clavos again to measure a minute of their impasse. She had always counted but only at moments like this was she conscious of it. Counting reassured her that the universe had not rearranged itself while her attention strayed. She counted steps, counted days, counted blessings, counted boys she had kissed instead of sheep. Counted beats to the measure, beads of the rosary, beans as she snapped them. She supposed she had been counting the weeds she pulled right up until Isaac's arrival. However, there was no counting Isaac. He did not add up.

She still loved him as the child she had raised but was also fearful of the stranger he had become. Such a beautiful boy—everyone had said so, going above and beyond the adoration to which all babies are entitled—and when he began to have problems everyone said, *look at all you've done, look at your other boys*, as if that proved she was not at fault, as if the other sons had not fled as soon as they could. Jacob went straight to the Navy, found a Japanese wife in Okinawa and established a life over unbridgeable waters. Joseph, off to a good journalism school, stayed for big city opportunities. The knock from the banished one came to her like the late-arriving light from an extinguished star.

≈

Isaac stared at the hulking door so dark and distressed it might've been salvaged from a sacked cathedral. The door did its job, making clear he was not welcome. All he had to do was request his birth certificate and walk back to town. But right now he had a calf's liver for a tongue; his skin, a salty rind, his scalp peppered with oily flakes; mush warmed in the spaces between his toes; each step produced a habanero burn in his crotch; bones flared in their sockets; every nerve begged to go off duty. If there were a name for this weary condition, his ransacking brain would have exhumed it by now.

A car shushed past on the road. The earth ticked toward sunset. The broken-necked phoebe said: *It's not so bad to give up.* He lowered himself to the concrete—a long delicious slide against the warm wall—and submitted his surrender.

The rattle of Joe's old four-banger Subaru woke him. His brother sat in the car so long Isaac wondered if he was expected to get in. "Is she home?" Isaac said.

Joe tucked a phone in his pocket and got out. "She's concerned. It's been a long time since she saw you. Are you okay?"

He was not okay but that was not the right answer. "I'm not freaking out, if that's what you mean."

"Your face."

"I tripped in the dark."

"You understand why she might be worried about you suddenly showing up out of nowhere."

"She's always worried about something. You know that."

"Isaac, I didn't drive out here to debate. What are you after?"

"My birth certificate."

Joe made a show of patience but his tone grew sharper. "Don't tell me you rode all the way out here for that. You could've called and asked her to mail it."

"It's the original. It could get lost in the mail. And I didn't ride all the way. I've had two flats today on that stupid bike."

Joe eyed the Raleigh. "Glad to see you're finally riding it. You should carry a repair kit. Everybody gets flats from the goatheads."

As if Isaac needed bicycle tips from Joe. It happened all the time, people assuming he must be stupid. He didn't need that deflating shit from his family, too.

"And why are there goatheads? They've invaded because the soil was disturbed by roads and shopping centers. They're deployed all around the city to keep me out."

"You're not making sense."

"Goat heads are *Tribulus terrestris*—it means affliction of the earth. They're in the caltrop family. The Romans invented the caltrop to cripple their enemy's horses and troops. Look it up."

"Jesus, Isaac! Why do you have to make everything so complicated?"

"Because everything is." Joe should know. That's why he had a job—to simplify the world, summarize the hard stuff and pull out the juicy parts.

"She's not opening the door unless I tell her it's safe. So far this conversation isn't helping you."

"It *is* safe. I have never, ever hurt anyone."

"If that's what you believe, brother, you have a pretty narrow definition of hurt."

※

Marian heard the boys talking on the...terrace, stoop? Sometimes she could still not retrieve the word she wanted. After her stroke names for things hid or showed up disguised as another word. People smiled at her sentences as if she were wearing unmatched socks. It helped doing crosswords and watching *Jeopardy!* Soon, she would write limericks to show she'd recovered.

> *There once were three boys all named Samson*
> *In varied degrees they were handsome*
> *They left home, to a man,*

One as far as Japan
Now the other two wait at her transom!

Carl's death had brought her sons back together only momentarily—so they could, in Jake's horrid phrase, *make sure he stays under.* It had taken more than her being alone for Joe to move back from Missouri with Shelly and the children. Her stroke, a stroke of luck. She remembered little from that two years of confusion. Soliciting rides to church and then insisting that Carl would take her. Returning calls she'd already returned while forgetting others. Wandering lost on the canal road behind the house, though there were only two directions she could go. Friends can only put up with that kind of nonsense for so long. She worked hard to become herself again. Thank God she didn't end up a vegetable, although if she had, Isaac might have taken an interest in her.

She had been fooled before. They both had. She had been soft and Carl hard, one forgiving, the other resolute. Marian had accepted Isaac's condition as an illness while Carl considered it a character flaw. Love did not cure him nor did tirades set him straight. She was resigned to her postcard returning one day. Or claiming his body. Well, here he was—the word alighted—on her *threshold.*

Marian slid the deadbolt and grasped the iron ring with both hands. Then she counted to twenty-eight and leaned back with all her might.

She should have welcomed Isaac, spoken his name first, but his appearance overwhelmed her. His face half-purpled. His clothes looked slept-in. He had not shaved for days. His bleary eyes shifted without making contact. She blurted, "Are you in some kind of trouble?"

"I'm not after money, if that's what you think. This is…an administrative matter."

"You could've called first."

"I thought you'd say no."

"I might have," she said.

"See."

He was still Isaac, maddening circumlocutions, argumentative, insisting on his peculiar logic. His eyes her shade of blue.

"You can't just expect everything to be fine after all that's happened." She didn't mean to lecture but it was how she felt.

Isaac rubbed his hair back and tilted his head toward the sky.

"Where are you staying?" she asked. Softer, trying not to provoke.

"There's no *staying* anywhere. I'm camping here and there."

"I wish you wouldn't camp. You're a grown man, not a Boy Scout."

"Mom, it's not the camping."

"What is it then?"

"Nothing. Everything. I can't explain. I came for my birth certificate, that's all."

Administrative matter, my foot. She saw the tension in him, one arm pinned rigid against his side, the fingers plucking invisible strings. Her baby, her pride, her failure, her phantom. The stitch in her chest, the knot in her stomach, the crick in her neck. A pregnancy she had carried going on forty years. A wedge, a conundrum, a timebomb, a scapegoat. All those words about to explode from her and out slipped *Oh, sweetie.*

She wasn't ready for him yet.

〰

I know I have it somewhere, she said, leaving him on the step. *Call me tomorrow.* Not, *wait a second and I'll be back.* She had always been so organized; she had to know right where his birth certificate was. Why did she think she could fool him? He had extensive practice sensing when he wasn't wanted.

Joe said, "Your showing up here's a big deal to her. When you talk to her next time, consider that she's your mother, not some random custodian of vital records."

That was Joe. The deadpan distance, the sincere tone, the after-the-fact advice. He had taken Isaac to breakfast once a week, given him the bike, let him stay in their guest room after Carl booted him for the last time. Even after the kitchen mess, Joe had talked Shelly into serving as Isaac's payee. In his own way, each brother had offered protection. Joe had played stepfather. Jake had given him a knife.

"Is there something else going on? You can get a copy of your birth certificate in town, you know."

"Sure, if I've got some identification. But I don't."

"It can't be that hard."

"It's not, as long as I've got an unexpired fishing license and a gun permit. Or a current pay stub with motor vehicle registration, or a Social Security card and Medicaid card. Oh, there's other ways if I bring a utility bill and voter registration card plus a booking photo and baptismal record. Or my tax return and a mortgage document plus a certified copy of my ass from my last employer's copy machine."

"Come on."

"Look it up. Colorado has a million ways to validate your identity—and I have like zero point five."

"What do you want me to do about it?" Joe asked.

"Nothing. Write the governor. Give me a ride back to town."

"Look, I know you're frustrated. But don't blow it with her."

"I always manage to piss people off, don't I?"

Joe cinched the Raleigh onto the Subaru's bike rack and checked it over as if they were about to drive across the country.

"You haven't pissed us off, Isaac—you've worn us down."

"There's a difference?"

"Pissed off is an emotional response. People don't stay pissed. Worn down is a long process. It's hard to repair something once it's been eroded away."

≈

Each filing cabinet drawer opened with a particular sound. Those fully loaded with invoices or tax records produced a rumble, while lighter drawers clacked on the rollers and whooshed when closed. To Marian's ear, the drawer labeled FAMILY, stuffed with non-uniform envelopes, construction paper, track ribbons, report cards and class pictures, rattled in the middle register. Its five tabs marked a series of subordinate files and accordion folders organized by birth order. Isaac's section bulged deepest in the drawer. AWARDS, EDUCATION and PICTURES sang of promise while FINANCE, LEGAL and the over-flowing MEDICAL teemed with complication and heartbreak. A single folder, MAIL, recorded his years since he last left the house. Mail had stopped coming for him and it was empty. Only the thin BIRTH folder seemed unburdened with connotation. It verified a male child, Isaac David, had been delivered, named, baptized and immunized. She set aside the birth certificate. Such a simple and matter-of-fact record, a boarding pass for a flight she thought had crashed. Perhaps it only had yet to land.

There were no files labeled UNEASY TRUCES, FALSE STARTS or DISASTERS. The documentation for those categories was largely anecdotal and unforgettable. The last qualifying disaster began with Carl's funeral, when she took Isaac out to buy a proper outfit. The helpful saleslady held up shirt and tie combinations for his consideration. But when Isaac tried to feel the fabric of one, she snatched it away. It was just a reflex but it made Marian mad, too, so she didn't blame her son for blowing up at the lady. He survived the mass and when he stepped up to the grave she had a fleeting hope that Carl's death might finally be their chance to reconcile. But grunting with the effort, Isaac flung down clots of earth until they pried the shovel from his hands.

Likewise, there were few records of her efforts at truce, as when she drove past the soup kitchen hoping to catch a glimpse of him.

She scanned the Blotter column daily in case his name should appear. On the freeway once, he materialized above her on an overpass and she couldn't even slow the car before he vanished. She wrote his name in the memo line of her monthly checks to Catholic Outreach and the Salvation Army, as if the aid would somehow find its way to him. She prayed novenas to Saint Jude over the postcards she stamped *Return to Sender*. Rosaries and votive offerings sent requests for his safety and peace of mind. She avoided conversations about her friends' children and did not burden them with her loss. She found no succor in the NAMI and Al-Anon meetings, where strangers told stories of their pain. She read *Courage to Change* and did not change.

For years she had believed that a cure for his illness would bring Isaac back whole. Then her stroke and slow transition out of numbness enlightened her. Her recovery was a stumbling forward, not a repossession. The absent, avoidant Isaac probably *was* himself—as she was herself now. Which was to say, the mother and son she remembered would never reunite except as ghosts wander-wafting through the rooms of this accursed house.

The kitchen. This was where she first suspected. Isaac had left for college from the house where he was raised. When returned to the new house, he seemed different but of course college was supposed to change people. He announced a plan to complete his studies online for the master's degree he would need to land a library job. Working at Safeway as a night stocker would cover his tuition and allow him to pay a modest rent to stay in their lower level. He seemed on a good path, and they agreed on a temporary arrangement that would help advance him to self-sufficiency, which seemed to be working until early one morning she found the kitchen in disarray. All the food had been removed from the refrigerator, cupboards and pantry. Dishes and glassware were stacked on the counters. Isaac claimed the entire kitchen had tilted out of balance when he emptied a box of Raisin Bran and he realized how much its equilibrium depended upon him. It had been the same way at school.

Nothing would stay where it belonged, he said. *Stacks of books and information someone else had ordered. The college was saving money by making me its library.*

He showed her a sheaf of medical records. Before coming home, he had checked himself into a hospital. He was taking medication and attending counseling sessions. He said he was getting better and he was an adult, so he would handle it.

He had always been a good worker when he was well. But one day he was transferred to Safeway's produce department after becoming distressed by the new planogram for the canned vegetables. The store manager stopped seeking her out when she shopped. The checkers who'd always mentioned Isaac when he was away in college kept their chat general. They must have known he was losing it. Why didn't she?

The guest room. When Carl pried open the bedroom door, the moist exhalation of mold, urine, armpit and root cellar had revolted them both. Isaac was curled in his sheets with a pillow over his head. Her first frantic thought was that he had died. Then she saw the skulls of cantaloupe. Liquefying asparagus. Blackened avocadoes and bananas. Blue lemons. Flaccid, disgusting cucumbers.

He answered with nonsense. His autonomic nervous system was paralyzed, so he had to stay awake to breathe. The Y2K Bug was not a programming error; it was part of the Pope's plan to prevent aliens from attacking in 2001. He flung a jar of pennies through the television screen *to bring the earth forty days of peace.*

While he was away, they fumigated the room, sent the mattress to the landfill and replaced the carpet. After he was discharged, they took him back. Where else could he go?

The office. She sat at Carl's desk, a polished hunk of mahogany made for signifying rank, not performing work. Carl had coveted this symbol of his rise from unplugging toilets but his plumber's temperament had ruled the desk too posh for the company offices. The scars on the surface had been filled in and the repair was apparent now only because she had seen where Isaac stood as he punched holes in the ceiling with a golf club.

She had heard a thudding deep in the house, which she first attributed to shoes tumbling in the washing machine. Then a crash and an arpeggio of glass. More thumps and thrashes. She isolated the racket and yanked open the office door. The blinds had been ripped down from a broken window and the walls had holes from his fists, the golf club and various items of Carl's Isaac had turned into projectiles. Drawers were upended on the floor. Carl's Rocky Mountain sheep was missing a horn. The other trophies had been pitched outdoors.

Get down this instant! Her command snapped his head around and he locked into her gaze with reddened eyes. His shoulders heaved from exertion and rage. He swung the golf club across the desk, spraying a burst of shattered glass and Jolly Ranchers.

Wh-y-y-y! One long word the way a thunderclap is one word. The way a gunshot is one word. The way goodbye is one word.

The shed. Isaac's abrupt departure left behind an array of meticulously organized junk—matchbooks from businesses in cities he'd never visited, their locations keyed to maps; a similar collection of promotional pens and mechanical pencils; a map with coins glued to it, accompanied by a spreadsheet that noted the date, location and heads-tails orientation of each discovery, tallied by month; swizzle-stick menageries of lobsters and monkeys, tropical fruits and Polynesian artifacts; flattened pasta cartons with cellophane windows; bus, train and airline schedules; many books, pamphlets and reams of files she couldn't bear to examine. Carl was ready to burn it all but Marian prevailed. They moved everything into the small storage shed that had been Carl's first workshop. Once they established contact with Isaac, she reasoned, they could arrange a deadline for him to clear it out.

In retrospect, they should have changed all the locks. Their motorhome disappeared from the pole barn while they were at mass. Carl launched a furious search of boat ramps, campgrounds and shopping center parking lots, certain he would find Isaac occupying the Winnebago somewhere in the valley. It surfaced finally in a California impoundment lot, encumbered by tickets, towing and storage fees, its interior infested and the sewage tank overflowing. Isaac was in a shelter, living under a restraining order that kept him away from the Reagan Presidential Library. Carl pressed for felony theft charges, which achieved the goal of bringing Isaac back to Colorado. The court ordered Isaac into another mental health program. Carl sent his men to haul the shed's contents to the landfill. Empty nesters at last.

The throne room, Carl had called it, reserved for the king, leaving the master bathroom for her. This was the most-scrubbed room in the house.

It was a given that Carl would not go out gently, but she had not imagined the final scene: her husband roaring as she groped her way out of a dream to shut off the deep-throated alarm clock. By the time she found him, he was silent on the floor, his boxers around his ankles. She pounded her bony fists against his chest before thinking to do compressions. The doctors later set her straight. If Carl's heart had restarted, he still would have gone under like a ship running its engines full speed ahead with a hole blasted in its hull. *There was nothing you could have done*, they said, as if their verdict were a comfort instead of the story of her life.

She lit a Parliament, as she did when she needed mental space. If she and Isaac had any future, it was shrinking fast. This cabinet mirror had always shown her a reflection especially timeworn and harsh, not the face in her head or the one she wore in other rooms; nevertheless, a prediction she had come to accept, the way of all flesh. Perhaps it was the effect of the glass and the lighting, and anyone who stepped in here saw their future selves and was appalled.

She had always read too much into things, seen what wasn't there. What was hope, if not that?

Empty hearts fill rooms to the fullest.

—"Home" with Meg Mogrin, *Grand Junction Style*

Meg had offered Pandora a room without considering how much of her mental and emotional space the girl would occupy. At various moments, she felt like a host, an aunt or a mother. Was Pandora allowed the run of the house? Did she get her own key? Were meals included? Were housekeeping duties reasonable to expect or was she a guest? Meg wouldn't impose a curfew, but what if Pandora brought someone home? And flip-flops were no way to go through life. Did she appreciate how Cody had hobbled her? Would it be too overbearing to buy her some sneakers?

Jeez, why don't you just ask her?

Whether she wants shoes?

About whether she wants you to fix her life. How did you get so angsty about what other people do?

How do you think?

Oh, it's my fault!

Let's just call it cause and effect. I'm trying to avert disaster.

As if it's worked so far. Avert your own disasters.

If you'd only listened.

Who wants their big sister's advice? I wanted your approval!

I thought I'd have time for that later.

Don't we all.

Pandora's real. I can actually help her. Ghosts are only thoughts.

Oh, ghosts're real, too. We just seem like thoughts because we can pass through walls.

To Meg's surprise, Pandora agreed to shop on Main Street instead of the mall. With little fuss, she picked out a pair of New Balance—purple and on sale. Did she know they were designed for running?

"Duh. Do you think I'm too fat to run?" She said it with a laugh and the slight flick of an edge. "I don't think you're too old."

Pandora wasn't fat. She was just…well, she defied expectations. Meg lifted another sample from the sale table. The running shoes seemed lighter these days, more advanced somehow. Like the girls. Meg was supposed to do yoga now. It was more spiritual and gauged for diminished expectations, more befitting a woman in her forties who still wanted to look good. Who could show up on time and stay on her mat and follow the leader. *Fuck yoga.*

Yes, the salesman said, he thought they had a pair in a seven-and-a-half.

Outside the store a boy sat on a brick planter tuning a mandolin. The girl beside him was blond, waifish and attractive in a still-child-like way. Her long sleeves hung past her knuckles and her thumbs protruded through holes cut in the cuffs. The boy looked older, with a dark fringe of beard and broad shoulders, a watch cap rolled onto his head. A square of cardboard propped in the open instrument case said: STARVING ARTIST'S. ANYTHING HELPS.

Pandora dropped in a few coins. Meg must have stared into the case too long because Pandora said, "I'll pay you back as soon as I get a job."

"Oh, that wasn't what I was thinking."

It was that vagrant apostrophe. Plus the illusion that starvation ennobled artistry—or vice versa. Pandora had been taken in and the boy hadn't even started to play. Meg spun down the sidewalk. Behind her, one string plucked over and over as the note rose in search of its twin tone.

For lunch, Meg chose the Italian bistro, where the music burbled at low decibels and there was no risk of loud wait-staff renditions of "Happy Birthday."

Pandora scanned the options. "What's a *panini*?"

"A pressed toast sandwich."

"Oh, like with a George Foreman grill. And *capicollo*?"

"Pork, dry cured and sliced very thin, sort of like a really lean bacon."

"Cooked?"

"I don't think so," Meg said.

"Well, I guess they wouldn't serve it if it could kill you."

Pandora talked about older friends in Las Vegas who were playing in a show band in one of the minor casinos. She was thinking about waitressing there until they had an opening for a backup singer. Meg shuddered. What were the chances Pandora would end up working in one of the other Vegas industries?

"The scholarship offer stands. You can still go to school. In a year everything will look different. Cody'll be history and maybe your parents will have eased up."

Pandora shook her head so vigorously her shoulders joined in. "You know what my father said when I left? *The difference between a happy dog and a miserable dog is obedience.* He and Cody were basically telling me the same thing—to just roll over. How did you get past all that? You're doing great on your own."

"I was lucky. My father wasn't that way. My husband wasn't either but he still became my ex. You're right not to let other people define you in the name of love or happiness—or success, for that matter."

Pandora's attention dropped to the cornichon on her plate. "Is that a pickle or is it just decoration?"

Meg wanted to laugh. "It's both. You can eat it."

Pandora chanced a nibble and her eyes widened. "You don't expect something so tiny to be that intense. It wouldn't be such a cool surprise if it was bigger."

When had she last enjoyed a small indulgence? It was as if that damn eye were a spot of noir film blood on her carpet and she couldn't let anyone in until it was gone.

Surely Pandora cleaned up worse messes in North Dakota. Maybe she could help Meg with this one.

Her tale unfolded so easily. A homeless man finds a glass eye. Believing it must be reunited with its counterpart, he has an overwhelming urge to find the owner. For weeks, he's been searching. He's covered the city with posters and handbills. The police won't take him seriously because of his history of mental problems. Isaac's caseworker is worried he can't take the stress. For all she knew, it was true.

"But maybe the eye's old and it's too late. Or the person who lost it isn't from around here," Pandora said. "Or he has a replacement, and getting it back doesn't matter any more."

"It matters to Isaac."

"But if nobody wants it..."

"Then we could just say it was ours. That will solve the mystery for him. Once the eye is in the right hands, he'll be okay."

Pandora's brows pinched. "Uh, I count four eyes at this table."

"We'd say it's a family member's—someone no longer with us. I'd been thinking about doing this myself but I'm so visible around town and I know his caseworker from the Homeless Coalition. He might suspect something funny was going on."

"So...basically, you want me to lie to a homeless man."

Well, if you want to put it that way.

"Not a lie. This is a situation where nobody knows the truth. We're filling the void with a comforting story."

"Sort of like believing in heaven, I guess."

"In a way. We're rewarding kindness with kindness—undoing his distress." *Which shall undo unto you.*

"He must be a nice man," Pandora said. "All right. Let me think up the rest of the story. Where did he find it?"

"A canyon in the Monument."

Pandora said her grandfather worked in the coalmines at Somerset, a good place to put out an eye. She conjured a drive over the Monument with this one-eyed grandfather, who wanted to teach her not to be afraid of heights. As he is hanging far over one of the overlook railings, "He sneezes. A big one. All of a sudden he's looking at us with his eye socket empty! Grandpa was always kidding around, so we think he's teasing. Now, which canyon? My story's no good if there's not an overlook."

"Your story's fine. He found it in Columbus Canyon, below Cold Shivers Point."

"Oh." Pandora's impish manner dissolved. She plucked her napkin from her lap and covered her mouth. "You must think I'm this clueless little brat. First, I blew off the scholarship. Now I make up this story about horsing around on a cliff. I didn't mean to be disrespectful. I am so, so sorry."

"Oh no, I didn't take it that way at all."

Pandora's jolly coalminer would get the job done. He was real enough and explained the facts of Isaac's discovery. Absolute truth was overrated. Even scientific truth was provisional, the best story available at the moment. Biblical truth, an all-time, all-purpose security blanket. That's all anyone wanted, the explanation that didn't raise other questions, the bedtime story that let you sleep. Before long she could sleep again.

She waved to the waiter, who knew her well. And as requested, he brought the check with cornichons instead of the customary Glitterati candies.

Pandora couldn't wait to try her new shoes and Meg felt the same. Happily, Meg offered to show her the path that wound through a spatter of trees down to the river trails.

Gravity coaxed them into an easy lope. Meg knew not to pound downhill and took care to let her body flow. No sense ruining a good start with jellied quadriceps. At the bottom, a footbridge crossed the Redlands Power Canal, a diversion from the Gunnison River that plunged through an electrical co-op's turbine before catching up with the merged waters of the Colorado. Pausing there, Pandora spotted a river otter swimming downstream with a large fish in its mouth. Meg, mindful of their feet in the new shoes, suggested they walk-run the dirt loops circling the Connected Lakes. Now, thanks to Donnie Barclay, Meg would forever think of the green fishing ponds as potholes bequeathed by gravel miners.

A heavy-set jogger, sweating and overdressed, reeled in his Labrador when he saw Meg and Pandora. Two intent bird watchers ignored them. A family on bicycles passed, crying *on your left* in four different voices. A pair of absorbed women on a bench dissected some bottomless woe.

"This is nice," Pandora said. "I hardly ever came down this far. We usually partied close to our cars."

Yes, it was great. Meg, too, was guilty of partying close to her car, her phone, her computer, her office. She came here only a few times a year.

They went as far as the owl tree, a cottonwood in which a wicker basket had been installed to support a nest. Each spring, a great horned owl pair returned to raise another hatch.

Pandora said, "I looked up some of the girls who won your scholarship. Artsy, all of them, but nobody seems to have made it. It made me think someday I might get tired of having crappy jobs just so I can do music in crappy bars. Maybe your first dream is like your first boyfriend. You have to go for it but you don't want to be stuck with him forever."

This kid. "Helen was the creative one. I was trying to be well-rounded. She was the one who went for it. I used to call her Hel and she called me Madge, if that gives you any clue."

"But you seem to love what you do now. Your tag line, *Helping you achieve the lifestyle of your dreams*, sounds creative. Tell me the best thing about it, what makes you happiest."

"I like helping people, smoothing their way." It sounded like a cliché, but wasn't happiness the realm of platitudes? "That's what real estate's about. The dream can be really different for people—a couple starting out, excited and in love; a growing, tumultuous family; a prosperous person broadcasting their success; a rancher who just wants to stay on his land after his wife dies." *A teacher in exile. A man who envisions a tent city.* "People going and coming, crossing life stages, families expanding and contracting. Finding a place to live can be a stressful time. Not always. Most of it's good."

"And the worst thing?"

The market after the bubble burst. When nothing was moving. When brokers pored over the foreclosures like chiropractors skimming ambulance call reports. When she thought she might go under. Then later, when she realized she had been a willing beneficiary from the rancid enterprise of sub-prime lending. She had ushered people to the brink of misfortune and taken her cut.

A second footbridge led over the canal to a longer, steadier slope up the bluff. It offered a good excuse to pause, to gather breath, to consider whether an eighteen-year-old mulling her future really needed to hear the worst.

Pandora made the call to Isaac. He refused her suggestion to meet at the library, insisting instead on Whitman Park. The park had a bad reputation, but with the police department in the next block, it was the most closely patrolled acre in the city. Meg parked in the museum lot across the street, which gave her a clear view. A dozen men and women idled on the grass or sat at scattered picnic tables. A plump woman sorted laundry, bright reds, yellowed whites and faded blues. She held up shirts against the leaf-filtered sunlight, crossed their sleeves one by one, and then folded each in an embrace against her chest, bowing to draw in the fragrance. Nearby, a man lay facedown in the grass, his head in the crook of one arm; the other arm splayed oddly over his back, as if disaster workers had found a detached limb and temporarily placed it with the nearest body.

"Are you certain you want to do this?" Meg offered Pandora the pepper spray she always carried to first appointments.

"Don't worry, I'm good," Pandora said. "We're going to make his day."

〰〰

Isaac was not comfortable describing himself, so to help Ann identify him he carried a book to the park, a history of Henry Ford's attempt to grow rubber in the Amazon, about the folly of men who have vision and don't care about facts. He felt the book made him seem harmless, although reading a book outdoors also marked him as a vagrant. As he crossed the street, a girl dismounted from an SUV parked in the museum lot and headed straight toward him. The purple shoes. It had to be Ann. She was younger than he'd expected from her voice on the phone and striking in a way that made him nervous. Her hair looked as if the last person to cut it had been angry with her.

"Isaac?" she said. She was smiling. Not that mask most teens wore. She seemed pleased to meet him.

"Who's driving your getaway car?"

Her laugh reassured him. She waved toward the SUV. The woman behind the wheel waved back. "Oh, my mom. You know how they worry."

He did and he didn't. Now he was hyperconscious of being observed, of being by himself with a girl. Last week, they'd arrested a man for cornering a teenager in the park bathroom and whacking off in front of her. He headed for one of the picnic tables where

Mother Ruth had parked her shopping cart. With a grey carpet pad cover and plastic cemetery garland wired to the chrome front, the cart always made him think of a Cadillac. Mother Ruth could be their chaperone. She professed to have one hundred and fourteen children, and the way she said Jesus was the father of each one sounded like a paternity claim, not a mangled Biblical reference. No matter. Mother Ruth's unreserved love for everyone was indisputable.

Mother Ruth ground tobacco shreds from her day's cigarette butt harvest. She beamed at Ann. "Did you come to see me? You look like one of my kids."

"No, we just want to sit," Isaac said.

"Well, sit. You can call me Mom anyway. You know the name of that roll you eat for breakfast? I was at the store and couldn't think of it this morning. If you're alone and all you have to go on are your thoughts, you don't even know if you're making sense when you speak. I thought it might be Danish, but that was my first husband. Or was he Flemish? Are those the same thing? I know Denmark but where's Flem?"

"It's Flanders, not Flem," said Isaac. "Flanders is a region, Flemish is their language."

"No, he didn't speak Flemish because I understood him. Is he your boyfriend, little girl?"

"We just met," Ann said. "My granddad lost his glass eye and I think Isaac found it."

"Oh, that's nice. I've lost apartments, husbands, jobs and my Supreme Court child custody case, but I always knew where to find them," said Mother Ruth. She fished a half-smoked cigarette out of the loose tobacco. "I found this but it wasn't lost. Interesting… easier than hunting for a needle in a haystack. I don't care, because I'm going to smoke it."

"Not now, please," Isaac said. Just the stench from her tobacco made him woozy.

Mother Ruth sniffed the butt and packed it straight before tucking it into her sleeve. "Okay, let's see that glass eyeball."

"Yes, let's," said Ann. She didn't seem at all bothered by Mother Ruth. In fact, they might be preparing to gang up on him.

Isaac retrieved the Band-Aid tin where he kept the eye swaddled in medicine-bottle cotton. To build anticipation, he slowly unwrapped the thick rubber bands securing the top. "I get tired of explaining this, but it's not glass and not a ball."

Mother Ruth nodded. "Just like how I always have to explain why Jesus won't wear a rubber. So what am I supposed to call it—and don't say look it up!" She waggled her eyebrows toward the girl. "He always says to look it up but you probably know that already."

"Ocular prosthesis," Isaac said.

"What did you say?" she whooped.

"*Oc*-ular pros-*the*-sis."

Mother Ruth howled and threw up her hands as if she'd been goosed. "I like glass eyeball better." Now Ann was laughing, too.

This was serious. He covered the tin with his hands and waited for quiet. Mother Ruth, however, continued to chuckle as she swept stray tobacco strands from the table, then raised the baggie above her head and peered at the sky through the plastic.

"You know the sun's magnetic field is going to flip pretty soon. The whole solar system is going to be radioactive with joy. I can feel it already." She drew the seal on the bag. "Tobacco means peace." She blew across her palms, peppering the air with scorched tobacco flakes. "Peace be on you, my children."

Mother Ruth slipped off the bench and leaned into her cart, struggling as one off-kilter wheel wobbled through the grass. Once on the sidewalk, the cart straightened and she proceeded toward the soup kitchen.

Ann waited until Mother Ruth was well away before she said, "What was that about? Is she all right?"

"I'm not sure," he said. Mother Ruth's mother-sweetness was fine in small doses, but she talked without listening. Isaac understood why. Fill the silence and drown out the voices. Act crazy and keep people at a distance. Your mind was a weapon they couldn't disarm.

Ann turned toward him now. He sensed expectation in her. Curiosity, perhaps. He felt victorious. The moment slowed, then expanded. He stood untouched at the center of a quiet explosion. Energy poured outward from him and connected with this girl. Despite everything, he had shepherded this treasure back to where it belonged. Finder and loser united! No, it was not victory he felt; it had to be happiness.

The eye was suddenly cool and insubstantial in his hand. He blew into the barrel of his fingers like a crapshooter, warming it for her first touch. He had never commanded such delicious attention. Now he desired to prolong it.

Raising his fist, he asked, "What color were his eyes?"

It was an obvious question, yet she paused.

"I was just a little girl then. I'm not sure I remember."

"Your mother must know," he said. That woman sitting in the SUV watching him as if he were a pervert. "Let's go ask her."

"She has an anxiety disorder," Ann said quickly. "That's why she sent me."

He could understand that. "Then what color are her eyes?"

"Brownish, like mine." No hesitation this time.

Could a grey-green-eyed father produce a brownish-eyed daughter? He should have looked up the genetics of eye color. He should have questioned Ann more closely when she called but it didn't occur to him until now that someone might try to deceive him. He should have taken the eye somewhere to have appraised. The lifelike detail that had startled him in the canyon now seemed artificial. That metal disk showing through the back—he had discovered it was magnetic and assumed it was to anchor the eye movement… but what if it was a transmitter?

Ann slid closer to him. "I'm sorry I don't have better proof. I appreciate all the trouble you've gone to."

Breathe.

"It wasn't trouble," he said. "Why do people call it trouble when someone does the right thing?"

She drew back a little.

"I didn't mean you," he said.

"It's a good question, though. May I see it?" She leaned close again.

Breathe.

"Oh, wow. It's amazing. Did you ever think about just keeping it?"

He did. But the glass eye song in his head kept telling him the *clutter you call a collection/A forest that's nothing but trees*. It was the forest he was after.

"I find things all the time. It's exciting at first but then it can be sad to realize that another person lost it or got rid of it because it doesn't mean the same thing any more." *Don't need eyes to cry.*

"You're right. It's my grandfather I miss, not the eye."

He held out the eye in his palm. "See this? The Muslims call it the *hamsa*, a symbol of awareness, conscience and protection. Pagans, Jews, Hindus, Christians—everybody has a version. You can look it up. And now its good fortune is back with your family."

~~~

Yoga Man.

As Meg followed the pantomime in the park, she lost any sense of having orchestrated the exchange. Isaac, Joe's brother now unveiled as Yoga Man. Pandora, a successor to Helen now impersonating Ann. Who was Meg Margaret Madge—their champion or their exploiter?

Pandora left Isaac at the picnic table. She marched straight across the grass, paused for a break in the traffic and trotted to the car, her carriage tense, her face solemn.

"Success?"

"It was easy. He was excited to give it to me."

"Did he take the reward?"

Pandora shook her head. "He thinks this is some kind of heartwarming family story. The only reward he wants is to have it told—so people will have more faith in each other, I guess. Jesus." She slumped against the door, her face pressed to the glass.

"No way." Meg had trusted Pandora to handle this. Had she softened and divulged something?

"No duh. I told him this was totally personal and private, but that I'd ask."

"Ask who?"

Pandora snapped around to glare at her. "My *mom*." The sarcasm was impeccable. "Don't you even want to see it?"

Meg wanted it gone but she held out her hand. Smooth as a polished agate, the eye cast a lifelike impression yet was inert to the touch. She sensed no emanations—of Neulan or any person. She had lost sleep, imposed herself in Brian's world, risked Pandora's safety and, worse, compromised her integrity for a piece of acrylic with an unknown history.

"I'm sorry if you felt used."

"I feel dis-*gust*-ing. He actually cared about what happened to that stupid eye, about our *family*. He trusted me and I lied to his face."

"We discussed that. It's a complicated situation."

"Why do you think it's okay to deceive someone if it's for their own good?"

"Have you ever lied to your parents to keep them from worrying?"

"Of course."

"And?"

"And to keep from getting my butt whipped."

"So there's not just one perspective to consider when you try to do something good. It's nice to believe your motives are pure and selfless, but they're always mixed up with what's good for you."

Pandora turned back to the window. "I see what you're saying but I'm not in the mood to have this conversation right now."

Pandora was right to keep caring about the good. To persist in doing right. But virtuousness could veil wickedness. Not everyone was gentle and truthful and striving for the light.

**Beware of fixer-uppers.
Nothing turns out the way you expect.**

—"Home" with Meg Mogrin, *Grand Junction Style*

The young man went door-to-door with exaggerated precision, heading up and down driveways instead of cutting straight across the lawns. A canvasser intent upon making a good impression. Meg's neighborhood was quietly prosperous, decent pickings for the right cause. She paused in her plant watering a moment too long and he caught her eye through the window, waved and raised his clipboard. A picture of a polar bear. She ducked out of the frame but it was too late. He was already coming up the drive. Good-looking in the unremarkable way that came with being dark and thin and in his early twenties. Idealistic young man plus eye contact plus polar bear argued for answering the door, and answering the door meant she'd soon be writing him a check. She wondered if this kid had learned how to keep people talking until they came around to what he wanted. A real estate continuing education class had covered the psychology of it. At first everyone resented the social pressure of being trapped. But once the solicitor became a person, they could redeem their resentment by making a generous gesture.

She answered the door with the brass watering can in her hand to show she had been interrupted doing something green already. It might get her off for twenty-five dollars.

Yes, she knew about global warming. Yes, the glaciers were shrinking and possums were heading north while polar bears had nowhere to go. Yes, powerful interests were at work before Congress and the oil companies didn't care about the earth. Okay, she would sign a petition. Sure, he could tell her what her neighbors had said on the issue.

He leaned toward her to share the confidence. "They told me you've got the biggest heart on the block," he said. "Giving scholarships. Serving on boards. Taking in strays."

"Strays?" she said. "No, that's not me. I don't have any pets."

He looked down the street as if to confirm his source. "I could've sworn. Well, here's the petition."

As she took the clipboard, he planted a foot in the threshold and grabbed her wrist, shoved inside the entry and closed the door. "Is she here?"

"Who?"

He dug his thumb into a point above her wrist and she followed the dot of pain into the living room. He called toward the back of the house. "Pandora! Pan?"

"There's no Pandora here," Meg said. "I'd appreciate it if you left right now."

Cody—it had to be Cody—lowered his voice but maintained his grip. "Please don't fuck with me."

At least he said please.

"I don't know where Pandora is. I heard she went to North Dakota with a guy she was in love with. Maybe you could ask him."

"That's it!" He dragged her into the kitchen, ripping open drawers. "You got any duct tape? I bet you'd like tape better than a dish rag down your throat."

"I'm not a screamer."

"No, sarcastic bitches think they don't have to be. I'm not going to hurt you, so just chill. Promise me you'll behave and I'll be nice, too." At her nod, he released her, took the telephone handset off the charger and slipped it in his shirt pocket. "See? Now that we're acquainted you can give me the tour."

She took him through—polite, efficient, the way she would treat any obvious non-prospect. Thinking ahead: when was Pandora due

back? Where was her cell? How fast would 911 respond? In the bedroom where Pandora was staying, Cody checked the closet, looked
under the bed and examined the t-shirt crumpled on the floor.

"So the old lady across the street was right," he said. "When's
Pandora due back?"

"I don't know."

He came close behind her so she had to move or feel his breath
on her neck. "The kitchen seems like a nice place to wait," he said.

Across the valley, the Book Cliffs had adopted a lavender glow. Small
birds flitted in the arbor, drawn by the memory of grapes. Meg sat
so Cody would have to turn away from the view in order to keep an
eye on her. If Pandora came in via the patio, she might see him first
and have a chance to run.

"Not a bad neighborhood. I figured you in something fancier,
though. I mean, looking at your website and you being in the business and all."

It made her ill to think of Cody probing her life more deeply
online, reading her website, checking the value of her home, esti-
mating her income. Doing what she did every day.

"The real estate business teaches you to live below your means,"
she said. "You see how fast the good times can turn around—for a
person, a neighborhood or a whole town. It sounds like Williston
was a rough place."

His eyes flashed agreement. "Land of opportunity but still a hell-
hole. Even worse if you're a girl, I guess. But why did she blame me
there's no Target? They have a Herberger's in Dickinson." He began
a circuit of the kitchen, opening cabinets, flicking light switches,
feeling the underside of the countertops, tapping the walls, joggling
the patio door on its rail. He had to be on something. "I was taking
care of her as good as conditions allowed, and I had a plan for us. I
was on track to make almost fifty-thou just driving a truck, plus my
paper route for some extra income."

"In that business, I imagine you have subscribers in good times and bad."

Cody checked her expression and smiled to see that Meg knew. He withdrew from his shirt pocket a green packet of gum that opened like a business card case. He thumbed up two pieces. Meg declined. His shrug said, *okay, more for Cody*, and he peeled off both wrappers.

"When you get the dry mouth, the acid goes to town. Saliva protects your teeth." Cody seemed to wait for her to thank him for this health tip.

"Would you like something to drink?" Distract him. Slow him down. Think of a way to warn Pandora.

"You got any beer?"

"I only have wine. Some Chardonnay?"

"Is that red or white?"

"White."

"I'm good."

"Cody, I honestly don't know when she'll be back. Rather than you waiting around, how about if I talk to her and she can call you, no pressure. Then ask her what she wants to do."

Cody's jaw stopped working the gum. "What choice does she have? We're engaged. And her family, hah. Look where she came to—to some lady who didn't even want to help her in the first place."

So that was the world according to Cody. Without a choice of men, Pandora didn't have a choice in life. Obey and serve. It did not seem productive to argue. Not unless she was prepared to be duct-taped to a chair.

"So what if going to school is the right thing? You can't force her to go back."

"Who said anything about force? She's upset with me, okay, but you and I should be able to talk rationally. We get how the world is. Pandora thinks it's all about her. About her becoming a singer, like if that's not her career, she'll never be happy. And she thinks if

I don't say go for it, I don't support her. As if working my ass off isn't supporting her. If she goes to Denver, I know what happens. She meets some guitar player dude. He starts writing her love songs while I'm driving a honeywagon in fucking North Dakota. I'm not going to find another girl like her. Not up there. A little patience, a little sympathy would be nice. I've got shit going on, too."

A car stopped on the street, doors slamming. Cody shot her a look—*Don't even think about it*—and stepped into the living room where he could spy through the front blinds. She should just walk out. She had nothing to do with his problems. This was her home, her neighborhood. She wasn't some browbeaten high school girl. What would he do? She'd half-risen when he returned.

"False alarm. Now please *sit*," Cody hissed. "I'm not here to harass you, so don't get your buns in an uproar." He strolled to the refrigerator and found a carton of orange juice, unscrewed the cap and raised it to his mouth before turning to Meg. "You have a boyfriend? You hate it when we drink out of the carton, right?"

He set the carton on a counter, took down a glass and extracted his chewing gum. "I should drink more juice. It's easy to eat like shit in the oil patch unless you've got someone fixing the meals for you. I had a girlfriend, but hey, no kitchen. She told you, right? I moved into the man camp and left her with the truck. What could I do? I needed to keep my strength up. She had all day to feed herself."

He drained the glass, replaced the gum and refreshed it with another tab. "Citrus has a lot of acid." He drifted back to sit across from Meg. The lunch nook filled with an acrid smell, half sweat and half spearmint.

"I'm saying girls aren't the only ones who have dreams. The patch is full of guys who are doing it for their family, and their wives or girlfriends back home're saying, *screw this, I'm not moving there*. So they stay where it's fucked up or go home where there's no work—they can't win. Eating alone, sleeping alone, trying to stay focused so they don't get killed on the job, trying to stay connected while they get further and further away inside. Who cares about the money then? They'll fork over hundreds for anything that makes them feel better. Men depressed out of their gourds, there's your moneymaker in oilfield services.

"My dad left the family to work in Alaska and never came back. He stopped sending child support and my mom didn't even bother reporting him. He died by himself in a fucking trailer in the pines. The funeral notice didn't say what he did for a living, who his family was, just *he enjoyed working on his Jeep and took advantage of everything the outdoors had to offer*. I mean, that's a man's life—a trailer, the outdoors and a Jeep?"

"Cody, it's good you want more out of life. But did you ever consider that maybe you and Pandora aren't compatible? That it's not a simple matter for her to change what she wants?"

"I do see now why she came here. You remind me of her, with your questions like put-downs I'm not supposed to notice. She didn't give me a chance."

"She didn't sign up for drug dealing and being held captive."

Cody stiffened. "Who said she was a captive?"

"Maybe those weren't her words…"

"Fuck!" Cody slapped the table, his eyes dark. "Are you a captive? No. I just need you to stay out of this so I can handle it." He yanked money from the pockets of his cargo pants and began throwing it on the table—rolls, wads, singles. "She wants to be a singer—fine! She can sing for me. Make recordings? How much does that cost? I'll pay. I'm not risking my ass because it's fun. Why doesn't she ask me what I want?"

"What *do* you want, Cody?" Pandora spoke quietly. She didn't appear afraid. Resigned, perhaps. "I hope you're not bothering my friend."

"We've been talking about life. You're looking good, Pan."

"I look like hell," she said. The truth was somewhere in between. She stuffed a windbreaker into the gym bag hanging from her shoulder. Her fingers touched her blistered forehead. "My whole face is going to peel off."

He reddened. "Where's my ring?"

"Your ring? I thought it was my ring."

Cody worked his wad of gum. His fists clenched. "We're not talking about this here. Let's go. I've got the truck parked in the next block."

"I saw it," she said. "I'm not getting in that thing ever again."

"It doesn't have to be back to North Dakota."

"I don't care where you go."

"You mean we."

"I mean you. Pick up the money, please."

Cody shook his head. He stepped back to where he could watch them both. "You pick it up. I earned it for you. So you could do what you want."

"I don't care. With you, it's money first, then live the way you want. I don't want to be like that."

"That's the way it works."

"No, it doesn't. That's just the way it's done."

Cody turned to Meg. *We're both in business,* his expression seemed to say, *help me straighten her out.* But Meg fixed on Pandora. Somehow her impulse to leave had transformed into the courage to face him down.

Cody's attention snapped back to Pandora. "Oh, so she's like your big protector now. You think so?" He snatched the house phone from his pocket and smashed it at Meg's feet.

"Cody, calm down," Meg said. She gauged the distance to the knife block on the counter but it seemed like a very bad idea. She was no one's protector.

"Where's your cell? Give me your cell!"

"Leave her alone," Pandora said. "She hasn't done anything to you."

"You two aren't telling me what to do."

"Three," said Pandora.

"What?"

"Three." She pointed at Meg, then herself. "One… two…" Her hand came out of the gym bag gripping a pistol. "Three. You said a girl's gun would be good enough for me."

Cody seemed aggrieved. He took a tentative step toward Pandora. "You won't shoot me."

"I won't *kill* you," she said. He moved again and she leveled the gun, letting it wander just enough to be worrisome. "Not on purpose."

Meg's words jumped between them. "She doesn't want to hurt you, Cody, and maybe you didn't mean to hurt her, but you can't undo the past. Now it's about how you both go forward."

"Stay out of this!"

"I'm in it. You both put me here. Pandora came to me for a safe place so she didn't have to use that gun. You came here to force her back. Think about where that's heading."

"What did I ever do that was so bad?" A demand. Another righteous man forcing her to the edge.

"It's not what you're doing, it's what you're becoming. I hope you'll enjoy working on your goddamn Jeep."

Meg saw Cody sway and she felt the gun in her own hands so acutely she had to pause. Wesley Chambers had flared up and then run off. Neulan had threatened and then surrendered. Hungerman had drifted away. Even Brian. She sensed the power of denial and condescension, how it only worked on those groping toward their better selves. She could push Cody over the edge or she could disarm this right now.

"Whatever good thing you're planning, you better be working on it now. Love is the work of a lifetime. Maybe you think you can start being your best self after you're through partying, after you get established, but I'm telling you, we don't get to choose our moment of judgment."

Cody grabbed the nape of his neck and crooked his head toward Pandora. "I need you."

Pandora had allowed the barrel to sag. "And I need myself. All the time, not just when you're through with me."

"Pan…"

"No. Go, please—out the back."

He turned toward the patio. The Book Cliffs had flattened to a charcoal backdrop hung beneath an indigo sky. Cody slid the door, admitting the surf of distant traffic. "You'll be sorry," he said.

Pandora's elbow twitched as if denying a fly a place to land. "Just don't try to make me. Let me be sorry on my own."

He flung his arms up and back, the aggressive shrug of a drunk dismissing a fight he'd pretended to want. After he lunged out, Meg snatched her cell phone.

"Don't," Pandora said. "Please. He's not coming back. What did he do, really? He left a pile of money on your table and asked me to go with him. I'm the one who pulled a gun."

"You're not thinking straight."

"Probably not. But I don't want to give him another reason to be angry. He's already humiliated. Oh, I'm so sorry I brought him into your home. Thank you for talking to him. I could have really screwed things up with this." Pandora ejected the magazine and cleared the round from the pistol's chamber. She knew what she was doing.

"You convinced him. The gun just made him listen. I don't believe you would have shot him."

"Cody thought I might, though, so what does that tell you?"

"Do you feel you need to keep it?"

"God, no."

"Then we're taking care of this tonight."

All of it.

For whatever crime-novel reason, the gun seemed to belong in the river. The Redlands Parkway bridge, only minutes away, felt too close to home. The Broadway bridge was already fraught with the memory of Brian helicoptering the baseball bat out of Neulan's Jeep. So Meg drove them west on the old U.S. highway. They traveled without speaking until the freeway, where two spotless truck stops attached to the newly rebuilt interchange glared at each other.

"This is where I got dropped by a semi driver," Pandora said. "I couldn't get a ride back into town. After I started walking, I decided it was just as close to your house."

Meg thought of Pandora faced with trudging five miles in those flip-flops, refusing to be pinned by a driver's whim or another man's unbending desires. Pandora would be dynamite at the office. Personality, wit, resourcefulness—with some guidance, she could go far. And her music? Well, there was the college here, and Meg knew the owners of two clubs.

At Fruita, where the old highway and Interstate converged again, she turned south toward the river. Once past the bright strip mall, the McDonald's and the Dinosaur Museum, the road plunged deep into the prior century, past trailers and a demolition-filled floodplain. Unlike the three-span iron truss bridge it had replaced, the utilitarian bridge with its knee-high guard rails afforded the disposal of evidence without the bother of slowing down.

Pandora took the gun from her bag, gripped the barrel and backhanded it with a practiced snap of the wrist. She settled, tilted the seat back as far as it would go and cradled a newborn smile. The gun was gone and so was her connection to Cody. Could release be that easy? Meg felt the hard nodule of the glass eye in her pocket, carried like a tumor. She wanted no more reminders of malignancy.

She turned the car around at Dinosaur Hill and placed the eye in Pandora's hand. "Put it out there as far as you can."

The girl cranked her seat upright as the car rolled down the hill. This time, they could see the dark river as they approached the bridge. Pandora flicked her arm hard toward the water. The eye might have been a bottle cap, gone in a blink. Meg powered up the windows. They peered at each other in the car's confessional darkness.

"Why?" Pandora said.

"It wasn't mine to keep." *True enough, but say something truer.* "I hate being reminded of loss."

Pandora pressed her forehead against the glass. After a moment she said, "Then what's left to remember?"

Ahead, the garish truck plaza lights presided over the duel of generic gasoline brands—yellow-and-red versus yellow-orange-and-red.

"Can we pull off here?" Pandora said.

"Are you not feeling okay?" Of course she wasn't. She'd hardly had time to process the breakup. Even cutting loose a bad boyfriend wasn't pure relief.

"Did you notice? The station on the north side—Loves. One says Pilot, the other one says Loves."

The names of the companies were everywhere. On the fuel price signs. The pump canopies. The building façades. Meg headed for the orange and yellow with red hearts, a citrus bowl of Love.

"The truck driver said hitchhikers can't be choosers. I thought he was being an asshole passing up the earlier exit but maybe coming here was a sign," Pandora said. "Pilot and Loves. It's sort of like *Jesus loves* or *God is my co-pilot.*"

"That heart is supposed to be an apostrophe," Meg said. "It makes the Love possessive."

She eased the car under the bright lights illuminating the concrete pad. Trucks idling. Air brakes releasing. Diesel exhaust. Hamburger grease. Gasoline vapors. Hot rubber. The atmosphere saturated with depletion.

Pandora said, "You've been so awesome to me."

"It's nothing. It's a pleasure to help."

"It's like having a big sister all of a sudden. I've learned so much from you in just a few days."

Just wait. You're only getting started.

"What you said to Cody, about trying to fix your mistakes before you know the person you're trying to be..."

Is that what I said?

"How life's about the way you go forward and you shouldn't try to undo the past."

But we just undid it. We're free.

"I know you were saying that to me, too. But I'm not like you. Music...music isn't about being in charge. I mean, you have to work and practice and pay your dues but then you release it and you have no more control over it. The music does what it does and it's different for everyone. All the singer does is find the spirit of it so someone else hears something they never heard before. Or maybe they won't feel so alone. Thanks for the ride. Thank you for all you've done."

It's barely a start.

"Going on to Las Vegas is what I should've done in the first place instead of thinking I could come home."

Your things, back at the house.

"Before he came, I'd already packed the gym bag to go. And now I have Cody's cash with me."

A thousand at most. It won't last very long.

"My friends in Las Vegas said I could stay with them. I know playing in a casino sounds gross but it might be fun."

Pandora opened the door and stepped out. "I wrote a song last night called 'Purple Shoes.' It's not finished, though. Listen for it someday on the radio."

The porch light was on as she'd left it. She drove past the house and through the subdivision on the lookout for Cody's pickup before returning to open the garage door. Casting lights ahead of her, she disarmed the beeping security system, stared hard at the panel and rearmed it in *Stay* mode for the first time in her life. Shrapnel from the house phone lay scattered on the kitchen tiles. Green gum wrappers. She took a boning knife from the block and placed it on the counter, then swept up the pieces, listening past the hiss of broom and plastic. She dumped the remains of the orange juice carton into the sink and picked up the knife. Seeing the stockade wall of books in the living room somehow fortified her. The house was substantial in a good neighborhood. She was not some vulnerable girl. She checked the front entry. Cody's phony polar bear clipboard was still in the corner where he had flung it. Venturing down the hallway, she regretted for the first time its low-intensity lighting, although tonight a searchlight would not have swept away her apprehension.

The guest room door was ajar. Pandora had removed the linens and mounded them at the foot of the bed. Crowning the peak, two flip-flops propped upright like stone tablets freshly inscribed:

Meg set down the knife and felt the room pass back into her hands. *Life's about the way you go forward*, she had advised, as if Pandora needed to be told. And the kid seemed to know the rest, too. Half the purpose of making plans was to gather courage to take the leap. You write the song and release it and then the music does what it does.

Curious how Pandora's brief occupancy had recharged the space. Though the room had never been a shrine, it would be good to complete the transformation—redecorate, donate the furniture and mix Helen's books in with hers.

Meg felt transported to that long ago instant when Hel's flight plucked Madge off the wall. To that flash of shock before they floated as one and tumbled, uproarious in the sand. To this moment when she knew that Helen's picture of the leaping sisters was gone.

Which factors have contributed to your homeless situation?

—Vulnerability Index Prescreen for Single Adults

His mother sat in front of the house as he wheeled up. Isaac didn't remember a chair outside before and now there were two. He walked his bike the last fifty yards of the driveway because he knew she'd want to finish her cigarette. Her shortened drags came closer together as she converted his pace into the number of puffs remaining. She had always been cancer-thin and her smoking made a point of it. Her yellow dress hung loose from her coat hanger collarbone. The tendons in her neck strained as if to keep her face moored to the jawbone.

He gently lowered his bicycle to the gravel rimming the entry. The bird he'd left under the bush was gone. Would a coyote eat a dead bird or had his mother buried it? He kept the question to himself. After his meltdown at Carl's funeral, burials might still be a sore topic between them. She ground out her cigarette, plucked the ashtray from the chair and cleared him a seat with a flutter of her free hand. No one bothered with hello in his family.

"You *are* doing better now. I can see it," she said, her voice brown around the edges. "Did you have a nice ride?"

As if he pedaled for recreation. It was his fault for riding out here the first time looking for sympathy. All he'd done was open up the past and now she had an excuse to rub his nose in it. "It was great—except for the speeding ticket."

"I know you're teasing," she said. "Joe told me you've been through a rough stretch and now you're pulling things together."

No, the rough still stretched before him and things were not together, he simply had fewer things to pull. Isaac thanked his brother for the spin. He was not going to butter her up or troll for pity. He'd overheard too many drunks hitting up their mothers for money, acting solicitous before ratcheting up tales of woe into demands that turned into the same old argument. Nobody, even mothers, liked supporting losers.

"Once I get my replacement ID I can look for work again. Then I can buy a new computer and find a place to get indoors for the winter."

"Shelly told me you just got a computer."

"Somebody stole it."

His mother looked at him hard, as if she could still see his bruises.

"So," she said and let hang the most terrifying word in the Samson language, with ten meanings depending on the inflection. This was not the insouciant *so* that comes with a question mark; not the exclamatory one; not the conclusive, ergo sum *so* or the inconclusive one that dangles at the end of a conversation. It was closer to the declarative yet elliptical *so*; a portentous, oxygen-sucking *so* that pitched him trembling into the ensuing silence to contemplate which of his sins was about to be chewed over. The Chinese would know what he was talking about.

"What did you ever think you were going to do with those mush melons?"

At least she wasn't going to beat him up over the computer. "They were cantaloupe."

"Thank you. Cantaloupes. It was quite a shock."

What made cantaloupes shocking, he didn't know. In a normal family, by this time the story would be a joke: *Remember when Isaac hid all those rotten fruits and vegetables in his room?* He had been fretting about the threat of global collapse posed by the Y2K software bug, but he was also distressed by the waste at work. The waste of pumping Colorado River water to grow crops in California that would be picked green and shipped back to Colorado, only to overripen and be pulled from the Safeway shelves and fed to pigs. The waste of treatment that used talk and medications to press him into a more sluggish and repressed version of himself. The waste of Johnny Depp's talents in *The Astronaut's Wife*. Petra—the first girl (and last) interested in him—took offense at his critique of Johnny Depp, and abandoned Isaac at the movie theater. How could he explain to his mother those terrible, out-of-body days that followed?

No one in the family was ever going to laugh at that story.

She said, "Will you come for a walk with me? I'm not supposed to go wandering off alone." She slid her arm through his and led him around to the back of the house, leaning into him as they climbed the slope to the canal road. Her tobacco-sweet smell surprised him. It felt strange to be trespassing with his mother. Canal roads were where kids sought escape from parents. Drinking, fighting, making out, canal surfing. For the first time, he conceived of his mother as a rebel.

The dirt road drew them west on a line scribed between Martian badland and earthling settlement. Where the irrigation water flowed south, greenery sputtered or sprawled according to the property owner's preferences. Mature cottonwoods shaded farmsteads surrounded by alfalfa; subdivided lots staked saplings against their wills to bluegrass carpets or allowed desert plantings to sip from gravel-covered drip systems. The unobstructed view behind the houses revealed grills, fire pits and meat smokers; dirt bikes, trailers and ATVs; trampolines, batting cages and play structures; dog runs, rabbit hutches and llama pens; spoked wagon wheels, rusty plows and broken-down wheelbarrows; birdbaths, pools and hot tubs. And sheds. Sheds for outdoor gear keeping, plant potting, car restoring, woodworking, junk collecting, pottery firing, RV screening and beer brewing. Sheds were where the owners fled to escape the gravity of those houses, where they were free to fiddle with a shortwave, grow weed, keep a hostage or store bulk food supplies in the event of end times.

At length, his mother spoke. "That GE business…I hope you're done with that, too."

So she wanted to plow up old history after all. She didn't understand that his problem was not with GE—not alone. GE was one lone sea monster pulled up from the deep. His problem was that people declared it a freak. They wouldn't admit that there had to be many other such giants living undisturbed in the depths of the ocean. Others saw a random universe or the hand of God in things, while Isaac, like the boy in the movie who saw dead people, saw systems. The universe was pulsing with them. Someone had to pay attention.

He began counting his breaths as he had learned to do when his brain sprang this snake of thoughts against him.

"I don't think about that any more, Mom." It was what she wanted to hear.

"And what about Mr. Garrison—is that all settled?"

William Garrison had seen promise in Isaac and offered him an interview and they had ruined his chances by not delivering the letter. So, no, that was not all settled. How could it be?

She read his silence. "Maybe it wasn't the best idea to keep that letter from you, but what else could we do? It was just an initial phone screening. You were in no shape to be interviewed, let alone take a job. You couldn't even make it in to Safeway. How would you survive in Maryland where you didn't know anybody? We were going to show you the letter once your condition improved—to give you some hope things could turn out for the better."

She couldn't possibly understand hope. She had married Carl Samson.

"That was for *me* to decide. When I saw it was too late to reply, I could feel you and dad sitting on my chest. I had to get you off."

"It was an anxiety attack, sweetie."

"No, it was an epiphany. I saw that this consciousness, which was so bright inside my head, was not required for the world to keep going. Like when a light goes out in a room and all the furniture is still there. The light doesn't matter."

He didn't cry, though he thought for a moment he would.

"And you thought Mr. Garrison appreciated the light."

"I needed to know!"

"But you never found him."

"No, I never did."

"But with your master's degree you could have gotten another job."

He hadn't wanted her to worry. He almost had it. He would have finished, but the system knew he was dangerous. It saw he had hold of the string and it waited. He let go for one second and away it went, all that work, like a helium balloon. He watched it disappear.

∿

Marian heard the distant chuff of an air brake that told her the driver from Barclay's Biffies had arrived at the house. Then the whine of the lift gate. Sound traveled far with nothing to absorb it. The vast landscape served as filter and amplifier both.

Isaac talked on and on. He could not help himself. He saw a poor cow across the canal and he was off to the races. The only way for that cow to escape the meat grinder system, he said, was to produce more calves. To be a mother of meat.

"Stop. We've gone far enough," she said.

Isaac quieted, tucked her arm through his and throttled the jitter in his stride. She did not understand her son. Oh, she gathered him as a general concept, in the way she knew the canal water would flow west and south from here and not in other directions. She knew his mind was crowded, his thoughts consuming, yet somehow he managed to function. Perhaps his library studies had helped him structure a medicating sense of order, and that was enough.

Nothing she had done to wrap him in safety and comfort had made a difference. Even for normal mothers with normal sons it was difficult to save them from spending too much, from driving like their fathers, from heartache, from getting stuck in the wrong job. They had tried so hard with Isaac, yet he floated between extremes— intelligent and proud, unpredictable and unmanageable. Doctors suggested institutional solutions. Friends advocated for detaching with love and allowing Isaac to hit bottom. Oh, how simple and necessary the advice had sounded. Self-preservation without guilt. The magical healing of neglect. None of it sank in, not until one terrible night when Carl brought his gun to their bedside, *just in case*, he said, *just in case*. Finally they looked at the terrifying blank of their son and had no choice but to cry in each other's arms.

∿

He was certain the portable toilet hadn't been standing there when they left the house. It was one of the old blue ones from when his father owned the business, now with a Barclay Biffies label covering Samson Sanitation. Contractors were good at helping old ladies spend their money.

"What's wrong with your house?"

His mother retrieved her Parliaments from a pocket. "Nothing. The biffy is for the shed."

There was nothing wrong with the shed, either. After they built the house, Carl's workshop overwhelmed the garage and he decided he needed a new one. Marian had told him it had better not be unsightly. This miniature country cottage prefab had been his vengeful compliance. He wired the shed with enough outlets to run an appliance store and filled it with power tools and big red Craftsman tool chests but his father must have felt his balls shrink every time he set foot inside. Outside it still resembled an oversized dollhouse: yellow vinyl clapboard siding, twin imitation casement windows flanked by tan ornamental shutters, two flower boxes and a hipped roof with a gabled dormer centered over the entry. All these features were jammed into fourteen feet of corner-to-corner symmetry with no sense of proportion.

His mother rapped the cigarette package against her hand. A key slipped from the cellophane. She restored the cigarettes to her pocket and fitted the key in the knob. There was hardly any point in locking the hollow fiberglass door. He peered into a window box, its bottom covered with a whitish crust. No flowers had ever bloomed there.

"We last used it to store your things. After you took the Winnebago, well, that was it for Carl. It didn't mean he didn't love you—that *we* didn't… Well, it's too late now. I'm sorry if any of it was precious to you."

She didn't have to apologize. His parents had freed him to survive without attachment. Now he and his friends lived off the town's discards and discarded in turn.

The interior was almost empty. The built-in workbench remained, the wood dinged and scarred and speckled with constellations of drips, rings and crescent moons. A folded card table tucked against a wall. A trunk. A broom stood in the corner. A whiff of Pine-Sol.

"What do you plan to do with it?" he said.

"An experiment. All I can offer you right now is shelter. If it works out, we'll see. If you fill it up with junk or burn it down—at least I'll know there was nothing more I could do."

What about my birth certificate? It was the first of a thousand questions plucking at him and he knew better than to ask any aloud now. Sometimes his mother misspoke. Shelter was not all she offered. Taking in someone was never one thing.

She touched his arm. He should hug her but his arms wouldn't move. She lifted his hand and placed the key in it.

"Sweetie, with so much flying at you, you've never had a moment to look very deep into anybody else. Why, when my brain popped, nobody mattered to me, either. I was working so hard to survive. But if you don't watch it, survivors end up alone."

This wasn't anything he didn't know. She was telling him she knew it, too.

"I'm not so proud of what I did to survive. You were the one drowning and I told myself I had to cut you loose for your own good. I thought you were going to drag me under."

She dabbed at her eyes but he didn't see any tears. He supposed he had dried her out.

"All you have to do is take care of yourself and keep out of trouble. No roommates or complaints from the neighbors. No run-ins with the police. No Isaac Samson showing up in my newspaper."

He couldn't tell her that if the eye story appeared, it should count in his favor. "Sometimes the paper won't print what somebody does."

"They do if you die." She probed for her cigarettes. "I bought an air mattress. It's in the trunk. You should have an armchair and a rug to make it homier. You could cook with a hot plate and you can have one of my bar stools to eat at the workbench. But a grown man probably doesn't want his mother decorating his room."

He could not stop himself. "It's not a room, Mom, it's a shed. A room is a divided part within a building."

A cigarette took up whatever lips she might have pursed. The rest of her expression sank deep in her skull. She turned away from him to hiss out a straw of smoke. "You might try a thank you."

"Thank you. It's just—I'm afraid. Afraid of screwing this up."

"You think I'm not?"

So.

Part Three

June

A home is less an investment than a reflection of what we include or exclude from our lives.

—"Home" with Meg Mogrin, *Grand Junction Style*

Once a month Meg had to deliver seven hundred words celebrating the acquisition, maintenance or disposition of beautiful spaces. With the next column due in three days, she had yet to begin. Ideas no longer descended from the clouds; they were increasingly wrenched from the tense crevice between panic and deadline. Her struggle of late owed to this realization: the magazine cared only that her musings reflected tasteful consumption and kept the advertising pages from flowing into each other.

With two free hours in the office, she had better take a hack at something.

At infertile moments like this she dipped into a file called Inspiration where she stocked article excerpts, quotes, news items and highlighted book passages. Once they lost their former context, the fragments might trip loose an original thought. It was not plagiarism, she told herself, but a sort of intellectual property flipping.

Sadly, the easy pickings had been harvested. Skimming, she found the dregs too self-conscious, obvious or banal. "Houses are vessels of desire." "The ache for home lives in all of us." "Put storage in otherwise wasted areas: above doorways, under stairs or between studs in interior walls." *No, no and no.*

Oh, well. She always came up with something. She opened a New Blank Document in Word. The *Blank* seemed superfluous. *Just start typing.*

The credit crunch that fell out of the recession is nowhere to be seen. Lenders are writing mortgages again, and the terms and rates raise questions of

Blah, blah. She struck the lines and tried again.

Real estate is an asset, and a home is the largest single investment you may ever make. However, until you pay off the mortgage your investment belongs to the bank.

She hit a triple return to distance herself from the irate call she'd receive from Jules Lodge the day that piece hit the stands.

Home draws the sharpest line between what we include or exclude from our lives.

She stared at the words, fingers on the keyboard. Where was she going with this? *Grand Junction Style* readers didn't want to be depressed about all the secrets and crap in their closets and the friends they never invited over.

This wasn't just a summer funk. Somehow, she had lost the groove.

It had been agonizing to watch the City Council's Vagrancy Committee crush the life out of the tent city idea. Eve, feeling blindsided by Winslowville and by Wesley's infatuation with the glue factory site, had rained her wrath on Meg and the ill feeling still festered. Jules was screwing Hungerman, or whatever it was they did under cover of their own little nondisclosure agreement. And Pandora's departure had left a surprising void in the house.

Dwelling on lost siblings—now, that was her forté. Family, nostalgia, nesting, security—home as a source of strength and a well of pain!

The home my parents left behind on Gunnison Avenue was not the darling craftsman cottage they had purchased the year before I was born... Over the years, they nudged it toward perfection, never expecting the life-wrenching changes

Oh, puke. You are not exploiting Helen's empty bedroom!

Who was she to pronounce upon the essence of home? The cursor taunted her to continue. If she typed any more in this frame of mind, it would have to be the letter resigning her column.

Ashley cracked Meg's door and peeped through the opening. The assistant's doll face contained only the essential features—bright eyes, nub of nose, molded lips—leaving Ashley to paint in the rest. The abbreviated eyebrows, stenciled a touch high, gave her an expression of perpetual surprise.

"Sorry to interrupt," Ashley said. "A gentleman is outside looking for someone named Ann. He won't listen when I tell him she's not here."

This was exactly the sort of thing Meg had called out in Ashley's performance review. The girl was baffled by any departure from the routine. The man probably got off the elevator on the wrong floor and was confused by the look-alike reception areas.

"Ann who?"

"He didn't give a last name."

Meg put her irritation on hold. Unfortunately, teachable moments called for teachable students. It would be quicker to deal with this herself. She looked into the lobby and saw a delivery person lingering with a sort of jittery indifference. No, it was Isaac Samson.

Ann. Isaac had a crush on Pandora. Or he'd changed his mind and wanted the eye back. Or—*he knows.*

The familiar churn of if-thens, might-buts and shouldn't-shoulds. Whatever this was about, she still had the advantage. There was no more glass eye; Isaac Samson was only a street character; she was Meg Mogrin. This was her office. Her company.

"I'll talk to him," she said. "Offer him some water and put him in the front conference room. Leave the inner blinds open. If anything threatening happens, call 911."

Ashley's brows arched even higher. "What should I say then?"

"Oh, God, never mind. Just put him in the room and I'll be out in a second."

Ashley made her way across the carpet with the deliberate steps of a bomb-squad specialist. The 911 thing was probably overkill. Isaac had given Pandora no problems. She had even been charmed. Meg had been, too, from a distance, once upon a time. She slipped on the bulky cardigan kept for when the air conditioning dropped too low. From her purse, cash went into the left pocket, pepper spray in the right. Just in case.

Ashley sat with fingertips poised on the desktop, impersonating a lab subject who awaited a random shock. Isaac was intent upon reading the High Country Living label on the water bottle. *Good. Stay calm. Don't give anything away.*

"I was right," he said when Meg entered. "I thought you looked semi-familiar. You already know me. It didn't seem that important until nothing happened."

"I'm sorry, I don't understand what you're talking about. What did you expect would happen?"

Isaac screwed up his face and drew out the name. "A-a-a-n said she would talk to her mother about the newspaper doing a story. She said it specifically. Months went by and no one from *The Clarion* contacted me. Had she forgotten? Did her so-called mother say no? Did the paper turn her idea down?"

"Excuse me..."

He made an agitated unravelling motion with his hands. "All I knew was Ann and the face of the woman in an SUV. I don't like half-knowing things. Then I noticed your ad in Sunday's paper. Yes, Meg Mogrin!" He raised a triumphant finger. "Coincidence rewards a prepared mind! I went to your website. Don't realtors parade their blessed family life? It said nothing about a daughter. So if Ann wasn't your daughter, maybe her name wasn't Ann, either, and maybe nothing was as presented that day. Even normal life can be unruly. Order is important. Disorder, well, that's what we call a disease, a disturbance of the norm. Not everything lines up in neat, orderly categories. In fact, categories are our invention imposed on the world to help us make sense of things."

He was nervous, scattered, speaking in a gentle, impersonal manner to the corner of the room.

"Still, it wasn't hard to locate your father—that would be Ann's supposed grandfather. It turns out he wasn't a miner and he's not dead. He was an American Family agent and he's still living in Arizona."

Isaac paused and finally made eye contact, as if expecting her to congratulate him.

"Obviously you have excellent research skills," she said. Fluency, not so much, but his meaning was clear enough. This was leading to uncomfortable places. She hoped the scotched story about a family reunited with a glass eye was all he cared about. "Did you consider that I was merely a friend giving Ann a ride that day?"

"That's a logical possibility." He took a long drink, then acted surprised his water bottle was almost empty. "But she pointed you out as her mother. Parent or not, I'm puzzled that someone of your stature would be involved in a prank."

Pandora had been upset at being used. Meg wouldn't use her again.

"It wasn't a prank. I involved her to protect my privacy."

"Privacy! Sometimes I forget there is such a thing." He rapped his temples with his fingertips. "I respected Ann's request for privacy. But you… didn't… respect… me." Isaac rocked as if processing an undulating signal.

This was not leading to a good place. She touched the lump of cash in her pocket. He'd already turned down a reward. She had no idea what a homeless man would consider a persuasive amount of money.

"Pandora did respect you. She told me so."

"Ah, Pandora, not Ann. I did like that girl. But I'm talking about you, now. The purported mother, the mastermind. I'm used to being underestimated. Dismissed. Excluded. I try not to pay attention, but you went out of your way."

"I'm sorry…"

Isaac stood abruptly, banging his chair hard into the wall. His hand shot up as if to block the words. "*Keep* your sorry! You don't even know me!"

The pepper-spray canister in her hand surprised them both. As if it had gone off, Isaac's face compressed. "Fake politeness is the worst."

He rapped his forehead with the soft nautilus of his fist and drew in a deep breath. Meg did the same until their lungs filled together, two accordions playing the same slow song. His body relaxed and his face became placid again but Meg only mirrored his calm. Her insides still throbbed from the race of adrenaline.

"When you and Ann—Pandora—came along to claim the eye, I was happy until I realized you'd lied to me. I have to be careful. Anger leads to problems. It's bad for the world. Okay, boo-hoo, move on. That's what they teach you; don't obsess about things you can't change. Most of the time, I just let other people's misperceptions go. I know I'm a very intelligent person. I understand many things automatically. I used to think it was voices. Now I know it's my mind reporting back from its wanderings. Many things, though, I look up. I have a degree in library sciences. I know how to find almost anything if it's written down. Suppose a question occurs to me, a puzzle presents itself, like a glass eye found in a canyon. What if I'm the only one to see it, the only one who can solve it? Everything is connected. Suppose the world collapsed because Isaac Samson didn't do his job.

"You asked for privacy and I respected that, but when an upright person like you lies to get something from me, I want to know why. I understand the creeps who stole my computer really were just after money. At least you didn't beat me up."

He smiled to show her he was making a joke. The threat seemed to have passed. Isaac's intensity was not physical; he vibrated from the thoughts blowing through the double reed of his mind. She would give him a few more minutes. She sat back down to show she was not afraid.

"If you've come here for the answer to your puzzle, I'm not going to satisfy your curiosity," she said.

"You don't have to. I know the answer."

So here it finally came. The moment between the drop of the trap door and the snap of the rope. Fear was irrelevant now. If this odd man had truly put everything together, all that remained was to hear what he planned to do—or had already done. Then she would decide.

"People aren't like books. Most of their thoughts remain inaccessible—unstructured and undocumented. Plus, they conceal and they lie. But their actions are out there somewhere. We think reality is solid, but it's mostly floating in a vacuum, like the Milky Way that seems so full of stars and comet dust and planets, inhabited or uninhabited. A house is mostly air. A family is defined by the invisible links between the people. That's where I look for the truth, in the spaces that seem empty. I found a glass eye in a canyon. I also found a bowling ball, a Frisbee, canned peaches, a barrel, even a car. And after a long time thinking about them, they drew me a picture. They all came from above!"

He looked up at an imaginary Cold Shivers Point. His ramblings were either mad or the comet dust of genius. Meg replaced the pepper spray and realized her hands were freezing. She placed them in the pockets of her sweater and drew it around her.

"I had started from the most random, untraceable fact. Forget the eye. Follow from the other end. I started with you. Through the scholarship it was easy to connect Mogrin to Vavoris, then to your father, as I told you, and your sister, of course, which raised the question of how she died, which led me to that canyon. Surprise, surprise. And also to a story my brother wrote ten years ago connecting her death to those of other women killed by Neulan Kornhauer. I did not know about your sister. That was a time I missed a great deal, even in my own life. But now...

"I know you're a good person. Most people don't lie because they're evil. They lie not to *appear* evil. They lie because they know what goodness is. I finally learned this on the river from the addicts and the drunks, the child molesters—all the people you would think are no good. I used to think, you people are not like me. What is *wrong* with you? But that's not how to talk to a person who is afraid. Do you know the right question? It's *what happened to you?* Even then, people who are afraid may not answer. They don't trust you or think you have the right to ask. They are *ashamed.*"

He clenched his water bottle and it gave a crackling sound that startled her. He frowned and set it down. The indented sides caused the bottle to rock. It pointed at her. She plucked it from the table and dropped it in the recycling container by the door.

He looked from Meg to the container, then back. "Where was I?"

She considered her answer. She was not sure she knew. *Trust, fear, shame.* No. "Knowing what goodness is."

He nodded slowly. "Something happened to you. You wanted the eye because you thought it would make you feel better, yes?" His words tumbled with increasing speed. "I never had a sister but I'm sure girls are different. A boy would play tricks, put his glass eye in somebody's mashed potatoes, make jokes to cover his shame. People would know. But I think a girl would want her disfigurement kept secret, if she could. That's why you wouldn't tell me the real story and no one else would either. You're guarding her memory and here I am butting in, dredging up this...this irrelevance, making a fuss about the eye, Craigslist, posters all over."

He stopped for breath. "I had no business causing you this grief. This is the last I will ever speak about it."

Did Isaac actually believe he'd found *Helen's* eye? This dear, sweet, crazy man!

Isaac stared at the table, uncomfortable now, as if waiting to be dismissed. What could she possibly say to him? The Isaac she had created in her head was nothing like the man who had just unburdened himself to her. And she was no longer the woman who had named him Yoga Man.

"Are there stairs? I don't care for elevators very much."

He shouldered his pack and came around the table. She stood and he edged sideways to pass with more room between them. For the first time, she sensed how difficult it was for him to be in this realty office speaking to a stranger. His consideration of her was a gift and she had almost pepper-sprayed him for his trouble.

"Isaac… I'm not sure I have the right to ask, but what happened to you?"

He was almost to the exit. He turned back. This time he looked fully at her with the blue eyes that had startled her that first day on Main Street.

"I wish…" He put his arm through the other strap of his pack and hunched it square. "I wish I knew."

She dropped back into the conference room chair and covered her face to shut out the bright lights. The aquarium gurgle, the ventilation whistle still plucked at her. A phone rang in a back office. She plugged her ears, trying to be certain of what she was feeling—what she no longer felt: Neulan, who had taken Helen, then her parents, then Brian from her, dragged them all down in one long pull, and there she was at the end of the rope, her heels planted in the unyielding ground, putting on this show of resistance for herself. But he wasn't really there any more.

Had she been wrong about the eye, too? Its provenance no

longer mattered to her, not because it was in the river and Isaac was deluded, but because she saw in full the woman who had sent Pandora to the park, the one who had let Wesley Chambers founder, Hungerman's little champion. A shameful body of work.

So many times she'd shaded the truth. Fibs, equivocations and evasions. All for a good cause, but what had she achieved? None of it meant to hurt anyone, yet she had. Isaac's visit confirmed it. Her column, a prancing sham. Her air-kiss relationships staving off real intimacy. Her mentoring, so well-meant, but also advertising her virtue. What had happened to her?

Ashley's voice penetrated the room. "Is everything all right?"

What a strange construct. How could everything ever be all right?

Ashley hovered, a worried look on her face. "Umm...one question. If you make a 911 call and you don't need the police any more, are you supposed to cancel—or should we just leave it up to the Lord?"

"Oh, please tell me you didn't call."

Ashley's face flushed. "He banged the chair. He was talking wild. You took out your pepper spray!"

Meg waved Ashley back to her post. Speaking, even moving from here, could endanger this precarious moment of clarity. Going back to the office routine of client care, she might forget what true compassion felt like, might slip back into a more calculating form of empathy that did unto others as you would have them do unto your business.

She might lose her nerve.

School on the reservation must be over by now. Brian seemed grounded there but he traveled light.

"Is this Chosposi?"

The reply was guarded. "It's Grace."

"We've met. I need to reach Brian Mogrin. You helped me before."

"Not another messeege..." Chosposi's laugh sparked through the wire.

"Can you give him this when he comes in? Or sooner? *You win. No, wait. You were right. It's time. Call me.* From Meg."

"Oh, he knows who. You think all the girls call him here?"

"It's important."

"Don't worry."

Meg heard a bustling in the lobby. Ashley's eyes widened, then squinted toward the conference room. Her entire face pitched in to broadcast three silent syllables: *The police.*

Tony Martin, Amy Hostetter's former outreach partner.

Thank you, Isaac. Yes, coincidence rewards a prepared mind.

Do you have planned activities each day other than just surviving that bring you happiness and fulfillment?

—Vulnerability Index Prescreen for Single Adults

Isaac's insulated shed had passed winter's tests, which were rarely severe in the valley. Overnight snow usually disappeared by noon except for lingering patches on north-facing slopes. A January inversion had trapped bitter cold and bad air, leaving the heights warmer than the lowlands, but the sunny days surrounding did not inspire prayers for winter's end. By every measure except the calendar, spring came in February and April morphed into summer. June might be too hot for him to live inside.

Events in town fell and melted before he saw them. The Winslowville protest did not survive chill weather and a police strategy that posted targeted streets in advance. An informant was suspected. A church offered to host the Thistletown tent city for the winter but neighbors rose up and the City required a costly temporary use permit. By the time the ACLU got involved, the numbers of willing campers had dwindled to a handful. They tried to occupy the glue factory land and Wesley was arrested as one of the leaders. Isaac had followed the stories in the newspaper but never visited the encampment. How could he, living in his own place for free, tell Wesley he was not welcome to join him? He had agreed to his mother's conditions. Obeying the rules always meant someone would be disappointed.

He and his mother had found equilibrium. She had started calling the shed the *casita*, as a joke or perhaps because it was a happier word. The biffy was gone and he was allowed to use the bathroom and the laundry. He had sprayed the halogetan that sprouted all through her yard and would soon tear out the old landscape fabric, put down a new layer and refresh the gravel. Twice a week she fixed him dinner; twice a week he made her breakfast. Beyond that, they had no schedule or transitional arrangement. He had no desire to live in her house and he could sense she did not want him there, at least, not yet. Trials longer than this one had failed, so...

The yellow Raleigh remained in service. With less to haul and further to ride, he found the road bike suitable, despite the pesky goatheads.

He was still adjusting to his work, to the miracle of its appearance.

A man named Gordon couldn't get the Colorado driver's license he needed for work. The license he'd lost was from Pennsylvania; he'd been born in New Jersey; an outstanding warrant for a parking ticket in Maryland somehow followed him to where no one else had. Isaac unwound the rules, found the forms and helped Gordon file the paperwork in the proper sequence. Next, he helped untangle a woman with four different names—birth, marriage, social security and an alias to hide from her abusive ex. Already having looked up four states, he kept going and created a national catalog of procedures and contacts. He had meant it as a self-help guide, but some cases were unique and people were still overwhelmed by the processes. Bureaucratic threads seemed less daunting to him when they bound someone else, so he continued, a walking encyclopedia of lost identity. He took such a load off Catholic Outreach that Sister Rose gave him a desk with a computer and office hours two days a week to handle miscellaneous questions: where to find a cheap haircut; how to get a bus pass; when the soup kitchen stopped serving; how often someone could visit the food shelf; who did free dental work; where to take a sick dog if you had no money; how to find out if your boyfriend was in jail; and how to get your heat back on when you couldn't pay the bill.

The library restored his privileges in April. Linda Cornish had heard about the database he had continued to build and asked him what he thought about manning a table next to the information desk. There was no budget to pay him but it was enough when she said *any question that comes in the library is a library question.*

The last time he'd heard an engine running outside his shed—the only time someone knocked—it was the driver from the House of Flowers come to deliver a thank you bouquet from Meg Mogrin. Now the door was rattling again.

Wesley.

"I heard you were living in a shed and I imagined some old shack. You're living the dream, my man."

The shed was Wesley's micro-house dream, except this was not Thistletown because Wesley couldn't live here. Isaac hoped he wouldn't ask.

"Your brother told me you were out here. He tracked me down, wanted to write a story about me. I told him I wasn't the point."

It seemed Joe specialized in stories people didn't want him to write.

"I heard you were at the glue factory," Isaac said. "I was looking for you there when some guys ripped me off."

"Sorry. I went underground for a while. I was dangerous to be around. The Winslowville thing pissed off the cops. And me telling the cops it was Dexter and Screech's booby trap pissed off their druggie friends. I thought at first they dropped those fusees on us for revenge. A meth head can be pretty truthful if you catch him right, especially after his head's going underwater for the third or fourth time. Anyway, the ones I visited swore they didn't know shit. It seemed kind of pointless to keep dunking people til I found out who actually burned us out. It was pretty plain half the town was happy to see it."

"The other half wasn't, though," Isaac said.

"The other half doesn't care. They want us gone, too. They just don't want to light the match. Instead, they gave me a deal. No jail time or probation." Wesley stretched out both arms as if measuring the shed. "Terrell's waiting in the car."

Terrell. Gravy, John, Doug. Isaac had lost track of everyone from the island. "Have him come in."

Wesley looked over his shoulder. "He has to keep his foot on the gas so the engine doesn't die."

"When did you get a car?"

"It was a recent donation."

"That's a big donation."

"I turned down a bus ticket to anywhere. Now we've got a Blazer with a full tank. Like I said..."

A brown Blazer, perhaps twenty years old. Its loosened sheet metal trembled slightly with the elevated rpms. Terrell nodded from behind the wheel.

"You're all loaded up," Isaac said. He saw one seat clear in the back. They could have said something before if they expected him to go along.

"We wanted to make sure things were going good with you before we took off. Looks like they are." Wesley cracked his neck bones, left and right.

They had been in the same situation and now their situations had changed. Sharing an island wasn't quite the same as being friends.

A light came on at the rear of the house. His mother's room. She must have seen the headlights, heard them talking. Now she was watching. Wondering.

"Where are you headed?" Isaac asked.

"We're thinking Utah," Terrell said.

Utah was only about one-percent black people, although, with Colorado only four-percent, Terrell probably wouldn't notice the difference.

"You sure? From here to Salt Lake there's only about four little towns, and the Mormons run the whole place." That was the flaw in Edison's plan to use technology to take over the country. He should have invented a religion.

"We heard things are changing there," said Wesley.

Religions didn't change. People were supposed to do the changing.

Terrell had been nursing the Blazer with sips of gasoline. Now he gave it a dose that made the engine growl. Wesley walked around to the passenger side and climbed in.

"We'll let you know," Wesley said. "You still get your mail at the Day Center?"

He didn't get much mail now that his mother had stopped sending the post cards, so what was the point of changing his address? It gave him a reason to stop in and see Sylvia. It let the others know he hadn't gone all normal on them.

Isaac's dream had once been to see the entire world, not one stop at a time like on the interstate or *Join the Navy and See the World*, but grasping all at once how everything connected to everything down to the atom particles, the same way when he spun the globe he could see the oceans and the land masses as one whole. Like he was an astronaut with x-ray vision. But there was simply no chance of that. Every new discovery that overturned the former schemes led humanity down some new rabbit hole. At some point, it seemed, you either had to believe the old book or just watch the movie.

Through his window Isaac could see his mother's silhouette in a yellow square of light. It resembled a stamp from some small country where artists had taken over the postal service and made postage look like art instead of money. She had no reason to continue her watch. Wesley and Terrell had left; he had stayed. He undressed, pulled back the coverlet and switched off the lights. Across the yard, as if awaiting his signal, the house went dark.

Nightly, dreams calibrated his mind to life's absurdity and irresolution. Tasks remained incomplete, shapes lost their integrity and actions defied logic. Paperwork got lost. Motion contradicted physics. Out of the blue, his dream self sometimes reacquired a forgotten ability to levitate. No one ever seemed to notice his power but at least it allowed him to float his way out of difficulties. Try as he might, he never felt whole in those dreams, never achieved full clarity or assurance, never reached his goals. Yet again and again his brain dispatched these impulses, as if his exploratory sparks could restore pathways between broken wires. And some mornings he awakened with pleasure, trusting that when the time came, his love of the world would lift him to a place where his bones would recall the lost secret of flight.

〰

The new banner had been placed on Meg's home page, her office number set to forwarding, her voicemail messages changed. After rehearsing the bullet points of the personal calls she intended, she found herself unready to manage the conversations. Instead, she composed a terse text. *Taking some time off. Focusing on personal stuff. Nothing fatal. No need to call. You'll hear when I know more.*

Caller ID let her divert the friends who called back, but her client-pleasing reflexes jumped at the unfamiliar number of Lew Hungerman's assistant, who asked her to hold. His voice echoed with the reverb of a bathroom stall. "Start your break right. Come to the home opener with Idaho Falls, it'll be great. It's my community relations kick off."

"It's baseball, not football," she said.

"You know what I mean," he said. "You've been a vital part of getting this blimp off the ground. Your ideas were brilliant. Adding the homeless veterans component to the project positioning."

"So you're doing the housing?" This was good to hear.

"Not really, but with Amy Hostetter throwing out the first pitch, I see both a friend-of-the-homeless angle and a great honoring-the-wounded-warrior aspect."

"Well, whatever you decide to do, I don't want any credit."

"That's what I love about you. You make huge contributions and don't care about personal recognition. I'm still disappointed you didn't run."

It was so like Hungerman to mistake revulsion for humility. But why hold his absorption against him? The project might still be good for the town. She could take comfort in that, despite her misgivings of how it got this far.

"Where are you calling from, the visitors' locker room?" she said.

"Now you're being sarcastic." The quality of the connection suddenly improved. "I *was* considering opening a call center in Idaho Falls."

She remembered what Jules had said about his business moving away from call centers. "I'm sure town fathers everywhere have appreciated your efforts to sow confusion."

He laughed. "Does your text mean you're still considering my offer?"

You prob'ly think this text is about you, don't you?

"You need a different kind of person in that job."

"That's for me to decide. About tonight, come. I'll leave your tickets at Will Call. They'll get you into the skybox. It'll be prime prospecting."

"You forget I already know all those people."

"But they don't know you as my new sales director."

"All I care about is seeing the pregame, Lew."

"The tickets'll be there. Bring some friends."

Meg drives the long gentle slope of Broadway from her house to the river, leaving time for a detour along Riverside Parkway. Spring rains have greened the grasses refreshed by last summer's fire, though expanses of Las Colonias remain bare. Car dealer-style pennants lag over the bricks of the sugar beet factory, and a sign zip-tied to the cyclone fence notes an upcoming public hearing. A billboard on Donnie Barclay's adjoining lot displays an architect's rendering of the proposed Betterment Institute campus. Sparkling buildings rise beyond a flank of mature trees where presently moribund spindles cling to wood-chip mounds.

Meg crosses Grand Avenue, like the city, named for the river before Congress rechristened it the Colorado. Next, Ouray Avenue, after the Ute chieftain who brokered the treaty tendering this valley from nomads to settlers, and then Chipeta Avenue, honoring his wife, who died far from home on a Utah reservation. As Meg approaches Lincoln Park, an alternate history of growth and prog-ress begins to take shape in her mind, the view of her hometown she should have presented to Hungerman last summer.

In a few short years bridging World War One, the Great Influenza Epidemic, falling farm prices and social unrest, local investment set in motion changes that still shaped the city. The county fairgrounds on the outskirts of town were purchased for an expansive city park that included sports fields, playgrounds, a zoo, exhibition hall and tourist camp. After an employee's son drowned in the river, a local department store owner financed a public swimming pool in Lincoln Park, stipulating free admission to children. The original pool and its Italianate bathhouse have been replaced, but the benefactor's name and a children's free-day tradition remain. An arboretum was envisioned on soils made arable by the new government canal; now sixty-nine varieties of trees leaf throughout the park. A municipal golf course opened nine holes; the forty acres reserved for a back nine were later dedicated to a VA hospital. Across North Avenue, a little two-year college opened its doors. Now a university campus sprawls around the original building. And tonight Lew Hungerman will talk up his vision for the neglected ground of Las Colonias in the ballpark suites overlooking verdant Lincoln Park.

Was the town any less divided then? Was financial speculation less rampant, the region's economy less fragile, its government less inept? She did not believe so. In those days, socialist workers wrangled with burghers who marched down Main Street with the KKK. Perhaps change had always been made from part sunshine and part graft.

In the parking lot, tributaries of fans leave their cars and merge to flow through the entry gate. Some linger, finishing beers and bratwursts and putting away their tailgate hibachis. Among them, eating from a plate set atop her wayward shopping cart, the old woman from Whitman Park, beaming at her fellow celebrants. Did one of them just call her *Mom*?

A horse trailer is parked near the exhibition hall. It's been nearly a year since she saw Amy. Vaughn had told her about Leonard and the rehab rides, but she could not bring herself to look into it. The Amy she wanted in her head was the woman from their softball days who hit laser line drives and knew there were more important things than winning a game.

Two boys chase past her, slapping each other with ball gloves. Ahead in line, Dan McCallam and his wife claim two of Hungerman's luxury box tickets. Passing through an incense of mustard, popcorn and beer, she heads for the general admission section. She scans the left field bleachers expecting to see Brian there already. Oh, well. His Jetta is the unreliable one. She has been warned by the attorney not to think too far ahead. The worst thing about going to the authorities will be surrendering her sense of control. They won't be jailed, he assured her, but it will seem as if they were while the investigation drags on. After all this time, the DA can only pursue a murder charge and must consider whether a jury will convict. Chances are, the case will never go to trial but the story will be all over the place. Resolution will come, he said, but if you expect absolution from the process, you will be disappointed.

Where is he?

A ballpark meeting before tomorrow's appointment felt less fraught than having Brian come to the house, but now it seems a mistake. Seeing the whole town has shown up to eavesdrop, perhaps he turned around. Or consulted his own lawyer. Or changed his mind and slipped further off the grid. Maybe Eco-Babe is not history after all. Why, that little pickup might be able to tow his *campito* if they drove slow, stayed south and avoided the passes.

Don't start in again!

I have to consider the possibilities.

No you don't. You worry too much. Just wait. It'll be like this baseball game. All the anticipation. It seems like nothing will happen and then something always does.

You've never said what happened to you that day.

Why does that matter now?

It would be nice to know the truth before I talk to the DA.

Well, my testimony will be unavailable, but try this: It was an accident. Call it a misadventure if that makes you feel better.

It doesn't. It makes me feel worse.

Gee, I'm sorry I don't have a bedtime story version of it.

It makes me feel…

Like you should have done something—say, thrown your body in front of the church bus that day? Spent the prior ten years hounding me into being a fraidy-cat? Nobody gets to foresee everything or tie up all the loose ends. You were an awesome sister.

Now try something you can actually achieve, like going on with your life. In the end, what you or Sister Rose or Mother Teresa accomplish all amounts to the same thing. Trust me, everyone here thinks so. Well, Shakespeare and Edison are being contrarian asses, but their last day of immortality is coming.

Will I get to keep my sense of humor after I die?

Yeah. It comes in handy. I'm not so sure, though, how well irony plays in jail.

There's a chance they might not even prosecute. Too much time has passed.

Thus vindicating procrastinators everywhere.

Oh, I miss you, Hel.

Enjoy the game, Madge.

Vaughn Hobart sits in full sunshine high in the cheap seats. She greets him with a peck on the cheek, which under other circumstances would never have entered her mind. The lofty perch gives her a good view of the late entrants.

The PA announcer directs attention to the right field corner and he clicks on a pre-recorded drum roll. The crowd rises as one to greet Officer Amy Hostetter mounted upon her therapy horse, riding without a tender, guiding its hooves through foul territory. The grounds crew, keeping their fingers crossed, joins the ovation.

Amy dismounts near the bullpen and Leonard Self takes the reins. The announcer introduces the police chief, Lew Hungerman and the director of the Wounded Warrior Riding Program, rolling out the names as if the Rockies cleanup hitter were coming to bat with the bases loaded. They conduct Amy to the pitcher's mound. She accepts one end of the foam board facsimile of Betterment Health's two-thousand-dollar check. The program director takes the other corner, freeing Hungerman to hug Amy and wave to his guests in the skybox. Applause ripples again.

The police chief salutes and hands Amy a baseball, then her entourage steps away from the mound. The crowd remains standing. Movement stops in the aisles. Amy turns to the fans in left-centerfield and waves all the way around to right. Instead of stepping in front of the mound, she aligns her foot with the pitching rubber. She gathers herself into the set position and looks down at the ball in her hands. Without a glove, the pose seems prayerful but perhaps the pause is to steady herself. Her arm draws back and sends the pitch looping to the catcher's target.

Cheers erupt. Across the stadium, men clap each other on the back, women examine the sky, noses blow into hot dog napkins and knuckles brush cheekbones. When the catcher tucks away the mask and walks the ball back, Meg sees it is Amy's old partner, Tony Martin.

After a singer wobbles through an over-embellished national anthem, Leonard walks the horse back to the trailer. The Grand Junction Rockies take the field against the Idaho Falls Chukars. The umpires confer with the managers. Amy Hostetter has disappeared, assimilated into the crowd.

By the scoreless sixth inning the upbeat tone set by Amy's public return has dissipated. With two outs and two strikes on the batter, two runners appear about to be stranded. Vaughn's back is aching from the bleachers and he takes a stroll to see if Leonard has left yet with the horse trailer. Meg checks her phone. Damn Brian's aversion to mobile devices. Once she'd thought it quirky, a consequence of his pared-down, out-of-the-way existence. Now it feels selfish and evasive, the way she must have seemed to him. Like those two men on base, they were both ready to run on anything.

The crowd's roar pulls her attention back to the play. A Chukar outfielder dashes back after a high fly slicing down the right-field line. He can only watch the ball soar over the fence, waving his glove toward foul territory, as if he could move the ball or sway the umpires. The runners, already racing at the crack of the bat, throttle back as the first base umpire points his finger skyward, indicating a home run, while the home plate umpire raises both hands to signal foul. Fielders throw up their arms; the runners continue home, then halt in confusion. Both managers emerge steaming from their dugouts. The umpires move away to deliberate. Home field fans scream that the ball was fair, obviously inside the foul pole. The less certain troop down to concessions for a final beer before the seventh-inning last call.

The conference drags on. There can be no compromise, provisional call or appeal to a replay. The umpires had a fleeting second to judge whether a three-inch-diameter baseball eclipsed a pole three-hundred-fifty feet away, and now they must be decisive even if in doubt. Either a foul ball returns the game to a scoreless deadlock or three runs score and perhaps determine the outcome.

Distracted in this equivocal twilight, Meg has no idea what the ruling should be. So how will they trace across the decades an arc that even she and Brian did not see the same? A system, so blinded, must conspire with the only witnesses to render justice.

She spies Brian now, shouldering against the flow, peering into the crowd. He will not see her high up behind the masses standing, stretching and departing, so she springs down the steps. The announcer urges everyone to stay for the fireworks after the game. Meg plunges through the throng, calling Brian's name. He stops to extract the familiar note from the hubbub. When he turns, his expression of relief delivers all she could ask of this night. *The Jetta's dead.* She hands him the keys to her car and points him toward the exit. When a clamor from the crowd arises behind them, Brian looks to her for an interpretation. He thought the game was over.

It seems like nothing happens and then something does.

Somewhere in the darkened lot a scuffed baseball lies under a car. The hero's bat is stuffed into a bag. He will use it again and again until it splinters one night in Missoula. In the morning, the anonymous ball will be found, join a sandlot game and be handed around until its cover falls off. The players will scatter but they will remember the grass they grew up on and when they return they will see the river has kept the valley green, though its edges remain brown as ever. The city lights will have washed out more of the night sky but the stars will still be up there with the planets, inhabited or not.

Across the asphalt, Meg sees her car's parking lamps blink and, if she is not mistaken, she hears the quiet thrum of an engine come to life.

Acknowledgements

Writing about one's semi-hometown is rich with resonance and fraught with peril. The Grand Junction that appears in *Inhabited* is reasonably accurate as a landscape, slightly altered as a built environment, approximate as to timelines and historical events, and invented once we get to characters and the story. For example, the tamarisk jungle on the Colorado River did exist when I set my first novel there. By the time I put it in *Inhabited* and wrote this note, it was a disc golf course.

The idea for *Inhabited* also grew out of my experiences as a volunteer at the Day Center run by Catholic Outreach of the Grand Valley. My interest in the issues began after being introduced to homeless families and children at People Serving People in Minneapolis. Working with kids in that shelter's preschool was inspiring, but I didn't find a similar opportunity in Colorado. At first, I thought it would be a comedown to be stuck in a day center handing out toothbrushes to street people. Ironically, it proved to be a great gift. *Inhabited* is in part a testament of how my mind continued to be opened. The place afforded me the chance to reflect on "the boundaries of kinship" and our human capacities for resilience and change.

While I made efforts to be accurate, the portrayal of homelessness in this novel represents a particular region and only a subset of the many people who live without stable shelter in our country. In parts of the west, a milder climate and open space means more people are willing to risk living outdoors. Rural or urban, homelessness is linked to the outdoors in a way that should expand our definition of what is an environmental issue. Although the political and economic tensions presented in the novel are real, the Grand

Junction community has come together in a much more compassionate and effective way than its fictional counterpart. To learn more, visit the Faces and Voices project at: www.facesandvoices.org.

Thanks in particular to Patricia Boom, who was director of the Day Center for most of my years there, Blair Weaver, the current director, and to the many individuals in the Grand Valley who opened up their lives to my questions and observation, including Carl Bartlett, James Easterling, Kelvin Gross, Tracy Gross, Brad Sweet, Rick Naimish, Marshall Harrow, Ken Halverson, Mark Hirschberg, Tracy Brado and John McDugle. Sherry Cole and Sandra Clark provided valuable insight from a social services perspective; Paul Quimby, Cindy Cohn and Cory Tomps helped me understand outreach from the law enforcement side.

I am also indebted to friends with family members who have experienced homelessness or extreme dysfunction. As with a loved one's suicide, relatives feel pain and guilt for feeling unable to help, and their stories often remain unspoken. Kate Ligare, Steve Hustead, Shirl McGuire-Belden, BK Loren and others, your hearts beat in this book.

Early readers Teresa Coons, Susan Fraker, George Orbanek, Margo Mejia and her book club helped me know I was on track. Jim Kalitowski, Bill Wagner, Jay Perkins, Gerry Cowhig, Jane Quimby and Margaret Chutich offered expert advice on content matters. Doug Quimby's multiple readings helped me refine a character and plot points.

Thanks also to Mark Bailey and Kirsten Allen of Torrey House Press for championing diverse writing about the environment in general and the West in particular, and to the always responsive Anne Terashima, to whom I still owe a beer. Nancy Stauffer Cahoon has generously given frank advice and Margie Wilson of Grand Valley Books has been an exemplar of the independent booksellers who support authors and enrich their communities' retail and cultural life.

About Charlie Quimby

Charlie Quimby is the author of *Monument Road*, an Indie Next pick and *Booklist* Editors' Choice in 2013. He began his writing career as playwright and arts journalist, veered into corporate communications and then founded a marketing agency that now purrs along without him. Along the way, he collected awards and developed the notion he had a few good novels in him. A native Coloradan and adopted Minnesotan, he is at home in both places.

TORREY HOUSE PRESS

VOICES FOR THE LAND

*The economy is a wholly owned subsidiary of the
environment, not the other way around.*
—Senator Gaylord Nelson, founder of Earth Day

Torrey House Press is an independent nonprofit publisher promoting environmental conservation through literature. We believe that culture is changed through conversation and that lively, contemporary literature is the cutting edge of social change. We strive to identify exceptional writers, nurture their work, and engage the widest possible audience; to publish diverse voices with transformative stories that illuminate important facets of our ever-changing planet; to develop literary resources for the conservation movement, educating and entertaining readers, inspiring action.

Visit **www.torreyhouse.org** for reading group discussion guides, author interviews, and more.